I DON'T
FORGIVE
YOU

I DON'T FORGIVE YOU

AGGIE BLUM THOMPSON

A TOM DOHERTY ASSOCIATES BOOK

NEW YORK

I DON'T FORGIVE YOU

Copyright © 2021 by Agnes Blum Thompson

A Forge Book
Published by Tom Doherty Associates
120 Broadway
New York, NY 10271

www.tor-forge.com

Forge® is a registered trademark of Macmillan Publishing Group, LLC.

Library of Congress Cataloging-in-Publication Data

Names: Thompson, Aggie Blum, author.
Title: I don't forgive you / Aggie Blum Thompson.
Description: First edition. | New York : Forge, 2021. | "A Tom Doherty Associates book."
Identifiers: LCCN 2021008752 (print) | LCCN 2021008753 (ebook) | ISBN 9781250818454 (hardcover) | ISBN 9781250773913 (trade paperback) | ISBN 9781250773920 (ebook)
Subjects: GSAFD: Suspense fiction.
Classification: LCC PS3620.H6477 I23 2021 (print) | LCC PS3620.H6477 (ebook) | DDC 813'.6—dc23
LC record available at https://lccn.loc.gov/2021008752
LC ebook record available at https://lccn.loc.gov/2021008753

Our books may be purchased in bulk for promotional, educational, or business use. Please contact your local bookseller or the Macmillan Corporate and Premium Sales Department at 1-800-221-7945, extension 5442, or by email at MacmillanSpecialMarkets@macmillan.com.

First Edition: June 2021

Printed in the United States of America

0 9 8 7 6 5 4 3 2 1

For John, Nina, and Roxy—always

I DON'T FORGIVE YOU

1

A little innocent flirting never killed anyone.

"You look like the sauvignon blanc type."

"Is that right?" The guy standing next to me fills my glass to the rim from a bottle of New Zealand's finest. I didn't catch Wine Guy's name. He's the same age as the other dads at the party, but he gives off a different energy, like the one house on a dilapidated block that has been painted.

Sharp laughter carries across the kitchen, and I shoot a glance at the corner from which it emanated. It's three moms from school who completely ignored me for twenty minutes while I listened to them debate Blue Apron versus Plated, with a dumb smile on my face, waiting for a chance to speak. I turn back to Wine Guy and smile. Men are so much easier.

"So there's a sauvignon blanc type?"

"Oh, definitely." He smirks, which makes his green eyes crinkle. We are at that age where men get sexier and women get Botox. "And you're it."

I glance over at Mark, but my husband hasn't paid attention to me since we arrived at the annual Eastbrook Neighborhood Social. I can see his dark hair and the back of his checkered shirt on the opposite side of the Gordons' kitchen; he's talking to some of the other men about the Washington Nationals' World Series chances.

"I'm *it*, huh?" We're flirting, no denying it, and I don't mind. It beats mingling and trying to make "mommy friends," as Mark put it earlier. I spent the first hour of the party wandering around, trying to slip into other women's conversations, feeling like a moth who keeps banging her head on the glass, a creature too dumb to know she's outside and is never getting in. "So just what is this sauvignon blanc type?"

I eye the blond streaks in his hair as I lift the glass to my lips, relishing the cool, tangy wine gliding down my throat. I wonder if they're produced by the sun or a salon. A squeal behind me makes me jump. I turn to see a blond woman in skinny jeans and buttery-brown riding boots embrace an identically dressed friend. I watch them kiss on both cheeks and am flooded with both contempt and jealousy. Aren't we too old for such conspicuous displays of cliquishness? Also, why don't I have any girlfriends who squeal when they see me?

"Sauvignon blanc folks like to think they're unique, creative."

"Creative, huh?" I pull at my skirt—the damn thing keeps riding up my thighs. I should have worn jeans like all the other moms here. The immense kitchen island offers cover for my wardrobe adjustment. It's large enough to lay two cadavers out side by side, the gleaming white expanse of marble daring partygoers to spill red wine on it.

"That's right," he says. "You look creative. Are you an artist or something?"

I can't help but smile. I'd like to think that I haven't lost that spark, even though I've become a mom and moved to the suburbs. I let myself indulge in the fantasy that this guy can see I've still got it. "Or something. A photographer."

"A photographer, like Ansel Adams?"

I have to laugh at that one. "More weddings and family portraits, fewer mountain ranges. Although recently I've done a bunch of headshots."

"Anyone famous?"

I laugh. "D.C. famous, maybe. Ever heard of Congressman Marcel Parks?"

"I think so."

"Did his headshot. There's a chance I might be doing Valerie Simmons's. She's got a new book coming out about her experience in the Obama administration."

His eyebrows shoot up. "Val Simmons? I watch her on CNN. She's a badass."

"If you're interested, you can follow me on Instagram. I'm Allie at allie-photo-dot-com." Then I blush, embarrassed at how automatic it's become. Ever since I took a class last year on branding and growing my online presence, I recite my Instagram address to everyone I meet.

"Well, that explains why you don't run with the chardonnay crowd."

"The chardonnay crowd? There's a whole crowd?" I giggle despite myself. And why not? It feels good to lose myself in wine and banter. Since we moved to Eastbrook, a tight-knit neighborhood in the close-in D.C. suburb of Bethesda, and our son, Cole, started kindergarten, my thoughts have been monopolized by to-do items: buying school supplies, arranging lawn service, vaccinations. The soul-crushing minutiae that are both mundane and urgent.

"Sure. Lifetime members of the comfort zone." He waves his arm around to encompass everyone else in the gleaming white kitchen, which is just smaller than an airplane hangar and boasts a stove the size of a Smart Car, as well as two Sub-Zero fridges. I wonder what the Gordons' monthly gas bill looks like.

"All chardonnay furniture is beige," he continues, not breaking eye contact with me, "and anything they're not familiar with is *weird*." He screws up his face when he says that last word.

But it isn't just that Eastbrook is chardonnay country through and through. It's me. I've never really fit in or belonged to a group. No #girlsquad for me. That wasn't a big deal in San Francisco, and in Chicago, no one really noticed, but here in the suburbs, you're nobody if you're not part of one of the mom tribes—the alpha career moms, the stay-at-home moms, the PTA contingent.

I've made one friend so far, my across-the-street neighbor

Leah, who has a daughter in the same kindergarten class as Cole. We bonded this summer, baking in the D.C. heat at the neighborhood pool, while our kids splashed around. Our running joke was that we were living in a zombie apocalypse, the only remaining moms thanks to a mass decampment for Nantucket or the Delaware shore.

Actually, I may have two friends if I count Daisy Gordon, but I believe Realtors are contractually obligated to be nice. Yes, she invited us to the party, but from the size of it, she invited the whole neighborhood.

"What else can you tell by looking at me?" I ask.

His gaze travels from my face, down to my breasts, and to my too-short skirt. Heat blooms within me. I cannot remember the last time a man examined me with such frank desire. It's like rediscovering a slinky red dress I had forgotten about in the back of my closet that still fits. I wouldn't trade my life with Mark and Cole for anything, but just a little taste of stranger danger won't hurt. In fact, maybe it could spice things up a little for Mark and me. The move to D.C. hasn't been great for our love life.

"What else? Let's see." Wine Guy narrows his eyes as if he's trying to read my mind like a boardwalk psychic. "You're not from D.C."

I scoff. "That's too easy. Who is?" Most of the people in this neighborhood come from around the country, around the world even, to work for the government or large international organizations such as the World Bank. Mark is a rarity in that he grew up around here.

"Fine. How about: you love Cardi B."

"I do love Cardi B." I keep sipping the wine, even though I know I am already buzzed. This is where tomorrow's headache begins, but I don't put my glass down. I'm sick of worrying about tomorrows. I want to enjoy the now. "But I can't be the only one who does."

"In this room?" He looks around and laughs. "You might very well be the only Cardi B fan."

"What else?" As I ask the question, I glance at Mark. He has not moved from his perch, still surrounded by the same three guys in baggy khakis and billowing polo shirts that do little to hide their dad bods. One of them is crouched like a batter at home plate. Still talking about baseball. If sports are the universal language for men, what do we women have? Maybe our kids or our exercise habits.

"Well, how about this?" he asks. "You'd rather be at home watching the new *John Wick 3* than at the annual neighborhood social."

I laugh because I said the exact same thing to Mark this evening as we were getting ready, even going so far as to offer to break it to Susan, our sitter, that her services wouldn't be needed. But Mark insisted we go after Daisy told him these neighborhood parties were mostly other parents. *You'll thank me later,* he said. *Maybe you'll meet your new best friend.*

"How did you know I love John Wick?"

"Lucky guess?"

Last week, I binge-watched the first two movies in the series while editing a tedious wedding shoot. "Have you been snooping in my Netflix queue?"

"Who, me?" His eyes widen in mock innocence, and he pushes on my collarbone with one finger. The heat from his touch radiates across my skin. I want more. This is good. I can take this home to Mark. It's been almost two months since we've had sex. "You should be more trusting, Lexi."

Lexi.

The sound of that old nickname snatches me from my fog. I've left Lexi far behind. "Wait, why did you call me that?"

"Me Rob." He leans in so close that his forehead almost touches mine. "You Lexi."

I jerk back. "I need to eat something."

As I weave through the crowded kitchen, I rack my brain. I might be saturated with wine, but I'm sure I would have introduced myself as Allie, maybe my full name—Alexis—but not Lexi.

Never Lexi.

2

Me Rob, you Lexi.

I shake it off. It's a common enough nickname for Alexis. It doesn't have to mean anything. But I feel exposed. Whatever fun we were having, it's dead now.

Too much wine, I decide, and too little food to absorb it. In search of nourishment to soak up all the alcohol, I push past a cluster of moms chatting in shorthand about swim team meets and times. Out of the corner of my eye, I see Daisy in her crisp, white button-down and door-knocker pearl earrings, waving me over. She's been nothing but kind to me, yet I can't tell if she is genuinely interested or if she sees me as another name to add to her LinkedIn network. Mark says I need to make more of an effort and not wait for everyone to come to me.

In a moment, Daisy is enveloping me in a cloud of cotton candy perfume.

"I'm so glad you and Mark came. The Eastbrook parties are where all the cool kids hang." She winks, hard. "And I'm not just saying that because I'm the president of the neighborhood association. Now, let me introduce you to some people!" Hand on my elbow, she guides me from the kitchen through the brightly lit foyer, which is wallpapered with gold loons preening their long necks against a black-and-white seascape. A modern glass chandelier resembling an illuminated octopus drips from the two-story ceiling.

"That's an authentic Chihuly." Daisy points to the chandelier as she whispers in my ear, her breath warm and gin-infused. "One of Trip's clients gave it to him. I think it's hideous, but I don't have the heart to tell him." She giggles like a schoolgirl and steers me past a yellow lacquered chest, so shiny that I can see our reflection in it. I try to remember what Trip does. Something with natural gas—lobbyist, I think.

"Is Leah here?" I ask as we enter the dining room.

"Not yet." Daisy rolls her eyes. "Some drama with Dustin. I think they might be getting a therapy dog."

"Got it." I'm not surprised there's drama. From what I have gleaned, Dustin, Leah's teenage son from her first marriage, is struggling—both socially and academically. A classic combination of off-the-charts intelligence and a lack of social skills. He radiates loneliness even when he's just taking out the trash.

I am happy to let Daisy lead me around the white tulip table, laden with food, although her attention makes me a little nervous. Beneath her kindhearted curiosity lies the probing scalpel of one of those journalists who gets you to cry on camera. The first time I met her, when she was showing Mark and me houses, I somehow ended up confiding in her that my mother did not consider me the pretty one.

"That is a lot of Le Creuset," I say, pointing to a wall of display shelves filled with the enameled, cast-iron pots in an array of bright colors. At three hundred dollars a pop, I estimate that I am looking at a week in Florida, or a used Honda.

Daisy's eye twitches, and for a moment, I worry that I've stepped in it. If there's one thing I've learned since marrying Mark, it's that rich people don't like to talk money.

"They're really beautiful," I hasten to add. "I've always wanted one, but I'm not really a cook."

"It's too much, right?" she asks, but doesn't wait for my response. "They're my indulgence. Every time I sell a house, I buy one in a new color. I have more in the basement, if you can believe it. I am obsessing over this season's new colors. I have to have sea salt—it's only available at Sur La Table, but the hubster says no way."

"They're lovely. They're like jelly beans. Jelly beans for grown-ups."

She leans in and whispers, "Take one home! Then I can replace it with the sea salt, and no one will be any wiser."

"Oh, I couldn't—"

"Melissa!" she calls over my shoulder. "Allie, I have to go say hi, but please, eat these for me." Daisy hands a plate of spanakopita to me. "You're so skinny, it's disgusting."

Then she leaves me to welcome a woman who is trying to wedge a tray of cut fruit onto the table. I turn to a woman beside me in tight pants and brown boots that ride up over her knees, accentuating her pin-like thighs. Just like the ones the two women in the kitchen were wearing. I've met her before, at back-to-school night, but I can't recall her name. Before I can say anything, the woman sticks out her hand at me. "Tanya. My Oliver is in Mrs. Liu's class." Her cool hand is limp, as if squeezing too hard would be a proletarian display of effort. "You look familiar," she says in a bored tone.

"Yes, we met at back-to-school night."

"No, that's not it. Did you go to Georgetown Law?"

"No, not me."

"You sure?"

"Yup, I'm sure I didn't go to Georgetown Law." I pop a few mini-quiches on my plate, hoping she doesn't ask me where I went to college. I doubt there are too many other art school dropouts here. "But our kids are in the same class. Cole is in Ms. Liu's class, as well. . . ."

But Tanya is no longer listening to me. Her eyes widen as she screeches with delight at something she has spotted. The smile and enthusiasm absent from our exchange are now on full display.

Tanya's voice booms out, "Edie! Sasha! Any other riding girls?"

Everyone in the vicinity freezes for a moment, flattening them-
selves against the edges of the room so the riding girls can enter.
I hover on the sideline like a parent at a child's soccer game and
make polite eye contact with the other bystanders as Tanya and
her friends, including the two I saw earlier in the kitchen, pose
for photos, angling this way and then turning that way in their
matching boots.

My throat tightens and I grip my wineglass, which is dan-
gerously close to being empty. A low-grade panic swells in me,
and I'm transported back to the day in fifth grade when my
three closest friends announced that my presence was no longer
needed at the lunch table. I'm almost tempted to seek out Rob,
the wine guy. At least he was friendly. But then I think of him
calling me Lexi, and I shudder. He's a creep.

Daisy sidles up to me, her plate covered in blueberries and
kiwi. "Allie, do you know the fabulous Karen Pearce? Karen is
not just a wonderful pediatrician, she is also the room-parent
coordinator for Eastbrook. Allie's a big-time photographer who
just moved into the neighborhood from Chicago. Her husband
Mark's a lawyer, and they have a kindergarten boy named Cole."

"Cole hasn't really done anything impressive yet," I say. "Unless you count finger painting." Daisy laughs, but Karen's smile
seems strained.

"Welcome to the neighborhood. Allie, is it?" A flicker of recognition crosses Karen's eyes. Had she heard something about
me, or was it just something in Daisy's detailed introduction that
resonated? "So where did you put the mini-buns?"

"The what?" I ask, unsure if I heard correctly.

"For the sliders?" It is then that I notice a platter stacked with
tiny round meat patties.

Karen is smiling, but her voice comes out strained. "The mini-
hamburger buns. You signed up to bring three dozen."

"I did? I don't think I did."

"Pickles are here, pickles are here!" A statuesque woman with long, curly brown hair strides in, carrying two oversize jars of pickle chips. She, too, wears brown boots. I want to tell her that she's missed the photo. "Hey, Karen, Daisy, where are we putting the pickles?"

"Right here." Karen moves a large wooden salad bowl to make room. "Allie, this is Vicki Armstrong, our incredible PTA president."

Vicki flashes me a thin smile and then, after a quick survey of the table, scowls. "Wait, where are the buns?"

"There might be a problem with the buns." Karen keeps her eyes fixed on Vicki, as if beaming a message to her in some special PTA language, inaudible to the rest of us.

"What are you talking about? Who was supposed to bring them?"

Karen says nothing, but the woman does not wait for an answer. She whips out her phone. *Tap tap tap.* "Who the hell is Allie Ross?"

"That's me." I hold up my hand, give a little wave.

"Right. So what's up with the hamburger buns?"

"I didn't sign up for hamburger buns."

Vicki thrusts her phone across the table at me in a pointless gesture, since I cannot read it from that far. "Well, this says you were supposed to bring buns."

Vicki looks to Daisy for backup, but she will not look up from the napkins she is busy arranging into a perfect spiral.

"Look, I'm sorry. There must have been a mix-up. I can run out and get some," I say. "I'd be happy to."

"No, it's not important," Daisy says. "Don't be silly. We have plenty of food."

"Right, it's not important that Karen took the time to make dozens of sliders, and that I brought the pickles, and that, like, you organize this Eastbrook tradition every year. That's not important."

"Vicki, really. It's fine," Daisy says.

"This," Vicki says, sweeping her hand over the table, "only works if everyone contributes."

"Ignore her," Daisy says and pulls me back into the foyer. "I swear, ever since she went Paleo, she's been a total bitch."

I offer a weak laugh, but my heart thumps wildly in my chest. I step back, as if pushed, my guts clenching. Vicki's hostility scares me. *You don't belong,* screams a little voice inside my head, one that I can usually muffle. But not tonight. Now it is raging. I knew we shouldn't have come.

All around me, people laugh, but I feel like I'm going to jump out of my own skin. Deep breaths do little to counteract the familiar tide of panic rising within me. I peel away from Daisy and work my way through the crowd toward the kitchen. I need more wine. But as soon as I cross the threshold, Rob, who is still standing by the wine, looks up and locks eyes with me.

He gives me a sly grin, a knowing nod. I pivot out of the room.

3

I need a quiet place to go. I feel the stirrings of a panic attack. I hadn't had one since last spring in Chicago, when I couldn't locate Cole at the grocery store. The walls seemed to close in. I need quiet and space. The powder room door is locked, and a woman directs me to the second floor. I start up the stairs, holding the banister for support.

My mind pings back and forth, hearing Rob call me *Lexi*, recalling the confrontation over the mini-buns. That awful, sneering woman. I'm certain I did not sign up to bring them. And even if I did forget, did she have to embarrass me like that? People make mistakes.

Inside the bathroom, my face is pink all the way to my hairline, outward proof that I am over my limit.

The past few weeks have been a blur—moving, filling out school papers, getting on the neighborhood's Facebook page—but I would have remembered signing up to bring mini-buns, wouldn't I? Maybe Mark did and forgot to tell me.

I wet my hands and tousle my short hair. Chopping it off had seemed like a good idea when we first moved to D.C. over the hot, sticky summer. I thought it might accentuate my small features, and I needed a refresh on my hair, which had been fried from so many years of highlights. But the truth is that my natural mousy brown makes me look washed out, and if I skip lipstick and mascara, I end up looking like an anemic Peter Pan.

I take my time powdering my face, trying to hide some of the shine. I'm in no hurry to return to the party, and this oversize bathroom is as good a place as any to kill some time. It's larger than the bedroom I shared with my sister growing up, and it's clearly been recently renovated, with a white porcelain farmhouse sink deep enough to bathe a golden retriever in. A stack of fluffy, white towels sits on a marble table beside a glass pedestal jar, the kind usually filled with candy. Only this one has tiny little soaps in the shape of seashells in pale pinks and creams. It reminds me of a scene from one of my mother's favorite movies, *The Flamingo Kid*. In it, a working-class guy goes to dinner at his boss's fancy house and stuffs the little soaps in his pocket.

I can't help myself. I take a photo and text it to my sister, Krystle. My mother would love it, but with the way her dementia is progressing, I'm lucky if she knows what year it is these days, forget being able to operate a smartphone.

But Krystle will get it, and that's almost as good.

My phone buzzes. It's a text from Leah: *Just got here. Where r u?*

Bathroom. I'll find you in five, I tap back. With Leah here, I may be able to handle the party a little longer. A former corporate lawyer turned stay-at-home mom, Leah glides effortlessly between the different tribes in the neighborhood—career moms, SAHMs, empty nesters—like some kind of goodwill ambassador. I need to find her—not just because she promised to introduce me to the moms who, in her words, "don't suck," but also because I want to stay in her good graces. I don't want to piss off the one friend I've made. I reapply lip gloss, ready to make some mommy friends.

I unlock the bathroom door, and it swings inward with such force that I am knocked back. Rob from the kitchen barges in. He kicks the door shut behind him, and in a split second has me pressed up against the sink, the cold porcelain jabbing my hip bone.

I freeze as his hands travel up and down my body, the air

trapped in my lungs. Then the adrenaline kicks in. I try to shove him away. It's like pushing against a brick wall.

"Jesus, you make me so fucking hot." His hands plunge up my skirt, warm fingers exploring. I swat at them to no effect. They crawl up my thighs like a dozen spiders. His mouth mashes my lips against my teeth. I slide my head to escape, to breathe. "You want me to fuck you right here?" His raspy cheek abrades mine like sandpaper.

There's no room to escape. He wedges one knee between my legs and pries them open. His fingers slip beneath my panties, delve inside me. "You're so wet."

Shame floods me as my back arches in response to his touch. My brain screams no. I wrangle one arm free and manage enough leverage to jam my elbow into him. He staggers back, hand to his chest.

We both stand still, stunned. "What the fuck was that?" he asks. "You could have hurt me."

I want to tell him I could hurt him a hell of a lot more. Instead, I yank open the bathroom door and stumble into the hall, pulling my skirt down and cursing myself again for wearing it.

I look up and see Mark halfway up the staircase. His eyes light up when he sees me.

"Hello. There you are." The singsong tone of his voice tells me he's drunk a bit too much. He glances past me, and his smile fades. I turn to see Rob emerging from the bathroom.

Rob shoves past me, knocking my shoulder, and then pauses at the top of the staircase. He turns, his face red with anger, and leans in to my ear so close I can smell his sweat. "Stay the fuck off Tinder, you cock tease."

I open my mouth. No sound comes out. Rob continues down the stairs, and Mark grabs him.

"What the hell did you just say to my wife?" Mark asks.

Rob shakes his arm free. "Why don't you ask Lexi?"

4

The foyer is empty when I retrieve our jackets from the coat closet.

Mark is on my heels. "Allie, what was that about? Who was that guy?"

"Shhh," I hiss. "I'll tell you later." I shove his jacket at him, ignoring the perplexed look on his face, and pull on my own coat. I just want to get out of here.

"Are you all right?" Mark's loud attempt at a whisper would be funny in other circumstances. He smells like beer.

"Can we just go?" My eyes dart from the living room to the dining room. No one pays us any mind. But Rob is in there somewhere, saying God knows what to people.

Moments later, we are picking our way across the flagstones to the car. The fresh night air fills my lungs, and I finally feel like I can breathe. Mark stops. "I'm not sure I should drive."

I nod. If he's saying that, he really is too drunk. And there's no way I want to get behind the wheel. My whole body is jangly.

"Fine. Let's walk." I turn away, not waiting for a response. We only live across Massachusetts Avenue, a fifteen-minute walk, tops.

"We could call an Uber," Mark calls after me.

I stop and pivot. "Can we please just go? By the time an Uber comes, we'll be home." I glance up at Daisy's house, the stone façade strategically lit by spotlights nestled among the azalea bushes. My eye lands on a figure in the front window, the large one in the dining room, backlit and unidentifiable. Is someone watching us? I shudder.

He jogs up to me and puts his arm on my shoulder as we hurry toward Mass Ave. At the curb, we wait for a chance to cross onto our side of the neighborhood. The distinction between the two sides is one of degrees. Both are upper-middle-class areas with single-family homes, but Daisy's side boasts sprawling houses with landscaped yards and accent lights, while our side is filled with more modest brick houses jammed onto small lots and front yards littered with kids' toys and worn Adirondack chairs.

"Allie, are you okay?" Mark asks. "What happened back there?"

"That guy was an asshole, that's what happened. A drunk asshole." My anger surprises both of us.

"What did he say to you?"

"Something about staying off Tinder."

"Tinder? The dating app?"

"I guess." After a car speeds by, I step into the four-lane road, pulling Mark after me.

"Why would he say that?" Mark asks, slightly out of breath, once we are on the other side.

"I don't know." I stop to face him. "Can we please just go home?"

He looks wounded.

"I just want to take a hot shower. Is that okay? Can we talk about it after that?"

He nods and we walk side by side through the empty suburban streets, Halloween decorations in almost every yard. It's mid-October and in the mid-sixties. Growing up in Connecticut, fall meant digging out your wool sweaters, and in Chicago, it meant winter coats. But my first autumn in D.C. has been one long extension of summer—blue skies and temperatures more appropriate for pool parties than apple-picking.

Relief fills me as our little house, illuminated in the moonlight, comes into view. The white paint peeling off the red brick could be interpreted as shabby chic, or simply shabby, but for me, it is home. More than that, it's tangible proof of success. It's the first house I have ever lived in, and my name is on the deed, alongside Mark's.

Mark glances up at Leah's house across the street, looking for the silhouette in the window.

"The Watcher's watching," Mark says with forced cheer. I look up and see a dark figure behind a curtain on the second floor. I think of the figure at Daisy's party. It's a part of the suburbs I am having trouble adjusting to, the total lack of anonymity.

The Watcher is Mark's nickname for Dustin, ever since he found Dustin lurking in our driveway the weekend we moved in, supposedly looking for his lost drone.

I force out a half-hearted laugh, trying to let Mark know that I appreciate his attempt to cheer me up. But inside, I am still reeling from what happened at the party.

We trudge along the path to the back door and enter the back of the house through the mudroom, a narrow room lined with deep cubbies that promised an organized life straight off a Pinterest board. It might have been the single biggest reason we bought this house.

When Mark flicks on the light, our sitter, Susan, pops up from the sofa in front of the TV, where a *Law and Order* spinoff is on. She's clutching her knitting in one hand, and her jangly Scotty-dog earrings swing from her ears.

"Oh, goodness, you startled me." She puts a hand to her heart. An elfish sixty-something retiree, Susan lives in the neighborhood with her West Highland terrier, Marnie. She's more than just a babysitter—she watches Cole after school until I get home from work and has become like an auntie to him. She knows how to talk to little boys. Her last job was sitting for the rambunctious Zoni triplets who live around the corner.

"Sorry, Susan," Mark says with a bit too much cheer. His

warmth toward others always seems to rise in direct proportion to how upset he is. I remember a trip to Florida one winter when the hotel screwed up our reservations. The more the situation worsened, the politer Mark became.

The heat of the kitchen hits me as soon as I walk in, which means Susan has been baking. Every time she babysits, she bakes something with Cole and then cleans the kitchen top to bottom, leaving it spiffier than before. Cole relishes these kitchen episodes—his favorite TV show is *The Great British Bake Off.*

"You're home early." Susan fixes me with her bright blue eyes.

"I know. Headache." The lie slides right out. It's not like I'm going to tell my babysitter that a guy I was flirting with tried to have sex with me at the neighborhood social. The scent of cinnamon hangs in the air, as well as something else I cannot put my finger on.

"Smells wonderful in here," Mark says, coming up behind me. He wraps me in his arms. "Doesn't it smell good, Allie?"

"Pumpkin bread." Susan gestures with a knitting needle toward two brown loaves on the kitchen counter. "Cole said he'd never tried it, so I thought, oh heck, why not?" Susan turns to me. "Do you need a cup of tea, Allie? Chamomile is good for a headache."

Her concern touches me. A part of me does want to let her mother me—no one else is doing it—but what I really want is a shower, the kind that's so hot it feels like it's taking off the top layer of skin.

"I think a shower and bed will do the trick," I say, disentangling myself from Mark. If not for Susan, I might strip out of this skirt and leave it in a puddle right here in the kitchen. My hip throbs where it met the hard sink. I'm sure there will be an ugly bruise.

Mark pulls out his wallet and lays a stack of twenties on the counter. Susan stands there smiling, clucking in a sympathetic manner and making no move to gather her things. I have the feeling that babysitting Cole is something of a highlight in her life. This might be unfair, but she comes off like a walking warning of what happens to a woman who dedicates her entire life to others.

When I finally get upstairs to my bathroom, I strip down and examine the pale purple bruise on my hip.

As I wait for the water to warm up, my greatest hits of unwanted touchings come rushing through my mind. The shift manager at the restaurant where I worked during art school, who would find me bent over doing some menial task and make comments like, *That's how I like to see you, ass in the air.*

The first photographer I worked for, the one who reeked of clove cigarettes and always found a reason to follow me into the supply room, breathing down my neck, accidentally grinding against me.

That man in a parking lot in Chicago who reached out and squeezed both my breasts as my arms hung useless by my side, laden with grocery bags. Stunned, I did nothing.

In fact, I didn't do anything about any of those incidents.

But at some point, I thought it would end. Navigating lecherous men is so commonplace as to be almost a rite of passage. But this, this was different.

I was a grown woman, married, a mother. I was Mark Ross's wife. I lived in Bethesda, Maryland, for Chrissakes.

Didn't any of those things offer me protection?

The wine guy, this Rob, lives in the same community, and we were at a neighborhood social event. Anger stirs within me. There's no way he could have thought this was acceptable behavior.

I climb into the shower. Under the warm water, I replay the night like a movie. I see myself in the dining room, the hamburger bun fiasco, in the kitchen, flirting, and then bam, Rob is in the bathroom with me, slamming me into the sink.

And that awful moment, when my body reacted despite me, when my back arched in response to his touch.

I shudder.

It's not your fault.

You didn't want this to happen.

I scrub hard with a washcloth, trying to scrape away the invisible grime his skin left on mine.

I shut off the water and lean my head against the cold tile, letting a wave of nausea wash over me. I feel tiny and insignificant, reduced by this stranger. I know it's not my fault, yet I feel a sickening dread. A tiny, ugly truth blooms in the swampiest corner of my soul. This rotten, little weed, begging for attention, wants me to know that inside of me is a broken thing, which he recognized. I thought I'd been clever enough to hide it. I've fooled so many people, people like Mark. But this guy smelled it on me.

Me. Not anyone else there.

5

Wrapped in the towel, I slip into Cole's darkened room. By the glow of the night-light, I watch his small chest rise and fall. He's flanked by a stuffed penguin and a pink giraffe, named, respectively, Penguin and Pink Giraffe. My little boy—who pretends to be a different animal baby every day, paints each of his fingernails a different color, and has an imaginary friend named Twizzle—chooses only the most literal names for his stuffed animals.

I bend down and inhale the dense tangle of his hair. It's dark and thick like Mark's, and I'm comforted by the familiar smell of Johnson's baby shampoo.

Before I leave, I pull the blanket over Cole's exposed shoulder, a symbolic act, since it will end up in a pile on the floor in the morning. Beside the pillow lies a dog-eared copy of *Pinkalicious*. Cole knows it by heart. I smile, picturing him pleading with Susan to read it to him one more time.

Back in my bedroom, I slip on an old Stanford Law T-shirt of Mark's that falls to my knees. It makes me feel about as sexy as an extra on *Little House on the Prairie*, but it's so worn it's almost see-through in parts, and despite being washed a hundred times, it still smells like him and I need that comfort. I need to wear something that isn't even a little sexy, that feels like a big hug.

Mark appears in the doorway, a mug of steaming liquid in hand. "Chamomile. Susan insisted." He puts the mug on my bedside table. "She's worried about you."

I DON'T FORGIVE YOU

"Susan's very sweet."

"So am I. Worried that is, not sweet."

I smile. "You're sweet."

"What happened back there? You came rushing down the stairs . . ." His voice trails off.

I shrug and avert my eyes from the intensity of his gaze. I know what he wants. Not just a recounting of what happened but to peer inside my psyche and listen in on my inner voice. In short, access to my soul. But my feelings are on lockdown. It's a vestigial skill, one I honed growing up in a household where I never knew which mother I would encounter—the sarcastic drunk or the silly flirt. Learning to pack up my emotions in a box that I could access later, in safety and privacy, was a tool I learned quite early.

Unlearning it is proving harder.

"Can we talk about this tomorrow?" Dragging it all out in our bedroom would be letting that man's ugliness into my safe and private space. I just want to put the whole thing behind me, pretend it didn't happen.

Mark sits down beside me.

"Allie, I want to understand what happened tonight." His tone is gentle, his face neutral. I have to tell him something. I believe this is what marriage is, taking the leap of faith into the void and having faith your partner will catch you. I take a deep breath.

"I don't want you to freak out or anything," I say, my words directed at the curtainless window. "But that guy? At the party? He basically came into the bathroom when I was in it, and he, umm, I don't know. Tried to kiss me?" My voice shakes as I speak, and I hate how tentative I sound, as if I am not exactly sure what happened, even though I am.

"He did what?" A hoarseness has crept into his voice.

"Please, please don't overreact." I place my hand atop Mark's and squeeze. I don't have the mental bandwidth for his feelings right now, only mine. "This guy was drunk and gross, and nothing happened—"

Mark bristles. "I don't call that nothing. He put his hands on you?"

"You're right. It's not nothing."

"Did he hurt you?" His eyes bore into me, unnerving me.

"No." The word shoots out of my mouth before I realize that I am lying. I want to protect Mark from his own anger. It's just a bruise, after all. It'll heal in a week. "I'm fine," I say. "It was just unsettling."

It's a lie. But I feel myself shutting down. I won't be forced into exploring all the awfulness of it right this second. Not even for Mark.

"Unsettling? That's illegal in the state of Maryland. Hell, it's illegal in all fifty states. It's called battery, and it's against the law." Mark stands up and runs his hands through his hair. "Do you know this guy's name?"

"Rob something. I don't know his last name."

"Rob, huh? I'm going to go talk to him."

"No, that's not a good idea."

He nods. "You're right. We should just go straight to the police."

The word *police* seizes me in my chest, making it hard to breathe. "No, no, no, Mark. Please, sit down."

But he's pacing back and forth, not listening to me. "Does Daisy know who this Rob guy is? Should I call her? No, it's late." He turns to me. "We can call Daisy in the morning. She'll know his full name, and then we can go to the police."

"No police, Mark. Stop saying the word *police*." My voice comes out thin and strained. He halts his pacing.

"Why not?"

"What do you think they are going to do?"

"I don't know. Investigate? Give this guy a warning?"

"You mean start interviewing every one of the people at that party? Our neighbors? The other parents? Is that what you want? We just moved here; I don't want to become the subject of neighborhood gossip." I don't tell him that I know what it's like to carry around that hot stone of shame in your body, that I have lived through that and have no desire to ever experience it again.

He stares up at the ceiling and then lets out a long, slow breath. "Fine. No police. But he shouldn't get away with this." Mark was an Eagle Scout when he was a teen. While other boys were binge-drinking and raising hell, he was building a handicapped ramp for the Chevy Chase library. In his world, there is right and wrong, black and white, truth and lies.

I stand up, and he does, too. I am so ready for this to be over. At least for now. "This kind of stuff happens to women all the time." I perch on my tiptoes and kiss him on his cheek. "All. The. Time. If women went to the cops every time some jerk came on to them at a party, the police wouldn't have time to do anything else."

I wrap my arms around him and hold him tight. I know I'm not being brave. If I were a superhero in the Marvel Universe, I would spring into action with righteous anger. I would be the one calling the police. But I know how things work in the real world and that this is a bell that can't be unrung. Slowly, he puts his arms around me, as well. I can feel the energy around him settle down. A few moments later, we disentangle, and it's as if a storm has passed.

"Let me lock up downstairs," Mark says. "And then I'll come to bed."

I head to the bathroom, where I dab cream made from Japanese mushrooms under my eyes and smooth a gelatinous firming serum that smells like bleach on my cheeks. These little potions cost more money than I used to spend on a week's worth of groceries when I was single.

I am lucky. I have a loving husband. A good job. A beautiful house and a healthy child. I don't want trouble.

Back in the bedroom, I wait for Mark under the duvet and watch the opening monologue of *Saturday Night Live* by myself.

The host is a middle-aged actor promoting a new action movie. I remember when he almost killed his career about fifteen years ago after being found nude and stoned, wandering around someone's backyard. But in the years since, he's made a comeback. No one ever mentions his past.

Lucky guy.

Finally, Mark arrives, apologizing for taking so long. "I forgot to set my fantasy football lineup," he says as he changes into his pajamas.

I snuggle beside him. During a commercial, he mutes the TV and turns to me.

"So what do you think that guy meant when he said *stay off Tinder?*" I look away from the television and directly at him. He looks like a huge version of Cole, right down to the shock of black hair falling across his forehead.

I tense up. "I have no idea, Mark."

"I mean, you're not on Tinder, are you?" I can tell he's trying to sound lighthearted, as if the question is a joke. I think of my sister and the horror stories she's told me about online dating sites—the married men looking for side action, the ubiquitous dick pics.

"That guy was drunk, Mark. He wasn't making any sense. Anyway, I don't even have time to hang curtains, much less trawl Tinder." I give his ribs a gentle nudge. "Now can we please watch *SNL?* You can tell me how much funnier it used to be in the old days."

"It *was* funnier," he says, turning the volume back up.

"I know. Everything was better in the eighties."

He settles back against the pillows, and I tuck myself up against his broad shoulder. He's put on at least ten pounds since we moved to D.C. and he started working at the law firm. Long hours mean takeout for dinner at work many nights, and he has no time for the gym. I don't mind the weight. I like him solid.

And solid is what I need. Sometimes I think of Mark as my

lighthouse in a raging sea, and I am a tiny boat keeping my eyes on him. It's true that lighthouses aren't warm and fuzzy, but I don't need warm and fuzzy. I need strength, stability. I need to know he is always there, my light in the dark.

Tension seeps from my body and sleep beckons, a delicious riptide dragging me under. The laughter from the TV ebbs and flows like the waves of the ocean. But then moments before I surrender to sleep, I hear that voice again. I feel that finger pressing against my collarbone.

Me Rob, the voice says. *You Lexi.*

Then another memory, unbidden, drifts across my consciousness. One that's been buried for years. A hand parting the curtain of hair that always hid my face. *You don't even know how sexy you are. Sexy Lexi, that's what I'm going to call you.*

6

I awake with a start at five fifteen, thoughts struggling to break the surface of my consciousness. My eyes are heavy in a familiar way. I am wide awake, yet still tired.

Stay the fuck off Tinder, you cock tease.

I roll over, and in the pale moonlight shining through our bare window, I make out the outline of the pile of books on my bedside table. I know the top one is a novel I am supposed to be reading for Leah's book club, but it seems a Herculean task. Somewhere beneath that is *The Friendship Crisis: Finding, Making, and Keeping Friends When You're Not a Kid Anymore.* Chapter 3 suggests that lonely grown-ups like me join a book club.

Sauvignon blanc.

John Wick.

Cardi B.

Lexi.

My heart begins to gallop in my chest. I sit up. There's no way I am falling back to sleep. I pull back the covers as quietly as I can, but nonetheless Mark stirs.

"Huh?" he asks, jerking his head a few inches from the pillow. "What's going on?"

"Shhh," I whisper. "Go back to sleep." He lies back down, throwing his forearm over his eyes, his mouth open, and within seconds, he is snoring gently.

After donning a robe and slippers, I pad downstairs and put the kettle on for a cup of tea. We keep the family computer in a little nook in the kitchen-slash-family-room, where the three of us spend about eighty percent of our waking hours. In fact, if a fire destroyed the rest of the house, we could happily live in this one room.

Having the computer in a central place means we can pay bills, check email, or search for a recipe without having to leave Cole unattended. And we can monitor his online activity, which for now consists of watching YouTube videos of other children building complicated structures with LEGOs.

I take my tea and settle in front of the computer, ready for it to give me answers to questions I'm not even sure I can articulate. I don't even know this Rob's last name.

Above the computer hangs a poster I've owned for ages, a re-production of a Mary Ellen Mark black-and-white photograph of a reed-thin girl in a black dress, arms crossed, a defiant ex-pression on her face as she peers out from behind a black veil. Mark hates the photo, finds it depressing and spooky. But I hang it in a prominent place every time we move. It reminds me that photography isn't only for the beautiful. Everyone deserves to be truly seen.

Our home page is Google, and I type in *Rob*, then *Eastbrook*, and then *Bethesda*. What comes back are a jumble of meaningless results. It's not a surprise that our D.C. suburb is filled with men named Robert. The sheer uselessness of this exercise leaves me defeated.

My fingers hover over the keyboard, reluctant to type the word that has flashed neon in my brain. It's as if doing so will conjure, voodoo-style, some spirit I won't be able to rid myself of.

I take a deep breath and type.

Tinder.

I click, but I can't get far without joining. And it seems that to join Tinder, you have to link your Facebook account, which I am not willing to do, even for purely research purposes.

Instead, I open Instagram and scroll mindlessly through the

likes I've received recently. I click on a new follower, and it takes a moment for it to register: Rob, the guy from last night.

I curse myself. Why did I tell him to follow me on Insta? He's gone back through my posts and liked dozens of pictures from the last few months. Mostly cityscapes, but some studio shots that clients have allowed me to post, along with selfies of me in my new surroundings—the neighborhood pool, the Farm Women's Market in downtown Bethesda. What he did takes time, and it creeps me out.

But it is his comments that make my skin crawl.

Under one selfie I took in front of a fiery red maple on our block, he wrote: *Not just beautiful, but talented, too.*

And on a shot I took of Leah and me before we headed out for a girls' night of drinks, he wrote: *Sexy Lexi.*

I freeze.

There it is again.

That nickname. It can't be a coincidence, but what connection could this Rob guy possibly have to Overton Academy?

I've been careful since I left Connecticut more than sixteen years ago. There's a demarcation in my life between then and now, and I am meticulous about not letting anything in from the past. I don't subscribe to any of the Overton alumni stuff, I throw away anything that comes in the mail, and I haven't stayed in touch with anyone from my two years at that school. If anyone from high school does manage to connect my past name, Alexis Healy, with my married name, Allie Ross, and asks to follow me on Instagram, or tries to friend me on Facebook, I offer the same response: radio silence.

I'm super careful to keep everything under Allie Ross.

Not Alexis, and certainly not Lexi.

Lexi was an experiment my senior year at Overton—a brief and desperate attempt to transform from an awkward scholarship student into someone sophisticated and alluring.

I can even recall the exact moment I decided to start calling myself Lexi. It was a chilly Friday night in late fall, the kind in New England where the wind is sharp and there's no doubt that a long, cold winter is around the corner. Madeline, my only true friend at the school, convinced me to come with her to crash a house party.

We'll be sociologists, Madeline said in that way she had of hiding her teenage insecurities behind faux intellectualism. She was one of a handful of African American girls at Overton and the only one in our grade. She often came across as uptight and rigid, unfriendly even, the only child of two stiff academics. She had mastered the art of rejecting the world first, before it got a chance to reject her. But when it was just us two, she was different—wry and vulnerable. *C'mon,* she cajoled, *we can stand off by ourselves and laugh at the sheeple in their J. Crew clothes getting drunk on Daddy's liquor.*

I can see us now—me dressed incongruously in a miniskirt and a hand-me-down men's parka, and Madeline, her shoulders stooped to minimize her height, dressed all in black—trudging up the steps to the grand Victorian a few blocks from the town square. I remember hoping that the party had reached that tipping point where everyone was too trashed to realize we had not been invited.

It wasn't long afterward that I was back on the street, pulling my parka tight against the wind, furious at Madeline for abandoning me for the attention of a wasted soccer player, the kind of vacuous bro we always mocked. Her transformation from cynical social observer to desperate groupie had been swift. All he did was offer her a red Solo cup full of beer and recite a few lines from a Dave Matthews song.

Disgusted and betrayed, I headed to the bus stop and settled in for a long wait. I was no stranger to the public transportation system. Unlike most of my classmates at Overton, who lived in the wealthy town in which the school was located, I had a thirty-minute bus ride every day from Norwalk. I would press my forehead against the glass and watch as our neighborhood of low-rise condos and large homes chopped into apartments receded, to be replaced by the stately houses with pillars and porches that led up to the leafy campus of Overton. It took the entire ride to gird myself for the day and to put on my invisible armor. No one was overtly mean to me. No one mocked my off-brand sneakers, or sneered when I said I had never been to Martha's Vineyard. It was all much subtler than that, and in a way that was worse. I didn't even merit teasing. I was invisible.

I sat at the bus stop with my camera on my lap. The public buses ran sporadically on weekend evenings, and that meant I might be sitting in the cold and dark for an hour or more. I was fiddling with the lens cap when a rusted BMW pulled up.

The passenger-side window rolled down to reveal my photography teacher sitting in the driver's seat, a lopsided smile on his face. Paul Adamson was almost thirty, but he still dressed like a prep school kid—worn-out chinos and beat-up Stan Smiths held together by duct tape. His hair was dark auburn; thick, spirited waves fell this way and that. He had green eyes and long lashes, and when he got really worked up about some brilliant photographer in class, his whole face would turn red, right down to his neck, where it disappeared in the V of his button-down collared shirt. He never wore anything but—sometimes an Oxford-blue one, sometimes white, and on rare occasion, pink.

"Well, well, well," he said, smiling. "What have we here—my star pupil."

I approached the car, my face flushing under his gaze. Without the buffer that other students usually provided, there was nothing between us but the cold night air.

"What in the world are you doing out here?" he asked. When he looked at me then, he ignited a small fire. No one had ever looked at me like that before, no high school boy, that was for sure. It was as if I had not existed until that moment. I burned red and hot then, even in the cold, and I was thankful for the cover of darkness.

Before I could answer, he shoved open the passenger-side door. "Hop in, Alexis. I'll drive you home."

I had always hated the name Alexis.

It sounded like I was trying too hard, overcompensating for our cramped apartment and lack of family money. It reminded me of my mother smoking menthols while poring over gossip magazines, as if wearing the same shade of lipstick as some actress would magically imbue her with class. My Overton classmates possessed carefree, almost dowdy nicknames—Kristen V. in my English class was known as Cricket. My year also had two Mollys, an Emsy, short for Emily, and even a Cookie.

As I climbed in the car, I improvised.

"Call me Lexi," I said.

7

"She's trying to kill me!" I hold the phone a few inches from my ear, as the panic in my mother's voice makes her sound more like a child than a fifty-seven-year-old woman.

"No one's trying to kill you, Sharon," I say and roll my eyes at Mark. He pauses, mid-flip of a pancake, and gives me a sympathetic smile. We've both become accustomed to these dramatic phone calls at all hours.

My mother received a diagnosis of early-onset dementia about eight years ago. For a while, I just attributed her cognitive problems to her drinking, and I overlooked her increasingly strange behavior. When you grow up with a mother who shows up at school in smeared lipstick and a leopard-print cocktail dress, it's easy to dismiss her twenty years later when the neighbor calls to inform you she's watering the roses in a negligee.

But then Sharon fell.

She was outside Westfair Fish & Chips, a three-table joint in a strip mall just outside Westport. Her version was that she went to say hello to a large dog, who jumped on her and knocked her down. But according to the dog owner, Sharon was teetering on high heels, clearly drunk, and collapsed of her own accord.

Sharon ended up in the ER with a concussion, a broken elbow, and a shattered shoulder. And most important—after a battery of tests—a diagnosis of early-onset dementia, alcohol-related.

A social worker and a neurologist got involved. We put together a "team." But her health degenerated from there.

She refused to allow aides to enter the house, locking them out and calling the police when they tried to get in. But she couldn't feed or bathe herself. She became paranoid, withdrawn. That's when I moved her into assisted living, but it only accelerated her deterioration.

"That witch was here, Alexis," Sharon insists. "She was in my room last night. Please come get me."

From the corner of my eye, I see Cole, in his little chef's hat, swatting Mark's bottom with a spatula.

"No one was in your room. You're perfectly safe, I promise." I plug my earbuds into the phone and turn the volume way down so I can use my hands to help get breakfast on the table while talking.

"Oh, really?" And just like that, my mother has traded the little-girl wheedling for cold sarcasm. "Since when are you such an expert?"

"Sharon, be nice." My mother has never let me call her Mom; it's been Sharon since I can remember. "It was probably just one of the aides checking on you."

"Don't you think I know the difference between an aide and an assassin?" I can imagine the spittle flying from her cherry-red lips. Revlon's Fire & Ice, of course, the same lipstick she's worn my whole life. "You've always been naive. Book-smart yes, street-smart no. Now your sister. She's another story."

The internet is filled with articles on how to gracefully handle parents whose dementia has transformed their lovable, sunny personalities into cauldrons of paranoia and vitriol. But what about when your mother has always been this way? What if you don't have reserves of good memories to call upon?

"If you're rude to me, I will hang up. You know the rules." I read that tip in an article called "When Anger Follows Dementia: Establishing Boundaries."

"The rules. That's a good one." Sharon lets out a sharp laugh that would make Cruella De Vil wince. "I don't remember agreeing to these rules, Madame."

Growing up, my mother and sister used to joke that I was like a fussy old lady. They called me Madame as in *Madame doesn't think we should park in the handicap spot* or *Madame doesn't think we should throw cigarette butts out the car window.*

Oh, are we offending Madame?

But I also knew that it made my mother proud that I was pulled out in middle school for the gifted-and-talented program. I once overheard her bragging about me to the old lady who lived in the apartment below us. Even if Sharon thought it was hysterical that I didn't want her using my library books as coasters for her evening whiskey sour, she was the one who pushed me to apply for the scholarship at Overton.

My mother launches into one of her tirades about how she doesn't deserve to be locked away like a criminal, and I turn my attention to Cole, who is crouched like a baseball player, hoisting his spatula over his shoulder. "I am ze bum smacker!" he howls and gives Mark's behind a good whack. "Smack! Smack! Smack!"

Mark recoils in mock pain and limps over to me, a cup of coffee in one hand and a plate in the other. "Les pancakes?" he asks in an exaggerated French accent. "And your cappuccino?"

Cole climbs onto the stool beside me.

"Get off the phone, Mommy." Cole grabs at the phone. I twist away.

"Sharon, I have to go. We're having breakfast."

"Are you coming to see me? I'd love to see you, Alexis. I haven't seen you in months." Her tone has shifted again. Now she is needy, cloying. I can picture her in front of her vanity, batting her eyes at her reflection.

"I saw you last weekend. I come every Sunday. I'll be there later today."

"But what time? What time exactly?" She lowers her voice to a whisper. "They try to hide me when you come, make up some malarkey about having to see the nurse so I'll miss your visit."

Only after making assurances that no one is going to keep us apart am I able to hang up.

She wasn't always this bad off. But the move from her assisted living facility in Connecticut to one in Maryland has triggered a precipitous decline in her mental state. I'd wanted her closer to us so that I could visit her more frequently and also to maintain her warm relationship with Cole.

I never knew any of my grandparents. My mom's parents died when she was a teenager, and after my father died, we moved away from the small Massachusetts town where my father's family, the entire extended Healy clan, had resided since James Healy took a boat over from Connaught in 1845. I have a few photos of me as an infant, sitting on my father's mother's lap, but no memory of her. Sharon maintained that she was never welcomed by the Healys and had always felt trapped living in a small town. I don't blame her for leaving—she was barely twenty-five when widowed, with a toddler and a baby, and staying in that small town must have felt suffocating.

But it's hard not to fault her for cutting ties with my father's family. Norwalk is less than a two-hour drive from that Massachusetts town. I remember Krystle and I received a few cards and gifts at Christmas over the years and then the news that my father's parents had passed. Essentially, Krystle and I grew up with no extended family.

So I suppose moving Sharon down here was competing in my own way with Mark's large family, which has tentacles in every suburb of Washington, D.C. Krystle opposed the move from the beginning and blames me for our mother's subsequent decline.

The worst part is that my mother's relationship with Cole has soured. The first time we visited Sharon in her new place, she barely acknowledged him. And two weeks ago, she flew into a rage while we were there and threw a bottle of L'Air du Temps at one of the aides, striking her in the shoulder. That episode terrified Cole and gave him nightmares. Mark, his sister, Caitlin, and their mother insisted that I stop bringing Cole to see Sharon until she settled down.

I peer into my coffee cup and smile. Mark has managed to create a delicate fern in the foam. He knows I love when he does that. "You're getting good at this foam art thing."

He bats his eyelashes. "Why, thank you. If this lawyer thing doesn't pan out, I might look for work at Compass Coffee."

"Mine are Mickey Mouse pancakes." Cole holds one up to show me. "I eat the ears first."

"Is that right?" I pour the syrup and swirl it on my own pancakes. Mark cleans the griddle, half-watching a soccer game on TV that he's recorded. Last night's drama seems far away. We are a portrait of domestic contentment.

Suddenly, my phone starts vibrating.

Ping. Ping. Ping. A cascade of text messages, one after another.

I look at the phone and realize quickly that I am the third in a three-way text conversation involving Daisy and Leah.

What's with the yellow police tape on Arleigh? Leah has typed. *Saw it walking dog this a.m.*

Didn't you see the ENFB? Daisy responds. It takes my groggy brain a moment to translate that as the Eastbrook Neighborhood Facebook page. I haven't looked at it since I woke up, hours ago now. *There was a break-in!*

Cops are EVERYWHERE!

Whose house?

5005 Arleigh Rd. Who lives there?

Averys. Daughter in fourth grade, I think. Parents divorced?

From across the room, Mark's phone emits a buzz, too. He frowns. "What the heck is going on?" he asks.

I glance at Cole, not wanting to freak him out with news there's been a break-in. "I think there's something police-related over on Arleigh Road. Apparently, the whole neighborhood is abuzz."

"What's police-related?" Cole asks.

"Buddy, go get dressed for church," Mark says, and after the obligatory whining, Cole heads upstairs.

Mark comes around the counter and kisses the top of my head. "How you doing this morning? Any better?"

"I guess I'm okay. Just groggy." I stand up and take my plate to the sink. My phone and Mark's both ping at the same time.

"What now?" he asks and grabs his phone.

I look up to see his expression turn sour.

"What is it?" I ask, but he does not look up from his phone. "Mark, you're scaring me."

"Apparently, it wasn't a break-in. The police thing over on Arleigh—somebody died."

The word hovers in my mind for a millisecond before clicking into place.

Someone in our neighborhood has died. I wonder if it was the older woman with the long, gray braids around the corner who feeds the raccoons. She always looked so frail.

"Oh my god," I say. "That's awful. Did we know the person?"

"Actually, yeah." Mark turns the phone toward me so I can see the screen. "You did know him."

I squint at the image. It's small, but I can easily make out the familiar face.

I'm looking right at Rob the Wine Guy.

8

"Robert Avery," Mark says, pulling the phone back and staring at it intently.

His tone is even and cool. I can't read his emotions at all. Inside, my thoughts swirl as I try to piece together everything I know.

"That is so crazy," I whisper. I am frozen in place, not sure what I am supposed to think or feel. I barely know the guy, and what I do know of him is not positive. But he's dead. And that means shifting my frame of mind. Whatever happened last night is irrelevant now.

"At least now we know the guy's name," Mark says.

"Do you know what happened?" I ask. "Was it natural causes? An accident?"

He squints at the phone. "Nope. That's all the message says. But I'm sure as soon as Daisy and Leah find out, we'll all know."

The doorbell rings, a tinny *ding-dong-ding* that echoes through the house. A small shriek escapes me.

"You okay?" Mark asks.

"I'm freaked out, honestly. I mean, aren't you?"

The doorbell shrills again. "We should get that. It's probably Caitlin."

I step over Cole's pink hoodie with the faux fur collar and five mismatched shoes. My son's penchant for pink has exploded in the past few months, bourgeoning from an occasional splash of rose to an all-out obsession. At first, it was just a preference, but lately, he gets hysterical if he doesn't have at least one pink thing on. We've decided on a more hands-off approach, chalking his demands up to possible anxiety caused by the move. That means bits and bobs of bubble gum pink all throughout the house, as if a Disney princess exploded into tiny pieces in our home.

I open the front door to Caitlin and immediately position my body to block her view of our dining room.

"Oh! You're still in your pajamas. Are you sick, Allie?"

"Nope." I cross my arms over myself, realizing I am still wearing Mark's old T-shirt. "Just lazy."

"Well, happy Sunday!" Caitlin says.

"You, too!" I force myself to put Rob Avery's death out of my mind and plaster on a big smile.

Cole runs past me, clutching a poker, and thrusts it at Caitlin. "Aaargh, matey," he says.

Caitlin throws her hands up in mock terror. Cole takes the poker and leaps onto the lawn, stabbing at the air.

"So I see you've been putting my housewarming present to good use." When we first moved in, Caitlin presented us with a monogrammed set of hand-forged brass-and-iron fire tools. "I mean, they're sort of an heirloom, not really a toy. But hey, whatever works for you."

Caitlin adjusts her wide, navy-blue headband, which matches her navy-blue dress. Over it she's wearing an unbelted trench coat, looking every bit the female lead of an Alfred Hitchcock movie.

"As soon as it gets chilly enough for a fire, I am sure we'll put them to good use," I say.

She bends down and picks up the poker, where Cole has abandoned it for a try at climbing the dogwood tree. Caitlin traces a manicured finger over the R on the handle of the poker. Caitlin would brand the whole world with an R if she could. Lucky for her, she married Charles Robideaux and did not have to change any of her monogrammed belongings. I wonder if his initials played a role in her accepting his proposal.

"I'll take it inside." I take the poker from her. "Do you want to come in and wait? Cup of coffee?"

Caitlin turns to look at Cole, who is a blur of pink and khaki as he jumps up and down trying to grab hold of the dogwood's lowest-hanging branch.

"He really does love pink, doesn't he?" Above, the sky is a milky-white, threatening rain.

"Nothing wrong with that," I say, keeping my voice light. Cole's preference for traditionally "girl" things seems to rankle Mark's side of the family. A few weeks ago, Mark told them in no uncertain terms to butt out, but clearly Caitlin has trouble doing that. "In France, pink is a boy's color," I add.

"Oh, Allie. You're silly. We're not in France, we're in America." I'm not sure whether Caitlin is being precise or purposefully obtuse. I give her the benefit of the doubt and decide it's precision, a quality that runs in her family. Like her brother, Caitlin is a lawyer. Whereas Mark works in arbitration, Caitlin is at one of the D.C. area's top divorce firms. "Anyway, I thought it might be nice if he wore navy. Like Mark and me."

I don't ask how she knows what color her brother will be wearing to church, because I'm not sure I want to know. St. Edmund's, a gloomy Gothic building less than a mile away that straddles the line between D.C. and Maryland, is one of the few remaining Episcopal churches in the region that won't consecrate gay marriage or allow women priests.

The fact that his family made a point of staying in this particular congregation after many left for more liberal Episcopal churches was something I laughed off in Chicago. But what was fodder for amusement from afar has become a source of tension up close.

Mark's family expects us to attend this church, and I flatly refuse. I don't go, and I do nothing church-related. Cole goes for now. When he decides he's had enough, as I'm sure he will, we're going to respect that. I know I am kicking the can down the road, but I can't take on his entire family. Besides, I need these mornings to visit my mother.

I tell her I'll go find Mark. I locate him in the family room, remote control in hand, setting a recording for the Nats game.

"Your sister's waiting. She made a comment about Cole's shirt. Apparently, you were all supposed to wear navy."

Mark grunts. He didn't hear me, not really. I grab a tote bag I've filled with goodies that Sharon likes. Or at least used to like. Fire & Ice nail polish. Copies of the latest gossip magazines. A huge box of Dots candy.

Mark clicks the power off and tosses the remote into a wicker basket next to the sofa. He turns to me.

"You look very handsome," I say. And he does, in his chinos and blue-and-white checkered shirt. His temples have gone gray, but I think it only makes him more attractive. He could easily play the president in some B-movie, with his square jaw and easy smile. But it wasn't really his looks that drew me to him. It was his unflappable confidence. The café I worked at in San Francisco was a magnet for the homeless, crazies, and anarchists, and I used to watch how Mark navigated the sometimes-tricky terrain like a diplomat, treating everyone with respect and dignity. He used to come in every Saturday morning, lugging his laptop and files on whatever case he was working on, and park himself at a table near the window. He'd spend all day nursing one scone but drinking coffee after coffee, tapping away. Turned out he had wandered in one day randomly and had been returning every Saturday since to work up the nerve to ask me out, even though it meant taking a twenty-minute Muni ride from his apartment.

"And you look lovely in my old shirt." He kisses the top of my head.

"Yeah, I need to change." We're halfway through the dining room when he stops and pivots. "Allie, is there anything you want to tell me?"

"Uh, no. Like what?"

"I don't know. About this whole Rob Avery thing. About last night."

"No. Why?"

"I just, well, I noticed that he follows—or followed, I should say—you on Instagram."

"Wait, you noticed that?" I am taken aback. Mark is not on Instagram, or any social media. "What do you mean?"

"You left your Instagram page up on the computer."

"No, I didn't."

"Yes, you did." He sounds so confident that I start to question myself.

"Fine, maybe I did. But that guy Rob, he just started following me. Like last night. I told him my Instagram info at the party."

"Then how did he like pictures of you from August?"

I inhale through my nose and smile. Mark knows nothing about social media. "You can do that, silly. You can go back and like people's posts from months ago."

A dark cloud crosses his face. "I'm not being silly, Allie. I have to be honest, I think it's a little odd."

"Mark, are you serious? It means nothing." A swell of panic surges in my chest.

"Nothing? The guy you say attacked you last night, who is now dead, has been following you on Instagram. That's not nothing, Allie. That's weird."

A creak of a floorboard grabs my attention. I look past Mark to see my sister-in-law standing half-hidden in the shadows of the foyer. I didn't hear her open the screen door, and I have no idea how long she has been standing there.

9

I notice that Mark's car, which we had left at Daisy's last night, is now parked behind Caitlin's.

"When did you get that?" I ask, craning my neck.

"This morning."

"This morning? When? I got up just after five, and you were still sleeping."

"I woke up around three, hungover, you know the drill. Couldn't sleep."

I nod, trying to work it out in my head. "So you went over to Daisy's and got the car?"

"Yeah, then I went back to bed."

"I can't believe I slept through all that." But Mark is not listening. He's shepherding Cole into the back seat of Caitlin's enormous Ford Explorer. I've noticed an inverse correlation between the size of the woman and her SUV in D.C., and birdlike Caitlin is no exception.

I get into my own car and watch them drive away, a fluttering panic in my rib cage. Everything feels off, and my anxiety is spiking. I miss Cole already, and the thought that Caitlin is taking Mark and my son away from me for good hits me. Irrational. I turn on the engine. The news of Rob Avery's death has thrown me for a loop, that's all. And I'm never in a good mood after seeing Caitlin. I try to see her through Mark's eyes. He knows she's difficult, but he loves her loyalty and intelligence. He's told me all these stories about her taking on school bullies on his behalf and of how she stood up to their overbearing father, who thought it was a waste of time for a pretty girl to go to law school. According to Mark, Caitlin also struggled to get pregnant, and her husband refused to do IVF or to adopt. I almost wish I didn't know these intimate details about her, because then I feel like a jerk.

But then I remember the things she's said over the years. During my first visit to D.C. with Mark for Thanksgiving, when I was seven months pregnant, I overheard Caitlin asking her mother in the kitchen, *How do we know it's even Mark's?*

A rap on the car window startles me, and I look up to see Heather, my next-door neighbor, cranking her hand in the universal *roll-down-your-window* gesture.

"Hey, neighbor!" she says, pushing an errant honey-blond strand back into her high ponytail. "Did you hear about what happened over on Arleigh?"

"Yes, it's really crazy." My words are measured, my tone even.

"Did you know him?" Heather asks.

The question startles me. Does she know something? "No," I offer tentatively, trying to remember if I saw Heather at the party last night. She had to have been there. She has two kids at Eastbrook—Sam and Isabella—and from the emails I get, it looks like she is on almost every committee the school offers. Maybe she saw Rob and me talking in the kitchen.

"Me, neither," Heather says. "I mean, I knew him to say hi. I'd seen him around, at like the Backyard Pub Crawl and school things, but I didn't *know him* know him. So sad. He has a daughter, you know, Tenley, who's in the fourth grade with Isabella. That poor kid."

"Terrible." Guilt washes over me. I hadn't even thought of his daughter when I heard the news. But of course, some little girl just lost her dad.

"Of course, from what I hear, the poor thing basically lives at her mom's apartment in D.C., and the dad stayed in the Bethesda house so she could go to school in this district."

I nod, amazed at the intel Heather has on a man she claims not to know. What does Heather do? I rack my brain and then remember. She handles communications for a senator from Rhode Island. She can sure sniff out a scandal.

"I wonder what happened," she muses. "You know, my boss's brother had a heart attack at forty-five. And he was a marathon runner, super-fit guy."

"I have no idea. I guess we'll find out soon enough."

"Just goes to show you. I mean, we're at that age, aren't we? Well, you've got a few years to go, but once you hit your forties, it's nuts. Cancer, heart attacks, strokes. It's really scary." Heather winces as her little dog yanks at the leash. "Cut it out, Thurston." She refocuses her attention on me. "So what are you up to this lovely fall day?"

"Just visiting my mother." It comes out more clipped than I'd like, and I immediately regret that. Heather is in my book club, a potential friend, and she's been nothing but kind to me. A few weeks ago, I came home to see her leaving through my front door. I wondered if I had found some dark side to Heather, but it turns out she was just bringing in some Amazon packages that were getting rained on, using the spare key I had given her for emergencies.

"So I'll see you at book club Tuesday?" she asks.

"See you at book club!"

She steps back and waves as I pull away. *No way*, I think. *No way am I going to book club*. After all, I'll never finish *Disheveled* in time, and I'm not sure I'm ready to face a room full of neighborhood women buzzing about Rob Avery's death. But as I pull onto Western Avenue, I realize I am being silly. No one knows what happened to me last night. And now that Rob Avery is dead, no one ever will. It would be weird not to go to book club. If I am going to make new friends, I need to step up.

On Connecticut Avenue, I make sure to stay below thirty miles an hour to avoid being caught on one of the many speed cameras. My mother's assisted living facility is a good thirty-minute drive away. Squinting, I focus on which Beltway entrance to take, since the signs don't offer clear instruction—one says Baltimore, the other Richmond, which always confuses me. The Beltway is a loop, so you'd arrive at both places eventually if you stayed on it long enough. Which I have. When I first moved here, I found myself doing loops around D.C. after a photo shoot in Alexandria, wondering where the heck to exit.

The traffic is reasonable, something I am grateful for, since at any moment of any day, the Beltway can come to a standstill.

I dial Krystle's number, and soon my sister's scratchy voice is booming through the speaker in the car. Her voice is sodden in the way it gets when she's hungover.

"Late night?" I ask. My mother was only twenty-two when I was born, and she was a huge *Dynasty* fan. I was named for the raven-haired villainess. Two years later, her second daughter was named after the platinum-blond power wife on the show. This was apparently a source of contention with my father and his family, who, being good Catholics, felt children should be named after saints, not soap opera characters.

"It's not even ten o'clock, Allie," she grumbles. "What the fuck? Oh, shit, sorry. Is Cole in the car?"

"He's not. He's at church with Caitlin and Mark."

"Barf."

"Be nice, Krys. I'm heading up to see Sharon."

"Yes, *Madame*. I'll be nice. Hey, did you bring her Dots?" I hear a sharp inhale of breath on the other line, and I can picture my sister inhaling from that little tube she carries everywhere. She and her on-again-off-again boyfriend, Ron, traded in cigarettes for vaping a few months ago.

"Yes."

"And *US* magazine. Sharon likes *US*, not *People*."

I glance at the basket next to me. *"People, US, Star, In Style.* I've got them all."

"You should have left her where she was. She doesn't like this new place. We should move her back," Krystle says without pausing for breath. "Sharon doesn't need to live in some fancy-schmancy place."

I bristle. Every time I think we've settled this argument, she brings it up with renewed vigor. Sharon was not the type to scrupulously save for retirement, but she lucked into an inheritance my senior year of high school. A long-forgotten relative left her an old house on the water in Westport, Connecticut, and by renting that out over the years, she's been able to pay for assisted living.

It's the one smart financial move she ever made.

Only now it looks like selling the place might be the best option.

We haven't had tenants in four months, and the house requires major repairs. The septic tank needs replacing to the tune of twenty-five thousand dollars, and the roof will need to be replaced in the next year—probably another fifteen grand. We'd have to pull money out of the house to pay for that. Frankly, the whole thing seems like a nightmare, and I'd rather just sell and invest the money. But Krystle freaks out whenever I mention selling.

"Morningside House is not fancy. It's what assisted living costs around here." Krystle never got behind the plan to move our mother down here, but she also never visited Sharon when Sharon was living in Connecticut, even though it was only about an hour from New York City. "Come down and see for yourself."

"I mean, I want to come down, but my shifts at the restaurant have changed, and now I don't have two days off in a row. Did I tell you I got a callback for *The Young and the Restless*? I'm this close, Allie."

"Is that still on the air?" Krystle's been *this close* to her big break for about ten years now. I'd hoped that once she turned thirty, she might realize she was not going to become a famous actress. I thought at least she'd get a day job with real earning potential and benefits.

"Don't be a bitch. This is a big deal for me." Even over the phone, I can see that sour look on her face—eyes narrowed, lips pressed together. "Look, it's not like I don't want to come," she wheedles, "but it's just harder for me."

I don't argue. My sister's narrative is that things have always been easier for me. In her mind, my scholarship to Overton Prep school is exhibit A in this fundamental unfairness. My hard work versus her hard partying do not play a role in her version of our life. My marrying a lawyer only cemented this belief. I change subjects. I'm not in the mood for an argument that I can't win. Instead, we chat for the rest of the ride. If she's in the right mood, Krystle can talk unabated about her life in New York City with the ease and comic timing of a cabaret star. She's always made me laugh. In fact, that's pretty much the only thing I can depend on her for.

Even though Krystle is two years younger than I am, as children, we were often mistaken for twins. I was short for my age, and she was tall. We shared everything: our clothes, our bed, our long, brown hair. But somewhere in high school, our responses to the same circumstances put us on divergent paths.

We have the same genetics and the same upbringing, but the chaos of our childhood made me cling to stability, while it made Krystle allergic to it.

I'll never forget the day—I was in fourth grade—that Krystle and I came home to my mother announcing with great cheer that she was no longer going to work as a receptionist to a local podiatrist, and that we were moving to a small apartment building where she would be the manager. I cried, while Krystle jumped on the sofa with glee that she would get to miss a day of school.

The apartment-managing stint lasted all of six months. We left that place in a hurry, the building's owner threatening to sue my mother for some damages that had taken place on her watch. When we packed in the middle of the night, Krystle and my mother giggled like they were Thelma and Louise, outwitting the law. I got a stomachache that lasted a year. Our next stop was a basement apartment near a CPA where my mother worked during the rush of tax season only to be laid off come spring. Krystle loved that Sharon was working late and we were unsupervised, whereas I was visited by nightmares of my mother being abducted on cold, dark March evenings as she walked home from work.

Rinse and repeat.

Finally, there is a pause in the conversation, and I fill her in on what happened at the party last night.

"Wait, so you're on Tinder now?" she asks.

"No. That's not what I said, Krys. The guy said that." The fact that she has missed this salient point irritates me.

"I don't get it, Allie. Why did he think that?"

"I don't know. That's why it's so crazy." Her doubting tone irritates me. "But that's not the point."

I hear the gurgle of the coffee machine, and I can picture her in the kitchen of that tiny studio apartment on East Eleventh Street that she moved into ten years ago, with the miniature fridge and sink small enough for an airplane bathroom. "There's no shame in looking for a little excitement, Allie. I don't blame you. If I had to live with Mark in the suburbs, I would've turned to Tinder a long time ago."

"A, that's not funny. And B, I didn't turn to Tinder." I brake and honk at a Volvo that has drifted into my lane at forty miles an hour. "That's not even the weirdest part. This guy, the one who did this? He died."

"Died? What do you mean, died?"

"I mean stopped breathing. I don't know how. Could be he

fell down the basement stairs, could be a heart attack. I only know that it happened late last night or early this morning."

"How do you know?"

I laugh. "Believe me, in my neighborhood everyone knows everything."

"That's so creepy, Allie. It's like karma or something. It's like the universe saw what he did and then, you know."

"No, I don't know. I don't know anything about this guy. I don't know why he came onto me like that, and I don't know what he meant when he told me to stay off Tinder. Do you think he had me confused with someone else?"

"You know, there are a lot of fake Tinder profiles," she says. "People set them up to try to get money from suckers."

"I'm not on Tinder." The exit for Damascus comes into view. I'm in rural Montgomery County now, just thirty miles outside D.C., where working farms outnumber office buildings.

"Maybe you don't think you are, but maybe there's a fake pro-file on you."

"So you think there might be a fake Tinder profile of me? And that's what this guy saw?"

"Definitely. Happened to my friend Lola." Confidence has always flowed from Krystle, justified or not. "They took some nude photos of her that she did when she was young and made a fake Tinder account."

"Who is *they*?" I turn onto Flamingo Lane, which curves through open pastures.

"Umm, hello, the Russians? Do you, like, even read the news? You should check on Tinder and see. I bet it's some photo they've grabbed off some website."

"I can't check. You need to have a Facebook account to look at Tinder profiles, and I don't want to link mine to it. Can you look into it for me?"

Through the phone, I hear the scream of an ambulance, and it makes me miss living in the anonymous chaos of a big city. For a moment, I experience a pang of longing, not just for Krystle's life—which seems so uncomplicated compared to mine—but for the way mine used to be. "Hello, you still there?"

She takes a loud slurp of coffee. "You want me to search Tinder for your fake account?"

"Please?"

"You know there's an app you can download; it's for suspicious spouses. I saw it on *The Today Show*."

I swallow a hard sigh. Krystle has always been this way, clever yet resistant to any kind of work, doubly so if it is someone else's idea.

"Take a look, please. A fake Tinder account makes more sense than my other theory." I pull into the Morningside House of Damascus parking lot and find a spot under a large oak tree that has yet to lose its leaves.

"Why, what was your other theory?"

"That this Rob guy knew me, from Connecticut."

"Why would you think that?"

"Well, he called me Lexi." From the corner of my eye, I see a woman and two children approach the building with a large bouquet of flowers. Flowers. Next time, I will bring Sharon some.

"That's weird. Why would he call you Lexi?"

"I don't know. I thought, maybe he went to Overton or something? But he's older, so he wouldn't have been at school the same time I was."

She laughs. "Well, don't ask me. Older guys were your thing, Allie. Not mine."

When I don't respond, she lets out a gruff laugh. "Oh, come on, you're so sensitive, Allie. Learn to take a joke."

"I'm here now. Bye, Kris." I hang up and grab the basket. Everything's a joke with her. But she's right that everything that has happened in the last twelve hours has left me feeling sensitive.

I wait at the front door for the concierge—the facility's choice of word—to buzz me in. The large foyer is straight out of a new model home, with fancy couches flanking a gas fireplace. But the people on those couches are not fancy or new. Beside the sofas, some sit in wheelchairs or hunch over walkers. Many are still clad in pajamas, hair unkempt. I take a deep breath and push last night's drama out of my head. I need all my mental energy to steel myself for whatever condition I might find Sharon in.

On entering her room, the first thing I notice about my mother is that she has lost weight. She's always been slender, but now her peacock-blue wrap dress, more appropriate for a nightclub circa 1984 than an assisted living facility, falls from her frame like it's on a hanger, exposing deep clavicles.

The second thing I notice is the yellowish bruise on her neck.

10

I try not to act alarmed as guilt washes over me. She's been convinced that someone is after her, a concern I had dismissed as dementia. But last week, she had a scratch, and now this. This makes two injuries in two weeks.

I put the bag of goodies on a table and walk over to the vanity, where she is teasing her thinning champagne-colored hair in front of the mirror.

"Sharon, what's going on with your neck?"

"Oh, this thing? I hate it." She looks up and catches my eye. Her long fingers flutter to the oval bruise on her slender neck. It's the exact shape and size of a thumb, as if someone had been trying to take her pulse and pressed way too hard. "I woke up with it. I tried to cover it with makeup, but this concealer is crap. I need the stuff they use on movie sets. Can you get that for me, Alexis? They sell it at Dan's Beauty Supply."

"Sure, I can do that." Dan's is about a twenty-minute drive from where we used to live in Connecticut. But I don't remind her that we now live in Maryland. I play along. All the experts say to do this with people suffering from dementia.

"I would say we should walk there, but I don't want to leave the house in case Georges comes by."

"Georges?" I have not heard that name in years. He was Sharon's boyfriend during my ninth- and tenth-grade years. A club promoter who drank Dubonnet on the rocks and smelled like mint and salami. As far as I know, Georges has not been resurrected after dying in a three-car pileup on the Merritt Parkway about ten years ago. "You're expecting Georges?"

"I don't trust her."

"Who don't you trust, Sharon?"

"She brings me Dots, but she doesn't fool me." She points to a jumbo-size box of Dots on her vanity, the kind you find at the movie theater. Not the size I buy at the grocery store.

"Where did you get those?" I pick up the box. "Sharon, can you answer me?"

But she doesn't. She turns her face upward toward mine, like a marigold tracking the sun.

"Don't ruin your life like I did. You have choices. It's better you're not too pretty. The boys will leave you alone at that school, let you get your work done. Look what happened to your sister. Too pretty for her own good." She crinkles her nose. "What did you do to your hair? You look like a deranged elf."

"I know you don't like my haircut." My hand goes straight to the back of my neck. "You said the same thing last week."

"Aww, I hurt your feelings." She frowns.

"It's all right, Sharon."

"Don't be mad. Here, let me do your nails." She takes one hand of mine in her bony fingers. "You're just as good as those girls."

We sit side by side on the bed, and I let her massage cocoa butter into my hands.

"What happened to your neck, Sharon?" I gesture toward the bruise. I wait a few moments, and when she does not respond, I try again. "Sharon, did you hear me? What happened to your neck?"

She shoots me an annoyed look. "I can't recall."

"Did someone do this to you?" From my handbag, my phone buzzes, but I don't answer it.

She tightens her grip on my hands. "Don't talk about it here," she says through clenched teeth. "They're listening." She stands up and walks over to her dresser, where she pulls out a green silk scarf and wraps it around her neck. "I'll tie it like so, and voilà. Georges loves green. He says it brings out my eyes."

"I agree, green looks lovely on you." I sneak a surreptitious look at my phone to see who called. Unfamiliar number. I check my voice mail and read the transcribed message. It's filled with errors, but I can make out the gist. Valerie Simmons's assistant wants to set up a time to chat next week. I can hardly hide my elation. Back in Chicago, I shot the wedding of the daughter of Illinois congressman Marcel Parks. When I moved to the D.C. area, we reconnected, and I did headshots for him. He's the one who mentioned Valerie Simmons from CNN was looking for a photographer. If I land that job, I might be able to quit Mike Chau's and start my own business sooner than I'd thought.

"Sharon, have you heard of Valerie Simmons?" I ask Sharon. "Former Obama advisor, and now she's on CNN?"

Sharon frowns and holds a bottle of pink polish next to my hands.

"African American?" I push. "Mid-fifties? Bright silver hair?"

Sharon begins to paint my nails with the precision of Jackson Pollock. I sigh and give up on trying to impress her. I'll have to wait and share my good news with Mark when I get home; he'll be proud of me. While my nails dry, Sharon turns the pages of the gossip magazines and giggles. I can't imagine what she gets out of them. At thirty-four, I already don't recognize half the names and faces in those magazines, but they seem to make her happy. She has a comment about everyone and how they look and whether their outfits are "doing them any favors" or not.

After, I try to convince my mother to walk with me outside. I think the fresh air will do her good. I hate thinking of her cooped up in this room every day. But she begs off. Her eyelids are drooping, and I can tell the visit has exhausted her. She agrees to let me escort her to the large foyer and deposit her on the sofa next to a dozing man who has drool dripping down his cheek.

The room is filling up. Lunch is served at eleven thirty, and an impatient crowd has gathered, like before a concert or big game. I go in search of someone in charge, trying to keep from inhaling the scent of urine mingled with disinfectant. I find an aide with a put-upon look. She knows nothing of my mother's injuries; she's just come on duty. But she scribbles my information on her clipboard and promises someone will call me.

It's the best I can do for now, and it's not much.

I head back to my car, deflated.

Spending time with Sharon takes me back to those dingy little apartments where she left me to watch over Krystle so she could go out and meet Mr. Right. After my father died, she couldn't bear to be alone, and that led to some questionable choices in male companions. I used to be bitter about the men she brought home, about her drinking, her inability to function like the other mothers I knew. But now that I am married and have my own child, I am more sympathetic. When my father died, she was thrust into a life for which she was totally unprepared. Sharon never went to college, but she was whip smart, and she had a way of charming men, making them feel protective of her. I remember men paying for our meals at diners, police officers giving her warnings instead of tickets. Job offers came easily, people took chances on her. But she could never stick with anything. Once the novelty wore off, she would give up. Now I can see that her rages and behavior were probably a result of depression, not selfishness. She was doing the best she could.

If I allow myself to remember, it still hurts. Like when she forgot my tenth birthday or how she never once came to parent night at school. So I try not to.

But I don't want this for her. I wouldn't want it for anyone.

They say forgiveness is giving up hope on having had a better past. I'm ready. I want to let it all go. I'm just not sure how to do it.

I'm about to pull out of the parking lot when my phone pings.

You and Cole coming to the park? It's Leah.

On my way. I text back.

Check this out. And following that is a link to a local news story.

I click and am taken to their website. Immediately, a picture of Rob Avery pops up.

The headline reads: BETHESDA DAD FOUND POISONED IN HOME.

11

By the time I've battled the Beltway traffic and arrived at the playground near my house, I am fried. The late-afternoon sun is low, and it's chilly. I've had the whole ride to chew over what the word *poisoned* means. Horrific images of swollen tongues and frothing mouths, wide frozen eyes and stiff limbs, have been floating through my mind. I feel guilty for even briefly hating Rob Avery. Could my anger Saturday night have morphed into some kind of cosmic rage that brought about his violent death? Ridiculous nonsense.

It's just a coincidence, I tell myself. I need to get out of my own head.

At the park, Cole has changed out of his church clothes, and he and Mark are both wearing red Nationals shirts, no jackets. Tonight is game two of the Nationals' playoff series. I don't think Cole could tell the difference between a baseball and a Frisbee, but he likes to yell at the TV alongside his dad.

I say hi to Mark, who is standing with David, Leah's husband. I try to catch his eye, to see if he has heard about Rob Avery, but he is deep in conversation with David. David is one of those nervous, wiry guys with zero body fat, always wearing a T-shirt from the last marathon he ran. He tells me Leah is at Starbucks and will be back soon.

I take a seat on the blue "buddy bench," knees jangling, impatient for Leah to arrive. I need to talk to someone about Rob Avery.

Before me, Cole and Leah's daughter, Ava, scramble to the top of a green contraption shaped like an eight-foot metal spider. The school made a big deal of these new benches at the beginning of the year. They're part of the county's new anti-bullying campaign. Children with no one to play with are supposed to sit on a "buddy bench" and wait for someone to offer them the hand of friendship. I asked Cole if he ever used it, and he recoiled in horror, telling me he'd rather walk the playground's periphery by himself during recess than be caught on the buddy bench.

I totally relate to that sentiment. No one wants to be that publicly vulnerable. And yet, here I am, a grown woman, sitting on the bench and waiting for a buddy.

Poisoned.

The word pops into my head. It implies such hate.

I shake my head to clear it, and in an effort to distract myself, I take out my camera and aim it at David and Mark. The two men are a contrast in all ways. David can't stop moving; he's rocking on his heels, hands flying as he talks. Mark stands stock-still; he could be carved out of stone.

I adjust the camera's sights onto Cole and Ava, who are on top of the spiderlike contraption. Ava wears her long, dark brown hair parted in the middle just like her mom, but she has her dad's relentless energy. Cole is more cautious, like me, I think, contemplating his every move.

Beyond them, a lone figure skulks on the edge of the softball field where it meets the woods. Adjusting the lens of my camera, I can make out Dustin, his face in the shadows of his large black hoodie. He's holding a leash attached to a trembling dog the size of an undernourished cat.

"Can you believe this? I can't stop thinking about it." Leah plops down next to me, cradling an enormous Starbucks cup. Leah had been a partner-track lawyer for one of D.C.'s most prestigious law firms, but never returned to work after taking maternity leave for Ava five years ago. In lieu of climbing up the

corporate ladder, she seems to have channeled that fierce intelligence and drive into being the most organized mother-slash-
volunteer-slash-neighbor I've encountered. "I mean, murdered?
I figured it was like a heart attack, or something, but murder?"

"I know, right?"

Leah begins to speculate on who could have done this, set-
tling on a theory she has about outsiders who come into the
neighborhood to sell magazine subscriptions but are really crim-
inals casing houses.

As she talks, a longing to tell her what happened last night
builds in me. Yet I am scared to share so much personal information. So far, we have not come to the point in our friendship
where we push past the superficial niceties and reveal our darker
side. Every female friendship has this scary moment, the crucible
of personal sharing. You reveal something you are ashamed of,
or embarrassed by, or something traumatic that happened. And
it's like staring over the edge of a cliff before you jump into the
water below, exhilarated and frightened at the same time. You
either come out the other side with your bathing suit so far up
the crack of your ass you swear you'll never jump again, or the
rush is incredible—you've made a real friend. When she finally
stops speaking, I think I am ready to spill, but after a pause, I
chicken out and ask, "Did you guys get a dog?"

Leah rolls her eyes. "Therapy dog. Not my idea, believe me.
Apparently, it's supposed to help Dustin develop some empathy."

"Is empathy a problem for him?"

A quick twitch of her mouth tells me I've hit a nerve. "He's on
the spectrum. Super bright, like off the charts. He just doesn't
always pick up on social cues." She grins. "But he loves you guys.
He was telling me the other day how great it is that you let Cole
wear whatever he wants and stuff. He's sensitive to that kind of
stuff. I wonder if he might try babysitting. What do you think?"

"We have Susan," I say, a bit too quickly.

"Oh, of course. I just meant, theoretically." Her tone is cheery, but it masks defensiveness.

I feel a stab of guilt. Yes, a teen boy can be trusted to babysit, and being on the autism spectrum shouldn't disqualify anyone from working with kids, but at the same time, I don't feel comfortable leaving Cole with Dustin. And I know that makes me a hypocrite.

"So how is the new dog?" I ask.

She shrugs. "We'll see. All I know is we got him Friday, and he's already left about a half dozen little turdlets around the house." She turns to me and narrows her eyes. "So what happened to you last night? I texted you and you said to meet you in the kitchen, and the next thing I see, you're running out the door."

It's now or never. A line from *The Friendship Crisis,* on my bedside table, comes to me: *Confidences are the glue that cement female friendships.* I take a step off the cliff.

"A dad at the party came on to me." I pause. Why am I sugar-coating it? Because I feel guilty for flirting. "No, more like kind of assaulted me, in the bathroom."

"Kind of assaulted you?" Leah's large brown eyes widen. "What does *kind of* mean?"

"We were in the kitchen, and then I went upstairs to the bathroom, and he followed me."

"Into the bathroom?"

I describe the whole incident—starting with how we had been talking in the kitchen, and finishing with the purple bruise on my hip, which I show Leah.

"What a fucking bastard. Who is it? I'll kill him."

I swallow hard. "Well, he told me his first name was Rob." I keep my gaze on Ava and Cole, who are hanging by their fingers from the metal spider. I wonder if I should run over and facilitate their safe landing. I resist. Mark and David, who are feet away, don't budge. I envy them their obliviousness.

"Which Rob? Is he Asian? Rob Zse? Ever since he lost weight, he thinks he's some kind of a Romeo."

"No, he isn't Asian." *Wasn't*, I almost say. I watch as Cole and Ava climb down and run, hands entwined, across the field toward Dustin and the dog. David and Mark remain chatting by the metal spider, oblivious that their charges have flown the coop.

"Let's see, it can't be Rob Morten. He's gay."

"Rob Morten's gay?" I turn to face her. "I thought he was married."

"Please. He's so deep in the closet, he's part of the drywall. What other Robs are there?" Before I can answer, her eyes widen and she puts a hand to her mouth. I widen my eyes. "Rob fucking Avery?" Leah slaps her thigh. "The guy who was just killed?"

"Shhh, keep your voice down."

"This is so insane! Have you told anyone?"

"Besides Mark? And you? No."

"Whoa. Are you going to call the police?"

"The police? Why would I call the police?"

Leah narrows her eyes, a wry look on her face. "Now I wasn't a litigator, only a patent lawyer, and I think I got a C-plus in criminal law, but there's going to be a murder investigation, Allie. Someone killed Rob Avery. And I'm pretty sure they're going to want to talk to you. I mean, maybe he was doing drugs or something, and that's why he acted so crazy at the party, and like his drug dealer killed him."

I stare at Leah. "That's a bit of a leap."

"That was a *for instance*. The point is, you need to tell the police what happened," Leah says. "Maybe he's done this to other women, and someone got mad. Like a husband."

An image of an angry Mark skulking through the streets of our neighborhood in the middle of the night pops into my head. I shake the thought away.

"The truth is going to come out, Allie. You might as well get ahead of it."

But I have no desire to insert myself, or Mark, into a murder investigation. After all, Rob Avery did assault me, or try to, last night. As far-fetched as it sounds, I don't want to risk the police thinking that I—or even worse, Mark—might be involved. I'm about to restate that I have no interest in talking to the police, and I'd appreciate her keeping this confidential, when in one swift move Leah has jumped up, passed me her coffee, and is springing across the field to a sobbing Ava. From here, I can see the little girl's jeans are torn at the knee. Cole runs past her to me.

"Mommy, Mommy, Ava fell on the blacktop."

Leah scoops up Ava. As she and David head off, she gives me a wave.

A queasy panic stirs in my gut, like when I've drunk too many espressos. Being a mom to young kids means never getting to finish your conversations, but I'm worried that I didn't make myself clear to Leah.

I send up a little prayer to the universe: *Please, Leah, keep your mouth shut.*

12

After I put Cole to bed on Sunday night, I navigate over to the swampland that is Facebook to see if anyone has posted more info on Rob Avery. Despite my best efforts to keep things simple, I've somehow joined so many groups that I am totally overwhelmed whenever I open up the website. All this information is supposed to keep me informed of things, but the opposite seems to happen. I often feel like I'm flailing around in the dark, thanks to information overload and algorithms I don't understand.

There's the Eastbrook Neighborhood Association page, as well as the Eastbrook Elementary School parents' page, not to mention Eastbrook Moments—a page just for Cole's kindergarten class filled with news updates and field trip logistics, as well as cute photos captioned with adorable out-of-the-mouths-of-babes quotes.

My other groups include D.C. Yard Sale—a great place to find gently used LEGO; Washington D.C. Photographers—a professional networking necessity; and Bethesda Patch—the local news outlet.

I scan the Eastbrook Neighborhood Association page. It is inundated with posts about Rob Avery's death. The buzz from the morning has increased exponentially, and all other facets of our neighborhood life—requests for used tennis racquets, recommendations for pediatric dentists—have been squeezed out to make room for rumor.

Ninety percent of homicide victims are killed by someone they know, one post reads. *So it's probably someone from the neighborhood.*

Does anyone know if Rob was dating anyone?

Who was he hanging out with at Daisy Gordon's party? Does anyone have pictures?

I scroll down to see if anyone has posted pictures from Daisy's party that show me with Rob. But the only other recent post is from someone named Julie who wants everyone to be really, really careful because she just spotted a fox in her backyard.

I shut the page. It feels like a tsunami of speculation and gossip threatening to overtake me. I make a note to myself to take a digital detox for a day or two until this whole thing subsides. I know intellectually that what happened to me at the party and Rob's death are not related. But I'm pretty sure that police won't see it that way. And I can imagine what the neighborhood gossip mill would make of it all. The accusations would be flying. I don't want to put myself and my family through all that. I had wanted to pretend the whole thing at Daisy's party never happened. And that was before Rob Avery was killed. The feeling is even stronger now. The last thing I want is to get sucked into a murder investigation.

Still, I have an itch in the back of my brain that begs to be scratched—why did Rob Avery call me Sexy Lexi? I go to bed trying to make peace with the fact that I may never know.

Monday morning starts off well when I find parking close to work. The Mike Chau Studio occupies the second floor of a building on H Street that houses an artisanal falafel shop. Our neighbors are a café that specializes in cold-pour coffee and a medical marijuana dispensary. When I come in, Mike is sitting at his desk tapping at his computer at a speed that would have wowed my ninth-grade typing teacher. He looks up and grins.

"Hey, Allie. Good weekend?" Mike is the same age, but unlike me, he's almost aggressively hip. He has the black, shaggy hair of an indie rocker, and colorful full-sleeve tattoos, with more characters and story lines than *Game of Thrones*. But I realized early on that he's not as laid-back as he pretends. He wouldn't have been able to start his own successful photography studio before the age of thirty if he were.

"Weekend was great. You?" I don't want Mike thinking there is anything in my personal life that would interfere with my job. I'm still on probation for the first ninety days of employment. Besides, work has always been a refuge for me, and the last thing I want to do is dwell on the weekend's drama.

The studio takes up the whole second floor, with the back half divided into two enclosed rooms for shoots. The front room is a combination office and waiting area, replete with knockoff mid-century furniture and exposed pipes. What it lacks in privacy, Mike likes to joke, it makes up for in style.

I spend the morning editing and pop out to pick up lunch—a dry falafel from Yael's Kebab House. I am back at my desk and wiping the crumbs off my face when Valerie Simmons's assistant calls.

"Valerie loves your work—very natural and spontaneous. You really managed to capture Marcel's warmth." Congressman Parks had been an easy shoot. He had that politician's gift of being able to light up from the inside on cue.

We talk for a few minutes about her boss's desire to showcase a softer side for her upcoming memoir, while still maintaining gravitas. I assure her I know how to do this.

"This all sounds very promising," she answers and says she'll touch base with me later in the week to set up an appointment. After we hang up, I jump up and fist pump the air.

"Good news?" Mike asks from across the room.

"Looks like I may have the Valerie Simmons job. I'm talking details with her on Monday, but I think we've got it."

Mike leans back, putting his hands behind his head to reveal matching orange snakes that wrap around the undersides of his well-formed biceps and disappear under his white T-shirt. "Nice. Very nice."

A flicker of something crosses his face. Jealousy? Irritation? Technically, jobs funnel through Mike and he assigns them. I doubt that he is annoyed that I pursued Valerie Simmons on my own—it would be a feather in the studio's cap to have someone of her caliber as a client. Maybe he suspects that I plan to build up a client base and leave.

I decide I'll worry about that another day and just enjoy the win.

My high spirits last the rest of the day and all the way home despite miserable traffic. But they dissipate as I pull up to my house after work, when I find a dark sedan parked in front of our walkway.

One of the unspoken laws of suburbia is you don't park right in front of someone else's house, much less block their walkway. I learned this the hard way the first week after we moved in, when I parked in front of Heather's house. I received a little note card with sunflowers on it and a message about parking etiquette.

As I pass by the car on my way to the front door, I peer inside. My stomach dips a little when I spot a radio.

It's an unmarked police car.

13

"There she is," Susan says as I rush through the back door into the mudroom. "I was just telling the detectives that you would be home any minute."

"What detectives?" I turn to see a boyish-looking man in an ill-fitting suit behind me. How had I missed him when I first came in?

"Hi," I say. "Can I help you?"

"Ma'am," he says, handing me a business card. "Detective Brian Katz of the Montgomery County Police." He doesn't look old enough to drive, much less carry a gun and arrest people.

"What's going on?" I ask. But inside, I know exactly why these detectives are in my kitchen: they've come to question me about Rob Avery.

Cole runs in and throws his arms around my legs, almost sending me toppling. "Yay, you're home. Now we can do the family tree. I need photographs of Sharon and Aunt Caitlin and Aunt Krystle and everyone."

Just then, a stout woman with dark skin and salt-and-pepper hair emerges from the bathroom. She strides toward me, wiping her wet hands on her blue pants.

"Detective Stephanie Lopez." She takes my hand and squeezes it a bit too hard, telegraphing the message that she is not to be toyed with. She gives Detective Katz a stern nod. "Ready?"

He nods back like a well-trained dog.

"What is this about?" I ask.

Detective Lopez glances at Cole, her nostrils flare, and I know at once that she is childless. She looks from me to Susan and then back to me. "Is there somewhere we can talk?" Detective Lopez asks. "Privately?"

Cole squeezes my thighs harder. "Mommy, you promised. This is due soon."

"I can stay a bit longer," Susan offers. Today, her earrings are dangling orange popsicles. "If that would help."

"Would you? You're a godsend." Susan has been picking up Cole from school and watching him until I get home from work since we moved here. I don't know what I would do without her.

"No!" Cole shouts. "I want you to make the family tree."

Susan bends down. "Cole, how would you like to walk to my house and feed Marnie? It's her dinnertime. And I have some poster board you can use for the family tree. It's neon green."

Cole narrows his eyes, looking for the trick. But he loves Marnie and will do almost anything to spend time with the little white dog. He looks up at me. "And then we'll do the family tree, Mommy?"

"Of course. Thank you, Susan." I send a little thanks heavenward that I managed to find a babysitter who keeps neon poster board in stock.

The detectives follow me into our living room. I can feel their eyes boring into the back of my head. As soon as we are in the living room, I regret coming in, too, and I'm sure it shows. The furnishings have been passed down to us from Mark's mom, and they are not my taste at all. I sit in one of two wingbacks that overlook the street through a bay window and point to the couch. Detective Lopez takes a seat, but the younger Detective Katz wanders over to the bookshelf and starts examining family photographs, to my consternation.

Lopez sits across from me, legs spread wide, and leans forward as if she's ready to spring into action at a moment's notice. A large black gun sits askew on her hip, revealed by her open jacket. I wonder if that's on purpose, letting me see her weapon. Her wide face is makeup-free, ageless in the way that women who refuse to play the appearance game can be. She could be anywhere from thirty-five to fifty.

"How can I help you?" She glances at my hands. I realize I've been twisting the edges of my long cardigan. I drop my hands flat on my lap.

She hands me a business card exactly like the one Detective Katz gave me, only with her own name on it, and then takes out a small spiral notebook and flips it open.

"We are investigating a homicide that occurred in the five hundred block of Wentworth early Sunday morning."

I swallow hard. "Yes, I heard about it. It's awful."

"Were you awake between the hours of midnight and 6:00 a.m. on Sunday, Ms. Ross?"

"No, I was sleeping." Then I remember. "Actually, I did get up around five."

"So you were awake. Did you leave the house?"

"No."

"Not to get the paper, let the dog out?"

"We don't have a dog."

She asks about my routine, then about Mark's, and about whether we have any security cameras that might offer footage. She wants to know if I've noticed anyone suspicious around, any work people who looked out of place in the past few weeks. I feel as relaxed as I can being questioned by a homicide detective when she begins asking about the alley in the back of the house.

"Your house backs up to an alley," she says without missing a beat. "As does the property on which the crime occurred. Have you ever walked down that alley?"

"Sure. It's the quickest way to get to the metro station at Friendship Heights." The defensive note in my voice makes me cringe. I have a right to walk down the alley behind my house.

"How often do you walk it?"

"I don't know. Once a week? Mark, my husband, walks it every day on his commute."

She jots something down on her pad.

"A lot of people in this neighborhood used that alley," I say. "Kids, people walking their dogs."

"When is the last time you used the alley?"

I let out a throaty laugh. "I don't know."

"Think, Ms. Ross."

"Umm, last Thursday? Walking Cole home from a playdate?"

"Have you ever stopped at the Avery residence?"

"Of course not. I didn't even know he lived there." I shift in my chair, feeling restless. "We just moved here a few months ago."

"But you knew Robert Avery."

I pause, unsure if this is a question. "No," I say. "I didn't know him."

"I see." But what does she see? Her face is impossible to read. The only sign of reaction is two deep grooves between her eyebrows. "You're telling us that you did not know Robert Avery?"

I shake my head.

She takes out her phone and pokes at it so loudly I can hear her finger hitting the glass. A look of recognition crosses her face, and she turns the screen to me. "Can you tell me a little about this photograph?"

I take her phone from her and examine the picture on the screen. It was taken in Daisy's kitchen on the night of the party. In the center of the photo, two women grin into the camera. But Rob and I are visible in the background. Zooming in on us, we are a portrait of intimacy—our heads so close, they almost touch.

Blood rushes to my head. I feel dizzy. How can I explain this photo? "Where did you get this?"

"I'm not at liberty to say, Ms. Ross. Can you describe the circumstances behind this photo?"

"There are no circumstances." I hand her phone back to her, trying to keep my hand from shaking as I do so. "We were at the same party. That's all."

"You look like you're engaged in intimate conversation here."

"Conversation? Yes. Intimate? No. People have conversations at parties."

"So you did, in fact, know Robert Avery."

"Well, I met him that night." I pause. It feels like a trick question. The old *"Have you stopped beating your wife?"* If you answer yes, you are admitting to previously beating your wife. If you answer no—well, then, you are still beating her.

"I see."

"Literally thirty minutes before this picture was taken." Sweat has begun to seep out from under my arms and bra line. I forgot that this room is the warmest in the house, and I debate taking off my cardigan. I don't want her to see my sweat stains, because I don't want her to know how nervous this whole conversation is making me.

"And you never had any communication with Mr. Avery before the night this photo was taken, either via text or email or some kind of phone application?"

"Phone application?" I swallow the lump in my throat. I know exactly what she means.

"An app, like Instagram or Tinder."

Just hearing that word makes my stomach curl. *Stay off Tinder.* "No."

From his spot in the corner, Detective Katz clears his throat. Both Detective Lopez and I turn to him.

"Nice picture," he says, tilting a framed photo of Mark and me at the Japanese Tea Garden in San Francisco. "How long have you and your husband been married?"

"Five years." I wonder if he is thinking of Cole and doing the math to figure out that our son was conceived out of wedlock.

"Marriage is tough these days," he says. "A lot of temptation."

"Half of all marriages end in divorce," Detective Lopez says. It takes a millisecond for me to realize that they have shifted into sympathetic, marriage counseling mode. They think I'm going to confess to sleeping with Rob Avery.

"Maybe," I say in as deliberate and calm a voice as I can manage. "But I still didn't know who Rob Avery was before I met him at this party. In fact, I didn't even know his last name until I saw the news yesterday."

The two detectives exchange a glance, and that silent look does more to scare me than anything they've said so far. I hear the back door open, and a few seconds later, Mark calls out from the kitchen, "Hello! Anyone home?"

"In here," I call back in a shaky voice. I stand up, wiping my sweaty palms on my jeans. "That's my husband. You should go now."

Out of the corner of my eye, I see Leah and Daisy across the street, standing at the curb, talking to Heather. They are all dressed in black yoga pants and colorful fleeces. I wonder if they have spoken to the police. Could Leah have said something about what I told her, about Rob attacking me in the bathroom?

Detective Lopez stands, snapping her little notebook shut. "If there's anything you remember, or anything you want to tell us, I strongly encourage you to reach out. Secrets have a way of outing, Ms. Ross. Especially in a murder investigation. In my experience, it's better to just come clean in the beginning."

"Come clean? What's this about?"

We all turn to see Mark at the doorway to the room, a plastic-wrapped bouquet of grocery store mums hanging by his side.

His eyes zip from me to the detectives and back to me again. "What's going on?"

Lopez pockets her notebook and pivots toward Mark.

"Detective Lopez, Montgomery County Police. This is Detective

Katz." She jerks her head in the other detective's direction. "We are canvassing the neighborhood in regard to Sunday's homicide. Do you have a minute, Mr. Ross?"

"Actually, I don't."

A slight wave of surprise crosses the detective's face, and I love Mark for standing up to her. He's a lawyer, albeit an arbitration lawyer, but he knows his rights.

"Then I'll leave you a card, and we can arrange another time to talk."

"Fine." His voice is crisp and officious.

An awkward silence ensues until Mark steps back and gestures with his arm toward the front door. "Let me show you out."

Mark and I trail them to the front. As they head down the walkway to the unmarked car, he puts a hand on my shoulder and squeezes. As soon as they drive off, Daisy, Leah, and Heather turn and smile at us, all three waving in unison.

14

Mark doesn't mention the police visit during dinner. I am unsure if he is avoiding the topic because Cole is there or if he really doesn't think it's a big deal. Instead, I tell him about the potential Valerie Simmons shoot, but I am unable to tap into the excitement I felt earlier.

The visit from the police has infused me with anxiety.

After dinner, Cole runs upstairs, and Mark and I get a moment alone while clearing the table.

"I'm freaking out about that visit," I say, passing him a stack of dirty plates. "Those detectives, especially the woman—"

"Lopez. Detective Lopez." Mark puts down the soapy sponge and focuses on me.

"Right. Detective Lopez. She was so suspicious."

"She was certainly very aggressive."

"Like she thought I actually was involved somehow."

"I'm not sure you should read too much into it, honey." He walks around the island and wraps his arms around me. "They're just doing their job. To a cop, everyone looks like a suspect."

In his arms, some of the tension I have been holding begins to melt. I lean my cheek against the cool poplin of his dress shirt, inhale his scent. "I guess so. I just got a weird feeling."

He pulls back a little. "I saw Trip Gordon. You know, Daisy's husband? On the metro. He said the police were at their house, too, if that makes you feel any better. I'm sure they're questioning everyone who had any contact with this guy."

"You're right. It's probably just routine." But it doesn't make me feel any better. It makes me feel like a noose is tightening around my throat.

Tuesday at work is uneventful. I take advantage of downtime at lunch to finish the last chapters of *Disheveled* for book club. After dinner, I leave Mark to give Cole his bath and head across the street.

At Leah's, Dustin answers the door when I knock, clutching his quivering chihuahua.

"Hi, Dustin," I say. "Is this your new pup?"

He tilts his long head, his eyes almost hidden by a swoop of thick, black hair. "Wozniak." Wozniak shivers at the sound of his name, his eyes bugging in different directions.

"Interesting name."

"Steve Wozniak cofounded Apple in 1976," Dustin says, nuzzling his nose in his dog's tiny back. "He created the first programmable universal remote, so yeah, we have him to thank for that."

"Cool. I did not know that." Dustin proceeds with a microlecture on the birth of personal computing, while I take in Leah's foyer. Her house is a center-hall colonial, an exact replica of our own, built by the same developer during the World War II boom that turned Washington from a sleepy town into a city. But whereas our house has maintained what I like to consider its shabby-chic charm, Leah's has been blinged out.

"Is that Allie? C'mon in!" Someone yells from the living room, interrupting Dustin mid-monologue.

"Guess I should go in." I hold up the book.

I enter Leah's living room, shelter-magazine ready with buttery yellow walls, white sofas, and gleaming mahogany end tables. Symmetry reigns here, and I am askew, especially tonight, after the visit from the police.

Daisy embraces me in a warm hug.

"Everybody read the book?" I ask.

Daisy rolls her eyes. "Couldn't get past chapter 1, but don't tell anyone. I had a situation with Gabriella this week. Her mom found some prescription pills in her backpack and automatically assumed they were mine. She showed up guns blazing."

"Oh no!" Heather shakes her head in disbelief. She's wearing a Marine Corps Marathon T-shirt over running tights, but not a hair is out of place on her blond bob, the default hairdo of the neighborhood.

"And then I told Trip, which I was apparently not supposed to do, and he confronted Gabriella, and I became the bad guy." She winced. "Forget this book, I should write a book about step-parenting a teen. I'd call it *This Wasn't My First Choice, Either.*" She lets out a shrill laugh. "Kidding, of course. I love Gabriella to bits."

Daisy turns her attention to me. "Now, Allie." She puts both her hands on my shoulders and squeezes. "The question is, how are you holding up, sweetie?"

In an instant, I am sure Leah told her about Rob Avery and what happened in the bathroom. Fury rises in me. "Where's Leah?"

"She's in the kitchen."

I leave the room and find Leah buzzing around the kitchen in yoga pants and a cropped sweatshirt that most teenagers wouldn't dare wear.

"Allie, honey! How are you holding up?" She hugs me. "I've been thinking about you all day. I called a friend of mine from law school who's a public defender. Want to know what she said?"

"Not really. You told Daisy, didn't you?"

Unfazed, Leah points at a bottle of white wine on the counter. "Can you open that for me?"

I grab the bottle and unscrew the cap.

"Leah, did you tell Daisy?"

Leah stops what she's doing. "I had to. Please don't hate me! She came in here saying that someone had told her that you had been making out with Rob Avery the night he was killed, and I said, no way, no how." Leah opens a can of smoked almonds and pours them into a bowl. "That is not what happened."

"She said I was making out?" I am trying to picture what Daisy could have seen that night.

"Well, maybe not those exact words. She said she heard someone else say that."

"Who?"

"I don't know." Leah stops her busywork and stands with her hands on her hips. "That's not the point. The point is, I said that son of a bitch forced himself on you." She hands me the bowl of almonds. "That's all. Nothing else. I didn't tell her about him calling you a cock tease or the whole Tinder thing, don't worry." She tilts her head to one side. "Do you hate me?"

"No, I don't hate you." But I can barely contain my composure. "I just don't like the whole neighborhood talking about this."

"I know, I get it. But trust me, it's better if they know the truth, right? I mean, with the investigation, it's all going to come out. I used to work in PR."

I frown. "I thought you used to be a lawyer."

She waves away the question. "That was before. It's better to get ahead of things." She picks up the tray with the glasses. "Grab the wine, will you?"

I follow Leah into the living room like an automaton. Daisy's sitting on one of two white damask sofas that flank a roaring fire. The rest of the group—Heather, Janelle, and Pam—is seated and chatting about rumors that the school art teacher is leaving.

Leah hands me a wineglass—really a bowl on a stem—with *Why limit happy to an hour?* etched on the side. I take a deep sip, then another.

Leah clears her throat and claps her hands together three times like a kindergarten teacher. "Okay, people, this is a book club. So stop chatting"—she pauses for dramatic effect—"and start drinking."

Everyone laughs. I watch Leah as she passes the wine around. Heather catches my eye and offers a bittersweet smile. I don't know if she is being her usual simpering self or if she knows, too.

Something about the conversation in the kitchen is bugging me. Something Leah said, which I cannot put my finger on.

I lean back into the soft, white cushions and will myself to relax. Leah has been nothing but a good friend. *Not every time someone talks about you are they trying to hurt you,* I tell myself.

"No, seriously, enough with the chitchat," Daisy says. "Let's discuss *Disheveled.* Janelle? I know you've got some opinions."

Heather titters.

"Well, I hated this," says Janelle. "Do we really need another novel about how hard it is to be alive in America in the twenty-first century?"

"Big surprise," Pam mutters. "You only like books about the Holocaust. Or slavery."

"At least they have something to really complain about." Janelle sips her wine. "This is the worst kind of self-indulgent garbage."

People start chiming in. I scan my memory for some salient detail from the book that I can contribute to the discussion, but all I can think about is who knows what about me and Rob Avery. Was it one of these women who told Daisy we were making out at the party?

I grab the bottle and fill my glass again.

"I'm sorry," Pam says. "Are we just going to ignore the elephant in the room?"

The energy seems to shift.

"I mean, hello!" Pam continues. "A man was murdered in our neighborhood."

"I heard he was drugged," Janelle says. "A friend of a friend works at the county pathologist's."

"What?" Heather gasps. "Drugged? What in the world does that even mean?"

"I think," Janelle says, "it means someone drugged him, Heather. And those drugs killed him."

And the conversation is off and running. I pull further into myself, focusing on the terrible manicure Sharon gave me, until something Daisy says catches my attention.

"—most certainly was not a *good guy*. He may have looked the part, but he did some shitty things. And I mean really shitty."

The room falls silent. I straighten up, on high alert.

"What the hell are you talking about, Daisy?" Pam asks.

"Let's just say he got drunk at my party and assaulted one of the moms in the neighborhood."

A collective gasp erupts.

"When?" Janelle demands.

"At my party. Saturday night."

"Right before he died?" Janelle asks.

I glare at Daisy, trying to silence her with my eyes. She stares straight ahead, impervious, her blond curls like a halo around her head. This is happening at warp speed, right in front of me. I thought they'd at least have the decency to talk behind my back. I look at Leah, who seems shocked.

"Is the poor woman okay?" Heather asks.

"Who was it? We need names, now." Pam leans forward in her chair like a puppy panting for a treat.

"No names," Leah says. I shoot her a grateful look.

"How do you know about this, Daisy?" Janelle asks.

"I just do." Daisy pops an almond in her mouth, pleased with herself.

Panic rises within me. I do not know what to do. I don't want to say a word or move a muscle, afraid my voice or my body might betray me. I am certain the truth is written on my face, were anyone to bother to look over at me. But all eyes are on

Daisy. I pray for someone to steer the conversation back to the book.

"Do the police know this?" Heather asks.

"Lisa Bratt," Janelle says. "She was a hot mess Saturday night. I saw her puking in the azaleas."

Leah shakes her head. "Stop guessing, Janelle."

"Wait, Leah knows? How does Leah know?" She pivots toward Daisy. "Is it Karen Pearce? I saw her yelling at someone."

"You heard Leah," Daisy says. "You can stop guessing, because we're not telling."

"C'mon, Daisy. Seriously. Do the police know?" Pam asks. "Because maybe the husband, I don't know, got angry and attacked Rob. I mean, my husband would go ballistic if someone assaulted me."

"Did he hit on you, Leah? When you first moved here? Before you and David got together?" Janelle asks. "I feel like he hit on all the divorced moms."

"That poor girl," Pam says. "What's her name? Tenley?"

"And now she's going to hear that her dead father was a rapist," Heather says.

I can't take it anymore. "No one's accusing anyone of rape." All eyes turn to me. I put my wineglass on the table and misjudge the edge. It tumbles. I manage to catch it, but not before the wine splashes on the rug. "Oh, shit!"

I fall to my knees and dab at the stain with a few pink-and-green napkins that read: *Today's Forecast: 100% Chance of Wine.*

"Don't worry." Leah runs out of the room. In a moment, she is back with a moist rag, kneeling beside me and dabbing the rug. "It's white wine. Do you have any idea how much wine this rug has absorbed over the years? Its blood-alcohol level would get it arrested."

A scattering of nervous laughter fills the room.

I scoot back out of Leah's way. Little bits of the paper napkin

I used have wedged into the carpet like specks of green-and-pink confetti. I've made things worse. "I should go. I need to get home."

"Don't go," Leah says, standing up. "You're upset."

"We're on your side, Allie," Daisy says. "No one blames you for what Rob Avery did."

"Oh my god." Heather's voice reverberates in the room. "It was you? Are you all right?"

I shove my book into my bag.

"Is this you and Rob?" Janelle passes her phone to me. I take it from her as Leah and Heather crowd over my shoulder to peer at the small screen.

It's the same photo the detective showed me—with Rob and me almost touching foreheads in Daisy's kitchen Saturday night. I scroll down and see it has been posted on the Eastbrook Neighborhood Facebook page.

There are dozens of comments nested below.

I toss the phone onto the coffee table with a clang. I'm halfway to the front door when someone, maybe Pam, calls after me, "We won't tell anyone."

I twist and pull on the front door locks. The door won't budge. Leah reaches from behind me and pulls it open for me.

"Allie, please don't be upset. We want to support you. We all have our own stories—hashtag MeToo, right?"

I push past her, desperate to fill my lungs with cool air. It's not until I am across the street, inside my own house, with the door shut and locked, that I remember what Leah said in the kitchen that's been bugging me.

She told me she had been discreet when she'd talked to Daisy—that she did not share that Rob had told me to stay off Tinder.

But I'm sure that I never mentioned anything about Tinder to Leah.

15

"*A-B-C-D-E-F-G, gummy bears are chasing me,*" Cole sings as he moves his toothbrush to the other side of his mouth. To my chagrin, Cole is not only wide awake when I return from book club, he's taken every single item of clothing he owns and strewn them around his room.

But I'm too jittery to clean. All I can think about is what happened at Leah's. The way the women reacted to the news reminded me of watching a cigarette that's tossed into the woods and ignites a raging wildfire.

And the embarrassing way I ran out of there.

Mark is prone in front of the TV downstairs, an inning away from unconsciousness. If I had known that, while I was at book club, he would plant himself on the couch while Cole destroyed the upstairs, I might not have gone. And he wonders why I don't want another child.

"*One is red, one is blue, one is peeing on my shoe.*"

"Keep brushing," I say, trying to keep the edge out of my voice. I don't want to take out my irritation with Mark on Cole. "Not just singing."

Cole spits into the sink and then attacks his bottom teeth with gusto. The dentist told Cole that he needed to brush for the entirety of the ABC song, or "Twinkle, Twinkle, Little Star."

"*Now I'm running for my life, 'cause the green one has a knife.*"

Cole spits again.

"Very good." I hand him a towel to wipe his mouth. Volcanic

impatience is bubbling just under the surface of my skin, ready to erupt. But I can't let it show. Cole is like a wild animal this way; if he sniffs out my desire to leave, it will trigger an intense clinginess in him. If I want a drama-free exit, I will need to be super affectionate, so that it is he who pushes me away. It's a lot like dating, I realize.

An image of that photo and all those comments on the East-brook Facebook page spring to mind, and I cringe. The whole neighborhood is talking about it. How long can what happened to me stay a secret?

But more than that, my image is now forever linked to a murder. The internet never forgets.

"Mommy, you be the mommy ocelot, and I'll be the baby ocelot."

"Great idea." I wince at my own sarcasm and take a deep breath. "Now let's get our jammers on." Hands on his bony little shoulders, I guide Cole out of the bathroom and toward the bedroom.

The whole evening has left me unmoored. I know that Leah and Daisy do care about me, but I feel so exposed, naked even. I hope Mark is still awake, because we need to talk. And not just about his not putting Cole to bed. All of this has unearthed long-ago feelings I thought I had cordoned off in my heart. Memories and experiences that I hoped I had moved on from and that I would never have to revisit.

There have been moments over the years when I was tempted to tell Mark about what happened in high school, but I never had the guts. Right after we moved from San Francisco to Chicago, I bumped into someone from back home at a farmers' market, someone who was at Overton the same time I was. My body was swollen with Cole—not just my belly but my ankles, even my face. I was only days from giving birth, although I didn't know that at the time. But that's why I did not turn and run. That evening, I almost told Mark about what happened at Overton. When I hesitated, he told me, "I don't care about your past; it's your future that I'm interested in."

At the time, it seemed like the most romantic thing anyone could say to me.

Cole climbs onto his bed, where I am sitting. At first, I cannot believe what I am seeing, but my son is wearing a T-shirt with the word *Overton* splayed across the chest.

Seeing the name of the school is a slap across my face. Bracing, accusatory. It's the mocking laugh of the other girls, the snide smiles of the boys. It's everything I've run away from.

"Cole, where did you get that?" My voice trembles.

"I found it."

"Take it off." I begin yanking his arms through the sleeves.

"Why? I like it!"

"Where did you get this? It's not ours." I struggle to sound even-keeled, even though inside my thoughts are swirling. *Someone's been here. In my house.*

"I found it in the laundry."

"Cole, tell the truth, where did you get this?"

Tears spring to his eyes. "I am telling the truth! You never believe me!" he wails.

"Okay, okay, honey. I believe you." He collapses, sobbing, onto my shoulder. There has to be a reasonable explanation. Maybe Mark bought it. Maybe it came in the mail, and he didn't tell me. Maybe the school mails these out to alumni.

I am itching to get downstairs and ask Mark, but first things first.

"How about bumblebee pajamas?" I ask. "You haven't worn those in a while."

Cole nods, eyes downcast. Once he's changed, I snuggle beside him in bed and read *There's a Nightmare in My Closet*. Cole recites the words from memory. Then we read *Pinkalicious*, twice, my legs twitching the whole time. When we're done, I kiss Cole on the forehead, kiss Giraffe on his neck, and start to stand up.

"Scratchy my backy," Cole says.

I lie down beside my son, tracing my fingers back and forth

between the little boy's shoulder blades a little too fast. I do it because this is the kind of thing my mother never did. Since I don't
really have a role model on which to base my parenting style, I've
developed a modus operandi: do the opposite of what Sharon
did. From downstairs, a roar from the television drifts up.

I watch for the steady rise and fall of Cole's small body, which
means that he is finally asleep. Through the bare window, the white
moon glows against the purple-black sky. The days are shorter. We
haven't bought curtains yet, or to be precise, we haven't bought
curtain rods yet. The curtains are sitting in a box in the attic. I
wonder if we will ever put them up. Maybe we'll move out of this
house twenty years from now when Cole graduates from college,
with the curtains still sitting in the attic.

Finally, Cole is asleep. I can't get downstairs fast enough, and
I am disappointed to see that Mark is dozing on the sofa, short,
gasping snores escaping from his open mouth.

"Mark," I whisper in a loud voice. "Mark, you awake?"

He opens his eyes groggily. "What's up?"

I hold up the T-shirt. "Did you buy this shirt?"

He blinks at the shirt and then at me. "What? No, Allie, I
didn't buy that shirt." His words are deliberate and slow, and I
am impatient. I want him to be as upset as I am.

"Who did?"

"Umm, I don't know. I'm sorry, I'm going to bed. You coming?"

"This is a big deal. I need to know where this came from."

"First of all, please stop yelling."

"I didn't yell." But he's right. My voice is loud, my tone stri-
dent. "How did this get here?" I shake the shirt at him.

He bats it away and stands up. "I have no clue, Allie. I'm not
sure what you want me to say."

"I want you to be concerned."

"About a T-shirt? I was asleep." He starts to leave the room.
"Why don't you ask Susan? It probably came in the mail or
something."

I don't answer, just watch him leave. The energy between us isn't good at the precipice of an argument. I know that when Mark is this tired, the only thing I'll get by pushing him is a massive fight.

I need to calm down. I sit in the empty room for a minute trying to inventory my thoughts. I wish I had a best friend whom I could tell everything to, someone who would help me sort out what are legitimate feelings and what are overreactions.

But maybe that person doesn't exist, it's just a trope from cheesy movies, as clichéd as true love. Mark and Krystle are the closest people to me. I know they love me, but I don't dare tell them everything, show them everything, about me.

I pour myself a glass of wine and sit down in front of the computer. Within moments, I am looking at the picture of Rob and me on the Eastbrook Neighborhood Facebook page. Someone named Barb McLaren posted it. I click on her profile. She looks to be in her early fifties, with a gray-streaked blond bob and a lot of pink-and-green resort wear.

I don't remember seeing her at Daisy's party, but clearly, she saw me.

Can anyone identify this woman talking with Rob?

I think her name is Allie Ross. Lives on Worthington. Husband Mark. New to the neighborhood.

Looks very chummy to me. Wouldn't want my wife talking to a man like that.

STOP GOSSIPING!!!

I shut down the page. I should never have opened it. What did I expect? Of course tongues would be wagging. I had the bad luck of being the last woman Rob Avery hit on before he was killed. As much as I do not wish Rob's boorish behavior on anyone else, I would love for some other women in the neighborhood to step up and share similar experiences.

But I'm not about to put any feelers out.

Instead, I take a brief look at the online calendar—tomorrow night is Mark's mom's birthday, which means dinner in downtown Bethesda with Mark's whole family.

As for work, tomorrow I have Heather's referral—Sarah Ramirez—on the schedule. Like Heather, Sarah also works for Senator Fielding from Rhode Island—Heather as the communications director and Sarah as a caseworker. But Sarah doesn't want a headshot. Sarah wants something romantic for her fiancé who is about to leave for Africa.

I can't help myself. I go back to Facebook and do a search for Robert Avery. I find his page easily, covered in condolence posts. From his photos, he looks like the perfect suburban dad who hadn't lost his youthful edge. A photo of him kayaking the Potomac in a Fugazi T-shirt. Another of him with a lithe blonde, hoisting beers at the Bluejacket microbrewery in D.C.

Good-looking, mid-forties. Not a monster.

Why did he pick me? And why did someone kill him?

I need to talk to someone, but who?

My computer, phone, and laptop are all Apple and linked through my Apple ID. That means photos, texts, almost anything I do on one appears on all the devices. I text Krystle from the computer: *Sorry about before.*

Krystle's reply is immediate: *NP. You know I love you, Allie.*
Have you had a chance to check for my fake Tinder account?
Will check Tinder tonight.

I hover over a photo of Rob and then click on it, saving it to the computer. Then I copy it into a message for Krystle.

Does the guy I am talking to in this pic look familiar? I pause and then take a chance. *Also, does the name Robert Avery ring any bells? From back home?*

Nope. Any yearbooks you want me to check?

For a while, my entire childhood and adolescence were condensed into three banker's boxes that sat in the house in Westport, Connecticut, about five miles from where I grew up in Norwalk.

But when I transferred my mother into assisted living three

years ago, I discarded those boxes, though I hadn't told Krystle. I was married, had a child. My past had no hold on me anymore.

Or so I'd thought. But for the first time in years, I have the urge to delve into those Overton yearbooks. Maybe somewhere, among the senior photos and candids of kids playing Frisbee on the great lawn, is some kind of clue as to what is happening to me.

I shut the computer and head upstairs. The wine has made me sleepy, and I climb into the warm bed beside Mark. He's on his back, and I slide my hand under his T-shirt, tracing my finger down his chest until it arrives at the elastic waistband of his boxers. Territory I haven't explored in months. I slip my hand inside. He lets out a low groan and rolls toward me, his body responsive even as his mind has not quite caught up.

A quote I once read comes to me: "There is love, of course. And then there's life, its enemy." You can find a pedestrian article on that theme in every women's magazine in every doctor's waiting room. How domestic routines can destroy romance. Mark's eyes open; his face is a question. Before he can articulate it, I lean in and we are kissing.

Soon he is inside me, and even though we haven't been together for almost two months, we move with the familiarity of bodies that instinctively recognize each other. We are quiet, efficient, practiced at the art of domestic sex.

"Harder," I whisper, and he complies. I want him to nail me down to the bed. I want to be stuck in place like a piece of paper under a rock on a windy day. Fuck the book club, the neighborhood gossips, the internet. Mark is my husband, Cole is my son, this is my house, my life.

But I can't shake the feeling there is more to this Rob Avery thing than just bad luck. The Overton shirt, him calling me Sexy Lexi. Those details are like bits and pieces of some complicated mathematical equation that I don't yet know how to solve.

And deep in my bones, I know when the answer comes, it will not be good.

16

In the photo, my breasts pour out of a cobalt-blue bikini top.

Below the picture, it says: *Alexis, but my friends call me Sexy Lexi. Married, but I don't mind if you don't.*

I look up from my phone to make sure Cole has paused at the corner to wait for my signal like he's supposed to. I nod at him and he runs ahead. The streets are empty this morning, we're running a bit late, and the rush of hurrying children has subsided.

"You there?" Krystle's voice sounds tinny coming through my phone at arm's length.

"I'm here," I say.

"You recognize the photo? That could be a clue."

The blue bikini had been a bad online purchase. I wore it to our local pool once, on Memorial Day, the day after we moved into our new house, before I decided it was not family-friendly.

My stomach churns. Someone has been stalking me since I moved in.

"How did you find this?" I ask.

"On Tinder," she says. "It was pretty easy, actually. I just looked for women seeking men within five miles of you. This is no random Russian hacker."

"No. Whoever made this page knows about Overton." My skin prickles with the electric sensation of being watched. My tormentor lives right here, I think, as I pass by a row of picture-perfect colonials with manicured lawns.

"Who?" Krystle asks. "Who lives near you that knows about that shit?"

I don't have an answer for that question. All I know is that I need to shut this Tinder account down, and fast. I tell Krystle I'll call her later and jog to catch up to Cole. He points to the last few riders spilling off the yellow school buses.

"We're not late!"

Then he stops short and screws up his face in outrage. Out comes a shriek, sent straight up to the milky-white sky. "It's Blue Day! I was supposed to dress in blue!" Tears spring from his eyes as if they have been ready on standby.

As I glance at the other children going in, I have a vague recollection of an email about Blue Day, a show of solidarity with all the endangered marine mammals of the earth.

"Your shirt has blue in it, look." I unzip his pink hoodie coat and run a finger along a sky-blue strip of material.

Cole snaps at me like a cornered dog. "No! It's striped. That doesn't count. I need to go home and change." He stomps his foot once and then, pleased with the sound, a few more times.

"Honey, it's too late."

"You forgot to tell me." He zeroes in on my face. "You forget everything."

His accusation stings. A woman in an orange safety vest approaches and, after a few tense words, ushers Cole inside the building.

I turn and hurry back up the hill toward home, passing a black Audi with Virginia plates. The car is parked across from the school on the side of the street that is supposed to remain clear during school hours. This is the kind of infraction that brings down the wrath of the PTA moms, and sure enough, Vicki comes striding across the street toward the car. The first three license plate letters are FCS, which remind me of Sharon's favorite expression—"For cripes' sake."

I have no desire to cross paths with the woman who humiliated me over mini–hamburger buns on Saturday night, so I quicken my step to avoid having to pass her. I'm feeling raw and vulnerable; I don't have the energy to even pretend to be friendly.

Vicki is sure to have heard about me and Rob Avery. Maybe she's even seen the photo. It's possible she even took it.

I chide myself for my paranoia. There has to be a reasonable explanation for everything.

I sense someone behind me and turn to see Daisy and another woman hurrying toward me. It's too late to turn away, so I offer a small smile, hoping they will walk past. But as they near me, they slow down. All the muscles in my neck tighten.

"Good morning, Allie," Daisy says, falling into step beside me. "Do you know Priya? Priya Carmichael, this is Allie Ross. Priya is Micah's mom. He's in first grade." Turning to Priya, she adds, "Allie and her family just moved into the Vanniers' old house."

I keep walking, sure that my distress shows on my face. I was photographed, without my knowledge, at the neighborhood pool. I remember the day well. The morning after we moved all our furniture and boxes in, Leah knocked on the door and introduced herself and Ava. *Come to the pool,* she said, explaining that although there was a seven-year wait list to become a member, we could be her guests. *It's going to be a hundred degrees.*

"I love the Vannier house," Priya says. Her long, thin face and black eyes remind me of a Modigliani painting. "It's so funny," she adds, "I've seen you at drop-off, but I figured you were a nanny, you look so young."

Priya reaches out a slender hand and touches me, sending a shudder down my forearm. I move my arm away, shoving my hands into my coat pocket.

"I want you to know that you should pay no attention to what people are saying about you and Rob Avery."

I stop short. "I'm sorry, what are people saying?"

Priya looks nervously to Daisy for guidance. "Oh, I didn't mean to upset you."

"I'm not upset," I say through clenched teeth. "I just don't know what you mean."

"Well, some people are saying you were having an affair, and now that there's attention being paid to his death, you're claiming he sexually assaulted you."

I gasp. "What? Who said that?"

"I don't believe it for a minute." She holds her hands to her chest.

"Priya is a counselor at Georgetown." Daisy wears an earnest expression on her round face. "Isn't that right, Priya?"

Priya nods. "Yes. I run the sexual assault survivors' program there. I always believe women."

"In fact, Priya's the one who found us a therapist for Gabriella."

"Is that working out?" Priya asks.

Daisy lets out a little guffaw. "Don't ask me. Gabriella tells me nothing. Although, I heard her throwing up in her bathroom last night, so I wonder if the bulimia is back."

"I'm sorry, ladies, but I have to get to work." I turn and continue walking. Ridiculous. Every woman in this neighborhood appears to know what happened at Daisy's party, and they seem to feel entitled to pick at my experiences the way little boys gleefully pick the legs off insects. And as sweet as Daisy is, it is obviously she cannot keep a confidence—whether it's about me or her stepdaughter's problems.

"Bye, Allie!" Daisy calls. I turn and wave goodbye.

A mucky sense of unease envelops me as I drive down Mass Ave. toward D.C. Things are spinning out of my control. I'd rather be a nobody to the moms in the neighborhood than a topic of gossip. What happened at Overton scarred me. How quickly everyone turned against me.

The whispers of *Sexy Lexi*.

The police showing up during math class.

I shake the awful memories away. Maybe I'm just not used to having girlfriends. Take Daisy: while she overshares, she is also kind and loyal and clearly knows how to make and keep friends. I will try to stop reacting so negatively to everyone's concern. I want friends. I need them. The kind of support network you read about in books, a group of women who show up for each other. And that begins with me giving people the benefit of the doubt.

The car speaker shrills with an incoming call startling me. It's Mark.

"Hey, hon," he says. "I'm heading into a meeting, but I wanted to let you know that I talked to a guy from law school who's now a criminal lawyer—"

"You did? Why?" The words *criminal lawyer* immediately trigger a sense of guilt.

"Hold on, I was just running the scenario by him. What happened to you at Daisy's party and what you should do."

"Let me guess. He says that I should tell the police everything."

"Actually, yes. You have nothing to hide."

A tiny laugh escapes me, not loud enough for Mark to hear. As if having nothing to hide has ever helped a woman who's been assaulted.

"He strongly recommends that you lay out the facts as soon as possible. He knows a criminal defense lawyer who can go to the police with you if that's what you want. The lawyer's name is Artie Zucker. I think we should call him."

"Right, because nothing sends the message that you have done nothing wrong like hiring a criminal defense lawyer."

"I know you don't want to talk to the police. And I don't blame you. If it were just a matter of what happened at Daisy's party, it would be one thing, but Allie, a guy is dead. Murdered."

"I'm not guilty of anything, Mark."

"This is D.C. Everybody has a lawyer. It's like having a dentist. Tell you what, I'll call him."

"No. I can do it. Just text me his info."

We say goodbye just as traffic slows to a halt outside the vice president's residence at the Naval Observatory. A caravan of black Lincoln Navigators emerges like a giant snake from the property onto Mass Ave. I know Mark is right, but I can't shake the sense of unease, a sort of dark, swampy feeling in my gut that I am being pulled into some dark vortex that is going to swallow me whole.

Those detectives are probably getting all kinds of "tips" about my supposed affair with Rob, and it would probably be better just to tell them what happened. Not that I'm looking forward to it.

And then I see it.

The black Audi with FCS on the Virginia plates. It's right behind me.

17

At Dupont Circle, I take a different route than normal, winding my way through the neighborhood. The Audi falls back, but never out of sight.

A flash of red before my eyes. I slam on the breaks just inches from a woman pushing a stroller across a marked intersection.

The woman stops and wags her finger at me. "You crazy bitch!" she shouts. "Watch where you're going!"

My heart thumps like a drum as I drive on, eyes glued to the road. She's right. I am crazy. I'm becoming paranoid. So a car from my neighborhood is heading in the same direction I am. Lots of people have reason to be driving into downtown D.C. this hour. It doesn't have to mean something.

Sure enough, by the time I get down to H Street, the Audi is nowhere in sight. *I need to get a grip,* I tell myself as I park the car and walk to my office. I can't let neighborhood gossips get to me.

"Good morning," I say and put my laptop down on an empty table. I want to contact Tinder as soon as possible, but I don't want to be rude to my boss.

"Hey, Allie. Any chance you could edit the Dwayne-and-Kylie shoot today? I told them we'd expedite it."

"Of course." I boot up my laptop. Dwayne and Kylie are planning the perfect wedding, and they want engagement pics that Dwayne can send to his family in Trinidad. Normally, engagement shoots are a breeze, but their newborn was being very fussy that day.

Mike grabs his jacket and stops in front of my desk. "I'm heading out for coffee. You want an espresso?"

"Yes, please. Double." I hand him my Chicago Art Institute travel mug. It turns from pink to blue when filled with hot liquid.

He laughs. "Rough night?"

"Yeah, drama in the suburbs." I mean my tone to sound light. Mike frowns.

"Everything all right at home?" Mike is a sensitive guy who likes to take the emotional temperature of everyone he meets. Divorced for about three years from his high school girlfriend, he had kids early, and now his twin daughters are already in middle school. I've heard him drop comments about his online dating experiences, and I consider mentioning the Tinder issue to see if he has any insight. But I decide against it, not because he wouldn't listen but because I want him to leave so I can email Tinder.

"Yeah, I'm fine. Believe it or not, we had a murder in our neighborhood this weekend."

"See, that's why I will never leave the city. Too dangerous in the burbs." He raps his knuckles on the table.

After he's gone, I turn my attention to my computer. I should be editing. Instead, I call Krystle.

"This is no Russian scam, Allie," she says as soon as I answer. "This shit is real. Personal."

"I don't need you to tell me that," I snap. Still, I am grateful. It confirms my innermost fears. I am not paranoid; I am being targeted.

"Who's doing this?"

"I feel like it has to be someone from Overton. I mean—Sexy Lexi?"

"Like who?" she asks. "I mean, you don't think it's Paul Adamson, do you?"

"Maybe. I think it's possible." Paul would be in his mid-forties now.

"Maybe his life hasn't turned out the way he'd planned. Maybe he blames you for what happened."

"He's not like that. He was a kind person."

"Allie! He slept with a student when he was a teacher. He was a total creep. Why are you defending him?"

"I'm not. But you make it sound like I was a victim."

"That's because you *were* a victim. You were seventeen. He committed a crime."

"I take responsibility for what happened."

"That's not how the law works. Trust me on this one."

"And now he lives in my neighborhood? I mean, it's been years, but I like to think that I'd recognize Paul Adamson if I saw him at my neighborhood pool."

"I'm texting you a link to a page set up specifically to address false accounts," Krystle says. "Email them."

My phone pings right away with her text. If Tinder has bothered to create a whole page of FAQs about false accounts, that means they've encountered this problem before. Maybe there will be a quick fix, although somehow, I doubt it.

I open the page Krystle sent me and follow Tinder's instructions. It takes all of three minutes, and then there's nothing else I can do for the moment.

I should be editing. I should throw myself into work. But all I can think about is Paul and the blue bikini. Worst of all is how queasy I feel, how Krystle made me feel. Is she right? Why does the idea of being a victim repel me?

I'm not like her and Sharon. I don't blame everyone else for my life's problems. I type *Paul Adamson* into the computer.

I know what I'll find even before I hit Return. It's not like I haven't searched for him over the years. I've typed his name into the void of the web dozens of times. After all, everyone is on the internet. Everyone, it turns out, but Paul Adamson. At least not the Paul Adamson I knew. The first four pages of any search are gummed up by a Minnesota Vikings player with the same name.

Once I found an apple-cheeked priest in the Midwest named Paul Adamson who was charged with molesting altar boys. But I've never found my Paul.

I turn my attention to the hundreds of photos of Dwayne and Kylie, trying to find one where their newborn, Jaden, isn't scowling. I'll be culling the ones that don't work and putting together Package C—twenty-five different images on a disc.

Back when I was struggling to make it as an artist in San Francisco, while waiting tables and bartending to make ends meet, I looked down on this kind of photography. I am embarrassed to remember mocking another photographer friend who did weddings.

I wasn't mature enough to bear witness to other people's peak happiness. Now I love my work and feel honored that people let me into their private moments.

Mike returns with my coffee and two packets of Splenda, which is how I like it. After about an hour of editing, I've managed to cull the lot down to thirty photos and decide to take a break. I open the Eastbrook Facebook page, an idea stirring in the back of my head. It feels like every moment of life in our neighborhood is documented and posted on the site. So maybe if I go back to the day that my picture was taken at the pool, I can figure out who else was there. It's a long shot, but it's worth a try.

It takes a while to scroll all the way back to Memorial Day weekend, but I finally find it. Picture after picture of my new neighbors and their kids, sunburned noses, big smiles. I can almost smell the chlorine and grilled meat. It was the first weekend the pool was open, and there was a potluck and barbecue, and the pool was packed.

Vicki, Priya, Daisy—they're all there. I didn't know half these people yet, of course. And then I find me. In the background of a shot of two teenage girls, arms flung over their shoulders, is me. I'm sitting by the edge of the pool in that bikini. I remember being there for what felt like an eternity as Cole dipped one foot and then the other in the pool, terrified to commit to going in but refusing to abandon the exercise altogether.

But it was more like twenty minutes.

The angle is basically the same as the photo of me in the Tinder photo.

A chill runs down my spine. Whoever took the photo of me was standing basically where this person stood. I check to see who posted it. Heather, my neighbor. Could she have taken that shot of me? But why?

On another screen, I pull up the Tinder photo that Krystle sent me. The angles are not just the same. They are identical. Either someone took a photo from the same place and at the same time as Heather did, or she took the Tinder photo.

I need to find out.

My phone pings with a text from Mark with the name of the lawyer. I look up the website. A banner overlaid across a photo of a gavel resting on a stack of law books reads: *Artie Zucker: Aggressive and Experienced!* A bald, middle-aged man with arms crossed over his barrel chest sneers at the camera. Below him are boxes to click on for more information, all with names.

Drug Crimes.

Domestic Violence.

Assault.

Sex Crimes.

Drunk Driving.

Is this what it's come to? I need the help of some guy who defends rapists and drug dealers? This doesn't feel right. I decide to double-check with Mark before I call. This isn't the right guy.

My phone rings, and the caller ID says Morningside House. When I answer, a woman introduces herself as Lydia, the head nurse. We talk a little about the bruise on my mother's neck and the scratch from last week and my concerns that I don't know where they are coming from. I don't accuse her staff of anything.

"We completely understand your concern, Ms. Ross. Your

I DON'T FORGIVE YOU   103

mother can become quite agitated, especially in the evenings. She's been trying to leave after dinner, and there have been some altercations. Have you heard of sundowning?"

I jot the word down on a pad of paper as Lydia explains to me that dementia patients often become confused, anxious, and even violent as the sun starts to set and night approaches. "Our first line of defense in this case is usually some kind of antianxiety drug. With your permission, we'd like her to see the staff psychiatrist, and maybe we can start her on some kind of regimen."

Drugging her into compliance. "What are the options besides drugs?"

"We may have to move your mother into Memory Care."

Memory Care is the locked ward on the first floor. I got a glimpse of it when I took the tour, and it scared the heck out of me. Semi-catatonic people slumped over in wheelchairs, staring at a TV blasting infomercials. Sharon might have her problems, but she does not belong there. Not yet.

I tell Lydia to go ahead and make the psychiatric appointment.

"Until then," Lydia says, "you'll have to hire an aide from the hours of 8:00 a.m. to 8:00 p.m. to shadow her—"

"Wait, eight until eight? I thought you said the problem was in the evening."

"This is Morningside policy, based on years of experience. If someone tries to escape, doesn't matter what time, an aide needs to be hired to shadow them until bedtime. We need to ensure your mother doesn't go out and become lost. We have no problem with residents leaving, as long as they are accompanied. If that works, she can stay on the assisted living floor. But if an aide doesn't work out, she will have to move to Memory Care."

She tells me the facility has a service they use that provides private aides, and she offers to call them for me and initiate the process.

"How much will that cost?"

She tells me, and I scribble down a few numbers on the pad. It adds up to another two grand a month, which takes Sharon's monthly expenses above the income that comes from renting her old house in Westport. Mark and I can make up the difference for now, but it is not sustainable.

This extra cost, along with the repairs the Westport house needs, means one thing to me—I'm selling the house, whether Krystle likes it or not. The fact that it's sitting there empty, not earning us any money, is just another reason to sell.

"We shouldn't have moved her," I say. "She didn't have these problems in Connecticut."

"Don't blame yourself. Yes, the move may have triggered some of this, but in my experience, these declines are inevitable," Lydia says. "They are a matter of when, not if. And if she had stayed where she was, how often would she see you? What kind of life would that be?"

I don't answer because my ten o'clock photo shoot arrives. Sarah Ramirez, late twenties, glows the way you do when you've just spent the last three days rolling around in bed with someone you love, which she informs me right away she has been doing. I take her into the private studio in the back where we do the boudoir shoots, and I flick the switch on the wall that lights a blue bulb above the outside door.

"No one will come in while that light is on. You can undress right here, or behind that screen if you want." I point to a red-and-black printed screen that stands in the corner.

"Here is fine, I guess." Sarah's fingers hover over the buttons on her swiss-dot blouse, which she has fastened all the way up to her neck. With her calf-length navy skirt and sturdy shoes, she seems an unlikely candidate to strip in front of a stranger. But love makes you do crazy things.

I connect my phone to the speaker and put on Lana Del Rey. "How's this for music?"

Sarah smiles and then, keeping her gaze on the floor, peels off her clothes. I busy myself setting up lights around the shell-pink velvet chaise we have chosen for the shoot.

Shoots like this involve a lot of trust. I ask questions about her fiancé, Jordan, who is about to leave for a stint on the east coast of Africa where he will research and write a report on water quality. Soon enough, she has unleashed her long black hair from its bun and donned a fuchsia merry widow she bought for the shoot. I take some test shots of her lounging on the chaise, adjusting her long, black hair so it falls over one shoulder, moving a leg here, an arm there.

The work makes me think of my fake Tinder account. I wonder if Sarah knows how vulnerable she is right now, and not from an aesthetic standpoint but from a privacy one. These photos could do serious damage if they fell into the wrong hands.

The camerawork is second nature to me by now. I've known I wanted to be an artist since I was young. I was that girl who oohed over a new set of Crayolas, opening the cardboard box reverently, inhaling the scent of fresh wax. But I had never thought much about photography before I took Paul's class my senior year of high school. If you had asked me then, I would have said a photographer is a man who takes pictures of beautiful things—women, mountains, buildings. I didn't know the names Richard Avedon or Ansel Adams.

It was Paul who taught me that he who controlled the camera controlled the truth. He introduced me to photographers like Mary Ellen Mark, Cindy Sherman, and Nan Goldin, women who had the guts to challenge the mainstream and interject their own worldviews into the conversation.

Whatever else happened, he gave that to me.

A weather-shredded American flag flapping in the wind on the side of an old farmhouse. That's what I was focusing the lens on when Paul Adamson first touched me, pulling my hair out of my face.

It was a windy March day, the icy mud soaking through my tennis shoes as we tromped through the farmland of rural Connecticut. We were still pretending to be teacher and student.

Paul had tacked up a sign-up sheet earlier that week, offering to take students out on a field trip to practice taking landscapes, to put what we had learned about hyperfocal distance into use.

I was the only one who signed up.

Paul put his hand over mine, which was stiff with cold, and adjusted the f-stop on my Nikkormat camera, which was a low-end, mass-produced, single-lens-reflex model from Nikon that could also accept the lenses that fit the company's coveted F series.

Of course, I didn't know all that at the time.

I knew only that the clunky camera had been my dad's, one of the few items that escaped my mother's purge after he died. It wasn't until I signed up for Introduction to Photography that I ever used it.

I remember Paul's hot breath on the back of my neck.

The way his lips brushed my ear as he whispered his instructions.

He had long, slender fingers like a pianist's. I used to love watching him handle the camera, twisting the f-stop, adjusting the focus. For months, I longed for him to turn those same competent hands on me.

And then, that afternoon, in the back seat of his BMW at the end of a quiet, muddy country road, he did.

I shake the memories from my head and turn my attention back to Sarah. "So how long have you known Heather?" I ask.

"Like, three years. I couldn't imagine working without her. She's been sort of like a big sister to me. She's the one who encouraged me to apply to law school. She's been so sweet."

"She's my neighbor," I say. "We moved in next door to her."

Sarah's face brightens. "I know. She's told me all about you."

I look up from the viewfinder. "Really? Like what?"

Sarah flicks her hair over her shoulder. "Just like how you're so pretty and nice and how you are from Connecticut, just like her."

I straighten up at the sound of the word *Connecticut*. "I thought she was from Rhode Island. Don't you have to be in order to work for a representative from Rhode Island?"

Sarah laughs. "No. I'm from New York. I mean, there are a lot of people from Rhode Island that work in our office, but not everyone."

"What else did she say?" I try to keep my voice steady.

Sarah shrugs. "I'm not sure."

The camera feels slippery in my hands, which have become sweaty.

Sarah shifts her position and scowls. "I'm not usually this fat," Sarah says, shaking me out of my reverie. "But I'm studying for my LSATs, so I'm eating like a pint of Breyers every night."

"You're beautiful." I need to push suspicions of Heather out of my head and refocus on the shoot.

"I look tired. I have these purple bags under my eyes."

"Any bags, pimples, or stretch marks will be gone by the time I'm done photoshopping, don't worry."

Sarah giggles. "Promise me I'll look gorgeous. I know I can send him selfies and stuff, but I want to have some really good pictures. Like, perfect."

It's in her eyes, a pleading insecurity. She doesn't think she deserves him just the way she is, untouched. I want to tell her that she does. I know words like that will roll right off her. Besides, that's not my job. My job is to create beautiful photographs.

"I promise," I say. "You'll be perfect." I show her some of the shots on the screen on my camera. Red blotches appear on her cheeks.

"Oh my god, if anyone at work ever saw these pictures, I would die. I mean, Congress is a very uptight place. You have no idea."

"Really? Senator Fielding seems so cool."

"Oh, she's amazing. But she runs a tight ship. Everything is very professional."

"No one besides you and me will ever see these."

"Promise?"

I cross my heart. "Promise."

"You know, the senator might be looking for a photographer."

"Really? For what?"

Sarah laughs. "Believe it or not, she's publishing a children's book. I mean, between you and me, it's ghostwritten. It's about women politicians throughout American history. I heard her saying she wanted to update her headshot. Do you ever do those, for like public figures?"

"Sure. I've shot Congressman Marcel Parks, and I may be shooting Valerie Simmons soon." My tone is neutral, as if it's not a big deal to photograph the former White House advisor turned CNN commentator, but I watch her eyes widen. She's impressed.

"That's amazing! I'll tell her that."

"Yes, please, pass along my info. I'd love to chat with her."

"I will!"

When she leaves, all bundled up for the fall weather, Sarah plants a kiss on my cheek. "You're the best."

I am buoyed after Sarah leaves. Whatever else is happening, my work is going well, and I have to remember to take comfort in that. Fielding would make three high-profile clients in a row, and three is a pattern, not a fluke.

I head to my computer and spend twenty minutes stalking Heather Grady on social media. Although she is on Facebook, Insta, and LinkedIn, I learn little of consequence. Heather is a runner, always has been. This year she is trying to qualify for the Boston Marathon. She loves ladies' nights—I see picture after picture of her with various combinations of women from our neighborhood: Priya, Daisy, Vicki, and others at bars and concerts and coffee shops.

Then I see it. A shot of her at the finish line of a race, her arms wrapped around another runner, a woman whose face is obscured by a cap and sunglasses. They both have numbers pinned to their shirts, but I can make out the words on Heather's friend's shirt: Overton Academy.

So thrilled to run Give a Child a Chance 10k with one of my besties, Jane Fuller.

But when I check, I see Jane Fuller doesn't have a Facebook

profile. An internet search reveals no signs of her, or rather there are so many Jane Fullers the search is pointless. Maybe she didn't even go to Overton. The T-shirt might belong to someone else.

Two Overton T-shirt sightings in two days. My gut tells me it has to mean something.

Next, I google Heather's name and Overton, but the only Connecticut connection I can find is that she went to college at Wesleyan. That means nothing. She could have gone to high school anywhere. I can't even find her maiden name. Stymied, I spend the rest of the day in a blur of editing and paperwork. I do a little research on Realtors in Westport. I have nothing to go on besides Yelp reviews, and I'm not in the mood to trust the internet. I decide I'll ask Daisy if she can recommend someone. I'm able to wrap up early. I want to be home in time to relax a bit before dinner tonight with Mark's family.

As I'm shutting down for the day, Mark texts me, *Did you call the lawyer?*

Not yet. I want to talk to Mark face-to-face about my concerns about this guy.

On my way out, Mike praises the package I put together for Dwayne and Kylie. My probation will be ending soon, and it feels good to be kicking ass at something, especially when so much else in life feels out of my control.

"Nice lighting. Nice eye in general," he says as I leave.

His kind words buoy me as I take the stairs to the ground floor of the building. I need the extra good juju before this dinner. I have plenty of time to get home and take a relaxing shower, maybe even a twenty-minute nap.

But when I push open the door to the street, my good mood is snuffed out like a candle. Waiting for me in front of their unmarked cruiser are Detectives Lopez and Katz.

"Afternoon, Ms. Ross," Detective Lopez says, straightening up. "We're going to need you to come down to the station with us."

18

The two detectives sit across a table from me in a sterile conference room in a modern building in downtown Bethesda. On the ride through the streets of rush-hour D.C., I stewed in the back of the unmarked police car like a guilty criminal. When I said I could drive my own car, Detective Katz told me it would be so much easier just to take theirs.

"We know all the back ways," he said with a wink. They said it was my choice, but it sure didn't feel that way.

"How are you doing today, Ms. Ross?" Detective Lopez jiggles the remaining ice in a giant plastic cup that says Dunkin' Donuts on the side. She places the empty cup next to a yellow legal pad and her cell phone. "Your babysitter can stay longer?"

I put my phone bag in my bag. "Yes, it's no problem. Should my lawyer be here?" I hope they can't tell that I'm bluffing.

Detective Katz looks surprised and then peeks at his watch. "We had just a few questions, maybe like ten, fifteen minutes. But if you want to call your lawyer, we can wait for them. I've got no plans."

I look at the clock. Mark's mom's dinner is tonight. Maybe I can handle this. After all, I didn't do anything wrong. I'll just tell the truth. "Okay, but I can't stay too long."

"Of course. We understand." Detective Katz opens up a manila folder and thumbs through the pages. "Here we go. We just want to go over a few of the details of your earlier statement. You said you met Mr. Avery for the first time on Saturday night, at

the party at Daisy Gordon's house. Is that correct?" Katz pushes
the paper toward Detective Lopez, who picks it up and scans it.

"Yes. That's right."

The two exchange a glance. "And you also stated that you had
no prior relationship with Mr. Avery," Detective Lopez says, "via
any applications or social media platforms, correct?"

I shift uncomfortably in my seat. "Yes."

"Are you on Tinder, Ms. Ross?" she asks, boring into me with
dark eyes.

"No, I am not." I take a deep breath. "I am aware, however,
that there is a fake profile of me on Tinder."

Detective Lopez puckers her lips as if she's just tasted something sour. "And when were you made aware of this fake profile?"

"This morning, actually. My sister found it."

Detective Katz pushes the yellow legal pad toward me. "Can
we get your sister's name and contact info, please?"

"Have you contacted Tinder?" Lopez asks.

"Yes, I have." I finish jotting down Krystle's info and push the
pad back across the table.

Lopez turns her phone face up and taps at it. Then she pushes
it across the table toward me. A quick glance confirms what I
suspected. Me in that damn bikini.

"That's it," I say without touching it.

"Is it your position that you did not write any of the messages
coming from this profile?"

"Yes."

"Were you aware that whoever made this profile has been in
regular contact with Robert Avery over the past five weeks?"

A warmth rises in me. I think of what Mark said about coming clean. "No. But I'm not totally surprised. On Saturday night,
Rob said something to me about staying off Tinder, and I had no
idea what he meant. Now it makes sense."

Detective Lopez leans back in her chair. "He told you to stay
off Tinder? You didn't mention that earlier."

"I didn't think it was relevant."

Lopez bites her lip hard. She doesn't have to say anything. My credibility has just tanked with her.

"All righty," Katz says. "Let's start at the beginning of the night, the party, and even if it seems completely irrelevant and minor, why don't you walk us through everything that happened?"

I tell them everything to the best of my recollection, stating the facts of what happened upstairs in the bathroom as coolly as I can. "And I was very upset, of course, so we left. We went home."

"You were upset because your husband saw you leaving the bathroom with Mr. Avery."

"No," I snap. And then add more calmly, "I was upset because of what Rob did. My husband has been wonderful. Very supportive."

"Ms. Ross, I'm going to ask you point-blank, one more time, were you having an affair with Robert Avery?"

I bristle. "I've answered that question several times now. The answer is no." I look at my phone. It's almost six. I need to get home now if I am going to make it to this birthday dinner on time. There will be no time for a shower, let alone a nap, but I don't want to stay here any longer. I pull my bag onto my lap, realizing my hands are trembling. "I have to go. I have dinner plans."

"We're not quite done here, Ms. Ross. Let me ask you, do you use zolpidem?"

The question stuns me. "Do I what?"

"Zolpidem, brand name Ambien. The sleep aid. Ever used it?"

I blink. I have used it a few times, in Chicago last year. A doctor prescribed it for me during the stress of readying for our move, but I stopped using it when I realized it made me groggy the next day. But the police couldn't know this, could they? "No, not really."

"Which is it?" Lopez asks. "No, or not really?"

I'm confused. "What does this have to do with anything?"

"Ms. Ross, did you order liquid zolpidem from a Canadian pharmacy and have it delivered to your house on September . . . hold on." Detective Lopez holds up a finger as she scans the legal pad in front of her. "September 20?"

"No. No I didn't." The specificity of the question chills me. I didn't even know liquid Ambien existed. But now it's obvious— Rob Avery was poisoned with it. Janelle from book club said her friend told her he had been drugged. I stand up, adrenaline rushing through me. "Am I allowed to leave or not?"

Lopez's eyes shoot up. "You're not under arrest, if that's what you're asking."

I nod. I guess that's what I was asking.

"We'll be in touch, Ms. Ross."

It's not until I am outside in the cool evening air, waiting for my Uber to come, that I stop shaking.

I realize that I made a terrible mistake not calling Artie Zucker.

As soon as I climb out of the Uber, Cole and Mark emerge from our house wearing khakis and pink dress shirts.

"Mommy!" Cole runs to me. I bend down and hug him a little harder than usual. "We're both wearing pink!" he yells in my ear. "Go put on something pink and we can all match."

Mark looks confused. "Where's your car?"

"At work." I look from Mark to Cole and back again. "I'll explain later."

I quickly run upstairs and wash my face. I trade in my sweaty clothes for a nice blouse. It's not as good as a shower. A little lip gloss and a spritz of perfume, and I am presentable. At least from the outside. Inside, I am churning.

A few minutes later, we are all in Mark's car heading toward downtown Bethesda. Cole is yammering on about his family tree, and as long as he is not peppering me with questions, I don't mind the chatter. I use the mental space to digest what the detectives said. Why did they ask about a package of liquid Ambien? That was no fishing expedition; they have some basis for the question. Did someone have Ambien delivered to my house? It's not out of the question. After all, someone developed an entire fake online relationship with Rob Avery, while pretending to be me. And now he's dead, poisoned—possibly from an overdose of Ambien.

Somehow, I've landed in the crosshairs of this homicide investigation. It's all linked, but how?

They say you can't prove a negative—I know I never ordered any Ambien, but I don't know how to prove it.

"And I need photos, Daddy," Cole says. "Of Aunt Caitlin, Grandma, and Grandpa."

"Tell you what, if you and Mom pick out some photos and send the files to CVS, I'll grab them on the way home from work."

"You won't forget? Because you guys forget things. Mommy forgot Blue Day."

"I got this one, buddy," Mark says. "I promise."

Convinced, anxiety assuaged, Cole leans back and sings along to the radio.

I stare out the window, trying to piece together what I know so far. Someone who was at the pool on Memorial Day made that account. But they also knew me back at Overton, or at least knew about the whole Sexy Lexi thing.

And that shirt? I still don't have any answers for how that shirt arrived in my house. My stomach churns as I think of all the people who have keys to our house—Heather next door and Leah across the street both have spare sets, as I do of theirs. Daisy could have a key; we didn't change the locks after we moved in. Susan, the babysitter, has a key.

"What did you end up getting my mom?" Mark pulls the car into a spot near the restaurant.

"Umm, a scented candle and some hand lotion?" Thank god Whole Foods sells overpriced knickknacks, and I was able to find a gift for Joan at the same time I grabbed lunch.

"Great, thanks for doing that, Allie." He gives my arm a squeeze and I smile in return.

"Can I put in the quarters?" Cole leans forward and holds out his hand. I watch them as they stand on the sidewalk and feed the meter, a father and son so perfect that they could be in a bank commercial. This is all I have ever wanted. Love, stability, a happy home.

But I have this horrible sense that a force has been unleashed that will destroy it all. Mark raps on the window and motions for me to join him. I grab the gift bag for Joan and take the kind of deep, cleansing breath my yoga instructor is always encouraging the class to take.

When we are almost to the door of the restaurant, I pull Mark back.

"We need to talk. The police questioned me today."

His eyes widen. "Did you call that Zucker guy, like I told you?"

I shake my head.

"Allie. I thought we agreed."

I bite my lip, tears welling in my eyes. "They think I killed Rob Avery."

"That's insane," Mark whispers and pulls me close. I lean my head against his chest and listen to the soothing *thump-thump* of his heart. "We'll figure this out, I promise. Look, let's call him now."

"Go in," I say. "I'll call him, and meet you inside."

"You sure? Maybe I should stay?"

From the corner of my eye, I can see Cole trying to climb into one of the jumbo planters overflowing with autumn flowers right outside the restaurant.

"No. Take Cole in. I can make the call." He starts to turn, and I grab his sleeve. "And Mark? Please don't say anything to anyone. Especially not Caitlin, okay?"

"Of course not."

Through the glass window, I watch Mark and Cole disappear into the back of the restaurant. I walk around the corner to where it is more private and dial. No one answers at the law firm.

"My name is Allie Ross," I say after the beep. "And I'd like to meet with Mr. Zucker. I'm involved in a murder investigation." The words sound surreal coming from my mouth. I swallow hard and then add, "I think I'm a suspect."

19

The table erupts in laughter, and I look up to see my brother-in-law, Charles, staring at me.

"Little spacey tonight, Allie?"

"Just tired is all." I take a deep gulp of red wine, not my usual choice, but Mark's dad practically insisted.

"Have the steak frites. You look like you could use a little red meat."

A darker undercurrent lurks beneath the glib charm of Caitlin's husband. His meanness pops to the surface like a throbbing forehead vein when he drinks. Once, at a Thanksgiving dinner a few years ago, I caught him eviscerating Caitlin in the kitchen because she had forgotten to turn the second oven on and there would be no rolls. She was crying as he berated her. When I rushed in, they both plastered smiles on their faces, making me feel like I was the crazy one.

At the end of the table, Joan clears her throat. "Allie, darling, I was just telling Mark that St. Edmund's has a wonderful new children's director. Auditions for the Christmas pageant are this week."

"That seems a little early." The waitress places a basket of bread in the middle of the table, and I lunge for it. I haven't eaten in hours, and I need something to absorb the alcohol.

"It's never too early to start getting ready for Christmas," Joan says. She's the type who enrobes every piece of shrubbery on her property in tasteful white fairy lights the day after Thanksgiving.

"I think Cole would make a wonderful Joseph. What do you think, Cole?" Joan nudges him, and he looks up from the iPad in his grip. "Do you want to be in the pageant?"

"Yeah, I want to be in the pageant." Cole cranes his neck down the table toward me. "Can I, Mommy?"

"Maybe." I glance to Mark for help. He usually intervenes when church comes up. He's studying a spot on his butter knife. Next to him, Caitlin trades her clean knife for his. She'd do anything for her brother. She started a whisper campaign in high school to undermine the boy who ran against Mark for class president, basically outing him as gay. At the time, the early nineties, that was enough to hand the election to Mark. Retelling that story is one of the few times I've seen Mark express disapproval of his sister.

"Of course, you can be in the pageant, sweetie," Joan says to Cole.

"I believe all it takes is one parent to be a member of the church for a child to be in the pageant," my father-in-law, Bob, says, chiming in for the first time.

"That's easy." Caitlin touches Mark's arm. "Mark can join."

"Right, but we're not sure we want to make that commitment, are we, Mark?" I ask. I shoot *shut-this-down* glares at Mark from across the table, but he remains oblivious. When Cole was born, the full-court press began to bring Cole up in the church. I relented and allowed him to be baptized, with Caitlin and Charles as godparents, thinking that would satisfy everyone, at least for a few years.

"I don't know." Mark pops a little bread in his mouth. "It's not the worst idea in the world."

"And then you'll already belong somewhere when you finally have a second," Joan says and then winks at me. "You don't want to wait too long between kids."

I turn away from Joan, my face hot with anger. My chest constricts as if someone has squeezed me hard. It's none of their damn business whether we have another child. I glance at Cole, but he is totally absorbed in his video game, thank god.

"Remember when Mark was Joseph, and he broke character to shush the baby Jesus to stop crying?" Caitlin asks.

"Oh, Mark was Joseph three years in a row—remember that, honey?" Joan lets out a warm laugh. "Church adds such a wonderful dimension to a child's life. And if you don't introduce Cole when he's young, he'll always feel cut off."

"I never went to church," I say. "And I turned out fine."

"Did you?" Caitlin says under her breath and then winks. "Kidding!"

I gasp. Did anyone else hear her? But no, they're on to discussing the Nationals now, and whether Max Scherzer is the best pitcher in the league.

A waiter places our food in front of us. I poke at the grilled salmon on my plate, my appetite gone, stewing over a clever retort I could have delivered to Caitlin.

"—so many selfish mothers out there." I look up to see Caitlin holding court. In the past few years, she has gone from being a general divorce attorney to one who specializes in men's rights. She's developed a niche helping men avoid alimony and get custody of children. The glee with which Caitlin seems to enjoy separating families makes my stomach churn. It's as though the disappointment in not being able to have her own kids has been weaponized.

"This latest one's going to be a slam dunk." She sticks a forkful of pink steak in her mouth. "We're going for full custody."

"Isn't that rare?" Joan asks. She asks the same questions every time Caitlin talks about her work. Besides the one year she worked as a Saks counter girl after college, Joan has never held a job. She dedicated her entire life to being Mark and Caitlin's mother and Bob's wife, and she cannot imagine a world in which women are not the primary caretakers. "To grant full custody to the father?"

"Not at all," Caitlin sniffs. "It's not the seventies anymore, Mother. And I've got the trifecta on his wife."

"The trifecta?" Bob asks.

Caitlin ticks off her fingers as she speaks. "One, reckless infidelity. You know, not just one boyfriend but quite a number of them."

"Goodness." Joan puts her hands over Cole's ears. He shakes her off without breaking eye contact with his iPad.

"These days, everything is online," Charles says. "People are idiots for thinking they can get away with this kind of stuff."

But not everything online is true, I want to scream.

"Two," Caitlin continues, "she can't hold a job, and three, substance abuse. Any one of these might be grounds for a less than fifty-fifty split, but put all three together and bam, Dad gets full custody."

My phone buzzes on the table, and I flip it over, wondering who it could be now. It's Leah, and she's texted three capitalized letters.

WTF.

A moment later, another text pings my phone—a screenshot. I tap on it to enlarge it. The blood rushes to my head as I make out what I am looking at. A post on the Eastbrook Neighborhood Facebook page. *Clarify . . . some of you in the community have seen a picture of me and Rob from Saturday's party . . . not an affair . . . sexually assaulted . . . #MeToo.*

20

The words swim in front of my eyes.

I push my chair back and rush to the women's restroom. I am grateful to find it empty. The din of the restaurant fades once the doors have shut, and I lock myself in a stall to examine my phone. Even before I zoom in to reveal the name and avatar of the person responsible for the post, I know who it's going to be.

Me.

In that blue bikini.

But that's not my Facebook account. My Facebook avatar is an old-fashioned Leica camera.

And I've never posted on the Eastbrook Neighborhood page.

Bile fills my throat, and I am sure I am going to vomit. But nothing comes up. After a few minutes of useless retching, my phone rings. It's Leah.

"Are you all right? What is going on, Allie? I mean, I get how annoying all those comments about that picture of you and Rob are, but is this a good idea?" The questions come tumbling out faster than I can answer them.

"I didn't. I didn't post that, Leah. That's not my Facebook account."

"This is insane."

"I know."

"I don't get it. Are you saying someone is *impersonating* you?"

"Yes, I guess that is what I'm saying." My knees buckle, and I lean against the stall wall so I don't collapse. "I have to get that post taken down."

"The Facebook page administrator is this older guy, Jeff Crosetti. Lives on Brookdale. Want me to try and reach out to him?"

"Please, Leah, can you? I need this taken down before anyone sees it."

"Too late for that. There are like a dozen—wait, hold on." I hear clicking in the background. "There are like twenty-five responses. It's like the whole neighborhood is on this thread." A sharp intake of breath. "Oh no, this isn't good."

"What? What is it?"

"Can you come over? You need to see this. I'd come to you, but David's working late, and Dustin's not home yet to watch Ava."

"I'm out at dinner. I can come by after."

Right after we say our goodbyes, I realize I never figured out how she learned about my fake Tinder account. I hear the bathroom door swoosh open and the sound of high heels click across the tiled floor. I peer under the stall door and recognize Caitlin's nude pumps.

"You in here, Allie?" Caitlin calls out in her singsong voice.

I flush the toilet, giving myself a few extra moments to pull myself together. "Yup, right here."

I open the door to see my sister-in-law preening in the mirror. She has Mark's coloring—dark brown hair and eyes, and the kind of skin that turns bronze while walking from the car to the house. She styles herself after Jackie Kennedy circa 1960—bobbed hair, pearls, and sheath dresses. "You've been in here a long time. We were getting worried." She takes out a tube of pink lip gloss and begins applying it.

At the sink next to her, I pump one, two, then three foamy globs of hand soap into my palms and take my time washing my hands, hoping Caitlin doesn't notice they are trembling.

She doesn't. She's too busy baring her teeth in the mirror, looking for food. "I found a great therapist for you and Mark."

My jaw drops open.

She turns from the mirror to me. "Oh gosh, I hope you're not upset that he told me you guys were having problems."

"We're not having problems," I say calmly, but inside, I am roiling. The thought of Mark discussing our problems with his sister galls me.

"I mean, I'm honestly so happy that you even made it this far. We always thought he would end up with Molly, you know?"

I blink hard. The name Molly stings. She was Mark's college girlfriend, an award-winning equestrian from an old-money Virginia family. There was talk of an engagement, but she broke it off.

"Mmmm," I say and pretend to search my bag for my lipstick.

"But then whoopsie!" She smacks her lips at the mirror. "An accidental pregnancy. I really applaud you guys for trying to make it work."

"Thank you."

"Seriously! At first, Mother and I were like, what is the deal? This girl gets pregnant right when Mark makes partner. Hello, gold digger alert!" Caitlin lets out a shrill laugh and pops her lipstick back in her bag. "Kidding! You know we're crazy about you and Cole. That's why we're worried." She turns and makes a frowny face.

"Well, I'm fine, thanks." One last look in the mirror tells me I'm doing a good job of hiding the rage building within. Mark needs to know he should not be talking to Caitlin about our private business.

"Cole looks adorbs in those teeny khakis," Caitlin says. "He's like a mini-Mark."

"We'd better head back. People will think we got lost." I'm done with being fake nice. I move toward the door, but Caitlin takes a quick step to block me. A former Division I field hockey player, Caitlin moves with grace and speed. She leans in to my face, so close I can see the powder collecting in the pores of her skin.

"Just a heads-up—when you and Mark get divorced, I'm going to fight to get Cole."

I jerk back, startled.

Caitlin throws her head back and roars. I can smell the wine on her. "Kidding! You should see the look on your face!"

21

On the drive home, Cole jabbers on about Piper, a girl in his class who has been keeping him from the monkey bars on the playground. Mark offers gentle guidance on how to handle bullies. I don't join in. My mind is swimming with thoughts of the forged Facebook post, the fake Tinder account, and Caitlin's confrontation in the bathroom.

When you and Mark get divorced. That's what Caitlin said. Not if, but when. *She's just needling you,* I tell myself. *It's not personal. It's who she is.*

Before I wrangle Cole upstairs, I remind Mark that we need to talk. He glances up at the large clock in the kitchen that looks like it belongs in a nineteenth-century railway station and sucks his breath through his teeth.

"I have a nine p.m. call with the Singapore office."

I try not to rush Cole, knowing that doing so will backfire. He's already acting out, tired from being up later than usual.

"I want to pick out the photos for my family tree."

"It's after eight, Cole. We can do that tomorrow."

"No, you'll forget."

Worn out, I let him wear the same clothes he wore all day to bed. We've just finished speed-reading *Pinkalicious* when my phone buzzes. It's Leah asking if I'm still planning on stopping by.

It's almost eight forty-five. I text her that I will be there soon, nine thirty at the latest. I still need to talk to Mark.

Cole bats at my phone with a stuffed bunny. "Mommy, stop

looking at your phone. I want cuddles." I tuck my phone in my pocket and lie down next to him. He scooches into me until the backs of his knees are pressed against mine, his head just beneath my chin, and his curved spine against me, a small spoon nestling into the bigger one.

"I love you," I whisper into his ear.

"But I love you more." He yawns. After a few moments, my shallow breaths begin to steady, matching the easy rhythm of the rise and fall of his little chest. And just like that, he's asleep.

I rush back downstairs, where Mark has set up his laptop and some work folders on the kitchen counter. His law firm has opened a new office in Singapore, which is twelve hours ahead of D.C., and that's meant a lot of these late-night calls.

I pour myself a glass of wine. Mark raises an eyebrow but doesn't say anything.

"What?" My tone is defensive. I'm a grown woman, entitled to a glass of wine after the day I've had.

"Nothing. Tell me what happened with the police."

I run down what happened at the station and wait for him to tell me it's routine stuff, that I shouldn't worry. But he lets out a long breath and shakes his head.

"I don't like it. I really wish you had called Artie Zucker when I asked you to."

"Okay, but I didn't."

"And why not? I mean, I texted you the info. You said you would."

"I don't know, Mark. I got busy. Does it matter now?" I finish off my wine and refill the glass. "I mean, I called him tonight, so can you stop harping on that?"

"I'm glad you called. I just wish you had done it sooner." He nods his chin toward my wineglass. "Didn't you have several glasses at dinner?"

"So?"

"Do you think maybe *that's* part of the problem?" he asks in a soft voice.

"What problem is that?"

"The problem of forgetting things? Of not being able to keep track." He sighs. "Like the other day when you put the car keys in the salad crisper."

"So?" I'm trying to figure out what the hell losing my keys has to do with anything. As soon as I told him about that, I'd regretted doing so. I had searched for hours, afraid I was going out of my mind. Cole found the keys when he went looking for baby carrots at dinner to replace the yucky broccoli. "People lose things, forget things, that's normal."

"Like the hamburger buns?"

I wince. "Jesus, Mark. You're kidding, right? I told you I didn't sign up to bring those."

"Okay, fine. I'm not attacking you, Allie. I'm on your side."

"Are you? Doesn't feel that way."

"Yes, I am. You don't have to do everything, you know. Like how I offered to call the lawyer, and you said no." There's no accusation or hostility in his voice, only resignation with a hint of sadness. "Look, I'm making enough money now."

"Not this again. I love photography. I enjoy the work."

"When we first met, you said you hated doing this kind of photography. That your dream was to quit your waitressing job and make art. Well, now you can."

"Why are you bringing this up now?"

"You're doing too much," he says. "We're supposed to host Thanksgiving dinner next month, and half our stuff is still in boxes in the guest room."

"Feel free to unpack them, Mark!" My tone is sharp, but I'm fed up. I feel like I've been doing everything around here.

"You fall asleep every night in Cole's bed."

"You fall asleep every night in front of the TV."

"I'm waiting there for you. I'll happily turn off the TV if you come downstairs." He leans over the kitchen counter and in a low voice says, "Last night was the second time we've made love since we moved into this house."

"I didn't realize you were keeping track." I swallow hard. "Look, we only have ten minutes before your call, and I still need to ask you something. Did you tell Caitlin we were having problems? Do you talk to her about our marriage?" I tell him what she said to me in the bathroom of the restaurant.

"She shouldn't have said that."

"Why would she think we needed a marriage counselor?" I ask. "Did you ask her for a recommendation?"

"No. I mean, I asked her if she knew any good therapists, but not for a marriage counselor."

"A therapist? For me?"

"Look, honey, don't be mad. I thought it might help if you had someone to talk to. You just seem so on edge lately. I know moving here hasn't been easy—"

"I can't believe you told Caitlin I needed therapy."

"I didn't say that. I just asked her for some names. She knows a place outside Baltimore called Bridgeways."

I stand up straight. "Bridgeways? Isn't that a rehab?"

"*Rehab* isn't the right word."

"Jesus, Mark. You guys want to send me away to *rehab*?"

"Allie, it's not a rehab. It's a place where people go when they need a little break. You know—a place you can sort things out. No one's sending you anywhere. It was just an idea." He looks at the clock. Eight fifty-seven. He throws up his hands. "I have to make this phone call. I can wrap it up in twenty minutes, thirty tops."

"Please. Don't let me stop you from what's important." I sound like a bratty teen, but I can't stop myself. I feel betrayed.

"You're what's important. I want to talk to you about this. I do. Tell me what you want me to do."

"How about the next time your mom asks why we don't have

a second kid, you tell her—" I finish my wine in one gulp, trying to ignore the hurt look on his face. "Just make your call."

I head toward the back door.

"Where are you going?" Mark calls after me.

"Out."

"Allie! I am so glad you came over, I've been really worried. This whole thing is so messed up." Leah's white marble kitchen is covered in bowls and dusted with flour. She peers up from a sheet of rolled-out dough and smiles. My body is jacked up on adrenaline from my fight with Mark. I don't like the way we left it, and I know tossing that line in about a second kid and then running out was dirty fighting. But it felt good to lash out. I've kept so much bottled up inside recently.

"Listen, Leah, the other day when I left book club—"

"I am really sorry about that. You probably felt ambushed."

"Thank you for saying that, but I need to know—how did you find out about the whole Tinder thing? That Rob Avery had told me to stay off Tinder?"

She frowns. "You told me."

I narrow my eyes, trying to replay our conversations in my head. "I did? Because I don't think I did."

"Yeah, sweetie. At the park. You said he told you to *stay off Tinder*. And he called you some nickname?"

"I don't remember that." But it makes sense—how else would she know?

A scraping noise, like a chair being dragged across a floor, echoes from above. Leah rolls her eyes at the ceiling. "God knows what Dustin is doing. He came home about an hour ago and has literally not left his room. Except to grab a piece of cold pizza, which he then took back upstairs. David's at a client dinner, so me and this bottle of wine are keeping up with the Kardashians." She points to a tray of tiny little spirals of dough.

"Rugelach for International Night. The Jewish table is totally random—hummus from Israel next to rugelach from Poland."

I sit down at a stool and try to let the domesticity of the scene calm me down. A Jo Malone candle is burning nearby, and some kind of acoustic music is playing from the small speakers in the ceiling. I search my brain for the file on International Night. There have been loads of emails, and I've gathered that International Night is a big deal at Eastbrook Elementary School. Parents set up tables in the cafeteria representing their cultural heritage and serve food and drink from their family's country of origin. Apparently, some even dress up in elaborate ethnic costumes. Cole and Mark have already been brainstorming what they can come up with to reflect Mark's Scottish heritage. Haggis is out, shortbread is a possibility.

"What do you think?" Leah asks. "It's a Martha Stewart recipe. Don't tell anyone it's not an authentic family recipe from Poland, especially not David's mother. She thinks I don't know how to cook authentic Jewish food. I mean, she's right, my mother was more the TV dinner type, but she's very judgy about the whole thing."

The words continue to flow, and I don't try to stop her from talking. She grabs a glass and empties the last of the bottle into it. "You want some?"

As she digs through the small wine fridge nestled beneath the kitchen counter, Leah keeps talking. "You know, she cannot get over my quitting law to stay at home. And I'm like, my choice. Get over it. But the truth is, maybe she's right." She unscrews the top and pours both of us a glass, her smile replaced by a concerned look. "Sorry, you've got real problems, and I'm complaining about being a suburban housewife."

"No, it's fine," I say. "I get really lonely when Mark works late, too. How long have you been a stay-at-home mom?"

"Going on three years. Basically, when I started having to pull Dustin out for testing and therapy. At first, it was great. It was like, ahhhh, relief. But nobody's around in this neighborhood during the day. You know how D.C. is, all these type A moms working crazy stressful jobs. No time to socialize. But I am so glad you moved in! That was a lucky break for me."

"Me, too," I say. "I feel really lucky you're my neighbor and not like Vicki or Karen."

She laughs. "And I love my kids to pieces, but I swear, Dustin is sending me to an early grave. He and David have just never clicked. And now he's in the *you're-not-my-real-father* stage."

"If you don't mind my asking, where is Dustin's biological father?"

Leah pinches the bridge of her nose. "He, umm, died. A long time ago."

"I'm so sorry."

"Yeah. Me, too." Leah sighs and clinks her nails against her wineglass. "It was suicide. I haven't told Dustin yet. I know I should, but I just can't." She sniffles. "On the one hand, I'm afraid he'll be angry that I haven't told him earlier, and on the other hand, I am terrified of giving him any ideas."

I walk around the island and put my arms around her. I've never seen this side of Leah. Her Insta and Facebook posts are filled with sun-drenched, spotless rooms. Neat piles of laundry on her gleaming wood dining room table, shoes lined up by the door, or cute kid artwork. A Pinterest-perfect suburban life. Nothing that would hint at mental illness, loss, troubled teens.

But that's the thing about social media—it's a curated version of reality.

Or a completely warped one, in the case of my fake accounts.

Behind us, a voice calls hello, and I turn to see Daisy. She's in full Realtor mode, in a smart charcoal-gray pantsuit, her wild blond hair barely contained in a chignon.

"You guys okay?" She puts her briefcase on the island. "What'd I miss?"

Leah steps back and wipes her eyes. "I told Allie about Dustin's dad. And how I feel like a shitty mom that I haven't told him the truth."

"Oh, sweetie, you're not a shitty mom." Daisy frowns. "If it makes you feel any better, Gabriella walked out of Earth Science yesterday and took an Uber to Montgomery Mall."

Leah puts her hand to her mouth. "No, she didn't."

"She did. And she used her dad's credit card to rack up four hundred dollars in charges at Nordstrom, thank you very much. Guess who had to leave work to pick her up when mall security called? Not her mom. Not her dad. No, *moi*, her evil stepmother."

Leah holds up her glass. "Here's to the shitty things that happen to good people."

"I'll drink to that," I say, raising my glass.

"Allie," Daisy says, turning her full attention to me. "What the heck is going on? I cannot believe that Patch story."

"What Patch story?" I ask. All I know about Patch is that it is the local news website.

Daisy frowns and turns to Leah. "You didn't tell her? I thought you told her."

Leah shakes her head.

"Tell me what?" I ask.

Daisy pops open her computer and begins typing. "It's been posted on the Eastbrook Facebook page. Steel yourself," she says to me. "It's not pretty." She turns the screen toward me, and I see the familiar Facebook logo and the Eastbrook Neighborhood banner.

The most recent post is an article: "Police Question Local Woman in Neighbor's Violent Death."

I scan it quickly to see if my name shows up, but it doesn't. The story is vague, with phrases such as *police are questioning* and *person of interest*.

But where the story left things nebulous, the comments are viciously specific. I find one written by Vicki, the PTA capo.

This is that woman who lives on Wentworth, Alexis Ross. I know for a fact she was having an affair with Rob Avery.

I look up at Daisy and Leah, who are watching me with concern. "What is wrong with this woman Vicki? It's like she has
some kind of agenda against me. She's spreading lies. That can't
be legal."

I scroll down through the comments, losing count at thirty-five,
before turning the computer back to Daisy. "I can't read any more."

"They fall into roughly two camps," Daisy says. "People scared
that a murderer is on the loose in our neighborhood, and others
who, you know, want to take a wait-and-see approach." She taps
on the keyboards and clucks her tongue. "While I get you were
trying to clear your name, I don't think posting the account of
what Rob did to you Saturday night was the best idea. Just added
fuel to the fire."

"I didn't post anything, Daisy." I turn to Leah. "Didn't you tell
her? Someone made a fake Facebook account and posted that."

Daisy's eyes widen. "Oh. My. God. What a nightmare. What
are you going to do?"

"I don't know," I say. "What can I do?"

"For starters, we can contact Jeff Crosetti, who moderates this
page," Leah says over her shoulder as she stirs something sweet-
smelling on the stove. She carries the pot over to the counter
and drizzles the steaming liquid into a bowl of chopped nuts,
dripping on the counter as she goes. "He's the only one who can
take down posts."

"So this is not your Facebook page?" Daisy flips the laptop
toward me so I can see the screen—a Facebook page with my
name on it and that shot of me in a bikini. The same person who
created the fake Tinder account must have made this as well.

"No. Absolutely not."

"Because I friended you. I mean, I friended this page, like a
month ago."

I scroll quickly, making myself dizzy trying to read everything
that I supposedly posted on "my" Facebook page. Most feature
memes about drinking wine and the annoyances of motherhood,

which are cringeworthy enough. But then there are the personal ones. My throat tightens at one that reads: *Tell me why I decided to have children again?*

Tears spring to my eyes.

"Oh, sweetie." Daisy hands me a tissue.

I shake my head, refusing it. "No, I'm fine."

Daisy pushes it into my hand. "It's okay to cry. This is totally fucked up."

Something about her permission undams a torrent of emotion that I've had bottled up for days. Before I know it, hot tears are falling from my eyes, and my shoulders are shaking uncontrollably. "I never wrote any of this," I say, wiping my runny nose. "Did you really think this was me?"

"I don't know." Daisy looks pained. "I guess I did. I didn't really know you that well."

My whole chest constricts, making each breath laborious. The effort that went into making this page reflects such a deep hatred of me. It's as if I can feel that venom radiating off the screen and infecting me.

But who hates me this much? And why? All these posters have to know they're crossing a line from petty gossip to implicating me in a murder.

Is that the goal?

"I figured you were going through a tough time," Daisy says.

Leah nods. "We've all been there. Overwhelmed."

I scroll down to a post where, printed in block letters, are the words: *Men, coffee, and chocolate—all better rich.* Below that another one reads: *Marriage is a workshop—the man works and the wife shops.*

The overall portrait of me is revolting. What must people in the neighborhood think of me? I click on the Friends link. I have more than three hundred, name after name that I do not recognize. As I scroll down, a few familiar names jump out at me. Photography clients, Mike Chau, neighbors.

Vicki.

Heather.

My face burns. My boss has seen this. No, just because he's friended me on Facebook doesn't mean he's read all these posts, but he might have.

I navigate back to the main page and let out a little cry. A new post has just popped up. Had I missed it before? No. It's shown up in the last minute.

My tormentor is posting in real time.

Two pictures, side by side. The first is the photo from the party, the one where Rob's head and mine are so close they almost touch, that damn skirt riding up my thighs.

But it's the second photo that takes my breath away. I haven't seen it in sixteen years. I took it myself.

In it, I am lying naked, curled against the sleeping body of a man. The photo is cropped precisely—only the bottom half of his face is visible, and just the tops of my breasts can be seen. But I don't need to see the whole photo to remember his dark eyelashes, the way his lips parted slightly as he slept. The way I thrust my naked breasts at the camera, a caricature of a young seductress.

I look at my younger self—sucking on one finger and staring intently into the camera, trying so hard to be sexy.

Below the two photos, the caption reads: *Have I still got it? Please vote!*

Eighteen people have voted so far.

Then Nineteen.

Then Twenty.

I watch the number grow before my eyes, and each addition feels like a hot fist clenching my gut tighter.

This is the second time this naked photo of me has been posted online. The last time, I was seventeen, and it led to a man's arrest.

22

In Leah's powder room, I lean over the sink. During a first-aid class I took years ago, I learned to apply ice or cold water to wrists and temples to bring an overheated body back to normal temperature. But it's not helping.

I'm burning up from the inside.

A deep, familiar shame grips me.

Those memories, the ones I've boxed up and tucked into a corner of my brain, come shooting through my thoughts like shards of glass.

The motel's clock radio was playing "Hanging by a Moment" so softly I could barely make out the words.

I hummed along, not daring to turn it up. I didn't want to wake Paul.

My old Nikkormat had no timer, so I decided to try out the cable he had bought for me earlier that day at B&H Photo in midtown Manhattan. Among the walls of lenses, special papers, and obscure photography esoterica, I had withered under the somber looks of the Hasidic man helping us, sure he could see the dirtiness within me.

I connected the long, black cable to the camera and placed it on the nightstand. Then I pulled off my bra and nestled my body against Paul's sleeping one, folding myself into a pose that was sexually wise beyond my actual experience. I wanted to matter, not simply to exist. I ached to feel special, and Paul's intense desire had breathed life into me.

So I mimicked what I saw—in the movies, in magazines, in my home.

In the first pictures, I covered my bare breasts. *Click.*

The photos would cement us, would tether Paul to me. Sex was simply the seed from which our love would grow. In time, he would come to love me.

I remember thinking of my favorite TV show, *Mad About You,* and how everyone said I looked a little like the actress who played the wife on the show. I didn't have blond hair, but I had the same squinty eyes that disappeared when I smiled. On the show, the couple met at a newsstand on West 81st Street, when they both wanted the last copy of the Sunday *Times.* While paying for it, the woman dropped a dry-cleaning ticket, which the guy used to hunt her down.

I longed for someone to desire me so much they would track me down like that.

For the next batch of photos, I positioned my arm above my head, knowing, the way all girls know, that this would make my breasts look more attractive.

In the last one, I lowered my eyelids just a little, and put one finger in my mouth.

Click.

And then, weeks later, it was posted on MySpace, and life as I knew it was ripped apart.

Daisy's loud laugh jolts me back to the present.

I join them back in the kitchen, where Daisy and Leah are spooning heaps of chopped nuts on the long rectangles of dough.

They stop what they're doing when I enter.

"Are you all right?" Daisy asks.

"Not really." I hover near the counter, not sure whether I want to stay or go. But the warmth from the oven and the sweet smells from the oven are so comforting that I don't dare move.

"Is that you?" Daisy asks.

I nod. "When I was a teenager."

"Well, Facebook has to take it down. That's against the rules. Putting up naked photos of teenagers, right, Leah?"

Leah shakes her head in disgust. "Totally. They have to take it down."

I am heartened by their indignation. Leah starts typing. "I'm going to fill out the complaint form right now."

"Who's the guy in the picture?" Daisy asks. "Do you think he's doing this?"

Leah stops typing, and they both turn to me expectantly. Somewhere, in the darkest corners of my imagination, I've always felt haunted by what happened all those years ago. I've carried a vague sense of doom, that I would someday pay a price. But I never expected this.

"He's an ex-boyfriend," I say, not ready to tell the whole truth.

A loud "Goddamn it" issues from upstairs. Leah looks up at the ceiling. "He's got to be playing Fortnite. That's the only thing that gets a rise out of him these days."

Daisy reaches a hand out and touches my arm. "You were saying. An ex-boyfriend?"

"From high school. But we haven't spoken since my senior year."

"Do you think he could be the one doing all of this?" Leah asks.

"Maybe." *Lexi.* I knew in my gut when I heard Rob use that nickname that it had something to do with Overton. But how could it all be connected?

"Did you have an ugly breakup?" I turn away from them and stare at the blackened window that looks out onto Leah's backyard. All I can see is a muddy reflection of myself. I remember the police detective asking me if I really wanted to ruin this young man's life. "You could say that."

"What's his name? Let's track him down."

I turn back and put on a brave smile. I do not want everyone in Eastbrook to know I slept with my teacher in high school, triggering a police investigation. I need to take care of this myself.

"Thank you, both of you, for being so supportive," I say.

"Look," Daisy says. "Jeff is a good guy. I'm sure he will take these posts down. I'll reach out to him tonight." She scribbles on the legal pad.

"As for the neighborhood gossips, screw 'em," Leah says. "Who cares what they think!"

"And you should think about going to the police," Daisy says, "if for no other reason than if this escalates, you've started a paper trail."

I nod, but there is no way in hell I want to go back to the police station. The last time I was there, the detectives all but accused me of murder. My plan in regard to the police is to lie low until they catch who really killed Rob Avery.

They both walk me to the front.

"You're being really sweet. Thank you."

"I've been there," Leah says. "After my first husband died, I dated this total creep. He kind of cyber-stalked me. No fake profiles or anything, but he managed to hack into my emails and would just show up at places, like concerts or restaurants. I had to go to the police."

"Did they help?"

She laughs. "Actually, not really, now that I think about it."

"So how did it end?"

Leah shrugged. "I moved to D.C. Not because of him," she adds. "And I changed all my passwords to everything. But he's out there somewhere. I still think about that sometimes."

"Let us know if there's anything," Daisy says.

"Actually, there is one random thing. I have to sell my mother's house in Westport, Connecticut. You wouldn't happen to know how I can find out who's the best Realtor up there, do you, Daisy?"

She blinks hard, just once, but then a large smile spreads across her face. "Of course! I know just the woman. Barb DeSoto. I'll text you her info."

I hug them both good night and thank them again. As I cross the street to my house, I can see a figure walking a small dog in the distance. I wonder if it's Susan. I can't tell from this far. I take a deep gulp of the cool night air. My neighbor Heather has put up a giant inflatable jack-o'-lantern on her front lawn. Halloween is around the corner, and this is the first year Cole is excited to go trick-or-treating.

I take a few steps onto the walkway that leads to our back door when I hear a crunch of footsteps in the leaves behind me. I spin around, heart pounding. I see no one.

I pick up the pace to the back of my house. As I'm approaching the back door, someone grabs my arm. I spin around, a shriek caught in my throat.

It's Dustin. He lets go of my arm and backs up a few feet, hands up. "I didn't mean to scare you." His voice quivers, wavering between child and man.

"Well, you did." I put my hand to my chest, where my heart is pounding like it's going to explode. "You can't sneak up on people like that, Dustin."

"Sorry." He digs his hands into the pockets of his skinny jeans and stares at the ground.

"It's fine, really. Just be more careful, huh?"

"I heard what you were saying in the kitchen."

"You were listening in on our conversation?" Annoyance floods me.

Dustin raises his head. The round, low moon illuminates his long face, his hawklike nose. He looks nothing like Leah. I think of what I learned this evening, that his father committed suicide and how he's not getting along with his stepfather. I let out a deep sigh. "Dustin, you shouldn't eavesdrop."

"Don't be mad," he says. "I can help you. I want to help you."

"That's all right, Dustin. Thank you, anyway." I turn to go.

"The police are not going to figure this out," he calls, and I stop. "Even if they had the time, they don't have the skills to find out who is trolling you, messing with you. I do. I can find out who made that Facebook page."

I turn back to face him. "Is that right?"

"Sure. But you know, I charge for this kind of thing. It's a lot of work."

I have to smile at that one. And to think Leah imagined him babysitting children. "How much?"

"Two grand."

"Thanks, but no thanks. Good night, Dustin." The doorknob is in my hand when he calls from the shadows once more.

"Just remember, the police won't help you, but I can."

23

I'm in bed, anxiously waiting for Mark to finish with work and come upstairs. I need to tell him about the pictures of me online, but I don't know how I am going to do that. A part of me thinks I can contact Facebook and get them taken down before he even knows. But I know that's crazy. He needs to know the truth.

But if I tell him about the photos, how can I not tell him about Paul?

Mark comes in.

"How did the call go?" I ask, gauging his mood. If he's still mad, there's no way I'll tell him. At least not tonight.

"Fine. Better than expected." His tone is terse, but is that because of me or work he's stressed about? "I'm going to be busy the next month or so preparing for some depositions. Looks like we may end up going to trial after all."

"Mark, I'm sorry about before."

He sits on the edge of our bed in just his pajama bottoms. "It's okay. I'm sorry about the whole Caitlin therapy thing. I shouldn't have talked to her about it."

"Yeah." I'd forgotten all about Caitlin. "I should have called Artie Zucker sooner. You were right."

He smiles stiffly. "I was thinking about what you said, about how someone made fake social media accounts for you. That's a lot of work. I mean, that seems very deliberate."

"And then there's the whole T-shirt thing."

"T-shirt thing?"

I glance at him, annoyed, but the open look on his face tells me he has forgotten about the T-shirt. "You know, how I found Cole wearing an Overton T-shirt the other day?"

"Right." He nods slowly. "Maybe I'm missing something, but that just doesn't seem like such a big deal compared to everything else that's going on."

You are missing something! I think. *This is my moment to tell him about Overton and Paul Adamson, the picture on MySpace and the arrest.*

"I think it might be someone from Overton who's doing all this."

"You think someone from your prep school is involved with Rob Avery's death?" His deliberate tone makes me feel crazy.

I shake my head. I know it sounds nuts. "I'm not sure. I had a boyfriend my senior year. It didn't end well."

"And you think he's the one making these social media accounts?"

I shrug. "I'm not sure. Maybe."

"What did the police say, exactly?"

"They were asking me all sorts of weird questions about Ambien. It was awful."

"Ambien?"

"Yeah, liquid Ambien. Had I ever used it. Did I have it delivered to the house."

"And have you?"

"No. I didn't even know they made liquid Ambien. And now there's a story on the Eastbrook Facebook page saying the police were talking to a woman, a person of interest. And pretty much everyone on the page thinks that's me. You know, I want to run my own studio one day, and I can't have this kind of garbage about me floating around online. Right now, Valerie Simmons's people are probably vetting me. I'm supposed to talk with her tomorrow to set up the shoot. What if she finds out about this Rob Avery stuff? What if my boss finds out?"

"Shhh, calm down, honey. No one's going to find anything out. We're going to put a stop to this." He runs his hands through the sides of his hair, where there are enough grays among the dark brown to merit the label *salt and pepper*. "We'll talk to the lawyer. He'll know what to do. If anybody can shed some light on this, he can. He's a local guy, went to Maryland for law school, was a prosecutor for a while, and is extremely well connected."

"That sounds good." I feel a little better.

"I trust this guy, Allie. That's our plan. Hire the best, and let him deal with it. And as for Valerie Simmons—she'd be lucky to have you shoot her."

I can barely manage a smile.

"In a year, you're going to be the go-to photographer for all the D.C. hotshots, and she'll be the one begging you to get back to her." He gives me a kiss and pulls on his pajama top before grabbing the remote and turning on the game.

I lean up next to him and will myself to absorb some of my husband's faith in the world. But for the first time in our relationship, I think Mark's optimism is misplaced.

I want to believe that this will all blow over. That the lawyer that Mark knows will swoop in and fix it all. That nothing worse is coming down the pike.

But I cannot shake the certainty that the worst is yet to come.

I don't know why, but someone is trying to destroy my life.

And I don't know how to tell my husband that I think the person who might be behind it all is the first man I ever fell in love with, the first I ever made love to.

I am toasting a bagel for Cole the next morning when Mark wanders in from outside, smiling triumphantly.

"This look familiar?" he asks, holding up a small white post office mailing box.

"No. Should it?" The toaster oven pings. "Cream cheese or butter, Cole?"

"Cream cheese."

"It's a box from Overton," Mark says, as proud of himself as a terrier who's dragged in a rat. "I found it in the recycling."

I freeze.

Mark puts the box on the counter in front of me. The return address is Overton Academy in Connecticut. *Alexis "Lexi" Ross* is written in block print on the front. I stare at the word *Lexi* until the letters swim before my eyes. This is no accident. This is someone who knew me. I push it back at him, bile rising in me. "I didn't order that."

Mark blows air loudly through his lips. "Maybe you ordered it a while ago and forgot about it."

"No, Mark," I turn to him. "I did not order a T-shirt from Overton and forget about it."

"Jeez, you don't have to yell at me."

"I'm not yelling. But I think I would know if I ordered a T-shirt from Overton."

Cole lets out a wail. "No more cream cheese?" He sticks an empty plastic tub in my face. I recoil at the residual smell.

"Hey, bud," Mark says. "I'll eat the bagel. How about Cheerios?"

I pick up the box, walk to the back door, and toss it outside.

"Whoa, that was a little unnecessary," Mark says. "It goes in recycling."

"How can you not get this? Someone sent that to me, Mark, to fuck with me."

"Mommy!" Cole squeals. "You said the f-word."

"Calm down, Allie."

"Don't tell me to calm down."

"I thought you'd be happy." Mark throws up his hands as if in surrender. "Heading to the shower."

I bite into the bagel he left behind, feeling awful for having snapped. He was just trying to help. And he was right, I need to check with Susan. She probably opened the package and put the shirt in the wash, the box in recycling. Maybe the school is mailing them out to everyone in my year. Maybe they are part of some fundraising campaign.

There has to be an explanation.

But I know it won't be a happy one.

Not with everything that's been going on.

No happy explanation includes the use of the nickname *Lexi*.

Jeff Crosetti lives two blocks away from us. The walkway to his front door lies beneath languorous plants leaning in from either side. Bushwhacking as I go, I stop halfway up the path when I spot an older gentleman kneeling in the yard, half-hidden by a huge bush as orange as a flame.

"Hello," I call out.

"Oh, I didn't see you." He stands up, cradling a clump of dirt-caked roots that give off an earthy scent. "Any use for *Rudbeckia goldsturm* in your yard, a.k.a. black-eyed Susans?"

"No, thank you." I shake my head.

"Can't interest you in Maryland's state flower? Unfortunately, they like my yard a little too much." When it becomes clear I'm not in the market for perennials, he drops the clump.

"I'm Allie Ross," I say. "My friend Leah called last night and left a message. About taking down some posts?"

The old man purses his lips together in thought, wiping his dirty hands on his jeans. His skin is pink, as though he's been scrubbed hard, and it sets off his bushy white eyebrows and crown of soft silver curls. "I'd shake, but you probably don't love the feeling of compost under your nails as much as I do."

"No problem. My hands are full anyway." I hoist my travel coffee mug as evidence.

He brushes past me, removes a pair of clippers from his back pocket, and begins deadheading a plant. "So you've changed your mind about being on the Eastbrook Facebook page?" He examines the base of a plant. "Maybe I should leave these up for the birds."

"No, that's not it. Someone is impersonating me with a fake Facebook page. There are two Allie Rosses, the real me and the fake one."

Crosetti's white eyebrows bop up and down like two fuzzy caterpillars. "The real you and the fake one, eh? Sounds complicated." His face lights up with a wide smile and he points. "Look—goldfinches," he whispers, and I turn to see two small yellow birds perched atop a half-dead clump of zinnias. I relax a little. At least this guy has not seen my Facebook page or the poll asking if I've still got it. But every face I passed this morning on the way to school with Cole had me wondering—had they seen the photo of me naked? Do they think I was sleeping with Rob Avery? And that I am involved in his murder?

"Mr. Crosetti, what I'm trying to tell you is someone made a fake Facebook page and joined the Eastbrook page under false pretenses."

He frowns. I can tell he doesn't get it.

"If you don't want to post anymore, why not just stop posting?"

I open my mouth to answer, but just then my phone rings. It's Artie Zucker, so I wave goodbye to Crosetti and answer as I begin the long walk to the metro, cursing yesterday's decision to go with the police and leave my car at work.

I'm disappointed when I realize that the person on the line is not the lawyer himself but a paralegal who wants only my basic information. I make an appointment to meet Zucker tomorrow after work, when I know Mark will be available, too.

"In the meantime," she says, "do not speak to the police. If they bring you in, call us and do not say anything until Mr. Zucker arrives." She gives me his personal cell phone number before saying goodbye.

By the time I am descending the steep escalator at the Friendship Heights station, I feel a little better knowing that I have set the wheels in motion with the lawyer. Maybe today, Tinder and Facebook will respond. Maybe they'll shutter those accounts. It won't answer the question of who is doing this or why, but it will stanch the bleeding.

But I still cannot figure out how that damn T-shirt got to my house.

Instead of taking the trolley that runs down H Street, I walk from the Union Station metro to the studio, using the time to call the Realtor in Westport whose name Daisy texted to me.

Barb DeSoto tells me fall is a tough time to put a house on the market. "Winters are slow. It really would be better if we wait for the spring market," Barb says.

"I don't want to leave it unoccupied the whole winter. That's income we need." Neither one of us bothers to say that we can't rent the house with a leaky roof and a wonky septic tank. I turn down the street where I parked the car yesterday. It's still there, but as I grow nearer I see there's a pink slip of paper under the windshield wiper. "Damn it."

"I know it's not ideal," Barb says.

"No, sorry. I just got a parking ticket. As far as selling the house, I have no choice. We need to do it now."

"Got it. I'll start running through the paperwork, making sure everything's in order, that there are no liens against the house, et cetera."

"There shouldn't be. My mother didn't even have a mortgage." I stop outside the coffee shop, in desperate need of a caffeine fix.

"Lucky you," Barb says. "That will make things easier."

I stuff the ticket in my pocket, feeling anything but lucky.

After I grab my coffee, I head upstairs to the studio. No one is in yet, and I take advantage of the privacy to call the Overton alumni office. Of all the insanity of the past few days, that T-shirt showing up bugs me the most, for reasons I can't really put my finger on. The phone rings four times, and I am about to give up when an exhausted-sounding woman answers.

"Overton Academy, please hold." The sound of Pachelbel's Canon wafts through the receiver. I use the time to practice what I am going to say. By the time the woman returns, I am ready.

"Now, how can I help you?" she asks.

"This is Alexis Healy," I say, using my maiden name, "and I received the most wonderful surprise in the mail yesterday, an Overton T-shirt. The thing is, I didn't order it, and I wanted to see if I could find out who did, so I could thank them."

"I'm afraid we wouldn't be able to help you, dear. All school merchandise is purchased through our online shop and billed through a third party."

"I just thought maybe there was some kind of reunion thing going on? Where everyone from my class got a T-shirt?" I don't add that I never made it to my graduation. The school mailed me my diploma because I had left in mid-May.

"No, hon. None that I know of. But maybe you should check with your alumni relations coordinator for your area. Where do you live now?"

"In Bethesda, Maryland. That's just outside D.C."

"Our National Capital Alumni Group is very active. If you give me your email address, I can send you the coordinator's contact information. They might be able to help you with your reunion idea."

I don't bother to correct her misinterpretation of the situation. I just provide my info. Once we are off, I check my email and find an automated response from Tinder:

Dear Allie,

Each Tinder profile is tied to a unique Facebook account. If someone is impersonating you, please contact Facebook's help center to file a report.

Kind regards,

Tinder Tech Support

I have contacted Facebook, I type back, teeth clenched. It's all I can do to stop from screaming. *I have filed a report.* I hit Send, although I know there is zero point in doing so.

When I log on to the Eastbrook Neighborhood Facebook page, the posts from last night are gone. To my surprise, Jeff Crosetti has gotten right on it.

Googling *fake Facebook account* brings up page after page of results. I learn there are eighteen million fake Facebook accounts. That's small comfort. According to one website, about one in eight Americans who have social media accounts has experienced revenge porn, the posting of nude pictures of them without their permission. The more I read, the more nauseated I become. It seems like so many women have experienced this and found little or no recourse from either the companies or the police.

I scan the comments below the article.

Help! Someone is using my name and photos on a multitude of casual-sex sites. I really need help on how to stop this! Tinder won't help!

This is happening to me right now! It's so scary . . . I feel like there's nothing really to do about it. Hopefully this psycho closes the account, but I am freaking out. Getting tons of emails about casual-sex hookups.

Tinder and Facebook are no help! I even went to the police. Help! This is ruining my life.

Dustin's words spring to mind.

The police won't help you, but I can.

My phone trills, and I see it's Valerie Simmons's assistant. I shut down the tab of ghastly horror stories and answer. After a few pleasantries, Valerie herself comes on. She talks for a few minutes about her expectations for the shoot in her familiar sonorous voice, which I associate with doctor's waiting rooms and other places where CNN is always on.

"Listen, Allie, I'll be frank with you. I'm looking to reach a younger audience, and I want someone whose work is fresh and new and exciting, but—and this is important—I need someone who also understands that D.C. is a conservative place."

"I totally get it. I'm talking with a senator who is putting out a children's book and has many of the same concerns." A small white lie. I haven't spoken to Senator Fielding yet, but I'm confident Sarah Ramirez will come through with that introduction.

"Really? That's exactly what I am talking about, straddling those two worlds. And I don't mind saying that I love the idea of using a woman. More sensitivity. More discretion."

Before getting off the phone, we make an appointment for me to meet her at her Kalorama town house on Monday morning. Finally, something is going right. After typing the details into the studio's scheduler, I open my edits, newly energized.

There are fewer great shots of Sarah than I had hoped for, and I'll be lucky to cull twenty good ones that are different enough from each other to justify the cost. I feel bad—Sarah is so sweet, but these photographs don't capture how pretty she is.

In most pictures, her wide smile appears strained. Her mouth is frozen in a semi-grimace, and there's panic in her eyes. In one, although her face looks pretty, her smile genuine and warm, the way her body contorts on the chaise compresses the flesh on the side of her bra into bulges of dreaded "armpit fat."

I am tweaking a shot of Sarah lying on her side when Krystle calls.

"That is insanely fucked up," my sister says, popping my good mood instantaneously. "Fake Facebook pages? A poll? I mean, that is so twisted. What does Mark say?"

"He says not to pay attention to online bullies." I drag my little Photoshop paintbrush over to Sarah's arm and magically do what no diet can: spot reduce.

She scoffs. "Typical guy bullshit advice."

I scowl at the image on the screen. Sarah now resembles an alien, with an enormous head and sticklike limbs reminiscent of the praying mantis tattoo on my ankle.

"Holy shit," Krystle says. "That's the photo? God, you were so young."

"You're looking at it now?" A flush warms my face. That photo represents so much to me, a low point in my judgment and self-esteem. I actually thought my photography teacher was in love with me. That we would end up together, living happily ever after.

"Yeah, all the settings on your page are public."

"It's not my page, remember?"

"Sorry, fake page."

With a few clicks, I restore Sarah's armpit fat. Her boyfriend loves her. I'm sure he doesn't care about a little superfluous pocket of flesh, even if Sarah does.

"You know, Allie, you should contact Facebook."

I snort. "Thanks, Krystle, I hadn't thought of that."

"By the way, I am voting that you still got it."

I grit my teeth. "That's not funny. This is serious."

"Do you think maybe, if it's not Paul, it might be, you know, Madeline?"

The name startles me. "Do you mean Madeline Ashford? Why in the world would she do this?"

"Because she's a little bitch, that's why."

"Was a little bitch. That was what, sixteen years ago? We were all little bitches then."

"Oh my god, don't tell me you forgive her."

"*Forgive*'s not the right word. I just get it. She was mad. She wanted to hurt me. She didn't realize what would happen." I shut the editing down. I need to come back to it later, when I have some perspective. Right now, I worry I might do more damage than good.

"Right." Krystle snorts. "She didn't realize if she put up a nude photo of you and your photography teacher on MySpace that the shit might hit the fan? If you ask me, she's suspect numero uno. Once a nutter, always a nutter."

I sit back and sip my now-lukewarm espresso. Even though almost two decades have passed since that weekend, thinking about it sends my heart racing. Madeline Ashford was my one real friend at Overton, another outsider, although not because she was a scholarship student and not just because she was one of the few students of color, although that certainly contributed. She had a graceless honesty about her that rubbed people the wrong way.

But I liked her bluntness. And her bravery. It was as though she had the guts to say the things that I barely had the courage to think.

Today, her inability to read social cues might land her on the autistic spectrum. Back then she was just considered weird. She wanted to be a writer. *Wanted* is too weak of a word. She craved it. She wrote like her life depended on it, during class, lunch, late at night, in longhand in those cheap marble notebooks you can buy at any grocery store. She mocked people's grammar and word choices to their faces, which endeared her to no one.

We spent hours fantasizing about our life after high school. We'd move to New York together, and I would take the art world by storm while she made her publishing debut. We did everything together, and we had no secrets, including my crush on Mr. Adamson. In the beginning, she helped me stalk him, find out where he took his coffee between classes, where he parked his boxy vintage BMW. She accompanied me on countless trips into town to skulk through the cobbled streets trying to spot his reddish-brown hair, a bit longer than the older male teachers wore theirs.

But then one day, I had a secret worth keeping.

Madeline was like one of those cats who knows when its owner has been visiting a house where another cat lives. She could sniff Paul's scent on me. I tried to keep the secret from her for as long as I could.

My secret felt as beautiful and fragile as an aqua robin's egg you might find in springtime. I wanted to protect it, even as much as I knew it wouldn't last.

Then came the weekend that I forgot plans with Madeline. Nothing special, not a birthday, just a date between friends. We were supposed to go see *The Sisterhood of the Traveling Pants*, which we claimed we were watching ironically, although we had both loved the books when we were younger. But I wasn't at my apartment when Madeline came to fetch me. I was at the Moonlight Motel, off Route 1, where they charged by the hour. Krystle let her go up to my bedroom. She couldn't have known what Madeline was going to do, because Krystle had no idea what I had been doing.

Krystle didn't know about the drawer where I kept the pictures and copies of all the letters I wrote to Paul. Letters written in a loopy, girlish hand, bursting with adolescent longing, expressed in graphic sexual language that I thought made me look sexy and alluring.

But Madeline's instincts were spot-on. Madeline found them.

I refresh my email, hoping for news from Facebook or Tinder, and to my surprise, I find an email from Overton. I hadn't expected her response to be so fast.

When I come to the third line of the message, my throat tightens. I force myself to read the line two more times to be sure I am not seeing things.

The National Capital Overton Alumni Group coordinator is Madeline Ashford-Brown.

24

The whole drive back to Bethesda, I can't stop thinking about Madeline.

Her betrayal cut me deeper than anything done by a guy I had been with. I trusted her, let her in. I told her things about my mother and my homelife that no one else knew. She was the only person from Overton who ever saw where I lived. And she exposed me—on the internet, at school—to ridicule.

And now she's Madeline Ashford-Brown, living in Alexandria, Virginia, just over the Potomac River, less than a thirty-minute drive from my house. It's true that loads of people end up in the D.C. area for a variety of reasons, but it shakes me that she is so close. My past is like a parallel life that I had come to believe would never intersect with my present. And here they were, not just crossing but marking a large *X*.

The worst part of her posting that picture was that I didn't have my best friend to turn to for support. I felt totally alone in my shame.

She scared me off female friendships for a long time.

I pull into the parking lot of the grocery store and shut off the engine. As much as I want to crawl under the covers until this nightmare ends, I have to keep normal life going for Cole. And that means keeping the pantry stocked with mac and cheese and blueberry granola bars, and buying ingredients to make shortbread for International Night next week.

I'm not a scared teenager anymore, and I need to know what

the hell is happening. Could she have sent that shirt? Could it have been an innocent gesture, or is it possible that she is behind everything else, too? There's only one way to find out.

Without overthinking it, I dash off an email.

Madeline, it's Alexis Ross (formerly Healy) from Overton. Turns out we're practically neighbors. Any chance you could meet me for a cup of coffee? I need to talk to you.

I hit Send before I chicken out.

I'm in the baking aisle, trying to decipher the difference between confectioner's sugar and superfine sugar, when Krystle calls me.

"Hey," I say as I put both in my cart. Susan, who has agreed to bake shortbread with Cole for next week's International Night, can sort it out.

"I got a call from the neighbors in Westport this morning," she says by way of greeting. "They said you hired someone to assess the house. That you're selling. That's not true, is it?"

My throat tightens. I knew this phone call was coming, but I didn't realize Barb DeSoto would move so fast. "It's true. I'm putting the house on the market." I move the phone away from my head an inch and wait for the screaming to begin.

"Are you kidding me? And you didn't think to mention this to me when we spoke earlier?" she yells. "What the fuck is wrong with you, Allie?"

Gone is my sister the ally, whom I spoke to this morning, replaced by Krystle the rage machine.

"Calm down. In case you don't remember, I have a lot going on here."

"Calm down? You want to sell our house."

"Sharon has to have an aide. It's going to cost us an additional two grand a month, which as you know, puts us over the income we get from the rent." I shoot a glare at a woman my age who is looking at pancake mixes while eavesdropping. She scoots away.

"You can't sell it. I won't let you."

"You can't stop me." I sigh and summon up a softer tone. "She needs the money, Krystle. And anyway, it's time. I can't manage a one-hundred-year-old house from this far away, and no offense, you're not going to do it either."

"There has to be another way, Allie."

"I don't get why you care so much. It's not like we grew up there." I push the cart down the aisle toward the dairy section. "We lucked into that house. It's incredibly stupid to let it fall apart beyond repair. We need to sell now, while we can still get good money for it."

"Allie, that's our inheritance. My inheritance."

I stop short in front of the endless wall of yogurt. Even for Krystle, that's heartless. "It's not up to us. It's her money."

Krystle snorts.

"It is, Krystle." I put both salted and unsalted butter in the cart, covering my bets.

"I need that money, Allie. I have no retirement savings, and I'm in debt from when I hurt my back two years ago. I'm really counting on it."

"You're not listening. The house is falling apart. It's penny-wise but pound-foolish to keep fixing it up. Look, Mark and I are happy to help if you need cash."

"I don't need you and your lawyer husband to help me," she says. "I just want my inheritance."

It's not yours, I want to say, but for some reason, I can't. I know she resents me for having married someone with money. Before Mark, we would commiserate about when our bank balances hit single digits. We were in the same boat, going to Planned Parenthood for routine pap smears because we had no health insurance, buying clothes off eBay. After I married Mark, that changed. In her eyes, marrying him was like winning the lottery—a stroke of luck, and just one more example of how life was easier for me.

As I turn down the cereal aisle toward the checkout lines, I see Janelle, the English major from book club. I back up. The last thing I want right now is to become entangled in a web of chitchat with a neighborhood mom.

"Do you want to spend your inheritance on keeping up an old house? Because that's what we'll have to do. Take out a mortgage and use the money. If we sell now, we can invest and make money. We'll probably end up ahead."

"Well, I don't want to sell it."

I grit my teeth. I didn't want to have to say this. "It's not up to you, though, is it? I'm her power of attorney."

"You're not really gonna pull rank on me, are you?"

"I'm not pulling rank, Krystle. But it's my responsibility. You are familiar with the concept of responsibility, right?"

And with that, Krystle hangs up on me. I drive home, my hands shaking. My sister's emotions rise and plummet like a roller coaster, and I hate how she takes me along for the ride.

25

I can't pull up right in front of my house, because there's a blue BMW parked outside. This is the second day this week that some car has parked in that spot. I frown, juggling the grocery bags and my laptop as I enter the house.

Grateful that the back door is unlocked, I push it open. "Hello?" I call out. "I've got baking supplies!"

No answer.

"Susan? Cole? I'm home." With a loud grunt, I manage to hoist all the bags onto the kitchen counter.

A noise behind me makes me jump.

When I turn, Vicki is there.

"How did you get in here?" A chill runs down my back.

"Your babysitter let me in." Her voice trembles with controlled rage. "You are not going to get away with this."

"With what?"

Cole rushes in, a yellow bath towel thrown over his shoulders like a cape, and wraps his arms around my legs.

"I'm Super Duck, and this is my costume."

Susan follows behind him. I try to push Cole off me, but that makes him cling harder. Despite his size, Cole is strong. I want him out of this room and as far away from this conversation as possible.

"Susan, get Cole out of here. Please. Take him outside."

"I don't want to go outside," Cole whines. "It's cold."

"Then go upstairs and watch a video. Anything you want."

With more effort than I'd like to use, I pry his arms off me and nudge him toward the dining room.

"I just need to add the carrots and celery to the soup." Susan points to the large pot on the stove. A heaping pile of chopped carrots and celery sits on a cutting board next to it. The air is rich with the smell of rosemary and chicken.

"I'll do that later, Susan." The terseness in my voice startles her, and her elfin face seems to crumple in rejection. "Please, take Cole out of here."

"But I want to stay." Cole stomps his foot.

"Now, damn it," I say, and Cole's eyes widen. Susan looks shocked. I'm sure she's never snapped at a child in her life.

"C'mon, sweetie, let's go watch *Dog with a Blog*." Susan takes my son by the hand and leads him out of the room. My stomach churns. I hate it when I snap at Cole, especially in front of witnesses.

"Look, I don't know what your problem is," I say as soon as they are gone, "but you need to leave."

"Rob Avery was a friend of mine, a good one," she says. "He was a good person, not a sexual predator. And I'll be damned if I let you slander him."

"You can't slander the dead," I say, pulling that factoid out of God knows what part of my brain. This seems to enrage her further. She straightens up, looming large on the other side of my kitchen island.

"I know you were having an affair with Rob."

"You don't know shit."

"Is that right?" She smiles, a vicious slash across her grim face, and pulls out her cell phone. "I have proof."

"You need to go." I start toward the door. I am sure she's talking about that fake Tinder profile, but I don't feel any need to explain anything to this woman. "Now, or I'll call the police."

"Do it," she spits out. "I dare you."

A sound at the back door distracts us both. Mark strides in, loosening his blue paisley tie. He catches a glimpse of Vicki and freezes mid-action, his hand at his throat. He turns to me. "What's going on?"

"Vicki was just leaving."

"Look, it's Mark, right?" Vicki fixes her gaze on my husband. "I don't know what you know or what your wife has been telling you. But she needs to stop talking trash about Rob. And if she doesn't"—she waves her cell phone in the air—"I'm going to be forced to make their texting history public."

Mark turns to me. "What is she talking about?"

"She's talking about that fake Tinder profile," I say.

"Is that what you're telling people?" Vicki asks, her voice dripping with derision. "Please."

"It's the truth. I've already contacted Tinder, and they're going to shut it down."

"*Saw you at the library*," Vicki reads from her phone. "*You make me so wet.*"

The words make me want to throw up.

"That's enough!" The timbre in Mark's voice seems to shock Vicki to attention. He walks to the back door and yanks it open, sending the bell clanging angrily. "Get out."

To my surprise, a chastened Vicki does as he says. At the doorway, she pauses and turns back. "This isn't the end of this."

Mark shuts the door on her, and we watch through the glass as her face melts into a mask of fury. Once she has stalked off, I throw myself into his arms.

"What a bitch," he murmurs into my hair. "How dare she come in here, hurling accusations."

I rub my face against his smooth dress shirt, inhaling his sweat and cologne, overwhelmed with gratitude that he defended me.

He pulls his head back so he can look me in the eye. "Did you make an appointment with Artie Zucker?"

"Yes. We have an appointment for tomorrow. He's coming to the house at six."

"He makes house calls, huh?"

"I want you to be there."

"Of course." A small grimace crosses his face. "I guess this is a bad time to remind you I was supposed to go to the Nationals game tonight."

I put on a brave face. Mark works hard and loves baseball, and his team is in the playoffs. I don't want our lives to revolve around Rob Avery's murder. "No problem. Go. Have fun."

"I don't have to go if you don't want me to."

"Please. I'll be fine."

"It's just that I told Miles—"

"Go."

"I'll keep my phone on, so call me if anything happens."

"Nothing's going to happen. I'm going to put Cole to bed and then watch some stupid TV."

"You don't want to drive me to the metro, do you? I'm meeting Miles at the Tenleytown station."

"Can't you just Uber? I really don't want to leave the house right now."

Marks wrinkles his nose. "And how do I do that, exactly?"

I take my phone from my bag. "Just open the app and it's pretty obvious."

He takes my phone from me. "How do I pay?"

"You're such a Gen Xer. It's already linked to my credit card."

Footsteps on the stairs tell me that Cole and Susan are on their way down. I leave Mark in the kitchen and head to the powder room. My face is a sweaty mess, and my chest is red and blotchy, which happens when I get really upset. I take a few moments to breathe deeply and exhale. I want to be calm and centered for Cole. I don't want him to sense my anxiety.

When I come out, Cole is at Susan's side by the stove, adding vegetables to the pot. Mark comes back into the kitchen, having changed into a Nats jersey over a long-sleeve T-shirt.

"Did you order the Uber?"

He nods, but doesn't smile. "Mind walking me out front?"

Something in his tone makes my stomach flutter. "Sure," I say and follow him out.

Once on our front stoop, he turns my phone to me. "What's this?"

I peer at the screen, where I can make out the small red flame for Tinder. "I don't know. I think it's Tinder."

"You don't know?"

"I swear, Mark, I did not download that on my phone. I have no idea how that got there. Can I see it?" He hands me the phone. The app is floating, singular, on its own page. I flip back to the main screen where my most-used apps are and then to the next screen, where I have relegated apps I either never use or cannot remove.

Tinder is hanging out all by itself on the third screen. "I never even go to this screen."

Mark takes it from me and taps the app. Immediately, my profile comes up, the close-up of me in the bikini.

"*Alexis, but my friends call me Sexy Lexi,*" Mark reads. "*Married, but I don't mind if you don't.*"

"Mark, you know this is fake, right? I mean, we talked about this."

He looks at my face, his brown eyes searching. "I just don't understand how this got on your phone."

"I don't know either! I swear."

He taps at the phone. "*M is working late,*" he reads in a monotone voice. "*And I am horny as hell.*" He looks up at me. "I suppose I'm M, right?"

"No, Mark. You're not M, because this is fake. I told you." My voice cracks with exasperation. Hasn't he been listening to what I've been telling him these past few days?

"How about this one?" He scrunches up his face and continues in that fake high-pitched tone. "*Can't wait until tonight. M will be there, so we'll have to be careful.*"

I put my hand on the phone. "Stop it. Enough."

He tosses me the phone, startling me, but I catch it.

"You know I didn't write that."

"I don't know what to think, Allie."

"Fine." I yank open the front door. "Just go to your baseball game. I'll keep dealing with this. I've contacted Tinder. I've contacted Facebook."

"You can't blame me for being upset." His face is red. "I mean, how would you feel if it were the other way around and you found this shit on my phone?" A man in a neon-green vest glares at us as he runs by pushing a jogging stroller.

"You can be upset and still believe me. I'm upset, too. This is happening to me, Mark. To me!"

A brown sedan with an Uber sticker pulls up.

"That's your ride."

Mark walks down the path to the car.

I am half hoping he leans in the open window and tells the driver to take off, that he's changed his mind and won't need an Uber after all. I want him to want to stay, not because there's anything he can do to fix this tonight but just because he doesn't want me to be alone. But I can't find the words to ask for what I want, and standing in the doorway with my arms crossed, I can feel the sour look on my face.

I wait at the open door until my husband climbs into the car and it drives away.

Then I look down at the phone in my hand, scanning all the messages, supposedly from me, to Rob Avery.

I want to feel you rub your cock against me.

I want your hands between my legs.

Be aggressive, don't take no for an answer.

Seeing these words, I realize that I lied to Mark.

Those are my words. Only I didn't type them to Rob Avery. I wrote them to Paul Adamson, sixteen years ago.

26

When I enter the kitchen, Susan stops unpacking the groceries I brought home earlier, a box of baking soda in one hand and a stick of butter in the other. "Everything all right?"

"Yes, I'm fine." I plaster a smile on my face.

"You don't look fine," she says.

"Long day, that's all." I go to the fridge, grateful for the half-full bottle of wine. I pour myself a tall glass, aware that she is watching me. But I don't care. Let her judge.

"Well, the soup's on the stove, ready to eat. My mother always said there's nothing a hot bowl of soup and a warm bath can't fix."

"You're probably right," I say. "Thank you for everything."

After Susan leaves, I ladle out two bowls of soup, one for Cole and another for me. Cole wrinkles his nose. "I don't like cooked vegetables," he says, peering into the bowl. "I want mac and cheese."

I am about to launch into a tirade about how *you get what you get, and you don't get upset,* when I realize I do not have the strength. "You got it."

"Really?" His eyes bulge with shock at my easy acquiescence. "With apple slices?"

"No problem."

"Skinny slices, not fat."

"Sure."

After dinner, I even let Cole have a bowl of Lucky Charms for dessert. Then I tuck him into my bed, along with about a dozen stuffed animals. When he asks if he can watch a PG-13 movie, I consent.

"Why not?" I ask. "I watched *Basic Instinct* when I was twelve, and I turned out all right."

He scrunches up his nose. "What's *Basic Instinct*?"

I tuck the blanket tight around his legs. "That was just a joke."

"Were you and Daddy fighting with that lady?"

I flinch. Cole was listening after all. "No, not fighting. Just discussing a few things." I brace myself for him to ask me what, but he changes tack.

"Are you getting divorced? Dylan's parents are getting divorced. She's moving to an aparterment."

"Apartment," I correct him. "But no, Mommy and Daddy are not getting divorced. Sometimes grown-ups get mad, just like sometimes kids get mad."

"But if you do get divorced, can I get a bunny? Dylan's getting a bunny."

"Watch the movie, Cole." I kiss his forehead and leave the room.

I'm on the landing, on my way down to the kitchen for more wine, when I hear a scraping sound come from the living room. I grip the banister and listen. The sound repeats. It's like something being dragged across the floor.

Could be Mark is home from the game, but it's way too early.

My skin prickles as I tiptoe down the stairs. From the foyer, I can see the lights are on in the living room. I can't imagine what he would be doing in there. My breath quickens. I enter the room. A crouching figure shoots up, and I let out a yelp.

It's Leah. She rushes to me. "Hey, you all right?" She embraces me. "I'm sorry I freaked you out. Your back door was unlocked."

I offer a weak smile, struggling to catch my breath. "No, it's okay, I'm just not used to—"

"I'm so sorry! I'm just used to popping in on friends."

"Right. I'm just a little . . . I'm not used to it is all. And with everything going on—"

"You're right. I'm sorry. I just wanted to check on you. See if you had any luck today, you know, with Facebook and everything." Then she hoists a bottle of white wine that was sitting on the coffee table. "And I wanted someone to drink this Kim Crawford with me."

I force a laugh, flooded with relief. "I'd love to split that with you. But hold on."

I run upstairs to make sure Cole is occupied with his movie and find him out cold, snoring, legs akimbo. I shut the television and lights off and close the door.

Back downstairs, Leah has found the wineglasses and is looking through a stack of framed photographs leaning against the wall.

"Haven't quite gotten around to hanging those," I say.

"These are wonderful. Did you take them?"

"Eons ago." I unscrew the wine and pour us each a glass.

Leah peers at the photographs, a series of outtakes from weddings in San Francisco. None are of brides, or bridesmaids, or grooms. There's the elderly aunt relegated to the corner of the reception room, leaning on her walker, in her brocade vest. The flower girl hiding beneath the rickety stairs of the old farmhouse, mud streaked across her dress, terrified her mother will be mad.

"You're really talented. I have zero creative ability. Former lawyer."

"Oh, I doubt that," I say, adding a "Thank you." Leah curls herself into one of the wingback chairs, and I sit on the floral sofa.

"Nice sofa," she says and laughs.

"It was my mother-in-law's." At night, the bare windows and minimal furniture lend the room the feel of a theater set after everyone has gone home. The awful cement-colored walls that Daisy once called "greige" don't help.

"How did the visit with Jeff Crosetti go? I noticed the posts are gone from the Eastbrook page." She sips her wine.

I describe my interaction with Crosetti.

"Well, that's good news, right?"

"Well, neither Facebook nor Tinder has been the least bit helpful." I bite my lower lip, a stinging sensation building behind my eyes. *Don't cry,* I tell myself. Leah frowns.

"But what?" she asks.

I hesitate. "Did you see the blue BMW that was parked outside my house earlier?"

She scrunches up her nose. "Maybe?"

"Well, it was Vicki."

"Vicki Armstrong? The PTA president?"

I fill her in on what happened, my face warming as I recount the conversation and the embarrassing texts. "The worst part is that Mark saw them."

"But he believes you, right? That you didn't write them."

I cringe. *I did write them. And Madeline found them and posted them online, where my entire school could read them.* "It was really awful."

"He's in shock; give him some time. I mean, what would you think if you were in his shoes, and some woman showed up at your house, and the Tinder app was on his phone?"

"The app is on my phone, but I swear, Leah, I did not put it there. I know that sounds crazy."

"I believe you, I really do." She gathers her thick dark hair over one shoulder and begins braiding it. "You know that apps can be remotely installed, right?"

"They can?"

"Sure. If your phone is synced to your computer. Is your phone synced to your home computer?"

"Yes, everything—all our iPads and iPhones—are all synced up."

"Well, there you go." She raises her glass and takes a sip.

"How do you know about all this?"

She fixes her large eyes on me. "Believe me, I wish I didn't. Let's just say parenting Dustin has meant learning more about technology than I would like."

"Got it." I wonder if I should mention Dustin's proposal to help me, but I don't. Something tells me she wouldn't like it.

"Basically," she says, "anyone who had access to your computer could have downloaded that onto your phone."

I squeeze my eyes shut. "This is so out of control. I don't know how to fix this."

"Hopefully, there will be a break in the case soon, the police will arrest someone, and all this gossip will die down."

I look at Leah and nod. But inside I am less confident. I'm worried about the way the police have focused on me and might not be looking at other suspects. I've read about that happening; it's how innocent people end up in prison.

"You have to find out who's doing this to you. Do you still think it might be that ex-boyfriend from high school?"

I pick at a loose thread on the arm of the sofa. "I do. It's the only person I can think of who might be angry with me. And also, there are just these little things that very few people know about."

"You mean the nude photo?"

"Yeah. And a few other things."

"Is he in the D.C. area now? It would have to be someone who knew you then and lives here now."

I take a large gulp of wine. I've been thinking the exact same thought, but to hear Leah articulate it makes me realize how strange it would be. "I've never had any luck tracking him down. His name is so common, I've never gotten anywhere online."

"What about other friends from high school? Anyone here now?"

"Actually, yeah. My closest friend from back then, Madeline Ashford, lives in Arlington. We haven't spoken in ages. I've reached out to her, but we haven't connected yet." I shake my head, trying to think. "There really isn't anyone else. I don't really have friends from school. I was only there for two years. After that nude photo made the rounds, I left the school. They let me graduate early. I think they wanted to avoid any kind of lawsuit. I left for California and never looked back."

"Lawsuit?" Leah frowns.

I've said too much. The wine has loosened my thoughts, and I'm having trouble remembering which bits of my story I've shared and which I've not.

"What happened, Allie? Was it something with that guy in the photo?"

My whole throat seizes. I don't want to lie anymore. I don't want to drag this cloak of shame with me everywhere I go. I want to lay it at my friend's feet and let her kindness begin to heal me. "He was my photography teacher."

Leah brings a hand to her mouth. I don't know if she's judging me or is just shocked. Now that I've started telling her the truth, I don't want to stop. "It was a huge deal. He got fired. The police got involved, although nothing ever came of that. I was gone by then."

"Oh, Allie. I'm so sorry." Leah slides forward in the chair and reaches out across the coffee table for my hand. I let her squeeze it for a few seconds and then pull back.

"I can't believe I just told you that. I have never told anyone since it happened."

"Anyone?"

I shake my head. "Nope. Not even Mark. I just wanted so badly for it to be in my past. And for a while I was able to even forget sometimes, you know? Like how they say you shed your skin every seven years and become a new person? That was the old me. I didn't want to bring that into my new life."

"I think you need to tell Mark." Her voice is very soft. "It's not your fault, you know. This guy took advantage of you."

"You don't know. I'm the one who pursued him. I used to write him these letters." I shudder, embarrassed at the memory. They were pornographic ramblings, the pathetic attempts of a high school girl to appear sexy and sophisticated. Never in a million years did I imagine those words would be used against me like this.

Leah shakes her head. "No, Allie, you can't believe that. Consent is meaningless in that situation."

A silence hangs between us. I have always held myself responsible for my part in what happened. It was what I wanted, after all. I didn't berate myself. But I did pride myself on not sugarcoating the role I played. I wasn't like my sister and mother, who never took responsibility for anything that went wrong in their lives. I was different than that.

"Allie, I'm the mother of a teenager. You have to know that you were just a kid. Kids do dumb things, and the adults are the ones who are supposed to help, not take advantage," Leah says. "You have to forgive yourself."

I try to smile. Instead, I burst into tears. Leah disappears into the powder room and returns with a wad of toilet paper. "You really need to tell Mark."

"You sound like my sister."

"Your sister's right."

I laugh. "That would be a first."

"What if he sees the photo?" Leah asks. "What are you going to say then?"

"You're right, that would be awful. I'm going to tell him." I am not sure how I am going to bring myself to explain to Mark that I slept with my teacher in high school. Mark had always said my past didn't matter, but he had no idea what was hidden there. Would he think of me differently if he knew the truth?

Leah pulls me close to her. She smells like vanilla cookies, warm and reassuring. "We're going to get to the bottom of this," she whispers. "Don't you worry."

Once Leah leaves, I wander from room to room, shutting off the lights except the one in the front hall, which I leave on for Mark. Then I go upstairs and ready myself for bed.

At ten, I give up on waiting for Mark to come home. I shut off the television. I drift off into a fitful sleep punctuated by vivid dreams. Sounds from the street wake me every so often, but Mark's side of the bed remains empty. Still not home.

Then I dream that I'm back in the Moonlight Motel, lying naked atop the seafoam-green bedspread. Paul kisses first my neck, then my shoulder, then moves down my torso, gaining fervor. I arch my back with each delicious sweep of his lips across my skin. Outside, the roar of the trucks on Route 1 sounds like waves breaking on the shore. I clutch at the popcorn chenille bedspread, balling it in my fist. We're safe here in our own little paradise.

I jolt awake. It's after midnight, and Mark's still not home. The game must have gone into extra innings.

Unable to sleep, I go downstairs to pour myself the last of the wine that Leah brought. I turn the lights down low and pace the kitchen in front of our huge picture window that lets in so much sun during the day. I hear distant laughter from the back, where a pedestrian alley cuts behind the houses. The one that connects my house to Rob Avery's. It would be a one-minute walk, two tops. Is that what the police think? That I snuck out in the middle of the night and went to his house and killed him?

The laughter rises and falls. It sounds like teenage boys, laughing in that cruel way of theirs. Up until a few weeks ago, the red twig dogwood provided a green curtain of privacy. Now, in October, the denuded shrubs leave me exposed. I wonder if the boys can see me and if it is me they find funny.

27

On Friday morning, I wake with a pounding headache to the whir of the blender. Mark is in the kitchen, making his breakfast smoothie. The morning light slices my eyes like a blade. My tongue sticks to the roof of my mouth. I look around, disoriented for a moment, until I realize I am on the living room couch. On the floor beside me lie an empty bottle of sauvignon blanc and my laptop. Bits of the night come back to me.

"Drink this." He hands me a tall glass with a thick green liquid in it.

"It looks gross." I sit up and take it from him. The first sip tastes like freshly mowed grass. Disgusting, but it's a peace offering, so I finish it.

"It's good for you."

I do as he says, chug it, and drag myself upstairs for a shower. Afterward, I stare at my dark-rimmed eyes and sallow skin in the mirror. The wine and disrupted sleep are catching up with me. I apply my makeup more thickly than usual, hoping to approximate the glow of a healthy woman. Back in the kitchen, Cole sits cross-legged on the floor in front of the TV, eating cereal, violating our established no-screens-before-breakfast rule. A large, animated pig with an English accent twirls on the screen.

"Where are the photos, Daddy?" Cole asks during a commercial. "Did you remember to pick them up?"

"I did, actually," Mark says. "They're in an envelope in my bag."

Cole rushes to Mark's cubby in the mudroom. He comes back holding a large manila envelope, struggling with the clasp. He hands it to me to open.

"Please?" I say and take the envelope from him.

"Please," he repeats.

The return address is not for Kane & Burrows, the law firm where Mark works, but LFW Research. "What's LFW Research?" I ask, looking up at Mark.

With a sudden jerk, Mark snatches the envelope from my hands and turns to Cole. "You can't just go through my bag, grabbing things."

"You told me to." Cole's lower lip quivers, and his eyes widen.

"I said *envelope*, not manila envelope." Mark goes to his bag and returns with a small white envelope.

"Yikes," I say to Mark. "You all right?"

"Sorry, buddy," Mark says. "Didn't mean to snap at you."

Cole gingerly takes the envelope, looking at Mark to see if it is really safe.

"Go ahead," Mark urges in a chummy tone. "Open it up."

Cole pulls out the photos of Caitlin and Charles, Bob and Joan. The Rosses are all accounted for.

"Can you help me glue them on?" he asks.

"I'd love to, buddy, but I have to leave for work," Mark says. "I can help you this evening."

Cole turns to me. "Can you help, Mommy?"

"Sure," I say. "*After* school. Now it's time to get dressed."

"Today's a half day."

"That right?" I suppress a grimace. I had completely forgotten. It seemed as though there hadn't been a full week of school this whole fall. "Cole, please go upstairs and get dressed."

Cole scowls and stomps upstairs with the photos.

"I guess I'll see if Susan can pick him up."

Mark stands up, takes Cole's empty cereal bowl to the sink, and begins rinsing it. "You forgot about the half day?"

"I'm sorry, did you remember?" I snap. I take a centering breath. I don't want to fight about domestic duties. "Look, Mark, I think we should talk."

"Good idea." He shuts the water off. "Listen, Allie, I'm not accusing you of anything, but I need you to help me understand something."

I swallow hard. "Fine. What is it?"

He wipes his hands on a dish towel and grabs his phone. After some typing, he turns it to me. I see the familiar blue Facebook logo. "Brian at work, of all people, sent it to me."

I groan. I should have prepared him for this. And maybe I would have if he had stayed to talk to me last night instead of going to the Nats game. "Listen, that is the fake Facebook page I told you about. I contacted Facebook, and they're looking into it."

"Who's Lexi?" The name smacks me with the force of a slap.

"It was a stupid nickname from high school."

"There are nude photos of you online." His voice is taut like a guitar string that's too tight and about to snap. "My colleagues from work have seen them."

"I know, I should have told you they were out there."

"Yes, you should have. Do you have any idea how embarrassing this is for me?"

His words stun me. "However you feel, believe me, it's worse for me, Mark."

He rolls his eyes. "Of course. But, Allie, c'mon. You never thought to tell me there were nude photos of you floating around the internet?"

"They're not floating around, Mark." My head begins to throb. This isn't going the way I wanted it to. I shouldn't have to defend myself. "They're from high school."

"It's not just the pictures. It's the posts."

"I know how terrible this looks. But please remember that I did not write any of that. I feel you're not getting it—this is happening *to* me."

"What does your boss think? Has he said anything?" His eyes are glued to the screen. I don't think he's listening to me. "I mean, aren't you supposed to be shooting Valerie Simmons next week? What if she sees this?"

His anxiety pricks me like a bee sting. I try to swallow the lump that is forming in my throat. "I don't know. I'm praying I can get these accounts shut down soon."

Mark taps at the phone, his eyes wide. "*I'm a prisoner in my own life,*" he reads and then lowers his voice. "It says you regret having kids." He looks up. "I know that's not true, but . . ."

"But what?" My guts clench and twist. "If you know it's not true, then what?"

"I remember you talking about an abortion."

"That's not fair. That was years ago." I glance at the stairs, terrified Cole might come down at any moment. "We weren't even married," I hiss. "We had only been together a few months."

"You said you weren't ready for kids. I kept thinking that at some point, you would warm to all this."

"What haven't I warmed to?" But the truth is, his accusation hits a nerve. I've never regretted having Cole, not for a minute. I have ruminated, however, on how motherhood has swallowed me whole, whereas Mark has managed to tack *father* onto his list of descriptors. But I've never said any of this aloud.

"To all of this." Mark waves his hands around the messy kitchen. "To being a mom, to having other mom friends. To cooking. Allie, you don't even know how to scramble an egg, for Chrissakes."

"That's the metric you judge me by? How well I cook eggs?"

"You're being oversensitive." He closes his eyes, and for a moment the only sound in the kitchen is that damn huge clock. Mark opens his eyes. "When Cole was little, we agreed we wanted him to have a brother or sister. I thought that was the plan, but now . . ."

"Now what?"

"Maybe this is all too much for you."

"Maybe it is sometimes. And yes, I am not sure if I want a second child. But that doesn't mean I don't love Cole or that I don't love our life together. Just because I don't scramble eggs . . . I mean, all parents get overwhelmed."

To this, Mark shrugs.

"What, you're saying you never do?" I ask.

"No. Not like you do." He shakes his head. "I like our life. I like our house, our neighborhood. This is what I want."

"I want it, too. But someone is trying to destroy me, Mark. Someone is framing me for Rob Avery's murder."

"You're being overdramatic."

"Am I? I don't think so. Tell me you'll at least be home by six."

"What's happening at six?"

"I told you." I am furious that he doesn't remember. "Artie Zucker is coming. Here."

"Of course I'll be here," he snaps. "Hiring him was my idea, remember?"

My cell phone rings, but I ignore it.

"Your phone, Allie." He nods in the direction of the ringing. "Aren't you going to answer it? Never know who it might be." There's no missing the snide insinuation.

When he sees I am making no move, he walks over and glances at it. "It's Morningside House." He tosses the phone at me a little too roughly, but I catch it.

"Allie Ross?" a woman asks once I bring the phone to my ear. "This is Lydia from Morningside. We've had an incident with your mother. She's attacked one of our aides."

28

Absorbed in my phone, I almost bump into a parked car as I walk Cole to school. Susan is not available to pick up Cole from early release, but thankfully, Leah can.

No problem! At doctor, will be home by noon. Ava will be thrilled.

Once that is sorted, I tap out a message to the Realtor in Westport.

GM! Please call me. Looks like I'm going to need to put house on market ASAP.

I press Send and pray that Barb DeSoto is the type who checks her work phone obsessively.

"Mommy, are you listening?" Cole tugs at my coat. "You're not even listening. Put away your screens."

I smile tightly. The first time he fed my own words back to me, it was cute. Now it's just grating. "I'm listening, Cole."

Lydia made it clear Sharon would have to be moved, and soon. My mind spins with calculations. The Memory Care unit will cost much more, putting us in a monthly deficit. One that I will have to cover until we sell the house. Where will I get the money?

"Cole, do you wish I made eggs more often?" I take his hand in mine.

Cole stops skipping for a moment and frowns in confusion. "Eggs?"

"You know," I press on. "Hard-boiled eggs. Scrambled eggs."

He screws up his nose in disgust. "Eww. I don't like eggs."

"Exactly."

"But I wish you would make pumpkin muffins like Susan. They're really, really good."

That stings a little. I plaster a smile on my face. "But we're so lucky that Susan bakes for us, so we don't need to, right?"

He narrows his eyes into slits, unconvinced. "We were supposed to bake last night."

"Yes, I know. But you can do it another time."

"For International Night? International Night is Tuesday, you know. Don't forget." His tone is that of a jaded office supervisor.

"I won't forget. Leah and Ava are bringing a Jewish pastry called rugelach, and you and Susan are—"

"We're going to make shortbread, because she says that's very English and Scottish. Shortbread is like cookies."

He lets go of my hand.

"Can I run to the stop sign?" He doesn't wait for an answer but takes off. I break into a half-hearted jog. At the stop sign, he pauses a moment and then continues on. I catch up to him at the edge of the playground. The monkey bars and climbing equipment are crawling with the younger kids. The fifth graders are huddled, staring at their phones.

A herd of moms stands in a cluster around the little lending library. These small structures, which resemble birdhouses on posts and can hold about a dozen books, are everywhere. It's ironic that in this community—where everyone can afford to buy as many books as they want and where there is an excellent public library down the road—these have popped up on every other corner.

The only books I remember in our home growing up were romance novels that came in boxes of Hefty garbage bags as part of a promotional campaign. I used to have to take two buses growing up to get to the library.

I scan the women with the acuity of a gazelle evaluating the dangers of the other animals at a watering hole. I find my whole body tensing, wondering who has heard what about me. I know none by name, but I recognize a few of the faces. I steel myself. I hold my chin up and squeeze Cole's hand tighter. It's pathetic. He feels like protection. There's no telling who has seen my fake Facebook page and that nude photo of me.

"Okay, honey, let's say goodbye now. I have to go." The drive up to Sharon's during rush hour won't be pretty. I may not make it into the studio at all.

"No! You have to wait for the bell like the other moms."

"Cole, c'mon, sweetie."

With no warning, Cole begins pulling me toward the group of women.

"That's Oliver's mommy." He points at a tall woman with a messy updo. I recognize her from Daisy's party—she insisted I had gone to law school. "I want a playdate with Oliver. Oliver said you should ask her."

"I'll ask her later. Today, you're going to have a playdate with Ava." I try to stand my ground.

Cole pulls harder. "No, ask her now, Mommy. Oliver said so."

He breaks free of my grip and makes a beeline toward the group. The circle of women parts to make way for Cole. They remind me of a pen-and-ink illustration from a book I read as a girl. It chronicled the death of a young Puritan girl at the hands of the other women in her village, who thought she was a witch. I remember how good and wholesome the women were rendered, with their plump cheeks and sparkling eyes, and how at odds it was with their vicious behavior.

Only these women are clad in black yoga pants and fleeces, not modest Puritan dresses.

A woman standing next to Oliver's mom bends down a little to say something to Cole. I wonder what my son is saying to her. I have no choice. I walk over.

"Hi," I say. "It's Tanya, right? We met at the Gordons' party."

The woman, ruddy-cheeked as if she's just run a half marathon, straightens up. "Yes, that's right."

"Cole was saying that Oliver and he had talked about having a playdate? I'm happy to host."

I sense the mood shift without anyone saying a word, like a cool front moving across a summer's day. They know, or they think they know. Tanya's wide mouth folds into a facsimile of a smile, but her eyes are cold. "I'm afraid today's not good."

"I didn't mean today. I just meant at some point."

"What about tomorrow?" Cole asks, tugging at my jacket sleeve.

"Aww, sorry, sweetie." Tanya bends down so she can look Cole in the eye. "This week is super busy for Oliver."

"Of course," I say, but Tanya has already turned her back on us, recompleting the circle.

Cole frowns. "Ask her about next week," he says.

With some effort, I steer him away from the group, heartbroken for him. My own rejection is hard enough, but it's far more painful to witness Cole on the receiving end. Before I am forced to make up an excuse as to why I won't be asking Oliver's mom about next week, or any week for that matter, Ava comes running up. She takes Cole by the hand, and I watch the two run down the hill until they are safely within the flock of children.

Every other week, Cole comes home with some worksheet on bullying—how to be an upstander instead of a bystander, for example. As if cruelty is some sort of isolated childhood affliction, a gauntlet you must run through on your way to adolescence, that disappears once you hit twenty-one.

I turn and trudge back up the hill, keeping my head down to avoid making eye contact with any of the parents. My stomach is in knots from my argument with Mark. Maybe things will be better once we meet the lawyer later today. We need to be united.

I am lost in thought when I sense someone behind me. Instinctively, my back stiffens. I glance back to see Karen Pearce, the woman I met at Daisy's, power walking and grimacing, her blond bob stiff and unmoving.

I catch her eye and smile. No acknowledgment from her at all.

I speed up, eager to get to my car before she reaches me. I open the door and toss my bag inside.

"Excuse me."

I jump. Karen is right behind me, panting from exertion. She wasn't just power walking; she was chasing me.

"Can I help you?"

She steps in so close to me that I can smell the mix of pungent sweat and fruity deodorant on her.

"Hi. I didn't want to say this in front of the other moms, but the room parents for Ms. Liu's class have contacted me as room-parent coordinator."

"Yes."

"Right. So I wanted to talk to you about the Halloween class party. I wanted to tell you in person . . . gosh, this is so awkward." She sighs and rolls her eyes skyward. "That they won't be needing you to help set up after all."

"All right. That's fine." I want to get out of here, but she's not done.

"Eastbrook is a pretty tight-knit community, and Rob Avery was a dear friend to a lot of us. Some of the other moms are just not comfortable with your involvement with everything. I mean, no one's accusing you of anything. We don't like to gossip. But we have to think of the children."

"I see. I won't help plan the party. Got it." I climb into my car, my pulse quickening. I need to get away from this woman before I do something that can't be undone. But when I try to shut the door, she wedges her hip so that I am unable to.

"And it's probably best for everyone if you didn't come to the Halloween party. Like, at all."

"For the record," I say, "I did not make any of those posts. I've been hacked, and someone has created false social media accounts impersonating me. Not that you gossip."

"Look, don't get upset. You can still send something in with Cole if you want to help. I think we still need black-and-orange sprinkles for the cupcake-decorating station."

"Terrific. Will do!" The words fly out of my mouth before I can even process what I am saying. She pivots back toward the playground. Just then, the whoop of a police siren sounds as two marked cars followed by a familiar sedan round the corner.

The three cars pull up in front of my house, effectively blocking me in.

Detective Lopez gets out of the sedan, a folded-up piece of paper in her pocket.

I get out of my car as well, and walk toward her, aware that Karen Pearce is watching from the edge of my peripheral vision.

"Ms. Ross." She passes me the paper. "We have a warrant to search the premises."

29

"Can you open the door for us, please?"

I nod and walk up the walkway. I open the front door. She holds out her hand. "And we'll need the keys to your car, too."

"What? I need my car. I need to go somewhere today."

"You're not going anywhere in this car." Detective Lopez flicks her eyes at the paper in my hand. "That warrant gives us the right to search your house, your garage, and your car." She holds out her hand. "And your cell phone."

I take it out. "Can I call my husband first?"

Lopez scowls. "Make it quick."

The call goes straight to voice mail. I try his office as well, but no luck. With D.C. traffic, he may not even be in yet. "Call me back as soon as you get this," I whisper into the phone. Before shutting it off and handing it over, I turn my back and make another call.

"Mr. Zucker?" I say into the voice mail, praying that he's the type who checks his messages compulsively. "This is Allie Ross. We're supposed to meet this evening. But I need your help. The police are at my house."

"I've called my lawyer," I say before giving Lopez my phone.

"That's within your rights." She hands the phone over to a squat, uniformed officer behind her. I watch as he jogs off with my phone, wondering what he plans to do with it.

"Don't you have to wait for my lawyer before you do the search?" I ask.

"No, ma'am, we do not."

"How long is all this supposed to take?"

The detective shrugs. "We'll get your cell phone back to you within the hour. As for the search, can't say."

"Can you estimate? I'm supposed to be at my mother's assisted living facility right now."

"Ma'am, I appreciate this is stressful for you. You have the choice to leave or to remain on the property, but you may not interfere with the search." She nods toward a young woman standing nearby in uniform. "Officer Michaelson?"

The woman takes a tiny step up the walkway toward me, her hands hooked in her pockets, her hips laden with a radio and a gun.

I walk past her and back to the curb. It's a beautiful autumn day, with crisp air and cloudless blue skies. A duo of young mothers with jogging strollers whizzes through the intersection toward the park. It's suburban bliss, but I am in my own personal hell. At the far end of the block, I can see a small group of dog walkers who have collected in the middle of the road and are staring in my direction. I can't blame them. This is the most exciting thing that's happened here since, well, since Rob Avery was murdered.

I shiver. The reality of it is closing in. A man was murdered, and the police think that I am involved. Even having a lawyer isn't going to stop them from going through my house, my personal things.

If there was a tiny part of me that thought this was all a sick prank, the truth is glaringly obvious: I am in deep trouble. I realize that if Artie Zucker does call back, I don't even have my phone on me. Like a swimmer far from shore, I cannot let myself panic, lest I go under and don't come up. A lump forms in my throat, making it all but impossible to swallow. I won't cry. Not in the street, not in front of my neighbors.

I watch as several uniformed officers and Detective Katz march into my house after Detective Lopez. What could they possibly find in my house? The first thing that pops into my head is whether the house is neat enough. Did I make the bed? Do

I have clothes, underwear, bras lying around? What about the dishes? I shake away those petty concerns and open the warrant. It looks like a standard form that has been filled in with my name and address and today's date. The middle section has space to write in the basis for the search. Someone has typed *Evidence relevant to the commission of an act of murder in violation of Maryland Criminal Law Code 2–201.*

The words swim before me. I sink down onto the curb and put my head between my knees. I stare at my feet, unsure of my next move.

Soon a pair of scuffed-up, black Converse high-tops moves into my field of vision. Shielding my eyes from the autumn sun, I look up to see Dustin looming above me.

"Do you want me to call my mom?" he asks.

"Isn't she at the doctor's?" I ask. He frowns, confused. "No, don't bother your mom. Shouldn't you be at school?"

He shrugs. "I don't have first period."

I nod as if I believe this. I have too much going on to parent someone else's child right now.

"I got arrested once," Dustin says. "It was pretty scary."

"I bet." I stand up, uncomfortable seated while Dustin hovers above me. For a few moments, we stand in an embarrassing silence, and it occurs to me that the way this neighborhood works, loads of people must already know the police are at my house, and the only person who has come by to offer support is my socially awkward teenage neighbor.

"Can I borrow your cell phone?" I ask. Dustin types in his password and hands it to me. I try Mark's numbers, but like before, there's no answer. I turn my back to Dustin to leave a message. "Mark, you need to call me as soon as you get this. Or come home. The police are searching the house."

I use Dustin's phone to search for Artie Zucker's office number. When his voice mail picks up, I leave another message even more frantic than the last. "Please call me, or just come to my house now."

"Police have your phone?" Dustin asks when I hand his back.

"Yeah."

"They can get all your data, deleted pictures, locations, everything, in a matter of minutes now."

"You know a lot about this stuff, don't you?"

He gives me a half grin. "Yeah. You know, if someone messes with you online, in that many different places, there's going to be crumbs left behind."

"Crumbs?" Despite myself, I am intrigued. "Like digital fingerprints?"

Dustin frowns. "Bad analogy. It's not unique to a person, but there'll be enough little traces that it'll all add up to something."

I toy with whether to tell him about the fake Facebook and Tinder pages.

"The question is," he says, "are they doing this remotely? I mean, how did they put the Tinder app on your phone?"

I feel the blood rush to my face. "How do you know about that?"

"I dunno." He shrugs. "Maybe I heard my mom talking about it? Anyway, if you change your mind about wanting help . . ."

"Thanks, Dustin, but I'm just trying to get through this." I wave my hand toward my house. What I need is a good lawyer, not a computer hacker.

A white Lexus screeches to a halt on the corner, and Daisy climbs out and jogs over to me.

"Oh, Allie! Are you okay?" She doesn't wait for an answer but wraps her arms around me and hugs.

"How did you know?" I ask, pulling back.

She rolls her eyes. "It's all over the Eastbrook Facebook page. There are even photos."

I swivel my head around. Photos? I didn't see anybody taking pictures. I realize Karen Pearce is gone. She was here when the police pulled up.

"Do you know who posted them?" I ask.

She frowns. "Didn't check. Just hopped in my car and came right over." She looks over at Dustin. "Dustin, what are you doing here? Don't you have school or something?"

He shrugs and gives me a quick glance before fixing his eyes on the ground.

"You should go," Daisy tells him, a stern note in her voice that I've never heard her use before.

We watch him amble back across the street, and Daisy shudders. "I know I shouldn't say this, but he gives me the creeps."

"I think underneath it all, he's a good kid," I say. "Adolescence is hard."

"Where's Mark?"

"Work. I tried calling him, but he's not picking up."

"And Cole's at school?"

I nod.

"You poor thing," she says. "Any idea what the police are looking for?"

"None. This whole thing is a total shock to me."

We turn and stare at the house. The door opens, and a uniformed officer steps out carrying our home computer. It sends a chill through me, although I can't put my finger on exactly why. I know in my heart I had nothing to do with Rob Avery's murder, and they can't possibly find something on there that doesn't exist. But what if my Google searches get misconstrued? Or even worse, what if someone else put something on there that implicates me, like the Tinder app on my phone? Leah and Dustin had both told me that files and apps could be installed remotely. Maybe that happened with my computer. I take a step forward.

"Hey, that's our computer." As soon as the words leave my mouth, I realize it's a stupid thing to say. At the same time, the female officer watching me takes a step in my direction as if she's going to physically stop me from moving forward. She holds her hand up like a traffic cop.

"Everything removed from the house will be accounted for."

"I just feel like I should be there when you look at it, to explain stuff."

"If the detectives need your assistance, they'll ask for it."

"But they won't know." I turn to Daisy. "They won't know what's real and what was put on there by someone else."

Daisy narrows her eyes, clearly confused. "Allie? You're not making sense."

"Someone remotely installed the Tinder app on my phone. I didn't do it, but it's there, and I'm worried whoever did that put something on my computer, too."

"Okay, okay, calm down." She rubs my arm. "It's going to be all right. Do you have a lawyer?"

"Sort of. I called and left messages, but I can't reach him. I don't know what to do. This is insane. They're taking my things! Can they just do this?" I sound hysterical, even to my own ears. I take a deep breath. Losing it on the street is not going to help. I glance down at the end of the block. What had been a few people has grown into a wall of onlookers. Daisy follows my gaze. "Ugh, why don't they go home? I'm just glad Cole isn't here to see this. He's been kind of anxious lately, and this would freak him out."

"C'mon," she says. "Let's go sit in my car."

I feel a bit better once we are safely ensconced in the warming leather seats of her car. Daisy taps on her phone, and soon dreamy synth music fills the car.

"This is my Spotify Chill Out playlist," she says. "I use this to lower my blood pressure when my stepdaughter, or a client, is driving me crazy."

She asks me how the sale of the house in Westport is going and whether Barb DeSoto has been helpful. I answer her questions curtly. I know she is just trying to help by taking my mind off what is happening, but I can't concentrate on anything other than the fact that the police are swarming my house. "I just wish I knew what they were looking for."

"I know I shouldn't be surprised," Daisy says, tapping at her phone, "but I can't believe how quickly this got on the Facebook page. And with photos." She tilts the small screen toward me. "Looks like it was Heather. She posts, *Does anyone know what's going on with the police on our block?*"

"I can't believe she did that. I mean, I was right there. Why didn't she just ask me?"

Daisy shrugs. "Probably didn't want to bother you."

I look out the window. I think of the picture Heather took at the pool, the one from the same angle as my fake Tinder profile shot. And the picture of her with that woman wearing an Overton shirt. Lots of strange little coincidences, but what could Heather, the woman who organizes trash-free lunch at Cole's school, possibly have to do with Overton? When I turn back to mention this to Daisy, to see what she thinks, I see an officer wearing mirrored sunglasses striding to the car, his face in a tight grimace.

"Showtime," Daisy says.

We follow him, a short bulldog of a man, back to the front of my house, where he hands me my cell phone. "We're about done here, ma'am. Just some paperwork." As he scribbles on a stack of papers on a clipboard, I check my phone. Two missed calls from Morningside House and one from Artie Zucker. Just seeing his name floods me with relief.

But that relief is short-lived. When I look up, I see an officer leaving the house carrying a small brown box, the kind Amazon leaves on neighborhood doorsteps every day.

"What's that box?" I ask the officer.

"The list of items seized is right here, ma'am." He taps his finger on one of the papers he just handed me.

I look at the list, which is not long. The third item is: *Brown cardboard box containing liquid Ambien.*

30

Twenty minutes after the police leave, I am driving around Chevy Chase Circle, on the phone with Artie Zucker.

"As soon as we hang up, I'm going to make some phone calls and find out exactly what's going on," he says in a booming voice. "By the time I come by your place this evening, I should have more information."

"I don't feel good about this."

"Of course you don't! Why would you? I'll see you tonight." With that, he hangs up. I appreciate his candor, at least. He's not telling me this is a prank or the police are just doing their jobs. He's taking it seriously.

I drive in silence for a few minutes. The shock of seeing the police on my front lawn and then inside my house has worn off a bit, and now I am plain terrified.

As I merge onto the Beltway to head toward my mother's facility, Mark finally calls me back. As soon as he answers, I blurt out what happened—starting with the police showing up and ending with a recap of my call with the lawyer. "Artie Zucker will be at our house by six."

"I know." His tone is curt.

"Fine. Just reminding you."

We agree to be back at the house by four to get ready for Artie.

I hang up and focus on the drive, a bit unsettled by Mark's abruptness. I have my phone and car back, as well as paperwork on the seat beside me detailing exactly what they took from the house—including our computer. How am I going to pay bills or check email? I do everything online. It's then that I realize they did not take my laptop. It was sitting in my tote the whole time, and the police never asked about it. I feel a bit of relief, but also a slight sense of having gotten away with something. Surely, they would have confiscated my laptop if it had been in the house.

Thank god for small things. All my work stuff is on my laptop. I don't know how I would have explained to Mike that I couldn't edit my photos.

When I glance at myself in the mirror, I see a wild-eyed, red-faced woman. I can't help but imagine the conversations that are taking place in the neighborhood about me. I try to relax and focus on staying under the absurdly low thirty-miles-an-hour speed limit on Connecticut Avenue. The last thing I need is a speeding ticket.

As I pass the Chevy Chase fire station, my phone pings with a text from Barb DeSoto in Westport: *We have a major problem. Call me ASAP.*

The words send another wave of shock through my all-too-sensitive system. Everything that can go wrong is. A car blares at me as I yank the wheel to the right and pull into the parking lot of a library.

"What kind of problem?" I ask Barb, who answers my call right away.

"I've stopped by the house, and there's no good way to say this, but putting it on the market now would be a disaster."

"Why?"

"Let me ask you, Allie," Barb says in a patient tone. "When was the last time you visited the place?"

"About a year and a half ago. My sister is the one who keeps an eye on it." Only one other car sits in the lot, a weathered gold Chrysler LeBaron, which triggers a memory of my father. In one of the few photos I have of him, he stands proudly in front of a similar sedan, the kind of wide, gas-guzzling dinosaur you never see on the roads anymore.

"Well, she hasn't been," Barb says, her voice sharp.

"I know, it needs a new roof and a new septic tank."

"That's not all it needs. The paint is peeling, the gutters are literally sagging, and that's just the outside. Inside, you have a serious mouse problem, and the banister is loose to the point of being dangerous." I can picture Barb ticking these problems off on her French-manicured fingers. I've never seen Barb's fingers, of course. What I do know of her I have gleaned from her website, but her glistening, white smile and shellacked blond bob suggest to me that Barb sports a flawless French manicure. "And don't get me started on that kitchen. I estimate there's at least fifty, if not seventy-five thousand dollars' worth of work to do on that house before you put it on the market. Of course, you could sell it as is, but that's a tough sell. At least there are no tenants—that always complicates a sale—but still, in the condition it's in, you may not even break even."

"Break even? What are you talking about? That house is worth at least a million."

"But the mortgage is almost eight hundred thousand."

"No, that's not right. My mother inherited that house sixteen years ago. There's no mortgage."

"I'm looking at the paperwork right here," Barb says. "Sharon Healy took out a jumbo reverse mortgage on the property. She's pulled almost eight hundred thousand dollars out of the house."

I shake my head in disbelief, even though I know she can't see me. "My mother is incompetent. She's been in an assisted living facility for years. I'm my mother's power of attorney, and I did not approve any mortgage."

"Well, if all that's true, we very well may be looking at fraud." Barb sighs. "I think you ought to contact the Westport police."

Some kind of event must be taking place at Morningside House, because when I arrive, the main lot is full, and I have to pull around to the side lot. I shoot off a text to Daisy: *What the hell is a reverse mortgage???*

Tension grips my neck as I walk to the front of the building, and I can feel my shoulders inching closer to my ears. The last thing I want to do right now is call the Westport police. Everything is going wrong at once. I pull my coat tight against a gust of wind that is whipping particles of dirt into my eyes.

Inside the facility, it looks like the Halloween section of a crafts store exploded. Glittering paper pumpkins hang from a garland that stretches the length of the large lobby. Gangly scarecrows sit atop bales of straw that flank the faux fireplace. The room even smells like fall, a cloying combination of pumpkin spice and candy corn, but it cannot completely mask the acrid odor of ammonia.

"Are you here for the apple bobbing?" the woman at the front—Desiree, according to her name tag—asks as I sign in.

"No. I'm here to see Lydia."

Desiree picks up a phone. I wonder how she's going to dial with such long nails, painted orange and overlaid with tiny black spiderwebs, but she uses a pencil. "Miss Lydia? Someone is here to see you."

Everyone is a *Miss* at Morningside, like at a preschool. After she hangs up, she passes an orange flyer to me that outlines the many Halloween activities coming up. I see pumpkin carving is scheduled for tomorrow.

"Pumpkin carving? Is it a good idea to give knives to these people?" I gesture behind me at the slack-jawed men and women.

My attempt at humor is lost on the receptionist. "Most of our residents prefer to use Sharpies to decorate pumpkins. You should come back with your kids! This is a multigenerational experience."

Lydia arrives and ushers me to the back offices. Round-shouldered and short, she seems to roll rather than walk. Her voluminous skirt may well be hiding wheels.

"Miss Sharon is very spirited, but you probably don't need me to tell you that. She's small, but boy, when she gets hold of an idea, there's no stopping her." Her melodious voice soothes me, a skill that must come in handy when dealing with irascible seniors.

I follow Lydia into a small, cluttered office. She glides behind a metal desk overflowing with stacks of paper and motions for me to move a pile of magazines off the one other chair in the room.

"Unfortunately, Miss Sharon assaulted one of my staff members." Lydia's nose twitches, making the freckles on her brown skin dance.

"What happened, exactly?"

"Your mother must have decided she wanted to go for a stroll after dinner last night. She must have gone into her room, opened a window, and kicked out the screen. My staff found her halfway out the window. When they tried to pull her back in, she choked one of them. Had to be pried off."

You could never accuse my mother of lacking moxie—or piss and vinegar, as she called it—but this doesn't sound like her. "Why was she trying to escape? She's never tried anything like this before."

"She was having delusions of persecution. She said someone was out to get her and had tracked her down. That she needed to escape."

"Did she have an altercation with another resident or an argument with a staff member?"

"We don't think that's it. Unfortunately, with dementia, a move into a new facility can precipitate this kind of degeneration." Lydia interlaces her long fingers together in front of her face. "We understand it can be difficult to watch a loved one's personality change so dramatically."

I shake my head. I know what Lydia is saying is true, but I can't bear the thought that my moving Sharon down here may have triggered all this.

"The reality is that we can no longer keep her in assisted living," Lydia says. "It's time for the memory ward."

Lydia explains what this means and produces paperwork that has already been filled out. She's been through this enough times to know that the families sitting where I am have little choice. I look over the papers with a pang of sadness. I wish Mark were with me. He's the one who's good at reading this kind of fine print, not me. The cost is more than what I am paying now and almost double what I was paying for her assisted living facility up in Connecticut.

Maybe Krystle is right. Maybe I should find a cheaper place.

"I know this is a hard decision," Lydia says, offering me a bowl of candy corn, as if sugar will distract me from the hefty cost of this place.

I demur. "It's a lot of money."

"I understand. You can cancel the contract at any time, as long as you give us thirty days' notice."

I pick up the pen and hesitate. Staying at Morningside House will be expensive. But a move to another facility would destroy my mom. I sign. I'll sell her house. I'll find the money.

After we're done, Lydia takes me down a hallway I have never been before, pausing in front of a keypad.

"Your mom's been here since breakfast, in the community room. We don't have a free room on the memory ward yet, so we won't be able to move her and her belongings until the end of the month. But we'll be taking her in here right after breakfast up until bedtime from now on." I nod. My mother will be on lockdown for her waking hours. Lydia punches the keypad. "We'll give you the code. We change it weekly, because otherwise the residents might learn it and try to leave."

The doors swing open to reveal a sitting room with a large-screen TV. Several women and one man sit slumped in front of a home-shopping show hawking cubic zirconia earrings. I see Sharon lying in a fetal position at one end of the sofa, and a wave of nausea hits me. She was always so tough. Now she looks helpless.

I touch her shoulder, and she lifts her head, her big, green eyes brightening.

"Alexis. I'm so happy to see you." She holds out her hands, and I take them. I can feel her tiny, birdlike bones beneath her cool, papery skin. She's lost so much weight since she had to move to D.C. that it's aged her prematurely. I want to let go, but I don't. I text Mike that I won't be in today and then sit beside her, not speaking, as we watch a bronzed blond woman model a pair of fake diamond earrings the size of ice cubes.

After a while, when I am sure she is dozing, I start to get up. But her hand clamps down on mine, and her eyes open. "She found me," she says in a barely audible voice.

"Who?"

"That woman." Sharon's lower lip trembles, whether with anger or fear I cannot tell. "She came to the house, wanted me to interfere. But I can't control Krystle, that's what I told her."

"Well, that's the truth." I pat her hand. She's time-traveling again. She moved out of the Westport house more than five years ago.

"I told her, if you're looking for someone to blame your problems on, don't blame my daughter. That's what I said. I told her, you made your own bed."

"Uh-huh. That sounds very wise, Sharon." I have no idea what she's referring to, but it isn't too hard to fill in the gaps. Krystle spent her twenties lurching from drama to drama, and I'm not surprised to hear there was blowback that reached all the way up to Westport, Connecticut. "Hopefully, that lady won't come back."

"Oh, but she did." Sharon's eyes dart from side to side. "Yesterday. She pretended she was in the wrong room. I played along. Kept my eyes closed like I was sleeping."

I frown. "Sharon, are you saying some strange woman came into your room yesterday when you were resting?"

She nods very slowly. "She's found me, Alexis. Margaret Cooper. She's back."

On my way outside, I ask the receptionist if my mother had any visitors yesterday. I doubt it, but I want to double-check. The receptionist, who is on the phone, pushes the visitor log at me. I scan the names on the two pages for yesterday, looking for this Margaret Cooper that my mother mentioned, but there is none. In fact, no one signed in to see my mother. I feel a little silly. Margaret Cooper is as likely to be a soap opera character from the eighties as a real person my mother once knew.

"Thank you," I say, pushing the book back. But as I walk through the front door, a woman carrying a small fern passes me and smiles. I hesitate and watch her walk right through the lobby and turn left without signing in.

The receptionist takes no notice.

I shake the thought from my head. My mother suffers from delusions. I need to accept that. I'm viewing her dementia through the lens of my own personal problems.

But I make a mental note to mention it to Krystle when I discuss the dismal state of the Westport house and what I have learned about there being a reverse mortgage. I am not looking forward to that conversation.

I get in my car, exhausted from the day's events. All I want to do is crawl home and get into a hot bath with a glass of wine, and then curl up all by myself and watch something dumb. But going home means facing reality—judgmental moms, an angry husband, and a needy kid. Not to mention meeting with that shark of a lawyer and going over this whole nightmare in detail. So much for self-care; tonight will be about self-preservation.

Trying to exit the parking lot, I get stuck waiting for a break in traffic. Finally I can pull out and turn left, shooting a quick glance behind me to see if I am holding anyone up.

That's when I see it.

Idling by the curb is that black Audi with Virginia plates, FCS.

31

I'm halfway into oncoming traffic. It's too late to stop and back up, so I pull into the left lane so that I can make a U-turn and drive back into the Morningside House parking lot.

I feel dizzy and hot. It's the same car, I am sure. In addition to the *F* and the *C* and the *S*, I can now add the last three digits—372.

I hold my breath, waiting for the car in front of me to make a left, doing everything in my power not to lay on the horn. Finally, I am zooming back in the direction I came from. It probably takes less than a minute, but when I get back to the parking lot, the Audi is gone.

My whole body shakes as I merge onto the Beltway and head back to Bethesda. There is no doubt in my mind—someone is following me, but who, and why?

The shrill ring of my phone vibrates through the car, startling me out of my thoughts. It's Daisy.

"Hey, sweetie, how are you holding up? What do you need to know?" Her disembodied voice bounces through the interior of the car. It takes a second to remember she is returning my call. The text I sent her about the reverse mortgage earlier today seems so long ago. I explain what Barb DeSoto told me.

"Walk me through this," I say. "Please."

"A reverse mortgage was designed so people who have tons of equity in their house can pull some money out and stay in the house," Daisy says. "Like senior citizens. Let's say your house is worth five hundred thousand—you can pull out three hundred thousand and use that money to pay for living expenses or a grandchild's tuition, or whatever."

"It's like a home equity line of credit?"

"Not exactly. You don't make monthly payments. Instead, when the owner dies, or when the house is sold, you pay back the lender. In the case of a senior who takes out three hundred thousand, when they die and their heirs sell the house, the heirs will need to pay back the lenders that money. With interest, of course."

"There's no way my mother took out that loan. She's been in assisted living for years."

"Sad to say that there is rampant fraud and identity theft these days. Anyone who has your mom's basic information—social security number, date of birth—would have been able to apply in her name. Any strange financial letters or weird phone calls?"

"My sister handles all the correspondence to the house," I tell her before saying goodbye. The whole drive home, I am stewing in a hot mix of guilt and anger. I should never have left Krystle in charge of the management of the house. She was in over her head. This is as much my fault as hers.

I'm only a few miles from my house when my phone trills. I don't recognize the number, so I let it go through to voice mail, and a moment later, my phone beeps letting me know whoever called has left a message.

"Hi, Alexis? This is Madeline. I just saw your email. I'd be happy to meet up with you. I'm actually around this weekend. Call or text me."

I immediately text her back and ask if she can meet me on Sunday. I wish I could do it sooner, but my Saturday is booked with shoots.

Madeline Ashford, the Madeline who destroyed my senior year and now runs the D.C.-area Overton alumni group. The woman who may be behind everything that is happening to me.

A rush of adrenaline courses through me. Maybe I can finally get some answers and put a stop to all this.

32

The smell of roast chicken hits me when I enter the kitchen. On the counter sits the telltale take-out bag from Nando's. When I see the yucca fries inside the bag, I smile. I always have to lobby hard for those as a side, since neither Mark nor Cole likes them.

"Hello?" I call out. "I'm home."

"Mommy!" Cole runs in from the direction of the powder room, holding out his hands. "I washed my hands. Smell them."

I bend down and take a deep breath of the floral soap.

Mark follows suit, smiling. "He's hopped up on sugar. Apparently, Leah let them have two boxes of candy at the movies."

"The movies, so that's where you were all day," I say, forcing his squirming body into a hug. "I was wondering."

"Just one box each," Cole says. "But we switched halfway through."

We eat a quick dinner at the island in the kitchen, all in a row, under the bright lights suspended from the ceiling. I keep eyeing the clock, cognizant that the lawyer will be arriving at six. Cole carries eighty percent of the conversation, reenacting each scene from the movie for us. Mark laughs and makes funny faces. I can see our reflection in the large plate-glass window across from us. To my eyes, or to anyone who might happen to be walking through the pedestrian alley that cuts behind our house, it would appear to be a scene of domestic bliss.

It's hard to enjoy the merry mood, however, knowing what's to come after—a meeting with a criminal defense lawyer. The desktop in our nook is glaringly clear, our computer gone. Cole has not noticed yet, thank god.

As we are cleaning up, Krystle calls. I leave Mark and Cole to finish with the kitchen.

"What's this reverse mortgage thing?" Krystle's words hit me rapid-fire. No *hello*, or *how are you*. "I didn't understand your message."

As I walk into the dining room, I begin to explain what has happened, but Krystle interrupts me right away.

"There's no money? I need that money, Allie. We're counting on it."

I ignore the *we*. I assume she means Ron, but I don't want to get into a fight about her boyfriend right now. "Do you remember any weird mail that might have come to the house in Westport?"

"Oh, so this is my fault? For not checking the mail enough? Good to know, *Madame*."

My body tightens. Her fuse has been lit, and it's just a matter of time until she explodes. "That's not what I'm saying. I'm just asking if you remember anything out of the ordinary." The truth is, a part of me wonders if Krystle found a way to get the reverse mortgage, but I don't want to believe it, and I certainly don't want to accuse her without proof.

"Seriously? That house gets a ton of junk mail. I'm supposed to sort through every piece of trash that comes there?"

"So that's a no." I circle the dining room table, picking up the detritus that Cole leaves in his wake. I can't imagine what the police thought when they walked through here this afternoon.

"Don't be mean. I know you think this is my fault. Just say it."

She's goading me into a fight, a habit she honed with our mother. I used to shrink into the shadows watching the two of them go at it like two fires feeding off each other. Their faces would glisten red, not just with anger but with excitement.

Normally, I am better at steering Krystle away from her rages. But I don't have the energy tonight, not right before I'm about to meet with a criminal defense lawyer.

"I'm not accusing you of anything," I say. "Look, Krys, we don't even know what happened. Is there any possibility that you might have signed something accidentally?"

"What kind of idiot do you think I am?" she screams.

I blink hard at her ferocity and plow forward. Mark and Cole pass through the dining room and head upstairs, the dinner dishes done, the kitchen lights shut off. They wave at me as they leave the room.

Mark is going to put Cole in front of the TV with a movie and then come back down to meet with the lawyer. I'm not happy about how much we've been using screens to distract Cole from what's been going on recently—our strict rules have been bent so far they've completely broken in the past week. But I don't feel like we have a choice. I'd rather him get lost in screens than learn his mother is being framed for murder.

"What about Ron?" I ask Krystle. "I know he's had money troubles."

"That's not true." I can picture her mouth pressed into a straight line as she says this, jaw locked.

"This is the same guy who pawned his blood glucose monitor."

"That was two years ago. He bought it back. God, I wish I'd never told you that. You can be such a judgmental cunt sometimes."

And just like that, I am done. I hang up and put the phone on vibrate.

With his shirt sleeves rolled up, Artie Zucker leans his elbows on our seldom-used dining room table and lets out a deep sigh.

"I don't like this, I'm gonna be honest."

Mark and I exchange a glance. Zucker, pushing sixty, is sweat-stained, has about two days' worth of growth on his face, and smells like day-old pizza. But Mark says he is one of the three best criminal defense lawyers in Montgomery County, so here he is in our dining room trying to help me understand why the police have focused their attention on me and what we're going to do about it.

Mark and I spent the better part of the last hour explaining in excruciating detail what happened at the party on Saturday night with Rob and me, and everything since, including the fake Tinder and Facebook pages.

"So tell me again," Artie says, "about talking to Avery in the kitchen. Can you characterize your conversation?"

"I would say it was flirtatious. We were having fun—"

"So now you admit that you were flirting with Rob Avery?" Mark snaps.

I turn to him, blindsided by his accusatory tone. "It was a party. Besides, he was doing most of the flirting."

"No, that's fine," he says, leaning back in his chair. "But your first story was that this random drunk guy followed you into the bathroom. And you had no idea why."

"My story?"

"Yes, your story." He is in full lawyer mode now, voice clipped and emotionless. "It's changed a bit, you have to admit."

"You found me out, Mark. I slightly flirted with a stranger at a suburban party." I reach for the bottle of wine to refill my glass. "Any takers?" I ask. But both men say no. I don't know how Mark can make it through this ordeal sober, but I need the gentle buzz of wine to help stop me from falling apart.

"I just find it curious that you left out that little detail until now," Mark says, his eyes trained on me.

"All right, kids. That's enough of that." Zucker picks up his pen and scribbles something on the yellow legal pad, something I can't read from my vantage point across the table. "We've established that Allie flirted a little. Can we move on? Let's talk Ambien. You have no idea where that liquid Ambien came from?"

I shake my head. "Neither Mark nor I ordered it."

"Could someone else have left it here? Or had it delivered here?" Zucker asks. "Without telling you?"

Mark grunts. "And how exactly would that work?"

Zucker leans back in his chair, twirling a well-chewed pen between his fingers. "You tell me. A relative?"

"Caitlin has a key," I say.

"You think my sister left a bottle of liquid Ambien in our house?"

"Any neighbors have a spare key?" Zucker asks.

"Half the neighborhood has a spare key to our house," I say.

"Well, let's make a list," Zucker says. "Mark, call your sister, find out if she left it here or had it delivered here."

"I can tell you now she didn't."

"Great," Zucker says. "Then we can cross her off. Do it in the other room, will ya?"

Mark gets up to make the phone call in the kitchen. While he's gone, Zucker turns to me. "Allie, were you having an affair with Rob Avery?"

The question stuns me. "No, of course not."

Zucker's eyes dart toward the kitchen. "I can't defend you if I don't know the truth."

"It is the truth. I met Rob Avery for the first time Saturday night. I swear to God."

He bites the end of his pen. "Fine. Question asked and answered."

"But there is someone from my past. An ex-boyfriend."

Zucker pushes the legal pad at me. "Write down his name. I'll look into it."

I write *Paul Adamson* on the pad and push it back across the table just as Mark comes back in and sits down. "My sister did not bring any liquid Ambien into our house. Or have it delivered here."

Zucker draws a line through her name on his legal pad. "That just leaves everyone with a spare key. Start naming them."

"Susan, our babysitter."

"Susan what?"

"Susan Doyle. Our neighbor Heather Grady. Our other neighbor Leah Rosenblum." I look at Mark. "Anyone else?"

He shakes his head. "I think that's it. But we didn't change the locks when we moved in this fall. Anyone who had keys to the house before would still be able to get in."

"Good, that's good."

"That's good?" Mark asks.

Zucker smiles. "Sure. Lots of possibilities of how this box ended up in your house."

"Why are we so focused on the liquid Ambien?" Mark asks.

"We're focused on liquid Ambien because the Montgomery County police are focused on the liquid Ambien. And until further notice, that's all we've got to go on. I've put in a call to this, uh"—he squints at his pad—"Detective Lopez. Just to let her know you've hired a lawyer. In my experience, the police are less than extremely forthcoming at this point in an investigation, but who knows. Maybe we'll get lucky and she'll call me back to let me know just what the hell is going on. Mark, you could be in trouble, too."

"Me?" Mark scoffs.

"You were out that morning," I say. I'm emboldened by the wine. "Getting the car from Daisy's house? Remember?"

"They can't think I had anything to do with Rob Avery's death."

I shrug. I don't think he did. But I'm enjoying watching him squirm. Getting a taste of what I've been dealing with.

"Well, we need to be ready, because I'm going to be honest,

this search warrant"—Zucker pauses to hold up the paper that the detective gave me earlier—"does not bode well. Not at all."

Although it is almost ten o'clock when the lawyer leaves, we find Cole wide awake on our bed, still watching TV.

I walk through to the bathroom, momentarily obstructing the screen as I go.

"Move!" Cole yells. "I can't see!"

I shut the bathroom door to muffle the sound of television chatter mingled with my son's laughter. My mind is saturated and exhausted from the day's events. The police search, my mother's deepening paranoia, the reverse mortgage, tonight's meeting with Artie Zucker. Even if I checked myself into the Four Seasons in Georgetown for a whole week, I don't think it would be enough time to process it all.

"Everything all right?" Mark comes into the bathroom and shuts the door behind him. "You've been in here a while."

"Just lost in thought." I rub makeup remover on my face a little too roughly. I'm worked up.

"I think it went pretty well," Mark says, leaning against the shower door. "I mean, as well as can be expected. He may not be the most polished guy, but he's super connected to law enforcement in Montgomery County, and I think he'll be a real asset in sorting all this out."

"Umm, I should hope so."

"Listen, about the flirting thing. I shouldn't have said that."

I look at him in the mirror, waiting to see if there's more to this anemic apology. But he doesn't add anything else. I know I should tell him about Paul Adamson. I've told the lawyer. I've told Leah. So why can't I tell my own husband? Because I'm afraid of his reaction, I realize, and I'm kind of pissed at him. He can barely handle that I flirted a little at a party. What would he say if he knew that I had slept with my teacher, my married teacher, in high school? I decide to let the tiniest drip of truth out. A test.

"There's this guy, kind of an ex, from high school?" I turn around to face him. "I think there's a chance he may be involved."

"Why do you think that?" Mark crosses his arms over his chest.

Not a good sign. But I plow ahead. "The Overton T-shirt—"

"Which you ordered."

"I didn't order it, Mark."

"I found the box, Allie."

"You know what? Forget it." I turn back to the mirror and open the medicine cabinet, slamming around expensive little glass bottles with satisfaction.

"Do you know you drank more than half a bottle of wine tonight?"

I spin around. "And? The police searched our house, Mark. I think if there was ever a time to drink, tonight was the night."

"I think you have a problem, Allie. A drinking problem."

"Is that right?" I stomp over to the shower and turn the water on. "I'd like to take a shower now. Please leave."

He stares at me, working his jaw.

I usually try so hard to keep him happy, to make peace, but tonight I just don't have it in me. "Now."

"This is why I think we ought to talk about the place Caitlin mentioned. The one outside Baltimore."

I let out a bitter laugh. "Oh, your rehab-that's-not-really-a-rehab? No thank you." I open the door and gesture for him to leave. He walks through, and I slam it shut.

A twinge of sadness runs through me, but only a twinge.

Mostly I am filled with anger.

33

Saturdays are often workdays for photographers, and despite what is going on in my personal life, I can't afford Mike thinking I'm not up to the job. I'm still on probation, after all.

I spend the day with back-to-back shoots—the first at Dumbarton Oaks, a historic estate in Georgetown—and the second on the cobbled pathways along the C&O Canal. By the time I am finished and get home, it's dark. Mark is parked in front of the TV watching the Nationals, studiously ignoring me, and Cole's glued to some animated film.

I don't disturb either of them. I am exhausted, mentally and physically. I don't have the energy to fight with Mark or the patience to nurture Cole tonight. I scrounge dinner—yogurt and a banana—take a quick shower, and fall asleep.

The next morning, I wake with a confirmation text from Madeline that she can meet me. Mark begrudgingly agrees to "watch Cole" even though I hate the way he says it. As if I am the default parent and he is doing me a favor by hanging out with his own kid.

I leave them still in their pajamas and, following the prompts from my phone, drive toward the coffee shop in Alexandria that Madeline suggested. Normally, on a Sunday morning, I would be driving up to meet Sharon. But I was just there on Friday, so I'm letting myself off the hook.

As I cross the Potomac into Virginia, I think of when we first told Mark's family we were moving back to D.C. Caitlin and her husband suggested we look for a house in Northern Virginia, and we acted like we might consider it. But in private, we agreed that putting a river between me and his sister was not such a bad idea.

I smile at the memory. It was only a few months ago, but it seems like ages. I thought adjusting to a new neighborhood and making new friends were problems. Now I wish that were all I was dealing with.

Soon my car is bumping along the cobbled streets of Old Town Alexandria. This is my first time here, and under other circumstances, I would allow myself to enjoy the quaint old buildings that now house shops and restaurants. Instead, I am walking briskly along a brick sidewalk buckling with age, looking for Compass Coffee. The shop is part of a local chain founded by two former Marines. There's one about a mile from my house, and just spotting the familiar orange-and-blue logo feels reassuring.

I order an espresso at the front counter, and once it is in my hand, I start toward the back, looking for a lone woman about my age. In the back corner, sitting at a table below a shelf of board games, is a woman in a navy fleece and mom jeans, staring intently at her phone—Madeline.

Gone is the severe blunt cut from high school that stopped at her chin and took hours of straightening each morning. She's wearing her dark hair naturally, cut short. But her square jaw and large, intense dark eyes are unmistakable.

I stare, fascinated by the ways she has changed and the ways in which she has not. It's silly. It's been sixteen years. Did I expect she would still have the same hairstyle and those plastic tortoiseshell glasses?

I approach with a smile that I hope is friendly, though it feels artificial. "Madeline?" I ask. "Madeline Ashford?"

She looks up from her phone, concern evident in the deep grooves between her eyebrows. "It's Ashford-Brown, actually."

She motions toward the empty chair like a prospective employer to an applicant. "Please sit."

I put my coffee down and take a seat, my nervousness at our reunion strangling me like a too-tight turtleneck.

"Alexis Healy," she says, cocking her head to one side. This close, I can see tiny lines around her eyes, proof of all the living she's done over the years. Do I look older to her, as well? "It's been what, sixteen years?"

"That sounds right." I am struggling to reconcile this composed woman with the high-strung teenager that I once knew. I decide to get straight to the point. "This is a weird question, but did you send me an Overton T-shirt?"

She blinks twice, taken aback. "No."

"One showed up at my house, and I didn't order it. I can't figure out who might have sent it. Then I heard you were the alumni coordinator, and I thought . . . Well, I don't know what I thought."

Madeline's mouth twists into a perfunctory smile. "I'm afraid my duties as coordinator are limited to updating the local chapter's email list and organizing the occasional happy hour."

"You must have been surprised to hear from me," I say.

A small smile passes over her thin, lipstick-free lips. "Not really, if I'm being honest. I fully expected that, at some point, you might reach out to me. In fact, I've thought of reaching out to you many times over the years."

"You have?"

She cups her hands around her oversize mug of coffee and shifts in her seat. "I'm a psychology professor now. At George Mason. My area of research is trauma and recovery. And I don't mean to sound grandiose, but what happened at Overton, well, it constituted a minor trauma for me. And, I imagine, a not-so-minor one for you?"

"It did."

"I wasn't my best self, Alexis." She holds my gaze for a moment before her eyes flit away. "I can list excuses. Insecurity, imma-turity, a lack of positive conflict resolution being modeled in my home, but you're probably not interested."

"I am interested in anything you have to say."

"I'm nervous." She laughs. It's a familiar laugh, sonorous with the slight hint of a braying donkey. I can't help but think of us sit-ting on the top of the hill that overlooked the sweeping grounds of Overton, cracking each other up with color commentary on all the preppy kids below. Madeline with her black-and-white composition notebook filled with biting observations. Me with my camera slung over my neck.

"I always tell my children to own their mistakes," she says.

"Children," I say, returning to the present. Of course she's married with children. Did I really think she would be frozen as a social outcast, always on the periphery of life?

"Yes. Three. So here I am owning mine. I apologize, Alexis. It was wrong what I did, and I'm sure it hurt you immensely."

She blinks and purses her lips, and I realize she is fighting back tears. Her professional façade seems to melt away. My own eyes begin to sting.

"It's okay. I'm all right now." I don't know who is framing me for murder, but I am convinced it can't be the thoughtful woman sitting across the table from me. "I'm married, too. I have a son."

She sniffs and takes a packet of tissues from her bag. "I'm very glad to hear that. You were always such a creative, sensitive soul. I always hoped that you would land where you belonged." She blows her nose loudly into a tissue and smiles apologetically. "I've carried the guilt with me over the years. For you and the others I ended up hurting."

I tilt my head, curious. "You mean Paul?"

She lets out a sharp laugh. "Well, I can't say I feel too bad about what happened to Paul Adamson. He was a predator, it's as simple as that. Even if I didn't see that at the time, now that I am a mother, I can see it clear as day. But it was a different time then, wasn't it?"

I meet her eyes for a moment and then look away, focusing on a print of a dandelion on the wall. *Predator* was not a term used to describe Paul when everything came to light. I don't remember much attention being paid to his role at all. As for me, there were plenty of words bandied about.

Slut.

Liar.

Nutcase.

Stalker.

"I guess he was a predator. I never really thought of him that way."

"An adult who uses his, or her, position of authority to enter into a sexual relationship with a teenager is the very definition of a predator."

"That sounds very official."

She laughs. "It is. Textbook."

"What if the teenager in question, you know, wanted it?" My cheeks burn hot as the words leave my mouth. Isn't this the question I've carried with me my whole life, the basis for all the guilt I've felt? And someone who was there is about to answer, someone who is an actual authority on these matters.

Madeline shakes her head. "No. Allie, the whole legal concept of consent is there for a reason. Children and teenagers are not mini-adults. Their brains aren't fully formed. They cannot consent."

I nod toward her packet of tissues. "Can I have one of those?"

She smiles and pushes the tissues toward me.

"And to answer your earlier question," Madeline says. "No, I don't feel particularly bad about him being fired. Or the whole police thing. Now his wife, that's another story. She was sort of collateral damage in the whole thing, wasn't she?"

34

You must resist the temptation to trust your own memories.

I read that recently in an article. Most people think of their memories as immutable, but in fact, they change. We are constantly editing them throughout our lives, unconsciously adding bits and cutting out other parts. What rarely changes is our confidence that we accurately remember an event.

I know this.

I have a memory of my father, for instance, buying me a second balloon at a park after my first one floated away into the sky. The second balloon is red. The first was yellow.

I don't even know if it's a true memory. I was barely three when he died. But my mother has told me this story so many times, I can see it in my mind like a faded Super 8 video.

"What wife? Paul wasn't married." I feel as if the air has been sucked out of the room. The growl of the coffee grinder, the hiss of the milk steamer, all other conversation in the café recedes.

"Yes, he was, Allie." Madeline's eyebrows crinkle together, creating two deep grooves in the flesh above her nose. "You know that."

"I don't remember a wife," I say. But as I reach back through time, grasping at memories, I realize maybe I do. Do I? One thing I am ashamed to admit is that at seventeen, I certainly didn't care.

"You remember," Madeline says in a matter-of-fact tone. "You used to spend hours in that darkroom blacking her out of all your photos."

I shiver, a chill running through me despite the warmth of the room. Her words resonate in my bones with ice-cold veracity.

"My mother knew the wife," she says. "Actually, she knew *her* mother. They were in some women's club together. It wasn't professional, nothing to do with the university, maybe some garden club? Either way, the scandal took a toll on them socially. They became pariahs, he deservedly so, but not she. I always felt somewhat responsible for that."

"What happened to her?"

Madeline frowns, stirring her spoon in her mug. "No idea. The two of them moved away pretty soon after."

"Do you know her name?"

A sad half smile forms on her lips, and she looks off in the distance as she speaks. "Funny you should ask. I don't. I've made half-hearted attempts at tracking her down on the internet, just to see what happened. Try googling *Mrs. Adamson.* You won't get very far. I suppose I could just ask my mother."

"Would you?" I can barely get the words out.

"Of course. I'll get back to you." Madeline frowns at me, alarm in her face. "Alexis, you don't look well. Was it something I said?"

As I rub Cole's back in bed at night, my mind drifts, wondering how Madeline viewed me earlier at the coffee shop. Did she look past my impulse chop of a haircut, my dark circles and sallow skin, and see the curious teenager I used to be? I still saw the insouciant know-it-all in her, beneath her composed professional demeanor.

It was bittersweet connecting with someone from my past. I wish I had a group of girlfriends who knew me back when, whose childhoods were intertwined with my own, and acted as an extended family. Whenever I see women like that—laughing together, making private jokes, posing for pictures—I am gripped by an intense, primal jealousy.

I lean down to check if Cole is asleep. It's always astounded me how he can be racing around the room one minute and snoring the next. I kiss his forehead and get up. As clichéd as it sounds, Cole has taught me about love. About the richness that comes from being hurt, but then forgiving.

I always blamed my lack of friends on having to leave Overton, but now I am willing to see that I've never really done the hard work of making and keeping female friends. I think of Leah—even though she has her own kids with issues—she's carved out space in her life to let me in. Or Daisy, who makes time for me while juggling a successful real estate business and problems with her stepdaughter.

It's not too late. I can create my own little tribe, or at least try to join one. And I will make an effort with Madeline, too. Who knows? Maybe there is enough goodwill that we can rekindle our friendship.

As I get ready for bed, I think about what she told me about Paul's wife. Is it possible I had just erased this woman from my memories? I heard a story on NPR a while ago about people who wrote about their experience during 9/11 the next day. A few years later, researchers showed these folks what they had written, and the majority denied that they had done so. Their recollections had changed dramatically, and they were adamant that while the written memories were in their own hand, the substance was less accurate than their later recollections.

I let myself think about her for a moment, this unidentifiable wife. In my mind, she is cut from the same cloth as Katharine Hepburn, a New England classic in khakis and crisp, white shirts and pearls. I have no reason to imagine her this way, but I do. What does this woman do when she discovers her husband is sleeping with his student? When the entire school where he works is on fire with this scandalous news? How does she move on?

And where is she now?

I wonder if Madeline will really follow through on her promise to ask her mother about Paul's wife. As I fall asleep, it occurs to me: if Madeline can get me info on the wife, I'll probably be able to locate Paul.

And that may be the thread that unravels this whole goddamn knot.

35

My phone rings Monday morning just as I am stepping out of the shower. I can hear Mark and Cole in the kitchen below, and I am tempted to send the call to voice mail. Mornings run on a tight schedule, and I need to get down to the kitchen so Mark can get to work.

But when I see the call is from Valerie Simmons's assistant, I take it.

"Hi, Ms. Ross, sorry for calling so early, but I'm going to have to cancel Ms. Simmons's appointment today."

Her clipped delivery and officious tone almost scare me off of asking any follow-up questions, but I forge ahead.

"Oh, I'm so sorry to hear that," I say. "Do you want to reschedule?"

"Maybe I wasn't clear. Ms. Simmons won't be using Mike Chau Studio, and she will not be working with you. Goodbye, Ms. Ross."

I put the phone on Mark's dresser and stand rooted to the floor, water dripping from me.

Something happened between our talk last week and this morning to sour Valerie Simmons on me. She must have heard about the police searching my house. That has to be it. She's in the news business, and somehow she found out.

My face burns with shame. As annoyed as Mike was that I brought in this job, he'll be furious that I lost it.

"Allie!" Mark calls from below. "I'm leaving!"

I dress and head down to the kitchen, brainstorming ways to salvage the situation. I can tell Mike that I will be pitching to Senator Fielding, Sarah Ramirez's boss. Maybe that will appease him.

On the counter, I find a cappuccino Mark has left me, emblazoned with a foam heart. But this small act of kindness does little to lift my spirits.

Mark needs to know it's going to take a lot more than a fancy coffee to patch things up between us.

Cole remains uncharacteristically calm when I inform him that we are out of peanut butter and he will have to settle for a Lunchable. I always have a few on hand for those mornings when making lunch from scratch seems a Herculean task.

I manage to pop one in his backpack without feeling like it is a strike against my mothering.

After dropping Cole off at school, I drive to work. The dread growing as I get closer to the studio. Parking along H Street to get to work is tight as usual, and I have to cruise around for a while before I find a spot. By the time I park on Tenth Street in front of a small French bistro that just opened, my palms are sweaty and I feel nauseated.

I speed-walk past the Gold Spot check-cashing joint, a reminder that this area was not always dotted with beer gardens and artisanal pickle shops.

Upstairs at the studio, a young, round-faced woman I've never seen before sits at one of the desks. She's fussing with a mass of streaked curls, trying to tuck them all into a topknot on her head as I approach.

"Hi." I stick out my hand. "I'm Allie."

Her small eyes dart back and forth behind her bright red glasses. "Rebecca. It's my first day." She stops fixing her hair to place a limp hand in mine.

"Oh, I didn't realize we were hiring anyone. Welcome."

Rebecca's chapped lips twitch, and she won't meet my gaze.

Does she know I lost the Valerie Simmons job? Ridiculous. I chide myself for being paranoid. We both turn as Mike steps out from one of the back rooms.

Mike gestures toward a young woman in leggings and an oversize Howard University sweatshirt sitting on one of the white pleather sofas. "Rebecca, why don't you get our client situated in room two? Allie and I are going next door."

"We are?" I ask. It's obvious something is up. He must know about Valerie Simmons.

"Let's not do this here." He grabs a leather jacket off a hook on the wall and gestures to my bag. "Bring your laptop."

My pulse quickens as I rush to catch up to Mike. He's already down the stairs and entering Drip, a coffee shop specializing in six-dollar cold brews. I try and think of how I am going to spin having my house searched by the police as a giant misunderstanding.

As we enter the coffee shop, I prepare a small speech about how I've contacted a lawyer and everything is under control.

Although it's almost ten, the café is full. I recognize several regulars who come here every day with their laptops, checking their emails or punching out the Great American Novel.

Mike doesn't bother to order, but goes straight toward a tiny two-top along the exposed brick wall and sits down. He doesn't bother to take off his coat.

"What's going on?" I ask in a low voice, nurturing a last flicker of hope that this is not about Valerie Simmons canceling. Mike stares at the table, tracing a groove in the worn wood with one finger. We sat here for my first interview just two months ago. It was a sweltering August day, humidity seeping into every nook of D.C. I remember ordering an iced coffee and the way the condensation dripped down the glass onto the table. Mike and I chatted as if we had known each other for years.

The hiss of the espresso machine punctuates the soothing electronic music coming from the ceiling speakers. I think of the standard advice to break up in a public place so your partner won't throw a scene. "Did I do something wrong, Mike?"

I flash back to my first week on the job in early September, when I had sent out a contact sheet to a client without letting Mike see it first. He was understanding, but he made it clear that I was on probation for my first ninety days and I needed to be more careful.

"I don't even know where to begin, Allie." He regards me as if I am a stranger to him.

"Is this about Valerie Simmons?"

He looks taken aback. "Valerie Simmons? What about Valerie Simmons?"

"Nothing. Never mind. Please just tell me what's up."

"What's up? Let's see. You violated the agreement you signed when you started here. That's just for starters."

I frown, racking my brain to remember the three-page document I signed. A typical contract. The only thing that stands out to me is the extra attention that was paid to forbidding the use of work I did as a Mike Chau employee for personal gain. "I haven't used the photos I've taken here for anything else, if that's what you're referring to."

Mike rubs the barbed-wire tattoo around his left wrist. "No? How about your Facebook page?"

My Facebook page. That's what this is about. That's why Valerie canceled. She must have seen the page. "Mike, I can explain. That page is fake."

But he's in no mood to listen. He motions to my bag. "Take out your laptop."

I put the laptop on the table. "I've already contacted Facebook, and they've—"

"Sign in to Facebook." This sharp command stuns me. The man sitting across from me is not the warm, easygoing Mike I thought I knew.

"Mike, listen to me." A tremor runs through me, one that has been all too familiar this past week. "An account exists, but I didn't create it, and I don't have the password."

He exhales loudly. "Fine, I'll get to it through mine." He turns my laptop toward him and begins stabbing at the keys. "It's beyond inappropriate, Allie. It's completely unprofessional," he says as he types. "And cruel to boot. Do you have any idea how much damage you've caused?"

He spins the laptop around. Facing me is one of the photos that I took of Sarah Ramirez the other day, one that I discarded for being unflattering.

I scroll down and see several more.

Sarah with a twisted sneer on her face, her belly fat flopping onto the pink velvet chaise.

Sarah with her eyes half-open, half-closed, her thighs a map of stretch marks and cellulite.

Below that, the caption reads, "I'm not a magician. How am I supposed to make this look good?"

The viciousness of the words hits me in my gut. It sickens me that anyone would think I would write that.

Heather, my neighbor, pops into my head. She's on Facebook. She'll have seen this, and if she hasn't, Sarah is bound to tell her about it. What was it that Sarah said to me? That Heather was like a sister to her?

Something is gnawing at me. Then I remember—I've never figured out whether Heather took that photo of me at the pool or if she saw who did.

And of course, Heather has keys to our house.

Crazy. Heather was the warmest person I'd met in our neighborhood. She baked us blueberry muffins when we first moved in. And anyway, what would be her connection to Paul Adamson? My mind is spinning.

"The first step is you need to take these posts down," Mike says. The disgust in his eyes sends a chill through me.

"I can't." I bite my cheek to stop from crying. "It's not my account, but I've contacted Facebook."

"Sarah Ramirez wants this down by the end of the day, or she's going to sue."

"Let me talk to her, Mike. I can fix this."

"Don't, Allie! She doesn't want to hear from you!"

"I know how this looks, Mike. But I did not post these."

"I'm trying to talk her down off the ledge, but obviously, the first move is you need to take these photos down."

"Are you listening? I didn't post them." I slam my open hand on the table, making the sugar bowl jump. "Someone must have hacked into my laptop and posted these pictures."

He takes a red USB thumb drive out of his coat pocket and plugs it into my laptop. "I'm downloading all the photos you took as an employee of the Mike Chau Studio."

Tears wet my eyes, and I bite down hard on my lower lip to stop from crying. Not here at Drip, in front of Mike.

"Don't bother trying to get into our databases remotely. We've changed the passwords," he says. "You're lucky I'm not calling the police. Now, tell me—what's going on with Valerie Simmons? You're supposed to shoot her when, exactly?"

I shake my head. "It's not happening. She canceled."

"Canceled? Tell me she wants to reschedule, Allie."

I don't speak.

"Christ, Allie. This is my business you're ruining, you know that? That's my name on the front door. Do you even care?"

"I can explain."

He holds up a hand to silence me and turns his attention to the progress bar on the computer screen. Silently, we watch it go from zero to one hundred percent as all the photos are transferred. It's like watching my professional life dissipate before my eyes. Then, for good measure, he moves all the files to the trash and empties it. Mike pulls out the flash drive and shuts the laptop. Then he looks past my shoulder and nods. I spin around to see the new girl, Rebecca, clomp across the café toward us, as ungainly as a newborn colt. She plops a white banker's box on the floor near my feet. A framed photo of Mark, Cole, and me sticks out of the top.

I turn back to face Mike. "What's going on?"

"What's going on is you've been terminated, Allie. Effective immediately."

36

My heart pounds as I stand under the vertical sign spelling POLICE affixed to a modern, nondescript office building. It's not just that I've been fired; my dreams for opening my own studio are shattered. The photography world is small; everyone talks. I doubt I could get a job as an assistant after this. I've violated a cardinal rule—betraying the trust of a client. And not just any client—sweet Sarah, riddled with insecurities about how she looked. I cringe remembering how I promised the pictures would be beautiful and not embarrass her. She must hate me, and I don't blame her.

I need help. And as awful as dealing with the police has been this last week, they may be the only ones who can provide it. I call Artie Zucker, but his assistant says he's in court and puts me through to his voice mail.

"Hi, Artie. It's Allie Ross. I know you said not to talk to the police without you, but I need to report some online harassment. I won't talk about Rob Avery or anything to do with that, but I've been fired from my job because of false social media postings, and I'm sorry, but I just can't sit here and do nothing—"

Beeeep. A woman's automated voice asks me if I am satisfied with my message or want to rerecord it. I leave it as is and enter the station.

Inside, I am directed to the third floor, where I give my name and reason for being here to a surly, older man in uniform and take a seat in a molded plastic chair. I tell myself not to think about the last time I was here, being grilled by detectives Katz and Lopez. I won't be going anywhere near the Homicide department; someone from Computer Crimes will be talking to me. The only other people are an elderly couple, huddled together as if they need the warmth of each other's bodies. The older man glances up at me and then looks away, whispering something into his companion's ear.

Above them is a poster that reads: "Financial Scams Targeting Seniors are the Crime of the 21st Century." I wonder if that's why they are here, but it could be anything. A robbery, a stolen car.

There are so many things that can go wrong in life.

Every once in a while, the door next to the reception window opens and someone leaves, but no one seems to go inside.

I take my laptop out and browse through the Applications folder, then the one marked Downloads, although I'm not sure what I expect to find. Something on this machine has betrayed me. There have to be clues here somewhere.

What did Dustin say? *If someone messes with you online . . . there's going to be crumbs left behind.*

I want a name—a face—to pin to all this. I remember what Madeline said about her mom knowing Paul Adamson's wife. It's a long shot, but I tap out a quick text reminding her of her promise to ask her mom.

"Ms. Ross?"

A mustachioed man in his mid-fifties stands in the doorway. He's rangy, except for a potbelly the size of a bowling ball that droops over his brown slacks. When I approach, he shifts some folders so he can stick out his hand. "Detective Gabe Khoury, Computer Crimes. Follow me, please."

I follow Detective Khoury into a conference room with a long oval table and blue upholstered swivel chairs. Despite the chill outside, the air-conditioning is on full blast. I pull my coat tighter around me. A wall of windows looks out at a brick office building across an alley. "Sorry it's so cold, but at least we can have some privacy here."

The detective sits and motions for me to take a seat as well. He takes out an iPad and a stylus.

"Can you tell me what's going on, Ms. Ross?"

"What's going on is that someone is trying to ruin my life."

"Can you be more specific?"

I take a deep breath. "First, someone made a fake Tinder account, complete with an inappropriate picture of me. A guy approached me at a party, thinking I had been texting him, which of course I had not been. Then they made a fake account and posted on my neighborhood Facebook group." I pause to see if Detective Khoury is getting all this. He narrows his eyes at the small screen in front of him, tapping away with his stylus like a chicken pecking for grub worms. When he doesn't look up, I continue. "And finally, someone hacked into my computer and posted photos from my work onto Facebook. I got fired for that. Today."

Still no response.

"Did you hear me, Detective? I've lost my job because of this." I feel that focusing on the damage done to my career, rather than my relationship with Mark and my neighbors, will appeal to the detective. Khoury doesn't strike me as the touchy-feely type. "Do you understand?"

His face betrays no reaction. He seems neither surprised nor disbelieving. "Any requests for money? Strange invoices or bills?"

"No."

"No unusual recent emails from your bank? Credit cards arriving that you never ordered?"

"No, nothing like that." The jumbo reverse mortgage springs to mind, but mentioning Sharon's house will just muddy the waters. This is about me. "I don't think this is about money. This feels more personal."

Tap-tap-tap. "Any ex-boyfriends or ex-husbands we should talk to? Disgruntled coworkers? Employees?"

I start to shake my head, but then stop. "There is someone from my past, a man I was involved with. But it was years ago."

"Why don't you give us his name?"

"Paul Adamson."

"And what makes you think this Paul Adamson may be involved?"

It's a good question, one that I am not sure I have an answer to. "Maybe because he lost his job due to our relationship."

Khoury's eyebrows shoot up. "And why is that, Ms. Ross?"

"That," I say, ice in my voice, "is because he was my high school teacher at the time."

"I see." He turns to his iPad. "And was he arrested and charged?"

I shift in my seat, uncomfortable. The details on this matter are muddy for me. "Yes, but charges were dropped."

"And when is the last time you had contact with Mr. Adamson?"

I press hard on my temples. "When it happened, which was more than sixteen years ago."

I don't tell Detective Khoury that every moment of the last day I ever saw Paul Adamson is seared into my memory.

He doesn't need to know that I had planned to meet Madeline at the movie theater that Sunday afternoon in May, but instead at the appointed hour I was miles away, wading into the Long Island Sound with Paul.

He doesn't need to hear how our brief excursion, to dip our toes in the water, had found us driving up the Connecticut coast in his rusted old BMW looking for a public beach that wouldn't charge us twenty dollars just to pull into the parking lot.

Or that by the time we finished dinner at a seafood shack overlooking brackish water, I was drunk on two beers and sucking the melted butter off my fingers.

Or that I never made it to the movie theater to meet Madeline.

That Paul and I stumbled across the restaurant parking lot to a motel.

That my mother did not notice that I never came home.

"I realize this is a sensitive topic, Ms. Ross. But can you think of someone else, maybe someone you've crossed paths with more recently?"

"No." I shake my head, clearing it of thoughts of long ago.

"If there is someone you are, or were, involved with more recently—romantically, that is—we won't have to share that information with your husband."

He twists the stylus in his slender fingers, a light smirk causing the left side of his mustache to rise. It hits me. He thinks I'm having an affair. Or that I've slept with some random psycho who's now out to get me.

"There's nobody, Detective. Just Paul Adamson."

"It's just, usually these things have one of two causes. One is financial, and the other is personal—revenge. We're seeing a lot of revenge porn these days, you know—exes posting nude pictures online after a breakup."

"That's not what this is!"

"Now calm down, Ms. Ross. I'm very sympathetic. You're not the first person who's come in here with this kind of complaint." He lifts his hands in resignation. "We're seeing a lot more of this online harassment. Most of it is harmless, people playing pranks."

"This isn't harmless!" I yell. "I just lost my damn job, and my whole neighborhood is turning against me. It's destroying my marriage, Detective." I close my laptop and put it back into my bag. In a calmer voice, I add, "Detective, this is ruining my life, and I don't feel safe. I've even thought, why don't we just move? But wherever I go, unless I change my identity and basically go into hiding, this person can find me and do it all over again."

"There's a saying in law enforcement: if they call first, they aren't coming."

"What the hell's that supposed to mean?"

"It means that the truly dangerous folks don't announce they are coming to harm you. This type, the type to make fake social media accounts, they get off on just harassing you."

"Just harassing? There's nothing *just* about this."

He looks at the iPad on his desk. "Tell you what, let me take a peek at this Paul Adamson fellow, and I'll be in touch. Unfortunately, there's no federal law, or Maryland law, that makes it illegal to set up an imposter social media account. I'll tell you what I say to the high school students during my cyberbullying presentation." He hoists up his pants and leans in to deliver his pearls of wisdom. "Three words, Ms. Ross. *Shut. It. Off.* Shut off the computer, the phone, the iPad. Shut the damn router off. Go outside for a bit. Take a bike ride, garden, do something, Ms. Ross. There's more to life than what's on these little screens—"

A knock at the door distracts him, and Detective Khoury stands up and answers it. I can't see whom he is talking to, but he glances back at me, shaking his head. "I'll be back in a jiff. Can I get you a coffee or soda?"

"No, thank you." A jiff. How long does a jiff last? Suddenly, my anger melts into paranoia. Coming here was a bad idea. I am gathering my things when the door opens and Detectives Katz and Lopez enter.

I stand frozen. This was a mistake, thinking I could come in here and file a complaint and not be questioned about Rob Avery.

"Mind if we have a few minutes of your time, Ms. Ross?" Detective Lopez asks, slipping into the seat across from me. She is wearing a light blue oxford with a dried coffee stain down the front. This is not the kind of woman who lets little inconveniences stop her.

"Actually, I have to be home," I say.

"This will only take a minute," Detective Katz says, and beams a warm smile. "We understand someone has been harassing you online?"

I slide back into my seat, harboring a tiny shred of hope that maybe, just maybe, she will take my concerns seriously. "Yes. That's right."

"Tell us," Detective Katz says.

"I already told you about this, the fake Tinder account?" I try to keep the annoyance out of my voice. "Remember?"

"Tell us again."

I launch into what has happened once more, detailing the fake Tinder and Facebook accounts, and finishing with the hacked photos at work. I am careful not to mention I have my laptop with me. I decide if they ask, I will turn it over, but I'm not going to offer it up.

"When would you say you became aware of the online harassment?"

I think back. "I guess I knew for sure a week ago, maybe Wednesday? When my sister found the fake Tinder page."

"So after Rob Avery's murder." Detective Katz does not meet my eye when he says this.

"Yes."

A small smile dances at the corners of his mouth. It seems like I've walked into a trap, but I don't know exactly to what I've confessed.

Detective Lopez leans her elbows on the table, her biceps clearly definable beneath the sleeves of her shirt. "Let me tell you what I think is going on, Ms. Ross. I think you and Rob Avery had an affair—"

"No."

"I think something happened—maybe he wanted to go public, maybe he threatened to tell your husband?"

I shake my head and open my mouth to speak, but she holds up her hand before I have a chance. "You were both at Daisy Gordon's party. People saw you flirting, tongues started wagging. You had an argument. Made you realize the clock was ticking on your little secret. So you went home, got up early, walked down the alley behind your house to his. He let you in—why wouldn't he?"

My throat is tight, and I can barely choke out an answer. "No. Wrong. That's not what happened."

She continues in a soothing monotone as if I hadn't spoken. "You fought. Maybe you didn't mean to hurt him. Maybe it was an accident. Didn't have your story fully fleshed out when we first interviewed you, but once you realized you were on our radar for Avery's death, you concocted this whole backstory. Explains the texting, the pictures you two traded."

"I'm not going to sit here and listen to this." But I don't make a move. I'm not sure what my rights are. "I want to call my lawyer."

Detective Katz frowns, gives me puppy-dog eyes. "I know you're freaking out, Allie. Can I call you Allie? You're a good person who got yourself into a jam. But all this lying, it's not going to help you in the end."

"I'd like to go home."

"Why do you want to do that?" Detective Katz furrows his brow. "Makes me think you have something to hide."

Detective Lopez cocks her head to one side, knitting her eyebrows in an aww-shucks way. "We're just having a conversation here. Why don't you want to cooperate with us?"

"It'll be easier for everyone if you just tell us what really happened," Detective Katz says. "We know you killed Rob Avery. We want to hear your side of the story."

Something in me snaps. I stand up. "Either you let me call my lawyer, or I'm going home."

The look of kindness on Detective Katz's face vanishes. He looks to Detective Lopez, who pushes back her chair and walks toward the door.

"You're not under arrest, Ms. Ross. You're free to go at any point."

37

"You what?" Artie Zucker's voice booms through the car's speaker. "What part of *never, never, never talk to the police without me present* didn't you understand? Jesus, what were you thinking?"

"I wasn't. I mean, I didn't think I'd see them," I say, cringing. "I was there about my computer getting hacked. I didn't kill Rob Avery. I had nothing to do with his death."

"They're trying to rattle you," he says in a calmer voice. "That's all. Get you to say something incriminating. They shouldn't be talking to you at all, frankly, but because you came in on your own, it's a gray area."

"They said they knew I killed him. Knew."

"Allie, listen to me, it's important you know that the police are allowed to lie and mislead during an investigation. They have a lot of leeway, and they use it to freak people out and get them to confess. Sometimes people confess to crimes they have not even committed. That's why I don't want you talking to anyone without me present. *Capeesh?*"

"Got it." I feel slightly reassured by this. The police can lie. It's all part of the investigation.

"Now, tell me every last little detail, and do not leave a single thing out."

I recount the whole episode, first meeting with Detective Khoury and then when the other two took his place. It takes the entire drive home, and I'm just winding up the story as I pull up in front of my house.

"Well, at least now we have a pretty good idea of the direction their investigation is going. I think you need to prepare yourself."

"For what?"

"That you may be arrested. Hopefully, I'll get a heads-up first."

I sit stunned in my car, shocked to my core. I guess I knew this was a possibility, but to hear him say it so bluntly terrifies me. How am I supposed to prepare myself to be arrested? The thought of what this will do to Cole sends me spiraling down into darkness. I've heard about innocent people getting caught up in the criminal justice system, but I never in a million years thought it would be me.

A rap on my window startles me, and I turn to see a scowling Heather standing by the door. I've never seen her without an ear-to-ear grin. At once, I think of Sarah. She knows. I get out of the car and brace myself for a confrontation.

"Hi, Heather. I'm guessing you talked to Sarah."

"Sarah is a mess. I don't blame her. She showed me screenshots of what you wrote. Allie, how could you? She trusted you. I trusted you."

"I know it looks bad—"

"Looks bad? Looks bad?" Her voice grows louder as her face turns a mottled red. "Is that what you care about? How this looks?"

"No. That's not what I meant. I did not write those things, Heather. Someone made a fake Facebook account."

"Ha!" She takes a small step back, a triumphant smile on her face. "Vicki Armstrong said you would say that."

"Vicki Armstrong doesn't know what she's talking about." Rage builds in me at the thought of that woman buzzing around the neighborhood trying to turn everyone against me.

"You know, I defended you," Heather says, stabbing the air with her pointer finger. "When people said you were having an affair with Rob, I told them no way. To think that I recommended you to Sarah, even to my boss! But I'm done. We're done."

She pivots and heads next door to her house.

"Hold up," I say, catching up to her. I grab her shoulder and spin her around. "Did you photograph the police at my house the other day?" I ask, ignoring the way she dramatically rubs her shoulder as if I'd hurt her. "And post it on Facebook?"

A flicker of something crosses her face. Guilt? "Yes. Yes, I did," she says, half sputtering. "So what? Aren't I entitled to know why the police are swarming my block?"

"And what about the pool, Memorial Day weekend?"

"What about it?" She sticks her chin out in defiance.

"Did you photograph me at the pool, Heather?"

She holds up both hands and starts backing away, her eyes wild. "What? You're crazy."

"And what about Overton Academy? Do you know someone who went there?"

"Stay away from me. I mean it."

"Why won't you answer the question, Heather? What's your connection to Overton?"

I watch Heather back up to her front path, then turn and speed-walk past a giant inflated jack-o'-lantern and into her house.

It's probably my imagination, but I swear I can hear the deadbolt lock.

No one is in the kitchen, but the scent of browning meat permeates the air. A quick peek in the oven reveals a roast nestled in a bed of potatoes and carrots. Susan's doing.

Upstairs, I find Cole lying on his floor, an island amid a sea of colorful LEGO pieces. They're tiny but can cause a surprising amount of pain when stepped on in the middle of the night.

"Hey, Cole, you know you're going to have to pick up all these before dinner, right?"

He grunts in response but does not look up.

"Where's Susan?"

He does not answer, keeping his eyes fixed on the little pieces in his hand.

I walk down the dark hallway to my bedroom. When I open the door, Susan is standing on the other side. She gasps, hand fluttering to her throat.

"You startled me!"

I step back, surprised myself. She looks so out of place in my bedroom, less than a foot from my unmade bed.

"I hope you don't mind," she says. "I was using your bathroom. Cole was in the other one."

"No, not at all." Suddenly, I think of the Overton T-shirt that found its way into my laundry.

I watch as Susan steps past me into the hall and then into Cole's room. There's nothing threatening or even remarkable about her. She's nondescript, with her mannish haircut and medium-wash jeans. But what do I really know about her? I never even checked her references. Just knowing that she had watched the Zoni triplets had been enough for me.

Maybe that was a mistake, I think, as I continue through the bedroom to the entrance of our bathroom. There, in the silence, an uneasy feeling settles on me. Our bathroom was renovated sometime in the eighties, when pink tile was in vogue. Whoever owned the house did a cheap job. They installed an oversize Jacuzzi tub that's impossible to clean and a toilet that grumbles for a full five minutes after you flush it. It's on our list of things to fix.

But now the toilet is quiet.

Susan couldn't have been using it, not recently.

Stop it, I tell myself. Maybe she was washing her hands. Or her face.

When I turn, I notice a slice of light under my closet door. I pull the door open and stare inside. My clothes hang as they always do. Nothing looks out of place. Did I forget to turn off the light this morning when I left? Maybe Cole was playing in here.

"I'm taking off," Susan calls from the hallway. "There's a pot roast in the oven."

I rush to the hall. "Thank you, Susan. You didn't have to do that."

She stops halfway down the landing and gives me a little smile. "Oh, it's my pleasure. I know how busy you are, and it's not easy with Mark working late."

I nod as if I already knew this. "Right."

"He called about an hour ago. Said he couldn't reach you."

Now I remember. The call I sent to voice mail while I was meeting with Detective Khoury. I forgot to listen to his message. Still, for some reason I can't quite pinpoint, I am irritated that he passed the message on through Susan.

"You or Cole weren't in my closet for any reason, were you?" I ask, hoping to sound casual and not accusatory. "Maybe playing hide-and-seek or something?"

She blinks twice. "No."

"It's just that the light was on. I'm sure I shut it off this morning."

Susan frowns. "Is everything all right, Allie? You look exhausted, if you don't mind my saying so."

I feel my eyes widen. What has she heard? It's naive to think some gossip has not reached her ears. "Everything's fine. Good night, Susan."

I let Cole watch television with dinner, something I am normally loath to do, while I surf the internet. To distract myself, I try to read an article that Leah sent me on the four styles of parenting and how only one of them does not damage your children. It's

the usual clickbait nonsense, but I can't focus enough to be out-
raged. Bits and pieces of the day swarm my mind like a sick collage. Mike firing me. Detective Khoury dismissing my concerns.
Being accused of murder. My confrontation with Heather. I
need to talk to Mark, but he won't be home until late, so to calm
my nerves, I pour myself a tall glass of cold sauvignon blanc, not
even trying to hide it from Cole.

After Cole is in bed, I come back down and pour myself another glass as fortification while I do the dishes.

I once read a story about a happy couple that lived in a cute,
little blue house for years until one morning, they came down to
discover the kitchen had fallen into a sinkhole. By the late afternoon, the entire house had been swallowed, their lives vanished
before their eyes.

That's how this feels.

And the worst part is that I am unsure of what to do next. Especially without Mark here to guide me. He's like my compass.
I don't know if I've always been this way, or if self-doubt is part
of the legacy Paul left me.

I don't trust my own instincts.

For years, I questioned whether I deserved to be in art school,
whether I was really any good like he had said. Maybe that had
been a lie, too, a part of the bigger lie: That I was special. That I
was lovable.

Stop it.

I turn off the water. I need to distract myself. Watch something silly on TV. I slosh a bit more wine into my glass, promising myself that three's the limit, and move through the house,
switching on all the lights as I go. I feel safer this way, electricity
bill be damned.

This is the first house I have lived in, except the one my family
lived in before my father died. I don't remember it, but I have a
photo of the narrow blue wooden house. It stood in a neighborhood packed with them, all different colors, each one close

enough to the others that you could lean out your kitchen window and pass a saltshaker to the person next door.

After my father died, everything changed. We moved to Connecticut and began a pattern of moving from apartment to apartment every few years. Sometimes we came home from school to see all our belongings packed and a lost look on Sharon's face, like she had wandered in from some other life and didn't know what she was doing. Other times, we moved in the middle of the night, all our clothes stuffed into giant black trash bags like we were sneaking out on our lives.

I blamed my mother at the time. Losing jobs, unable to make rent. But she was overwhelmed trying to raise two little girls on her own.

When Daisy showed Mark and me the house we live in now, she declared, "This is not a starter house. This is a forever house."

If this were happening to Sharon, she would pack us up in the middle of the night and we'd be in a new part of town by morning. But I'm not Sharon, and I don't want to run. I want to face whoever is doing this.

In the dining room, I turn on the two slender lamps that grace the credenza when a noise from outside crashes my thoughts. I stop to listen. Just as I am about to write it off as typical suburban nighttime noise, I hear something again. Like the dragging of metal across concrete. It sounds close enough that, if I could reach through the dining room wall to the outside, I might touch whatever was causing it.

In the mudroom, I open the back door and look outside but see nothing, only an empty bird feeder swaying in the night wind. The wind swishes in the trees, but there is no sound of metal against concrete.

"Hello?" I call into the darkness.

I take a tentative step down the walkway that runs alongside the house toward the street. My skin prickles. There's someone here, even if I can't see him.

I remember what the detective said. *If they call first, they aren't coming.* But that does nothing to alleviate the drumming of my heart.

A flash of movement across my sight line makes me jump. A shriek escapes my throat.

Then my vision focuses on a figure by the curb.

It's a raccoon, rounded on its haunches, gazing at me with two mirror discs for eyes. We stare at each other for a second, and then the creature trots off into the darkness.

My heart thwacks in my rib cage. I begin to collect the garbage strewn on the walkway. That was the clang I heard, the animal knocking the metal garbage can lid to the ground.

He's done a good bit of damage. Following the contents of the ripped garbage bag takes me halfway to the street.

I'm picking up the last piece of debris, an old take-out container, when I see him.

Dustin is standing across the street, something in his hand.

"Hey," he whispers loudly and begins to cross.

I freeze, unsure of what to do. Before I can decide, he is right in front of me, raising his arm, his hand gripping something. A weapon?

"It's a universal remote," he says. "Like the one Steve Wozniak invented?"

I laugh nervously and take it from him. "Thank you, Dustin."

"Did you ever figure out who was behind all that online stuff?"

Something at the end of the street catches my eye—a familiar car on the corner.

The black Audi with FCS plates.

"I have to go." I turn and run back inside and lock the door. Rushing from room to room, I shut off all the lights. Once I am sure I cannot be seen, I peer out the front bay window. The Audi lurks there in the dark, but I cannot see if anyone is inside.

I have to do something. I call Mark.

"When are you coming home?" I try to keep the panic out of my voice.

"Soon. I just have about another hour of work to do. What's going on? Cole all right?"

No! I want to shout. *The police think I killed Rob Avery. Someone hacked my computer, and I lost my job. There's a black Audi following me.* Instead I say, "Cole's fine." I step away from the window, wondering how much I should share.

"What's going on, Allie?" Just hearing the warmth in his voice relaxes me a little. I remember how in Chicago he used to walk beside me so his body blocked the wind.

"There's a car on our block that doesn't belong there."

"It's probably someone visiting Leah or Heather."

"No. I've seen this car before, Mark. I think it's been following me." I hate how I sound. Overdramatic, like a shut-in who can no longer discern reality from fantasy. But I know what I know.

"Following you? Is it possible maybe you're just spooked? Letting your imagination run wild?"

"No, I don't think so. I recognize the plates."

"Allie, don't get mad, but have you been drinking?"

I open my mouth in disbelief. His question deflates me like air being let out of a tire. "Forget it. Forget I even called."

"No, I'm glad you called." He sounds genuine, but I can't tell if he's condescending to me, or if he takes me seriously. "Describe the car to me."

"It's a black Audi."

"Can you see who's driving it?" he asks with the patient tone he uses when planning birthday parties with Cole for our son's imaginary friends.

"I don't know, Mark." I sound snippy. My nerves are jangly and raw. Instead of soothing me, this conversation has left me feeling more isolated.

"Tell you what: lock the doors and go to bed, and I'll be home as soon as I can. I'm sure it's just someone visiting a neighbor."

When I peer out the window again, the street is empty. "It's gone."

"See?" he says. "Nothing to worry about. Now go to bed. I'll be home soon."

After hanging up with Mark, I break my own promise and down a fourth glass of wine. I need to pass out, not just fall asleep.

I am jolted awake and sit up, disoriented. The clock reads just after midnight. Alcohol does this to me—it sends me off to sleep but can't keep me there. Like a boat that's been launched, I lose speed halfway across my journey and end up drifting across the dark ocean.

I've been asleep about two hours. My head feels heavy on my neck. I look beside me and see Mark is not there.

I sit in my bed for a few moments, gauging whether I will be able to fall back asleep. But the day's events come rushing at me.

Maybe a cup of tea will help. I throw back the covers and step into the hallway. From the darkened second floor, I can see the bright lights in the kitchen. I'm sure I turned them off, so Mark must be home.

I am halfway down the stairs when the low murmur of Mark's voice reaches me. I pause and then continue softly, not wanting to be heard, although I cannot articulate to myself why. It's not that I want to spy on him, yet I am cautious. At the bottom of the staircase, I can hear Mark's voice coming clearly from the kitchen.

"—and I'm telling you, she knows. She described the car."

The shock of his words sends me reeling back a step. I grip the banister to right myself, and as my weight shifts from one leg to the other, the stair emits the tiniest of creaks. I hold my breath, praying he did not hear.

"Hello?" Mark calls, and then a few footsteps. "Allie? That you?"

I turn and run up the stairs as quietly as possible like a naughty child. I slip under the covers and squeeze my eyes tight. My heart feels like it is throwing itself against my rib cage, pounding so loudly I am sure Mark would hear it if he entered the room.

Moments later, he does enter.

The door squeaks as it is cracked ajar. I peer through the black bars of my eyelashes of one partially opened eye, not daring to move my head for a better view. All I can see is a sliver of light on the ceiling. I watch it grow wider as the door opens farther, Mark's elongated shadow stretching taller and taller.

I squeeze my eyes ferociously and breathe in deeply. Time seems to slow down, and the seconds tick by. Finally, the door clicks shut.

I am alone.

38

On Tuesday morning, neither Mark nor I mention what happened the night before. I'm not sure what's stopping me from just asking him about it, but I want time to think about how I am going to formulate my questions.

And maybe a part of me just does not want to face any more disappointments.

What if his answers are ones I cannot handle?

We stick to the familiar morning dialogue that goes on in suburban households across the country. During our morning routine, I see no good time to announce that I've been fired. That's not a five-minute conversation. It's not that I want to lie to Mark, but between finding a shirt that doesn't make Cole itch and packing lunch, it's easier just to avoid the topic.

Mark does not ask me anything.

He seems preoccupied and distant.

"I'm distracted," he says when I catch him putting the box of Grape-Nuts in the refrigerator and the milk in the cupboard. "This deposition is turning out more complicated than we thought it would be."

We both know it's more than that.

Mark leaves without saying anything, and I can't help but take it personally. He never leaves without kissing me goodbye.

Curiosity gnaws at me. I rush through getting Cole off to school, allowing him to walk the last half block by himself so I can get home quickly. I'm not sure where to begin or what I am looking for, exactly. I start by opening random drawers, looking for anything that might be a clue as to whom Mark might have been talking to last night. If only I could access his cell phone.

Then I realize I can.

I open my laptop and log in to our shared cell phone account. It takes a while, but I finally navigate to the page with the call logs associated with Mark's phone.

Nothing. No calls last night.

I frown. Then it hits me. His work phone. Of course he would make any private calls on that. I have no way of checking it.

I hate that I suspect Mark, but I know what I heard last night.

I continue my search in the third bedroom, for which Mark and I have yet to find a use. When we toured the house, Mark said it would be perfect for a nursery, and I said that I'd like to make it a home office for when I start my own studio. Now it looks like neither of us may get our wish.

One side of the room is stacked with moving boxes I haven't unpacked. They are filled with the sort of knickknacks and odds and ends that stymie even the most type A people, which I most decidedly am not. After two months, I still cannot seem to find the time to tackle them. Where to put the twine, the extra furniture pads, the fifty-dollar collapsible picnic basket we have used once?

I do a preliminary search of Mark's boxes. Old yearbooks from high school and college. Baseball trophies. Papers he wrote in law school.

But no answers to my gnawing questions.

No hint as to whom he might have been talking to last night.

In a far corner, I find a box marked *Allie's photo stuff.* I sit down and pull out film-developing canisters, tongs, and plastic trays that I once slipped paper into and watched as images emerged bit by bit. All rendered obsolete in the digital age.

Mark suggested many times that I should let it all go, sell it on eBay. But I can't.

Something flat sits at the bottom of the box. I hook one finger under the object and yank it out. In my hands, I hold a scrapbook, one I haven't opened in more than sixteen years. I stare at the familiar, plain black cover, a bittersweet mixture of nostalgia and shame sweeping over me. I was sure I had thrown this out when we moved Sharon out of the Westport house.

The thick cover, coated with dust, resists as I turn it.

There he is—Paul Adamson.

The shrill sound of my cell phone ringing from downstairs startles me. I ignore it and turn back to the photo album.

Each stiff black page features one single photograph of Paul, as if he were the only person on earth. The photos are devoid of all other humans.

Madeline's words come back to me. *You used to spend hours in that darkroom blacking her out of all your photos.*

She and I would spend afternoons skulking around the cobbled streets of the historic New England town where our school was located, I like a sharpshooter, armed with my camera, hunting my crush.

Then I'd head to the darkroom and excise anyone besides Paul who wound up in the frame of my photos. I remember the meticulous scissoring of card stock in the exact shape of Paul's outline and placing it precisely over his image as I exposed the photographic paper for such a long period of time that everything else around him turned black.

Goodbye, students or colleagues he was talking with.

Goodbye, innocent bystanders.

Goodbye, wife.

I had created a universe in which no one but Paul existed. In which I could pretend he did not have a wife. After all, if she wasn't in the pictures, maybe she didn't really exist. Maybe he was all mine.

I shut the album. Where is Paul now? Could he be somewhere nearby? Is that him in the black Audi?

And why now, after all these years?

The phone rings again. This time, I get up to answer it. Somebody wants to reach me, and it might be important.

I'm able to make it to my cell in the kitchen before voice mail picks up.

"Hello?" I ask, slightly out of breath.

"This is Ms. Lippman from Eastbrook Elementary School," a woman says. "Principal Flowers would like to see you."

39

Cole lies curled up like a newborn kitten on the bench in the school's main office.

I rush to him and kneel down. "Are you okay, sweetie?"

He throws his arms around me and buries his head in my neck. "I miss you. I hate school." I breathe in his scent, lavender shampoo mixed with his tangy sweat.

"It's all right, baby. I'm here now."

"It wasn't my fault," he says in a tiny voice.

I pull back and look straight into his brown eyes, Mark's eyes. "I believe you."

Mark taps me on the shoulder, and I stand up.

A plump woman wearing a corduroy dress and bright red clogs introduces herself as Principal Flowers. She looks like a character on a kids' PBS program from the seventies. "Mr. and Mrs. Ross? Please follow me." Then she turns to a girl in braids who looks to be about ten, who is dropping off a folder of papers. "Gigi, could you please walk Cole back to Mrs. Liu's class?"

Cole grabs the sleeve of my coat and shakes his head.

"It's all right, honey." But a part of me just wants to grab him and head home. I watch as, shoulders slumped, he shuffles out the door after Gigi. Mark and I follow Principal Flowers into her office, where she shuts the door and motions for us to sit. Plastic daisies, chrysanthemums, and sunflowers adorn the room—stuck to the wall, poking out of vases, attached to pens, staplers, every conceivable surface.

"People just give them to me," she says. "At least I don't use my maiden name—Dix." She guffaws at her own joke. Mark and I exchange a look. I place her in her fifties, the kind of woman who would rather bleed to death than be considered unpleasant. She reminds me of Susan in that way.

"So Cole was involved in an altercation today." Her words have the cadence of a child's rhyme.

"Let's define *altercation*." Mark's voice cuts through her Kumbaya bubble like a sharp knife. I love him for it.

Flowers blinks twice before continuing. "In this particular case, it means your son cut off the ponytail of another child."

"He what?" I look to Mark to see how he is taking this news, but he is staring straight ahead.

Flowers's tiny, blinking eyes shift back and forth from Mark to me like one of those old-fashioned Kit-Cat clocks whose bulging eyes flit with every passing second. "He took a pair of scissors—a pair of adult scissors, I might add, which he must have taken from the teacher's desk—and he cut off a fellow student's ponytail."

Mark remains as still as a statue. "And you know this how?" he asks.

"We know this, Mr. Ross, because the victim informed Ms. Liu what happened, and we found her severed ponytail in Cole's backpack."

Mark snickers. "I see. And we're supposed to take this girl's word for it?"

"Noooooo." Principal Flowers stretches out the word, a sappy smile plastered on her face. "We don't need to take her word for it. Cole has confessed."

"Why would he cut off some girl's ponytail?" I ask.

"Well, and this is not to excuse Cole's behavior in any way," the principal says. "But apparently, this other child had been picking on Cole."

Mark shifts in his chair. "What do you mean, picking on him?"

Flowers offers up a toothy smile. "This is a tight-knit community.

Word travels fast. Kids hear things, they see things. They don't always understand what they're seeing and hearing, but that doesn't stop them from trying to process it or discuss it with other children."

"Just tell us what's going on," Mark says, impatience bursting through his words.

Flowers straightens an already tidy stack of papers on her desk and looks at me. "Look, Tenley Avery is a student here, too."

I flinch. During this entire ordeal, I have given no thought to the little girl who lost her father. "You're saying Tenley Avery was involved in this? She's not even in Cole's grade."

"No, I am not saying Tenley Avery is involved. I am simply pointing out that children talk. And from what I understand, Ms. Ross, you're involved in the investigation of her father's death in some capacity."

My face flushes. I open my mouth to speak, but Mark beats me to it.

"That is frankly none of your business," Mark says, "and should have no bearing on Cole's education."

"Of course, Mr. Ross." The principal's voice breaks. She knows she has pissed him off. "I realize that this is not really any of my business—"

"No. It isn't."

"But children don't live in a vacuum. They hear things on the playground, they eavesdrop on their parents—"

"What does any of this have to do with what happened this morning?" I ask. "With the scissors?"

She clears her throat. "Apparently, a little girl in Cole's class said some unkind things to your son—"

"Now I get it," I say. "What's this girl's name?"

Flowers lets out the teeniest squeak of a laugh. "Ms. Ross, you must know that here at Eastbrook, we maintain the strictest confidentiality. We have zero tolerance for gossip."

"It's that Piper girl, isn't it?" My voice sounds shrill, but I don't care. They're scapegoating my son. I turn to Mark. "Cole has complained about her before. She won't let him play on the monkey bars. She makes fun of him for wearing pink."

"That's harassment," Mark says. "Are you bringing her parents in, as well?"

Flowers nods, acquiescing. "The other child's parents have been notified. But you need to understand that there will be . . . Procedures need to be followed."

"Such as?" I ask.

"Cole will have to be evaluated by an outside therapist."

"What?" I stand up. "That's insane. My kid has to see a therapist because he stood up to some little bully?"

Mark puts his hand on my wrist. "I think what my wife's saying is that seems disproportionate. Isn't there someone he can see at school?" he asks. "You have a guidance counselor, right?"

Flowers's strained smile suggests that she's running out of patience. "We have limited resources available. We are simply not equipped to handle these situations. We have Mrs. Jelly Bean—"

"Mrs. Jelly Bean?" Mark scoffs.

"That's what the kids call Mrs. Genbenito. She sends weekly Jelly Bean blasts in our school emails?" Flowers's tone implies this is the sort of thing that involved parents already know. "Mrs. Jelly Bean is our resource counselor. She can help to some extent, but she cannot do the evaluation necessary to regain access to school. I have a list of local counselors who are usually quite accommodating in these situations. Cole is welcome to attend school for now, but he'll need an evaluation within ten business days. After that, if you haven't turned in an evaluation, he won't be permitted to attend Eastbrook until you do."

"This is outrageous!" I say, turning to Mark. I wait for him to object, but he just gives the principal a perfunctory nod.

I follow Mark, and as soon as we are outside in the cold where no one can hear us, I say, "Why didn't you say more? I felt like I was the only one doing any fighting!"

He spins around. "Maybe fighting isn't the right response."

"What does that mean?"

"Allie, do you even see your role in this? This is happening because of you."

"Me?" My chest tightens, and I start to feel hot. Mark's comment has awoken my most primal fear: that I am damaging my own son. In my gut, I know that Cole might be responding to everything that's happening to me. He is so sensitive, and he picks up on everything. There's no way he hasn't noticed how freaked out I've been this week.

I've always joked that Cole got his brown eyes from his dad and inherited his anxiety from me. I really hoped that once we had adjusted to our new neighborhood, his issues would recede, imperceptibly, the way snow melts into the ground and then one day is simply gone. But if anything, his anxiety has gotten worse. He's become more rigid, more demanding.

And now it's spilled over into school.

Cole needs me to be balanced and strong, but I feel the opposite, like I can't find solid footing. I'm stretched so thin, between his needs and Sharon's dementia care, the house in Westport, and my problems with Mark.

I'm trying to keep it all together, but this Robert Avery thing might be what cracks me apart.

40

"We need to talk." I am breathless as I catch up to him at the top of the hill. "It's not my fault some bully attacked our son."

"I can't do this right now. I have to be at a meeting in forty minutes." He stops in front of my car. "Can you give me a ride to the metro? I Ubered here."

"Sure."

A look of confusion crosses his face. "Wait, how did you get here so fast? Weren't you at work?"

For a split second, I consider telling him what happened yesterday, that I have been fired. But the last thing I want is to give him more ammunition against me. Not after overhearing him on the phone last night. Whether I like it or not, Mark is holding something back from me. He's playing a game, for which I don't know all the rules. Some instinct tells me not to cede what little power I have. "I'm heading in later."

Neither of us speaks on the way to the Friendship Heights metro station. I pull in to the driveway entrance to a shopping mall, next to a No Stopping Any Time sign, and put my hazard lights on. This is a popular pickup and drop-off spot for commuters using the metro, and the police usually won't bother you if you're fast.

Mark takes a glossy, colorful brochure out of his briefcase and lays it on the console between our seats. On the cover, a woman with a contemplative look on her face stares out at a lake as the wind blows her hair back.

I pick it up.

"What's this?"

He doesn't answer.

"*Bridgeways Treatment Center,*" I read aloud. "*We can help.*"

"It's on twenty acres, with hiking trails, on an estuary of the Chesapeake Bay. They have kayaking."

"You make it sound like summer camp." I open the brochure. Certain words jump out at me—*addiction, mental health, residential program.* "This is rehab, Mark. I thought you said you didn't think I needed rehab, remember?" I put the brochure back on the console.

"You're taking this the wrong way. Bridgeways is a facility with outpatient counseling, experts who deal with all kinds of mental health issues, including substance abuse." He sounds like he's practiced this little speech in front of the mirror. "You don't have to check in."

"Mental health issues? I don't have mental health issues."

He bites his lower lip as if he is forcing himself not to answer. His silence infuriates me.

"Substance abuse?" I ask him. "You think I have a substance abuse issue?"

"Allie, a whole bottle of wine every night—it's not ideal. We can agree on that, right?"

"It's not every night. I'm under a lot of stress, in case you hadn't noticed."

He exhales a deep breath. "I didn't want to tell you this, but the other day Cole came home with this worksheet from school. Mommy's favorite this, Daddy's favorite that. Your favorite food? He wrote down *wine.*"

"I didn't know that." A burning sensation tingles at the edges of my scalp. I wonder if the teacher saw it, too.

"I knew you wouldn't like this idea—"

"Well, you're right." The words fly out of my mouth like bullets.

"I'm at a loss. I feel like I'm watching you disintegrate in slow motion."

"I'm sorry you feel that way." My tone is icy.

"I am, too. But now it involves Cole. So I have to step in."

"I see."

"I actually think marriage counseling might help, but Caitlin says that marriage counselors will not see couples where alcohol is a factor. They insist the alcohol issue must be treated first."

"Caitlin said that, huh?"

"Caitlin says this place is one of the best. Very upscale, very discreet. They have a seven-day program and a fourteen-day program."

"Fuck Caitlin."

His head jerks back. "My sister is not the problem here."

"I'm the problem, is that it?"

"No, you're not a problem." He reaches out and squeezes my hand. "But if you can't see that things have gotten out of control, I don't know what to say. You're a suspect in a murder investigation, Allie. And I want to believe you, I do. I want to be on your side, but then you do things that I just don't understand. You need help. This family needs help."

"You want to help?" I am practically shouting, but I can't help it. "Find out who launched an online campaign to destroy my life!" I pull my hand out from under his. "Do you have any idea how frustrating it is that you don't believe me?" In my rearview mirror, I see a white police car pull up behind us, and my heart begins to pound. I know it's only a traffic cop, but Artie Zucker's warning about being prepared to be arrested rings in my ears. "You should go."

"This isn't about believing you, Allie."

"Who were you talking to on the phone last night?"

"What?" He jerks his head back. "No one."

"Bullshit. I heard you, Mark. Around midnight. You were on the phone."

"Oh, that. That was Caitlin. She wanted to talk about Thanksgiving."

"You were talking about me. You said something about a car following me? About how I recognized it?"

He blinks at me, expressionless. "You're being paranoid, Allie."

"Can I see your phone? Your work phone?"

"Excuse me?"

I hold out my hand. "Can I see your work phone? I want to see that it was Caitlin."

Mark lets out a low whistle. "I'd better go. That cop is headed here." He opens the door and extends his long legs, but before he climbs out, he looks back at me. "Think about making an appointment, Allie."

I watch as he disappears down the escalator into the metro and then put the car in drive just as the traffic cop is almost to my car.

My guts twist all the way home with the knowledge that Mark has betrayed me. He's been talking with Caitlin behind my back, plotting. What was it she said in the bathroom at the restaurant last week? *When you and Mark get divorced.*

The question hovers in my mind: How long have they been cooking this up?

Stop.

I tell myself to stop, remind myself that this is Mark, that yes, even though we're going through a horrible time, he loves me.

But what about that phone call last night?

My head hurts from trying to sort it all out. Back at home, I put the kettle on in the kitchen and give the brochure Mark gave me a closer look.

What to expect on your first day. You will meet with a counselor during intake and be given a complete examination to assess your physical wellness.

You will then be screened to determine if there are drugs or alcohol in your system. If you test positive for drugs or alcohol, you will be taken to detox, which usually lasts three to ten days. If no substances are found in your system, you will go straight to the rehabilitation center.

Think about making an appointment, Allie.

His plea could be coming from the heart, out of love and concern. Or it could be something darker. I cannot overlook that Caitlin's specialty is getting full custody for fathers.

The kettle shrieks, and I pour hot water into a mug. I pick up the phone and put it back down. A part of me is willing to make the bargain—an appointment at the treatment center in exchange for preserving my marriage and family.

But what would I say once I arrived at Bridgeways? That my husband thinks I have a drinking problem, but I don't? That the police think I've killed my neighbor? That somebody is out to get me and no one believes me? It sounds crazy. They'd lock me up.

I saw a documentary once about a man who was wrongly convicted of rape. Every time he'd come up for parole, he couldn't bring himself to apologize for something he had not done. *Just show remorse to the parole board,* his lawyer would tell him every year, *and you'll be released.*

But he couldn't do it.

Could I show remorse for something I hadn't done? God knows I'm not a perfect mother. I forgot Blue Day. I can't bake to save my life. But I'm not the person Mark has painted me out to be.

I pick up my cell phone and see the voice mail notification from earlier. I don't recognize the number and hit Play.

"Ms. Ross? Detective Khoury here from the Montgomery County Police Department. I have some news for you. We located the Paul Adamson that you mentioned." A shiver runs through me at the sound of Paul's name. With trembling fingers,

I pause the message, not quite ready to hear what the detective has found.

I realize I have been waiting for this moment for more than sixteen years. It's a small hole in my soul, a tear that has never been mended. Where is he? What has he become? A part of me does not want him to be the one behind all this. It's pathetic, but I want a happy ending to the Paul Adamson story. Maybe he's living in Alaska with that wife I erased and their children. Maybe this whole thing has nothing to do with him.

I listen to the rest of the message. And then I replay it once more as key phrases jab at my brain like ice picks. "—cannot be responsible . . . a resident of the Mt. Auburn Cemetery . . . car crash on the Jamaicaway in Boston."

The third time I play it, the words devolve into white noise as the serpentine, tree-lined roadway springs forth in my mind. I've driven that winding route through Boston a few times. I couldn't help but notice the small piles of teddy bears and plastic flowers that dot it, shrines to those who perished on the notoriously dangerous road.

Had one of them been for Paul?

The last thing Detective Khoury says before hanging up is, "That should put your mind at ease."

But the detective is wrong. I do not feel at ease. I feel unmoored, adrift. That rip can never be sewn up now. Paul's been dead all these years. I'll never learn why he did that to me. Was there something defective about me, some kind of high-pitched whistle that only predators can hear, that led him to me?

I was twelve years younger, his student. I was clearly troubled. A different teacher might have rebuffed me, called my mother, notified the school counselor. But he didn't help me. Instead, he took me to a motel room where I traded my virginity and my innocence for a few hours of uninterrupted adult attention.

For the first time, I feel a disgust for him.

But now I know: Paul can't possibly be behind what's been happening.

But Paul had a wife.

Correction, a widow.

I stare at my phone for a moment, then at the brochure for Bridgeways, before I dial. I don't want to do this, but I have no choice.

The phone on the other end clicks on the first ring.

"This is Allie Ross," I say, trying to keep my voice from trembling. "I need your help."

"I figured you'd call," Dustin says. "It was just a matter of time."

41

I brake suddenly to avoid hitting an enormous black Mercedes SUV that's trying to cut in front of me. Construction workers have torn up the left lane on Wisconsin Avenue so that the two lanes must merge into one. All the drivers had been taking turns in a civil manner, alternating one car from each lane, until this guy came barreling along.

I'm supposed to meet Dustin at a Starbucks near his high school in twenty minutes, and I don't want to be late. I'm almost there when my phone rings. It's Krystle. We have not spoken since the other night when she called me a cunt and I hung up on her.

I hesitate, but then accept the call.

"Are you still mad at me?" Krystle asks as soon as I answer. "I hate the way we left things."

"Yeah, me, too." I note that feeling bad doesn't equate to an apology for her. But then again, I never ask her to provide one. When we were kids, we would fight like drunken dockworkers, kicking and biting, scratching and screaming. I would retreat to our room, while she would camp out on the sofa in the living room in front of the TV. But at some point in the night, she would crawl into my single bed without saying a word. We would wake up in a tangle of limbs, whatever storm that had raged the night before having passed.

"I know you think the mortgage thing is my fault, and I promise I am going to fix it," she says, her words bursting forth like a current. "I'm going to find out what happened to that money."

I sigh as I turn right onto Montgomery Avenue and into a public parking garage.

"Honestly, Sharon's house is the last thing on my mind right now," I say. "The past few days have been hell."

"Tell me everything." This is typical Krystle, swinging from one polarity to the other. One day she's a raging bitch, the next she's the most empathic confidante. It's enough to give me whiplash, but today, I need support wherever I can find it.

I tell Krystle everything, about the police investigating me, about the phone call I overheard last night. And Mark's urging me to go to Bridgeways.

"This is a nightmare. What are you going to do?"

"I'm going to meet Dustin."

"That weird kid that lives across the street from you?"

"I feel like he might be able to help. It can't hurt."

She doesn't respond.

"Krystle? You there?"

"Yeah, I'm here. I'm just not sure that's a great idea."

"Meaning what, exactly?" I get out of the car and lock it, keeping my phone to my ear. I look around, making a mental note of where I've parked.

"Meaning, no offense, but this all sounds really crazy. You're a suspect in a murder investigation? Someone leaked photos and got you fired, and now a car is following you. So you've hired your freak neighbor to hack into your computer?"

"He's not a freak. Well, not more than any other teenager is," I say as I head down the stairs. "He's the first person who might really be able to help me."

I get a bitter laugh in response. "Did it ever occur to you that this kid might be who's behind all this online harassment? And now you're paying him money to quote-unquote fix it?"

With my shoulder, I push open the garage's exit door and find myself on an unfamiliar street. It takes me a moment to orient myself. I've never been to this part of downtown Bethesda.

Then I spot the Starbucks on the ground floor of a soulless office building on the corner.

"I mean, it sounds like a pretty good scam to me," Krystle says. "Harass the new neighbor and then offer to fix it—for a few thousand dollars, of course."

"That's not what's happening." I walk as fast as I can without breaking into a jog. I'm five minutes late, and I have no idea if Dustin will wait around for me or if he has to get back to class.

"I mean, this stuff all started when you moved in across the street from him, right? And wasn't it his mom who took you to the pool that day someone took your picture in that bikini? Was this Dustin kid there?"

I pause. I don't know if he was there. I hadn't thought about it. I brush the question away. It's a distraction. "Forget Dustin. Dustin isn't following me in an Audi. Have you heard anything else I said?"

Inside Starbucks, I scan the room for Dustin in his familiar hoodie. Bethesda High School is a few blocks away and, judging from the number of teenagers sipping from white paper cups, this is a popular hangout. But no Dustin. I get in line for an espresso. I need it. It'll be my third dose of the day. The other two didn't even put a dent in my grogginess.

"Allie, have you considered that maybe, just maybe, it's not the worst idea to go check out this Bridgeways place? Not because this stuff is all your fault but because you seem really stressed."

"Whose side are you on?" I snap and then offer a smile to the confused-looking barista, a young pockmarked guy with a gray beanie pulled low over his forehead. "Espresso. Actually, double espresso, please."

I step aside to wait for my coffee.

"I am on your side," Krystle says. "I want to help you. But is now the time to run off and play Nancy Drew? Listen, do you want me to take over Sharon's affairs? I'd be happy to become power of attorney if that would help."

I bite the inside of my cheek, thinking of what Mark said about Krystle being the one who took out the reverse mortgage. It's true that her requests for emergency cash infusions have morphed over the years from midnight runs to Western Union to curt texts asking for me to Venmo her. But I know my sister. She's not a great money manager, and maybe she doesn't exactly have her shit together yet, but she wouldn't do this to me. She wouldn't put me through this. "If you want to help me, you can look into what's going on with the house in Westport."

"Already on it. In fact, I spoke to a detective in Westport this morning about the reverse mortgage."

"You did?" A barista calls my name. I grab my small cup and head toward two unoccupied chairs.

"Don't sound so surprised. I'm not an idiot, Allie." Her tone is terse. I've offended her. But I have to admit that I am surprised.

"I know you're not an idiot. I think that's awesome that you're doing this."

"You think this is all my fault," Krystle says.

"No, I don't." I hope the brusqueness in my voice cuts this short. I can't get into this again. Yes, if she had been more alert, maybe this wouldn't have happened. But it's just as much my fault for expecting her to be on top of it. "So this detective, what did he say?"

"He said this kind of fraud is very common. They get your social security number and date of birth, and that's all they need. They said this kind of thing happens to people in nursing homes all the time. They get scammed like this."

"What's the next step?"

I see the familiar, stooped figure enter. Dustin pulls off his hoodie and looks around the room until his eyes lock with mine.

"They open an investigation," Krystle says. "He asked me for a bunch of information—"

"Look, I've got to go, Krystle. Dustin's here. Just give the police whatever they need and keep me posted."

Dustin lurches toward me, his backpack slung over one shoulder. I clear my stuff off the beat-up, upholstered chair next to me that I've been saving for him.

"Well, call me later," Krystle says. "And be careful. I don't trust this freak."

42

"Rule number one is you can't tell my mom." Dustin pulls a laptop covered in stickers from his bag.

"And why not?" I wasn't planning on mentioning our meeting to Leah, but I want to hear his reasoning.

"She wouldn't understand." Up close, I can see that his ever-present black hoodie is filthy, with dark grease stains on the sleeves. A smattering of white dots, like a dusting of snow, lies across his shoulders. Dandruff, maybe. For a split second, I wonder if Krystle's right, if maybe this isn't such a good idea. Dustin grunts. "She thinks I spend too much time on computers as it is. She wants me to have hobbies. Like *sports*."

He spits out that last word with the same scorn as if Leah had nagged him to take up belly dancing.

"Dustin, I'm not going to lie to your mother. We're friends."

"I didn't say you should lie." He crosses and uncrosses his long, spidery legs. "But you don't have to, like, tell her, if she doesn't ask, right?"

"I guess not."

"How about this. You tell me what's happened, and then I tell you what I can do, and then you can decide if you want to hire me."

I sigh, not sure where to start. I feel as if I have run down this list so many times in the past few days—to friends, Krystle, the police—and no one has been able to help. But I do it again, making sure to hit the details I think Dustin's savviness can be applied to.

As I recount all this, I watch Dustin's face for signs that he finds all this far-fetched—a roll of the eyes, a smirk. But besides the occasional twitch of his beak-like nose, he stares straight at me.

"It sounds crazy, I know." I break off a bit of the dry blueberry scone I have no interest in eating and pop it in my mouth. Too much caffeine on an empty stomach can do a number on my guts.

"Nah, doesn't sound crazy to me. Sounds pretty straightforward. Someone wants to fuck with you, but they want to do it from the safety of their computer."

I am flooded with gratitude that he believes me.

"So do you think you can help me track down who is doing this?"

"Oh yeah, no prob." He opens his battered laptop. "We know that it's someone in the neighborhood, someone who belongs to the pool, or at least was at the pool that day."

I think of what Krystle said, how Dustin might be the one behind all this. "Were you at the pool that day? I mean, maybe you saw something."

He shudders. "I hate the pool. Hate everything about it, the sun, the noise. My mom used to force me to be on the swim team when I was a kid."

"You know Heather? Lives across the street from you? She took a photo that day that looks just like the one in the fake profiles." I explain in detail what I mean about the angle.

"Hmm." He types something into his laptop. "That could be a clue. I can look at her photos."

"You can do that?"

"Sure, if she stores them in the cloud or on Shutterfly."

I am struck by the realization of what I am asking Dustin to do. Hack into other people's computers.

"Look, if someone's been attacking you online, there will be evidence." He's revved up like an engine that's been gunned. "I mean, how did they get into your computer to access your work photos, for example?"

"I have no idea."

"I know you don't." Dustin rubs his knuckles together fe-verishly, his high-pitched words running together. "But I do. I mean, I will if I look at your devices. I'll be able to tell you if they have physical access—like, are they in your house, using your computer—or if they've installed a program that's being activated remotely."

Dustin's agitated state unnerves me, making it hard to focus on what he's saying.

"So we're looking for someone who has a fair amount of expe-rience with computers?"

"Not necessarily. They could just have money and have hired someone to do their dirty work."

"That's a thing?"

He guffaws as if he can't believe my stupidity. "I can name like half a dozen dudes who could do this stuff in their sleep." He grins, showcasing two rows of small, square teeth that remind me of corn kernels. "It's what I plan to do when I graduate. I'm gonna skip college—don't tell my mom—and be a paid hacker." He waves an arm toward the other customers in Starbucks. "There's probably at least one, maybe even two or three, guys in this room right now. Starbucks is a perfect phishing pond."

I look around at all the people. Whether young, old, or middle-aged, almost all are bent over some kind of device, whether it's a phone, an iPad, or a laptop.

"A phishing pond?"

"Let's say your nemesis wants to fuck you over. Let's say they hired me. I would follow you to a place where there's public Wi-Fi—like Starbucks or the library or the pool—and bring my own portable network."

I smile as if I am able to follow him. "All right. Those are all places where I've used the Wi-Fi, but I only sign on to the public Wi-Fi when I'm at Starbucks or wherever."

He snorts. "That's what you think. Let's say I camp out here with my laptop and my own open Wi-Fi network, which I re-name 'Starbucks Wi-Fi,' or if I'm at the pool, I call it 'Bethesda Pool Wi-Fi.' A certain number of customers are going to think they're connecting to the real Starbucks or pool network; but in fact, it's a trap."

"Okay. Then what happens?"

"Well, since I control the router, and my router can store data, anything you access while you're connected to my Wi-Fi net-work can be captured," he says, his knuckles twitching at warp speed. I can see red blisters along the sides of his fingers from all that rubbing. "Info like credit card numbers, usernames, and passwords—and not just for email accounts but for bank ac-counts, social media. Anything."

"I had no idea."

"Of course you didn't. Most people are complete idiots about online security."

I open my mouth to object, but he continues. "And that's not the biggest danger. The biggest danger is that someone installs either malware or spyware on your device."

I remove my laptop from my bag and put it on the low table in front of us. I may have been carrying around the instrument of my own torture. "Would you be able to figure that out by look-ing at my computer?"

Dustin nods.

"How long will you need it?"

He rolls his eyes in irritation. "A few hours? A few days? I don't know what I'm going to find. But I'll need your phone, too."

The request sends a shot of panic through me. Giving up my laptop is one thing, but my life is on my phone. I turn the small device over in my hand. "Is that really necessary? All my con-tacts, my calendar, everything is on here." I wonder how anyone will reach me in an emergency. What if something happens to Cole?

"You don't have another phone you can use?"

"No."

"You know you can buy a pay-as-you-go phone. Then have your calls forwarded to that phone."

"You mean like a burner phone?"

"Yeah. You can get them at any convenience store."

I think about it for a moment, but the thought of being separated from my phone fills me with dread.

"I'm not ready." I shake my head. "I can't just give up my phone. Can we start with my computer and see what's there? That's where my work photos were stored. If you find something, then we'll go through my phone."

He snorts. "Suit yourself. But if I were you, I wouldn't use that phone for anything sensitive for now. I'll ping you later after I look at your laptop."

"And if I need to reach you?"

"Text me, or if you have documents to show me, email me at dude@theabyss.com."

"Abyss.com?"

He titters. "It's just me and a few friends. We have our own server, so you don't need to worry about confidentiality. I'm not going to say it's unhackable, but let's just say security is tight."

"How much do you want for this?"

"It'll be five hundred up front, and then another hundred dollars an hour. If I'm going to work more than five hours on this, I'll contact you and let you decide if you want to keep going."

I knew Dustin's services were going to cost me, but I am galled by his rates. I charge half of that for my photography work, and I turn over a portion of that to Mike Chau. Or I did. Back when I had a job. "Fine. Do you want me to Venmo you?"

He scoffs. "Did you hear what I said? Don't do any financial transactions via the internet."

"Well, I don't have a checkbook with me."

"That's cool because I wouldn't take a check. Cash only."

He stands up and downs the rest of his drink, then tosses the empty cup on the table. I grab all the garbage, including his cup, and toss it on the way out.

We leave together and head to a bank around the corner. The air is crisp, proper autumn weather, and the tall office buildings create a wind tunnel that we have to lean into while we walk. We're just far enough apart from each other that no one would suspect we are together. I'm not sure if he's trying to maintain some kind of discretion or if it's just a teenager's natural reluctance to be seen with an adult.

Dustin waits behind a brick column while I withdraw the five hundred, the maximum the ATM will allow me. I wonder if he knew that.

"Here you go." I hand him the wad of cash. He turns to go, but I call him back. "One other thing. I think that someone's been following me. I have a license plate number, and I want to find the person it belongs to. The police won't help me—"

A sharp laugh like a kitten's yelp escapes his throat. "I told you so."

I jot down the info on a scrap of paper, which he plucks from my fingertips.

"So you think you can find something out?"

"Of course I can. Bring me more stuff like this—licenses, credit card numbers, cell phone numbers, email addresses—and I'll have this figured out in no time. People think they're anonymous, but there's no such thing as privacy anymore. Whether you're on the web or running around town, you are constantly being tracked, watched, and monitored."

He pulls his black hood over his head and walks off.

The wind has picked up, and a few errant drops of rain start to fall. The forecast is for rain tonight and a windstorm tomorrow. I pull the collar of my coat tight.

My car is on the second floor of the public parking garage. I take the stairs two at a time, holding my breath to keep out the stench of piss. As I round the second landing, the thud of foot-steps below echoes up through the stairwell. I pick up the pace.

My body relaxes once I'm out of the stairwell and on the sec-ond floor of the parking garage—that is, until I realize I've made an error. I've entered through the wrong staircase and will have to traverse the entire length of the dim garage to get to my car. I've just begun walking when I hear the click of the stairway door behind me. I glance over my shoulder. It's a man in a black puffy jacket, head down. He's walking right toward me.

My steps quicken. Not quite running, but I'm walking as fast as I can.

The garage is filled with cars. I'm safe, I tell myself. *Completely normal for other people to be here. It's the middle of the day.*

I take a peek over my shoulder. He's right there, just behind me. I pull my bag to my chest. I can see my car. It's so close. If I can just get inside and lock the doors, I'll be fine.

A dip in the pavement causes my ankle to twist and give out. I stumble and fall to my knees. The palms of my hands make contact with something wet and greasy. The man leans down and grabs my arm, lifting me up with the same ease with which I lift Cole. I feel helpless. My legs are like jelly as I force myself upright.

I push him back and open my mouth to scream, but nothing comes out, just a gasping for air.

He pulls his hood back, revealing a young, dark-skinned face. He holds his hands up, wide-eyed. "I'm not going to hurt you, lady." Hurt interlaced with anger fills his voice.

I try to smile, but my whole body shakes. The young man walks to a Honda minivan parked across from me. I limp to my car, the pain from my ankle radiating up my leg, my face burning with shame.

I can't go on like this. If Dustin doesn't come through for me, I have no idea what I will do.

43

"Where were you?" Cole says as soon as I walk in the door at home. "We have to go. We can't be late."

"Oh, shit," I say when I see the kitchen. I completely forgot about International Night.

"Mommy! You said the s-word."

The island is covered in trays filled with squares of shortbread. Each one boasts a toothpick hoisting a little blue rectangle with a white *X* on it. I am not up for this. Not with everything that's going on.

"That's Scotland's flag," Susan says, her voice brimming with pride.

"Terrific." I force a smile.

"I thought it would be a nice touch," Susan says. "These gave me the idea." Susan cups her ears to showcase her Union Jack earrings. "I printed them out, and we cut and taped them together, didn't we, Cole?"

Cole doesn't answer. He's returned to the task at hand—taping the unused toothpicks together end-to-end with the focus of a neurosurgeon.

Susan points to a plate filled with overbaked edges and broken cookie pieces. "These are the ones that didn't make the cut. Help yourself; they're still delicious."

Susan pushes the plate toward me. I get the feeling she won't stop until I try one, so I pop a piece in my mouth.

I wonder if there's some way I can get out of going tonight. Maybe Mark can take Cole, and I can stay home.

Cole looks up at me from his work. "Where's Daddy? Is he coming with us or meeting us at school? Ava said I could walk around with her. Can we walk around alone together, Mommy? No grown-ups? Please."

Amid this torrent of words, my phone chimes. I glance at it. It's a text from Dustin.

Found name connected to license plate: Jon Block.

I type back: *Name means nothing to me.*

"Mommy, are you listening?" Cole pulls at my sleeve. "I want to walk around with Ava. Her mom said it was okay with her if it's okay with you."

Dustin texts: *He works for a private investigation company called LFW Research.*

"Mommy!" Cole yells.

I put down the phone, sure I have seen the name LFW Research somewhere recently.

"What? Yeah, that's fine, hon." I don't really know what I have agreed to, but it elicits a fist pump from Cole. He jumps off his stool, making his pink tulle princess dress rustle.

"Why don't you get changed, and I'll see if Leah can take you and Ava over."

He frowns. "What do you mean? You're not coming?"

"I mean, Dad will be there, later." I remember how ticked Mark got when Cole pulled an envelope from his briefcase thinking it contained family photos. It had LFW Research as the return address.

Cole's chin trembles. "No, no, no. You have to be there. What if I don't like it? What if I want to come home? You said you would be at the England table. Mommy, you promised."

"Okay, sweetie, I'll go." I give his tiny little shoulders a squeeze. I can go for a little while, until Mark shows. "Let's get changed."

"I don't want to change," Cole says.

"Cole, go change. It's cold out there."

He rolls his eyes, but the iron in my voice sends him stomping upstairs. Knowing Cole, it will take him at least twenty minutes to pick out an outfit. Twenty minutes I can use to search the house for that envelope.

Now I just need to get rid of Susan.

"So, thanks for everything, Susan." I pour myself a glass of wine and stand there expectantly.

"Not a problem." Susan flits around the kitchen, tidying and chatting, oblivious to my chilliness. Her bubbly cheer, normally so reassuring, grates on me today like the tinny tune of a jack-in-the-box playing over and over. The clock on the wall ticks. I'm not sure how to make her leave without seeming rude.

"You probably want to get home to walk Marnie. I can take it from here."

"Oh." She straightens up, sponge in mid-swipe. "You sure? I feel like I've left you a mess here."

"You're sweet, but I can clean up later."

As soon as she's gone, I head to the guest room and begin looking through the boxes that contain our files. Even in moving boxes, Mark is a meticulous filer. No months-old receipts or scraps of paper with mysterious numbers scrawled on them. Each file gets its own folder, labeled *Utilities, Health Care, House,* et cetera. Nothing out of place.

And nothing that says LFW Research.

I sit on the floor and drink my wine. Who was I kidding? He wouldn't just file it away under *L*.

I stand up, wondering where to look next. In the bedroom, I rummage through Mark's dresser drawers, sliding my hands between his neatly folded clothing, searching for something out of the norm. In his bottom drawer, beneath plaid flannel pajamas, my fingers touch something crinkly.

I pull out a manila envelope, the same one that I saw in the kitchen, marked with a return address for LFW Research.

My heart thumps as I open it.

On top are several recent photographs of me—walking Cole to school, entering my mother's assisted living facility, leaving the Mike Chau studio. It all falls into place. This must be who Mark was talking to the other night. The private investigator he hired.

As disturbing as these images are, in some way they comfort me. I wasn't being paranoid. I *was* being followed.

A woman's shrill laugh from downstairs catches me off guard. Someone is in the house. I flip past the photos to a photocopy of two newspaper articles laid side by side, both from the *Stamford Advocate*. The first headline reads: POPULAR PREP-SCHOOL TEACHER CHARGED WITH STATUTORY RAPE.

My eyes drop to the second headline: RAPE CHARGES DROPPED.

My breath is ripped from my lungs. I struggle to breathe deeply. I know the articles well. I cut them out when they were first published sixteen years ago and took them into my room, weeping.

"What are you doing?" Cole asks, appearing in the doorway of the bedroom.

Quickly, I try to stuff the papers back into the envelope. "Nothing."

He tugs at the waistband of the sweatpants he's pulled on beneath his dress. "What're those? I want to see."

I shove the envelope under Mark's flannel pajamas and shut the drawer. "Did I hear someone downstairs?"

He nods solemnly, still eyeing the drawer.

"Let's go say hi." I stand up and take his hand.

But all I can think of on the way down is: *Mark knows.*

In my kitchen, I find Daisy, Leah, and Ava. Mother and daughter wear skinny jeans and light blue tees with blue Hebrew letters on them.

"What does your shirt say?" Cole asks.

Leah puts one hand on her hip and bends down. "They say *shalom,* which is the Hebrew word for peace."

"And hello," Ava says, jutting out one tiny hip and flipping her long, dark hair.

Leah laughs. "And goodbye, too."

Daisy waves a bottle of champagne.

"Guess who just sold the Beckerman house?"

I turn to Ava. "Honey, can you take Cole upstairs and help him change out of his dress? Cole, can you please put on a proper shirt?"

This time, he doesn't resist.

"But don't hurry," Daisy says, patting Ava on the head as she waltzes by. "The mommies need to drink this first."

Ava runs off, and Daisy pops the champagne, letting out a whoop. "Thought I would never sell that damn house. It's been on the market since mid-June."

Leah grabs two coffee mugs, fills them, and hands one to Daisy and one to me. My phone beeps with an incoming text. When I see it's from Madeline, my chest tightens. I open my messages, holding my breath. I may be about to learn who Paul Adamson's wife is. A part of me thinks I will be looking at a familiar face, like Vicki's. But when I read the message, all it says is that Madeline asked her mother, who promised she would look through her old garden club newsletters tonight.

I put the phone down.

"Everything all right?" Leah asks.

I stretch my lips into a tight smile and reach for my mug of champagne.

"We're keepin' it classy, right?" Daisy giggles.

I sip at mine, aware that I am getting buzzed. I don't want to be drunk at International Night, but I'd be lying if I didn't admit I loved how the cool, sparkling bubbles soothe my throat.

Leah juts her chin at me, a sad smile on her face. "How are you holding up, Allie? Doing okay?"

I shake my head. "Not really." I haven't told them about the police homing in on me as a suspect.

She refills my mug. "What's going on?"

I look at these two women, wondering how much to tell them. I am tempted to shut down, pull into my shell like a turtle. But I need support now; I can't handle this latest bombshell on my own. And Daisy and Leah are real friends. They have been nothing but empathic.

Daisy frowns. "Not another online thing, is it?"

I shake my head. She places one soft hand over mine. The heat from her body radiates through me, uncorking all my bottled-up feelings. "Mark hired a private detective to follow me, and I don't know why. I would tell him anything he wanted to know, so why would he do that? It makes no sense to me."

They both step closer to me and hug me at the same time. I feel the tears come to my eyes and blink them away. I'm just glad Cole is upstairs with Ava and can't see me lose it like this.

"How did you find out?" Daisy asks.

"I found an envelope with pictures," I say, careful to leave Dustin's involvement out of my explanation. "I thought someone had been following me."

Leah squeezes my shoulder. "Do you think it's because of the whole Rob Avery thing? Like maybe he's trying to clear your name?"

"Maybe. I hadn't thought of that." I straighten up so her hand falls back. The idea cheers me up a bit. Maybe that's what it is, an effort to exonerate me. But if that's the case, why not tell me?

"Did you ever go to the police?" Daisy asks. "About the harassment?"

I let out a sharp laugh. "They were zero help. Told me to stay off screens and go ride a bike."

"Super helpful," Daisy chortles.

"Dustin was right about them—totally useless." I tip my coffee mug toward Leah.

"Dustin?" She snaps her head back and wrinkles her nose. "When were you talking to my son?"

I clear my throat, my antennae on alert. "The other day. He must have heard us talking in your kitchen. He said the police wouldn't be able to help me."

"But let me guess: He said he could?" Leah's lower lip twitches.

"He did offer."

"But you said no, right?" Leah's voice has an insistent edge to it.

I look to Daisy for guidance, but she's picking crumbs of shortbread off the counter with her thumb.

"Right." I cradle the mug in my hand, unable to meet Leah's intense gaze.

"Good," Leah says. Her emphatic response makes me question whether hiring him was the right move. No, I tell myself, he's already produced some good information. Even if he is a little off, he knows what he's doing.

Daisy reaches across Leah and pops another piece of shortbread in her mouth.

"Stop it." Leah slaps Daisy's hand. "Allie worked hard on those." At the same time, Cole runs in, having traded in his pink tulle gown for his dinosaur pajama shirt.

"Mommy didn't bake those," Cole says. "Susan did. Mommy can't bake."

"My mommy is a really good baker," Ava says.

I wince inwardly. No matter how much I do, it never feels like enough. Daisy gives me a sympathetic look. We pack everything up, grab our coats, and usher the kids outside. Leah and Ava climb into their car across the street. I shudder in the cool air. The temperatures are supposed to dip below freezing tonight for the first time this fall. Daisy starts to place the trays of shortbread in the front seat, but when she sees the banker's box full of my things from work, she heads to the trunk. I'm grateful she does not ask any questions.

"See you at school," Leah calls through her open car window as she drives by. Ava sticks her arm out the back window and waves.

I buckle Cole into his car seat, then go to help Daisy make room in the trunk for the cookie trays.

"So glad I don't have to do any of this elementary school crap anymore. Listen." She fixes her bright blue eyes on me. "Please tell me that you didn't hire Dustin."

I don't answer. I can't even meet her eyes.

"Oh, Allie. That's not a great idea."

"What? The police can't help me, and I need help." I sound brash and defensive, but everything I am saying is true. "I need to find out who is trying to ruin my life. And I think he can do it. In fact, he's already started."

Daisy raises one eyebrow. "How so?"

"C'mon, Mommy!" Cole yells from the back seat. "We're gonna be late!"

"He's the one who figured out that Mark hired a private investigator."

"There's no doubt in my mind that Dustin is smart and can do what he says, but . . ."

"But what?"

"Leah would kill me if she knew I was telling you this, but he got in trouble last year. There was a teacher whom he had it in for, and he went to town on her. Made a fake Twitter profile and had her tweeting all sorts of inappropriate stuff. She got fired, Allie. It was all sorted out in the end, but not until the damage was done."

"What happened to her?"

"I don't know the details. She's teaching at a different school now. Private."

"And Dustin?"

Cole pounds on the rear window with his fists.

Daisy shakes her head. "I don't know the details. There was some level of punishment. He finished last spring semester at home, which practically killed Leah. Had to stay off computers for like six months, something like that. Anyway, I think you should be careful is all."

44

I ease the car into the parking lot, my head fuzzy. Although I didn't drink much more than one mug back at the house, I'm having trouble concentrating. I'm not used to champagne. Apparently, it makes me loose-jointed, like a marionette with slack strings. I'll have to be careful. The last thing I want to do is embarrass myself on International Night in front of every parent at Eastbrook Elementary School.

Once I get some food in my stomach, I'll feel better.

I peer at myself in the mirror. A quick swipe of lipstick helps, but not a lot. I pull at my short hair. My mother is right: I do look like a deranged elf.

"Mommy, why aren't we going in?"

"Just a second." I glance at Cole in the rearview mirror. My mini-Mark. I cannot reconcile the Mark who hired a private investigator with the trusting man I married. He always acted as though he loved me so much that my past didn't matter. He never wanted to discuss it. This just doesn't make sense.

"I want to go! Ava is waiting for me."

Once we are out of the car, Cole rushes to the front door without me. I lag behind, struggling with the two platters of shortbread. I focus on not tripping on the uneven pavement in the dark. I can see other parents pass by in my peripheral vision, but I keep my head down and avoid eye contact.

Mark will be here. He's meeting us straight from work. What

will I say? I want to ask him about the envelope I found in his dresser, but I don't want to seem confrontational or accusatory in case he really is just trying to help me.

A trio of women in Japanese kimonos standing just inside the front door turns to appraise me. I keep my chin up and ignore them, but I wonder who knows what. Who has seen my Facebook page with that nude photo of me? The buzzing fluorescent lights are like little electric needles in my brain.

Cole and I enter the all-purpose room. During the school day, the cavernous room serves as lunch hall, assembly room, and indoor gymnasium. But tonight, it has been transformed into a miniature Epcot.

When Mark was selling me on the move back to Bethesda, he would trot out certain key facts: its population is the most educated in America; the proximity to the nation's capital puts it minutes away from great museums, landmarks, and historical sites; and finally, its immense international presence. Because many of the foreign diplomats and World Bank officials in the D.C. area live in Bethesda, Cole would be attending school with children from around the world.

The result is International Night on steroids. If my own elementary school in Connecticut had a similar event, it would probably mean mostly white moms nuking some egg rolls and enchiladas purchased at Trader Joe's. Not here at Eastbrook.

The din crashes inside my brain like cymbals, making my head ache. Chinese pop music blasts from the front of the room. What look like professional dancers are swirling around with scarves. Then I remember an email I read saying that somebody's father who works at the Chinese embassy had secured dancers to perform the traditional lion dance.

Punctuating the loud flute music are the shrieks of children and laughter of parents. Mingling together in an unholy cacophony, these sounds bounce off the linoleum floor and reverberate in my brain. Cole has complained that he can't finish lunch at school because it's too loud to eat. Now I understand what he means.

Someone has gone to great lengths to hang regulation-size flags from different countries on the painted cinder block walls. These are no paper printouts but the real deal. I locate the Union Jack and begin picking my way across the packed room to the United Kingdom table, sandwiched between the Jewish table and Bolivia.

As I pass Nigeria, someone grabs my arm. It takes me a moment to recognize Janelle from book club. She's traded in her austere pantsuit for a turquoise robe and head wrap.

"I've been wondering about you," she says, offering what looks like a plantain on a toothpick to Cole and one to me. "I wasn't sure if you'd show tonight."

"Well, I did." I take the food from her, unsure of how to gauge her concern. I can't tell how much she knows or whether she is sympathetic or not.

"Don't let that queen bee get under your skin."

"Vicki," I say. "You're talking about Vicki Armstrong."

She shakes her head. "I mean Karen Pearce. She thinks she's a better mom because she's the school room–parent coordinator and a doctor, but the truth is she just feels guilty for working too much. It's like, stop overcompensating, please."

I nod.

"When I heard she kicked you off the Halloween party because you slept with Rob Avery, I was like, whaaaaaat? If you ask me, you dodged a bullet." She turns and flashes a huge smile at a little girl who is reaching for the plantains.

"Wait, I didn't sleep with Rob Avery. Is that what you think?"

Janelle twists her head to me. "Huh? Hon, your business is your business. I'm not judging."

"*Abole!*" Janelle beams at the little girl. "Would you like to try one?"

I back away with Cole, slightly sickened at just how much everyone is talking about me. When I get to the United Kingdom table, I slide my trays onto a table next to cupcake liners filled with miniature shepherd's pies.

"I'm so glad you're next to me," I whisper to Leah, who is manning her table along with a father I don't know. She gives me a funny look.

"Hello there! I'm Clare. I don't think we've met officially." I spin around to face a petite blonde in a plaid button-down. Even in teeteringly high boots, Clare comes up to my shoulders.

Her fingernails tap the triple strand of pearls on her neck. Staring at those perfect pink nails tap-tap-tapping the gleaming beads, I wonder how such tiny beads produce such a loud noise. Clare announces that she needs a "loo break" and tells me she will be back soon.

"We've got shepherd's pie, your shortbread, and these lovely little watercress tea sandwiches."

After about twenty minutes of handing out samples of British food to parents and children, I realize that I am slowing down. It's taking me a moment to understand what people are saying when they talk to me, as if their words can't find entry into my sodden brain. The loud laughter and voices reverberating through the big room ping around my skull. I need some air.

Clare reappears. Cole sees his chance and drags me into the throng.

He pulls me by the arm through the crowds around the room, stopping long enough to sample the offerings at each table. *Maybe food will wake me up,* I think, popping little morsels into my mouth. At the Italy table, we find Holly Zoni in a green, red, and white apron, offering mini-meatballs in tiny paper cups.

"*Buon appetito!*" she trills.

I realize this is the first time I have come face-to-face with Holly Zoni, although her triplets are legendary in the neighborhood. The trio of fifth-grade boys are notorious for tearing around corners on their dirt bikes, terrorizing the elderly out walking with their aides. I've read more than one thinly veiled complaint on the Facebook group.

Holly, all décolletage and flashing white smile, bends down to Cole's eye level. "And what did you make, handsome?"

"We made shortbread," Cole says.

"Actually, Susan baked it." I give her an appreciative smile. "And we have you to thank for that."

"Pardon?" Holly straightens up.

"Susan Doyle? She works for us now." Her smile remains frozen on her face, but there is no recognition in her eyes. Maybe I am not making sense. My brain feels sluggish, the thoughts ill-formed. "She used to watch the boys, right?"

"I don't know what you're talking about."

"Susan Doyle? She nannied for your triplets." I know Susan said the Zoni triplets. I am sure of it.

"Nope, not us. Never had a nanny or a sitter. I could never leave my children with a stranger. Not that I'm judging. Whatever works for you, but I just could never do that."

45

I step back, confused, as Holly turns from us to a father and daughter who have just arrived. *"Benvenuto!"*

Cole pulls at my arm. "There she is! There's Ava!" He takes off across the room, leaving me to fend for myself. The noise in the room begins to cloud out my thoughts. Did I have it wrong all this time about Susan? I had never bothered to check her references. Maybe she was talking about an entirely different set of triplets and I assumed she meant the Zonis.

Oh god, oh god, I've screwed that up, too.

A buzzing vibration emanates from my hip. It's Krystle.

"I'm in trouble," she sobs. "I need to talk to you, Allie."

"Hold on. I can't hear you that well." It's not just the din of the room. My ears feel like they're stuffed with cotton. I look for the closest exit to step outside and talk. Cole will be fine for a few minutes. It's less than fifty feet away, but it feels like I'd have to push through thousands of people to get there. Shoulder down, I delve into the crowd. Someone's elbow sends me staggering into the Korea table. I manage to right myself without knocking over the bowl of kimchi.

A woman in a shiny purple skirt glares at me. "What?" I bark at her.

"You don't sound normal," Krystle says. "What's going on?"

"Hold on!" I shout into the phone. As I try to steady myself, a tray of naan on the India table catches on my sweater and goes flying. The platter skids a few feet across the floor. I stumble toward it, but a woman with a dark topknot beats me to it. I realize it's Priya, the counselor from Georgetown who wanted me to come in the other day, and I scuttle away before she can greet me, like a feral animal caught in headlights.

"What the hell is going on, Allie?" Krystle's voice echoes in my ears. My head weighs a lot, I realize. More than normal.

"Too many people here. I need space," I say.

"Allie, this is important. I need you to focus. I spoke to the detective, and they tracked the money that was taken out in the reverse mortgage."

"Go on."

"It went to an account in Queens. They have a name."

I lean against a bulletin board, careful not to rip down any of the artwork. "Queens. Is that good?"

"No, listen, it's not good, Allie."

"Why? Who took the money?"

"Well, the name on the account is Krystle Healy. But I swear, I swear I didn't do it."

I pull the phone away from my head, so Krystle's voice is garbled and unintelligible. I'm having trouble following what she's saying. My thoughts keep drifting away from me before they are fully formed. "You took the money?"

"No, I didn't! That's what I'm trying to tell you." She's yelling through tears now, and I'm having trouble understanding what she is saying. "The detective, he thinks . . . He told me to get a lawyer. I'm so scared, Allie. What should I do?"

My phone beeps. I have another call. The screen reads: *Artie Zucker.* Out of the corner of my eye, I see the sign for the girls' bathroom. I need quiet, room to breathe. "Let me call you later." I hang up.

I answer the call from Zucker.

"Hello?" My voice sounds slurry. I must have drunk more champagne than I'd thought.

"Allie, this is Artie Zucker. I'm sorry to have to tell you this, but I think police officers are going before a judge tomorrow to get a felony warrant for your arrest."

"My arrest." I lean my shoulder against a cinder block wall and let those words sink in.

"We have to be prepared. I'll let you know more tomorrow, but it's a good idea for you and Mark to get your financing in order. Chances are bail is going to be high."

I stare at the phone after Artie hangs up, cold fear gripping me. *An arrest warrant. Bail.* I'm overheated. I need to splash cold water on my face.

The door to the girls' restroom is within reach when someone grabs my shoulder. I stumble, but right myself against the water fountain.

"What the hell?" My words bleed together as if embroidered with one piece of thread.

An enraged face zooms into view, a few inches from my own. It's Vicki, her curly hair piled into a tower atop her head. She's wearing a red peasant dress that clings in all the wrong places, but I can't identify what country she is representing.

"We need to talk," she declares.

"I don't think so."

"I did a little research on you, Allie Ross. Or should I say, Alexis Healy?"

She spits out my maiden name as if it's venom and can wound me, and she seems disappointed that I don't collapse immediately. *I've been called worse,* I want to say.

"Calm down, Vicki," says a woman whom I've just noticed standing next to her. She adjusts her cat-eye glasses. "Don't let her get to you."

"Yeah," I slur. "Calm down, *Vicki.*" I'm in no mood for her bullying.

"You think this is funny?" Vicki's face shines with sweat. A blue snakelike vein throbs along the left side of her temple. I stare at it, tempted to touch it.

Behind her, a small crowd has gathered, Karen Pearce and Oliver's mother at the center of it. They are far enough away for plausible deniability, but they are obviously rubbernecking. I see two figures approaching. The one with long, glossy hair is Leah, and the other is Janelle in her African gown and head wrap. My friends are coming to help me.

Vicki puckers her thin lips into a tiny circle as pink and wrinkly as a cat's asshole. "I know you had something to do with Rob's death. You're not going to get away with this—"

"Shut. Up. Just shut up."

Vicki's mouth opens in shock. "Did you just tell me to *shut up?*" She stretches her thin lips into a sneer and turns to the woman standing behind her. "Her whole 'I'm a victim of sexual assault' story is bullshit."

"*Survivors,* Vicki," the woman behind her whispers. "The term is *survivors.*"

"Rob isn't the first man she's falsely accused of rape." Her words silence the crowd. I don't need to look up to feel the glares. "She did it to her teacher in high school, didn't you, *Sexy Lexi?*"

"How do you know about that?" Wooziness washes over me.

Vicki holds up her phone and begins to read in a clear loud voice. "*All day long I daydream about your hands on my body. I want to feel you rub your cock against me. Your hot pulsing—*"

"Shut up!" I slap at the phone. "Just stop!"

"Does that sound like a victim to you?" she asks the crowd.

I pinch the bridge of my nose in an attempt to focus. I don't remember a Vicki from Overton. But with those words comes thundering a memory of walking into French class one late spring morning and the entire room falling quiet, all eyes on me. It was a few days after I had missed my movie date with Madeline. She had been giving me the cold shoulder since then.

I'd thought it was because she was so hurt, but now I know it was because she had lit a fuse on a bomb that would soon detonate my life, and she couldn't bear to look me in the eye.

Someone whispered, *Sexy Lexi*.

The entire class exploded in laughter.

Our teacher, Madame Saheb, came in and shushed everyone into silence, but it did nothing to stop the horrible shame growing in me like a cancer during the lesson. My naked photograph on-line was bad enough, but worse were those letters, laying out my innermost desires, naked and vulnerable for the world to mock.

I had signed them all *Sexy Lexi*.

It was a private joke, which now everyone knew.

"I have a friend who went to Overton Academy," Vicki says. "She told me everything. How you got him fired. Arrested. And then it all turned out to be bullshit."

"No." I shake my head. "That's not what happened."

She exchanges a knowing glance with her friend and snorts. "I told you she was mental."

I lean in close to her face and watch her beady eyes expand in fear. "You know what?" I say. "Fuck. You."

I turn my back on her and her friend and head into the girls' bathroom, which is empty, thank god. The only sound is the old radiator near the window, clanking as it belches out copious amounts of steamy heat.

Bone-deep fatigue grips me. My eyelids droop, and the urge to close them is impossible to resist.

"Fuck you," I repeat in a soft voice. Fuck Rob Avery for as-saulting me in the bathroom. Fuck the police for not believing me. Fuck Paul Adamson for seducing me. And most of all, fuck whoever is doing all this to me.

I take refuge in the handicapped stall. I slide down into a corner, pulling my knees to my chest. The cool tiles feel so good against my hot skin.

I will rest for just a moment. Then I can figure all this out. No one will notice if I'm gone for a minute. Cole is running around with his friends. Clare can handle the UK table.

My eyelids are so heavy. I'll let them close, just for a few moments.

46

When I crack open my crusted eyes, daylight is pouring through the window. I am in my bed, but I don't remember how I got here. I'm wearing only underwear and a bra. I try to move my legs, but they are trapped, tangled in the sheets.

My lips crack when I open my mouth. I'm so thirsty.

Someone presses a damp washcloth into my hand. I wipe it across my lips, desperate for a drop of water.

The world comes into focus. I'm lying on my side at the edge of the bed. Before me are Mark's feet, wearing socks with pictures of little tacos on them, a gift from Cole last Christmas. He passes me a cup of water. I bring it to my mouth and sip eagerly.

"What happened?" The words grate against my sore throat. Even in incremental movements, sitting up hurts. "I don't remember anything."

"What happened?" Mark glares at me, radiating fury. I search my brain for what I could have done. "Let's see, you passed out drunk at International Night. Leah found you in the bathroom. She was about to call an ambulance when someone came and got me."

Bits of the night bounce around in my brain in an incoherent collage—the articles in Mark's drawer, the confrontation with Vicki, Krystle and the reverse mortgage.

"I kind of remember going into the girls' bathroom."

"I had to carry you out fireman-style," Mark says. "In front of the entire school community. Cole watched."

"Is he all right?" I cringe, thinking of Cole seeing me that way.

"Not really. He was hysterical. He wanted to know if you were dead."

"Where is he?" I swing my legs over the edge of the bed. Bad idea to move so fast. The sudden action makes me feel like I'm going to puke.

"Don't worry about Cole. He's all right now."

I look at the clock. "It's almost ten. He's at school?"

"He didn't want to leave you, he was so worried about you."

"This doesn't make sense. I didn't drink enough to get drunk, let alone pass out for this long." I push back the covers and try to stand up. I make it on my second try, with no help from Mark. I'm unsteady on my feet. "I don't know what happened."

"You don't? Let's see if I can fill in the blanks. For starters, there was an empty bottle of wine in your back seat. You'll need to do a better job of hiding those, Allie."

"Bottle of wine?" I shake my head. "That's not right."

"And the travel mug trick. It only works if you rinse it out, Allie."

"What travel mug trick?" I pull on my terry cloth robe. Unable to locate the belt, I leave it hanging open.

"Your travel mug? You almost emptied it, but it stank to high heaven. I just thank god that you didn't get into an accident. When I think of what could have happened to Cole."

"Travel mug? You're not making sense." I sit back down on the edge of the bed.

"The travel mug you drank the wine out of, Allie! I found it. In the car. Stinking of booze."

I recognize the words, but the meaning eludes me. "Are you saying you think I was drinking and driving? Never. You know that." Even as I say it, I remember feeling a little tipsy as I pulled into the school parking lot. But I wasn't drunk. "I had a little bit to drink with Daisy and Leah, but not enough to get drunk."

"Stop."

"Listen, Mark. I don't know what you think you found, but if there was a bottle of wine in the car, I did not put it there."

"Enough, Allie."

"Someone else did. In fact, I think someone might have drugged me."

"Drugged you? Are you serious? No one else put an empty bottle of Matua in your car. No one else put your travel mug in the car."

"Listen to me, Mark. Someone is doing this to me. I swear—"

"Shut up! Just shut up!" He slams his open hand on the wall. The impact sends a black-and-white framed Man Ray photograph onto the floor. I freeze, staring at her cheeks, dotted with round tears. Neither of us makes a move to pick it up. Mark takes a deep breath. "I called the studio today to let them know that you'd be out sick. Imagine my surprise to find you don't work there anymore. That you were fired."

His face is beet red, his anger unfurled like a flag.

"I was going to tell you," I say evenly. "I swear. It just happened."

"Bullshit. You lied to my face yesterday. When I asked why you weren't at work."

"I wanted to tell you, but there were so many other things going on—"

"Uh-huh. And what about this, Allie?" He pulls a silvery object out of his pocket and flicks it at me. It lands on the floor. "How do you explain that?"

The sunlight streaming through the window glints off the object. I bend down and pick it up. It's an empty condom wrapper, the top torn off.

"Where did you find this?" My voice is so soft, I can barely hear it.

"Under the front passenger's seat." He sinks down into a crouching position, his head in his hands. "I can't do this anymore, Allie."

"You can't think that was mine. Mark. Someone must have put it there."

"Please stop acting like you are the victim here."

"I *am* the victim, Mark. That's what I'm trying to tell you. And if you loved me, you would listen."

"That's not fair. You know I love you. I have tried to be understanding. I have tried to help." He stands up and clears his throat. "I'm heading out to the Eastern Shore to meet Caitlin. She's already taken Cole. I've made an appointment for you at Bridgeways for this afternoon—"

"You did what? Listen, you can't do this. There's a chance I'm going to be arrested."

He jerks his head back. "What?"

"That's what Artie Zucker told me last night. He said to be ready."

"That's convenient."

His cold reaction stuns me. I know he's upset, but still, I expected sympathy. "It's true." I spit the words at him. "You think I'm lying about being arrested?"

"Honestly, I don't know what to think. If you're arrested, obviously you can't meet me at—"

"That's very understanding, Mark."

He ignores my sarcasm. "Let me finish. I plan on meeting you there, at Bridgeways, at five p.m. Of course, if something happens, and you physically can't make it . . ." He exhales deeply. "But I'm telling you, Allie, if you're not there at five, and you don't have a damn good reason, I'm filing for emergency temporary custody."

Emergency custody. The two words knock the wind out of me. My chest feels concave, sucking in on itself. I open my mouth to take in air, but my lungs won't expand.

He's going to take Cole.

When I look up, Mark has left the room. I can't let him do

this. I force myself to stand despite the dizziness and follow him down the stairs.

"You can't do this!" I yell at his back as we pass through the dining room. In the kitchen, he pauses at the refrigerator to take out a bottle of water.

"I want to help you. I'm trying to help you. But I can't let Cole see you like this. I don't want to do this, believe me, but—"

"If you don't want to, don't."

He shuts the fridge and continues to the mudroom, where he tucks the water bottle into his overnight bag. It's packed full of clothing. This is a fait accompli. There was never going to be a discussion. He opens the back door and walks out. Bits of stone and twigs dig into my bare feet as I stumble after him, my robe flapping around me, the cold air hitting my bare torso.

"Emergency custody?" I have to force the words out as I run.

Mark pops open the trunk of his car and places his bag inside.

"I found the file," I say, out of breath. "I know you hired someone to follow me. To spy on me."

He slams the trunk shut. "You went through my things?"

"That's what matters to you? That I went through your things? You hired a private detective, Mark. To spy on your wife."

"You don't know what you're talking about."

"Then explain it." We stare at each other for a moment that stretches on. We are like two actors on a stage who have forgotten our lines. I, the accommodating wife. He, the stalwart husband. If only someone from backstage could whisper them to us.

"Caitlin hired that detective," Mark says, a tremor in his voice. "I didn't ask her to. I didn't even read the file."

"I don't believe you. I heard you on the phone the other night. The night I told you that car was on our block?"

He lets out an anemic laugh. "Allie, you've got this all wrong. Caitlin hired the guy without asking me, but once she told me about the detective, I asked him to look into everything that has been going on. To try to find out who is doing this to you. Caitlin said he's the best."

"Caitlin. Did she put this in my car, too?" I toss the condom wrapper at him. "Maybe she's the one who's been behind all this online crap."

"That's crazy. Why would she do that?"

"She never liked me. Maybe she's trying to split us up."

Mark pushes me aside so he can open the driver-side door.

"To guarantee custody of Cole? Or maybe she wants him for herself."

He snorts. "Do you even hear yourself? You sound crazy."

"Do I?" I say, positioning my body so he can't shut the door. "What is it that Caitlin said about her precious trifecta? No job, substance abuse, infidelity. Is that what you want? What your family wants?"

"You know it's not what I want." He starts the engine and reaches to close the door. "I have to go, Allie. I don't want to fight with you."

I don't budge.

"Now please, move back before you get hurt."

47

But I am hurt already. Watching Mark drive away, my whole body begins to ache like I have the flu. I am alone on my street, my robe flapping around me. I yank it tight as his ultimatum rings in my ears: check into rehab or he'll file for custody.

I fall to the wet asphalt, feeling like the earth is dropping out from under me, and I'm scared I might be sick right there on the street. From the corner of my eye, I see two figures and a small dog coming this way. I wipe away my tears, and the forms take shape. Daisy is bundled into a yellow slicker, like the kind old-fashioned fishermen wear, and Leah is holding a thin leash attached to Dustin's therapy dog.

Daisy and Leah, Leah and Daisy, always there at every turn. A strange mixture of comfort and unease fills me. A notion lurks in the shadows of my thoughts, but before I can pinch it and pull it into the light, they are beside me, cooing kind words and lifting me up.

Arms around me, they sweep me inside, clucking over me. I let myself be carried along by their confident concern like a broken tree branch being swept down a river. I haven't even had time to process what happened with Mark. They get straight to work in my kitchen, putting the kettle on, banging cabinet doors, looking for tea and honey and mugs.

Dustin's small, yippy dog, whose name I can't recall, runs around the kitchen sniffing everything in sight.

Custody. The very word makes my stomach curdle. I don't know if he can even do that. And I don't know whom to ask. Whatever happens, I cannot lose Cole.

Daisy puts a steaming mug in front of me. "You poor thing," she says. She could be referring to any number of things—my public fight with Mark just now or my passing out at International Night. I cringe at the thought.

Leah puts the condom wrapper on the counter. She must have picked it up from the street after I tossed it.

"Do you want to talk about this?"

"Not really."

"What happened last night?" Leah's eyes scan my face for an answer. "Had you taken a Xanax or an Ativan?"

I shake my head.

"We were so worried about you." Daisy purses her cupid-bow lips together.

"I think someone drugged me."

They shoot each other a look. It's quick, so quick I could easily have missed it. They don't believe me.

"You think someone drugged you?" Leah asks, her voice as soft and gentle as a cotton ball.

"I don't know. It could have been anyone. I ate a ton of different food."

No one speaks. The only sound is the *click–click–click* of the little dog's nails on my wooden floor.

"So you think someone made food for International Night," Leah says slowly, "and put aside a little bit with drugs in it for you?" She keeps glancing over at Daisy when she says this.

"I don't know. Maybe." I jut my chin out, challenging them to question me.

"Allie, we're trying to help."

"Well, it's not helping. I don't need friends who don't believe me."

"We believe you," Leah says. Daisy nods in agreement and puts her hand on my back. My defenses melt, as does any effort at staying composed. Tears pour forth, and I can't stop them. I put my face in my hands as my whole body convulses with deep sobs. Leah presses a paper towel into my hand, and Daisy rubs my back, which just makes me cry harder. The past ten days have been like hurtling up and down a monster roller coaster. Just when I think things are winding down, I find myself perched on the brink of disaster once again. "Mark took Cole for the weekend. He's given me an ultimatum," I say through tears. "If I don't go to rehab, he's going to file for emergency custody of Cole." I look up at their faces. "Can he do that?"

I scan their faces for answers, but they offer none. "Well, I'm not going. That's for sure," I say.

Leah chews her lip. Daisy shrugs.

"What?" I ask. "You think I should go?"

"I don't know." Leah sighs. "I'm not saying he's handling this the best way possible—"

"Definitely not," Daisy says, making circles on my back with her palm.

"But maybe some time away wouldn't be the worst idea. You need a break, Allie."

Her touch, which had soothed me moments before, now feels oppressive to me, and I shake her hand off. I stand up straight. "You guys think I need to go to rehab?"

"That's not what we're saying," Daisy says. "It's just . . ."

"It's just what?"

"Would it hurt to go talk to someone? Take a little vacation from all this craziness?"

"Maybe it'll be good to get away for a few days," Daisy says. "Talk to a professional, someone who can be objective about everything that's been going on?"

Before I can answer, the tinny sound of a cell phone rings from the mudroom. "That's my phone," I say. "I should get it."

Leah steps toward me. "Sweetie, we only want what's best for you."

I grab my phone and groan. It's Morningside House. The last thing I need is more drama with my mother. "Hold on, please," I say as soon as I answer. Then I hold the phone to my chest. "I need to take this."

Daisy's mouth drops open, but she doesn't speak. I wait until they are gone before I put the phone to my ear.

"This is Lydia from Morningside House. Your mother has been taken to the emergency room."

48

Once upon a time, a call that my mother was in the emergency room would have sent me into a tailspin. But over the past few years, I have gotten used to getting one every few months. Stumbles and falls, mostly. The problem with a dementia patient is that when she falls, she often has no memory of it, and she can even have difficulty expressing that she is in pain.

That's where the emergency room visits come in. If the patient can't communicate, most facilities send their residents to the hospital to run every test known to man, just in case.

A total CYA move.

I'd been through this with Sharon a dozen times, and as I drive to the hospital, I say a little prayer that this is one of those times. A routine fall. Nothing more. I am grateful that her assisted living center sent her to Suburban, like I specified on her forms. It's only a ten-minute drive from my house.

I don't think I can handle anything more right now.

As I drive, I dial Krystle's number, but the call goes straight to voice mail. I dial again and again, without success. I know my sister. She is never more than ten feet away from her phone. If she could have it surgically attached to her body, she would.

A fat raindrop plops on the windshield. I look up at the milky white sky, which perfectly reflects the gloom suffocating me. It's only a matter of minutes until it pours. Bits of last night's conversation with Krystle float back to me as I wait at a red light. Something about an account opened up in her name.

It feels like the three of us—Krystle, Sharon, and me—are all cursed.

I turn into Suburban Hospital's large parking lot and find a spot. I dash through the hospital's sliding doors just as the rain comes pouring down. I get in line behind an elderly man at the information desk. My phone buzzes, and I pull it out, hoping it is Krystle, but it's Leah. I send the call to voice mail.

"I'm here to see my mother, Sharon Healy. Is she all right?"

The woman assures me my mother is in good hands. She takes my name, gives me a visitor's sticker, and sends me around the corner to wait. I sit below a television turned to the news and pick up a *Redbook* magazine from last winter. *Five Easy Fifteen-Minute Dinners for Weekday Nights.* I put it down, unable to concentrate.

I keep looking at my phone, willing Krystle to call. A crack of thunder makes me jump in my seat. A young woman sitting across from me tenderly holding her arm gives me a wan smile.

At this moment, Cole and Caitlin may be driving over the Bay Bridge on their way to the Eastern Shore. The first time I crossed the massive steel-and-concrete arc, I almost had a panic attack. The drive was endless, and though the bright blue Chesapeake spreading out on either side was beautiful, I was filled with visions of the car hurtling off the bridge into the water.

I hate the idea of Cole driving over it in this storm. Have they crossed yet? Did they stop somewhere to wait out the rain? I want to call Caitlin, but I don't dare. Nor can I call Mark after this morning. There's only one call Mark would want from me, one confirming that I will meet him at Bridgeways this afternoon.

My phone rings, jolting me out of my thoughts.

"Hi, Allie," Barb DeSoto says. "Is this a good time to talk?"

I almost laugh at the question, but I answer yes.

"I know this isn't what you want to hear, but now that there's a criminal investigation into the mortgage on the house, we're going to bow out. At least until things have been resolved."

"I understand." And I do understand. She has a business to run, and we cannot sell a house under these conditions. Still, it is confirmation that the reverse mortgage is more than just a wrench in the works. It's a complete disaster. I may never get that money back.

I panic, realizing that if I get arrested, I'll be leaving behind a huge mess. Who will deal with Sharon and the Westport house? Krystle?

"Please get back in touch with us once you've cleared all this up," Barb says. "I am sorry. We always knew this would be a tough one. The house had a whole host of issues to overcome even before this—being a rental property for so long, the dilapidated condition, and the ridiculously low price your mother paid for it back in 2005—"

"My mother didn't buy it," I interject. "It was an inheritance."

"I'm sure I saw in the records that she bought it for some nominal fee, something like twenty dollars. Wait, hold on, I have the deed right here." I can hear her shuffling papers in the background. "She was probably just using the word *inheritance* loosely. It's a pretty common way to pass a house down to a relative. Here we go—she purchased it for the grand sum of five dollars from Margaret Cooper."

I look up to see a woman in purple scrubs scowling at me. "Can't you read?" she hisses, pointing to a sign on the wall: No Cell Phone Use Permitted in Waiting Room.

I say goodbye quickly and put my phone on vibrate. The nurse, satisfied, walks away muttering under her breath about selfishness.

Margaret Cooper. I know that I've heard that name before, and I don't think it was in connection with the Westport house. Then I remember—that was the name of the woman Sharon said had come into her room and tried to hurt her.

If that was the name of the great-aunt who left my mother the Westport house, then Sharon must have experienced a dementia-induced episode where she thought her late aunt visited her.

I was unaware of the details of my mother inheriting the house until it was all over. At the time, I never learned the name of the relative who left it to Sharon, and there was no one else to ask. The whole thing happened while I was in San Francisco, and my mother was never very forthcoming about the details. All I knew was that an elderly aunt had died, one whom my mother had never mentioned, whom we had never met, and who had no other living relatives. That was all Sharon ever said when I pressed her. That wasn't unusual for my mother; she could be as tight-lipped as a Cold War spy when she wanted to be.

I guess that aunt must have been named Margaret Cooper. A quick search on my phone brings up nothing useful. The world abounds with Margaret Coopers. What had my mother said about that imaginary visit? It had something to do with Krystle, but I can't recall what exactly.

"Alexis Ross?" I look up to see a man in a white coat adjusting his glasses. "Dr. Ahmed."

He doesn't offer his hand or lead me to a more private place to talk but launches immediately into an emotionless recitation of my mother's condition.

"Your mother is in stable condition after ingesting a substantial amount of ethylene glycol. Not that any amount of ethylene glycol is safe for ingestion, but—"

"I'm sorry to interrupt, but what is ethylene glycol?"

His brown eyes widen behind his round glasses. "It's the main component in antifreeze."

"Antifreeze?" The word sends a chill through me. "Where the hell did she get antifreeze?"

He shrugs. "At the levels found in her, she is lucky to be alive. She was found unconscious and convulsing this morning. We have stabilized her, but we need to run some further tests and to keep an eye on her. Her heart rate was quite elevated, and she is dehydrated from all the vomiting. She's also developed metabolic acidosis as a result of the accumulation of organic acids."

I bite hard on my lip to stop from crying out. How did this happen? The doctor's increasingly obscure jargon blends into the rhythmic beating of the rain against the windows.

"Do you have any questions?" He glances at the clock above me, tapping one foot in a not-so-subtle reminder that he'd like to get back to work.

"I'd like to know how antifreeze got into my mother's system."

He holds his hands open and shrugs his slender shoulders. "I cannot answer that for certain. Along with the ethylene glycol, we did find a substantial amount of what appear to be undigested gummy candies in her stomach. But that is going to be a question for the police."

"The police?" The word reminds me that at any moment I could hear from Artie Zucker that the police have filed a warrant for my arrest.

"Yes." He nods. "This is being referred to the Montgomery County police as a matter of procedure."

"Can I see her?"

"Soon, but I'm afraid not right now. She's in the process of being transferred out of the ER, and I know the nephrologist wants to run a few tests on her kidneys. It may be a few more hours before you can see her."

He gives me a little bow of his head and then disappears behind two large double doors. I stare out at the rain, which has slowed to a drizzle, trying to process what he has told me. They found poison, along with undigested gummy candies, in my mother's stomach. I think of that box of Dots—the one I am sure I did not buy her.

I need to call Lydia at Morningside to see what they know. I have to reach Krystle, too. My stomach growls. I have not eaten anything all day, and I'm not thinking straight. The doctor said it would be a few hours. Maybe I should leave, get some food, and come back.

A text comes in from Dustin.

Wi-Fi network named EastLove. Mean anything?

EastLove. I frown. Could be any parents of an Eastbrook student.

No, I text back. *Why?*

Whoever made your Tinder account did it from EastLove.

A few seconds later, he sends me an address. I know the street; it's about four blocks from my house.

49

Wet leaves lie flattened against my windshield. I push them off and climb in my car. Adrenaline pumps through my veins as I wind my way back from the hospital toward my neighborhood.

I know I should be by my mother's side, but the urge to find out who has been torturing me is overwhelming. I promise myself that I will return to the hospital as soon as I can. But I have to go—learning the truth could keep me out of jail.

A quick glance at a map on my phone tells me that 304 Glenview sits about a quarter mile from my house, just on the other side of the community pool.

The pool where that photo of me in the blue bikini was taken. I can feel it in my bones—I'm finally going to find out who has been behind all this.

Glenview is one of a handful of short streets that make up a corner of our neighborhood untouched by the wave of demolitions and McMansions that has plagued the area. The houses here are original—modest redbrick ramblers set back from the street with identical black wrought iron railings on either side of white cement steps. Daisy had showed us a house here, a "starter" home in her vernacular, unlike our "forever" home.

I slow down, peering at the numbers as I drive. Past a house with a pumpkin flag flapping in the breeze, and past one with pots of faded purple mums outside the front door.

As I pull the car to a stop in front of 304, my phone rings. It's Artie Zucker—I have no choice but to answer.

"Don't panic, but a warrant has been entered into the system for your arrest. First-degree murder."

I gasp as if I've been sucker punched. I knew this was a possibility, but to hear it out loud still comes as a shock. A kid around Cole's age wobbles by on his bike, his father jogging after him. Stinging tears flood my eyes. "I can't go to jail."

"Take a deep breath. Calm down."

"Calm down? I'm going to be arrested for a crime I didn't commit. What the hell is going on? How can they do this?"

"Look, this is just the first step in the process—"

"I don't give a shit about the process!" I slam my fist onto the steering wheel, sending a wave of pain radiating up my arm. "I'm sorry, Artie. It's not your fault."

"I've arranged for you to turn yourself in," Artie continues as if my outburst had never taken place. "At seven a.m. tomorrow morning."

"I can do that? Turn myself in?"

"Absolutely. Police prefer when you turn yourself in, and frankly, the courts look fondly on that. Nobody wants to scoop you up in front of your kids."

I think of Cole, grateful that he is not in town to see his mother arrested. The news will devastate him. We won't be able to keep it a secret very long. My efforts to protect him from the kind of chaos I endured as a child have failed.

"I think we ought to meet later today and go over a few things," Artie says. "Like what to bring and not to bring and what you can expect. Lay out what your day is going to look like because it's going to be a long one."

I nod.

"Allie, you there?"

"Yup. I'm here."

"The good thing about turning yourself in early is that you will almost certainly be arraigned on the same day. So if bail is an option, we'll know tomorrow."

"You mean bail might not be an option?"

"We'll talk about all that later today. Does five work? It won't be a long meeting. Can Mark be there?"

"He's out of town." I don't mention that Mark thinks I will be meeting him at rehab at five.

"Fine. Then just you. My office in Rockville at five."

"I just don't understand how this is happening. I mean, what are they basing this on?"

"Apparently, they have an eyewitness."

"An eyewitness? That's impossible. An eyewitness to what?"

"I don't know. We'll know more tomorrow. I'll see you at five."

I sit there a moment, letting what Zucker said sink in. Eyewitness? Could one of these women, one of these neighborhood gossips, actually think they saw something? Or is someone so hell-bent on destroying me that they would lie to the police? But who, and why?

The answer may be on this street.

I know I need to call Mark and tell him what's happening, but the urgency to find out the truth compels me to get out of the car. I am certain in my bones that I am about to draw a direct line between what happened all those years ago and the nightmare I found myself in today.

Paul Adamson is dead.

It has to be his wife. It's the only thing that makes sense.

Sexy Lexi.

The Overton shirt.

Someone who knew about Paul Adamson, someone angry enough to want to destroy me. It makes sense in a twisted way. In the yard next door, a middle-aged woman in jeans and a down vest drags a tarp filled with leaves to the curb.

She gives me a friendly wave as I get out of my car. I wave back and practically run up the long set of cement steps to the front door. I can feel the blood pumping through my body. I am prepared for anything. I just want answers.

Gone is the shame I felt this morning when Mark told me that I had passed out at International Night. In its place is white-hot anger electrifying me to the tips of my fingers and toes.

I knock on the paneled door and wait. I can see out of the corner of my eye that the neighbor with the tarp is staring at me. I shoot her a look, telegraphing her to mind her own business.

I knock on the door again, this time with a closed fist.

A black metal mailbox molded into the shape of a giant envelope hangs on the brick wall next to the front door. I lift the flap. Maybe I'll find a letter with a name on it. But it's empty save for a flyer from Greener Pastures Landscaping. It's four o'clock. Either the mail has not yet been delivered or whoever lives here has taken it in.

A tall pane of wavy glass flanks the left side of the front door, but it is difficult to see through. All I can make out is a long, dark hallway, a slate floor, and a narrow console. This time, I bang on the door with all I've got.

Impatience gnaws at me. I step back to assess the house and yard. A mulched pathway laid with round concrete stepping-stones runs alongside the house to the back.

"They're not home," the neighbor calls.

I ignore her and head around back, taking giant half hops on the stones, which are set just far enough apart to make simple steps impossible. With a little finagling, the back-gate latch opens, and I find myself in a wide but shallow backyard. It's really just a stretch of grass parallel to a tall privacy fence. Most of the back is taken up by a slate patio, upon which sits a rusted wrought iron table and chairs.

Nothing here to identify the occupants of the house. Only a plastic blue watering can, bleached by the sun, lying on its side next to a few terra-cotta pots.

A wide sliding-glass door offers a view of the kitchen. I cup my hands over my eyes and peer inside, looking for clues. It's dark. I can make out blond wooden cabinets and yellow laminate countertops that look original to the house.

Suddenly, something lunges from the darkness inside the house and hurtles itself against the plate glass. I stumble back, trip on the edge of a chair, and fall down.

A dog's muffled yapping fills the air. Shock gives way to annoyance. I've fallen on wet leaves, which now cling to my jeans. The dampness soaks through my pants to my rear end and thighs.

"Damn it." I pick myself up, peeling off the leaves. On the other side of the glass, a small white dog propels itself at the glass once again.

A West Highland Terrier.

Marnie.

50

In an instant, the truth crystallizes. Susan lives here.

How could I not know that? My face flushes hot as it hits me how careless I have been. I allowed this woman into my home and into my life, and I never even bothered to learn her address. I spent more time researching scooters for Cole than I did checking on Susan.

I trusted her implicitly, and why wouldn't I? An older woman, so warm and maternal, always ready with the right recipe or a piece of poster board. How easy it was for her to infiltrate my chaotic life. She must have been laughing at me the whole time.

I gave her the key to our house.

I entrusted my son to her.

Could she have been married to Paul? Impossible. She would have been a good twenty years older, at least.

Then it hits me—she is Paul's mother. She blames me for his death. What would I do if I thought someone had been responsible for Cole's death? Would I track that person down and claw their life to shreds?

I might.

Bits of data zip across my brain.

It would have been easy for her to plant the liquid Ambien. She had access to my home computer, too, no password required.

I've seen her at the pool.

She lied about the Zoni triplets.

The Overton T-shirt—it could all easily be her doing.

From the front of the house comes the sound of a car with squeaky brakes pulling to a stop. In seconds, I am through the gate and running back down the wood-chip path to the front of the house. I emerge into the front yard just as Susan is opening the trunk of her car. I run down the hill to her.

"Hey!" I yell. "Susan!"

Susan steps out from behind the trunk, her cheeks twitching nervously. "Allie. What are you doing here?" She holds a bag of groceries in front of her as if for protection.

"I know," I say.

"You know what, dear?" Her eyes dart around, unable to focus.

"Cut the bullshit, Susan."

She seems frozen in place, not a muscle moving. "I see," she says in a soft voice. "Can we please discuss this inside? The neighbors are watching."

"I don't care. I want answers." I pull out my cell phone. "Before I call the police."

My skin tingles. Behind me, someone is approaching. I know it is Susan's neighbor even before I turn to see her pinched face.

"What's going on?" she asks, her brow furrowed. "Susan, is everything all right?"

"If you don't mind," I say, "we're in the middle of something."

"Susan?" The neighbor cranes her neck to look past me.

"She's fine! Mind your own fucking business." I turn back to Susan. "Well? Anything you want to tell me before I call the cops?"

"Don't call the police, please." Susan grabs at my phone, and I pull it away. She loses balance and tips toward me, flailing her arms before falling to the asphalt.

"Oh my god!" the neighbor exclaims and drops to her knees next to Susan. Out of the corner of my eye, I see two more people rushing toward us.

Susan lies crumpled on the ground. "I'm sorry, Allie." She peers up at me. "I can explain everything."

"You just assaulted her," the neighbor says. "I saw it with my own eyes. I should call the police."

"No!" Susan shouts and struggles to her feet, using the trunk of the car to help her up. "Please don't call the police, Nancy. I'm fine. Please."

"You're bleeding," Nancy says. "Hold on. I have a first aid kit in my car."

Susan touches her chin and looks at the blood on her hand in wonder. She turns her gaze on me. "Can we go inside, Allie?" she pleads. "I'll tell you everything, I swear."

The events of the last two weeks swirl in my head. "You're going to tell me now."

"In front of all these people?"

"Yes."

The neighbor has returned, clutching a small red nylon bag with a large white cross on it.

"Show some mercy, Allie," Susan says.

"You want mercy? Where was my mercy, Susan? Why have you been doing this to me? Are you related to Paul Adamson?"

"Paul Adamson? Who's Paul Adamson?"

"You almost ruined my life!" Behind me, a small crowd has gathered. *Let them stare,* I think. For once, I have nothing to be ashamed of. "I might lose my son because of you."

Susan's eyes fill with tears. "I just wanted the job. I knew you wouldn't hire me if you knew the truth. It was wrong to lie. I know that." She lets out a sob that seems to reduce her to even smaller stature. "I just wanted to start over."

My adrenaline drops down to zero, replaced by a sickening hunch. Something is wrong here. This isn't adding up. I search Susan's red, tear-streaked face for answers.

"I couldn't give you a reference," she says in such a small voice that I have to step closer to hear her. "I haven't held a job in years. Nothing at all. After Samuel died . . ." Her voice trails off.

Susan and I are having two different conversations.

I take a step back, and she takes one toward me as if we are dancing. "I'm good with kids," she continues. "I worked at the Montessori in Bannockburn for almost twenty years, until the drinking got to be too much. But I swear, Allie, I haven't had a drink in eighteen months. I just wanted a second chance. That's why I lied about the Zoni children."

"You lied about your references to get hired?"

"I tried telling people the truth." She hiccups. "But no one would hire a sixty-year-old woman with no references. I adore Cole. I really do. Please don't fire me."

Trembling hands outstretched, Susan wobbles toward me.

"Forgive me for lying, Allie." Snot runs down her nose. She's been transformed into a character from a children's tale, haggard, sniveling, and I'm the one who has reduced her to this. I open my mouth to speak, but no words fall from my lips. The onlookers surge past me, comforting and embracing Susan. I step back, pushed out of the circle of warmth and comfort.

Nancy with the first aid kit whips her head around.

"Aren't you that woman? The one from the internet?" she asks. "You should be ashamed of yourself."

"I didn't . . . " I start to say. "I thought . . ."

I hurry to my car, fighting back tears. I drive away, feeling as if I have left some part of my humanity behind. At the end of the block, I look in the rearview mirror through blurry eyes. The street has emptied. All the neighbors have gone inside.

Ashamed of yourself.

It hurts because it's true. I don't recognize who I've become.

Then it hits me. Dustin.

He sent me here.

But why?

51

I grip the steering wheel tightly as I drive home, wondering how I could have gotten it all so wrong.

Was Dustin toying with me? Playing a game?

Maybe Krystle was right: he was just out to make money, and I was an easy mark. Or maybe he was simply a spiteful little shit. Either way, I fell for it like an idiot.

Even after Daisy warned me.

I pull up in front of my house and stare at Leah's front door, wondering if Dustin is home. I dial his number, but he doesn't answer.

"What the hell was that?" I practically yell into the phone. "I want some answers, Dustin. You need to call me as soon as you get this message."

I text him: *WTF? Call me.*

Inside my kitchen, I pace around.

The Bridgeways brochure stares up at me from the counter. Suddenly, a week at a fancy rehab doesn't seem like such a bad idea. I'm unraveling like a cheap sweater. But I won't be making that five o'clock appointment at Bridgeways that Mark made for me. I'll be meeting with Artie Zucker to discuss the details of turning myself in to the police for murder.

I call Mark, but the call goes straight to voice mail.

"I can't meet you today at Bridgeways. Artie Zucker called. There's a warrant for my arrest, and I have to turn myself in tomorrow morning." My voice cracks on that last word, and I take a deep breath. "I'm sorry, Mark. I'm meeting him at his office at five, if you want to meet us." I pause. "I'd like you to be there if you can."

I tuck the phone in my back pocket and wander upstairs and into my bedroom. I'll need a suit or something presentable to wear in court when I am arraigned tomorrow. I open my closet, searching for an outfit that says *not guilty*.

My cell phone rings, and I lunge for it. It's not Dustin, though, it's Krystle. "Finally," I say. "Where the hell have you been?"

"With a lawyer. Allie, I'm in big trouble. It doesn't look good." The words come pouring out. "The account in Queens? The one under my name where the mortgage company sent the check to? It's been emptied out. The money's gone." Her voice catches. "Allie, I think I might go to jail. And I swear I didn't take the money."

"It's okay. It's going to be all right," I say, but even as I say the words, I know it's not. My mother's been poisoned, my sister's under suspicion for mortgage fraud, and I'm about to be arrested for murder. Someone is trying to destroy my whole family.

"No, it's not." Krystle's voice catches, surprising me. I can count on one hand the times I've seen her cry, and it was always because she was bleeding or had a broken bone. She was the one to go get my superball back from the tough boys on the corner or kick Colin MacDougal in the shins for calling me flat-chested.

"You're right. It's not." I tell her about what's happening with me, how I have to turn myself in tomorrow morning. "I'm leaving soon to meet with my lawyer to discuss the details."

"That's insane! We will fight this. If your lawyer's not good enough, we'll get you a better one. We won't let you go to jail."

"But I am going, Krystle. That's where they put you when they arrest you for first-degree murder. I may not make bail." My eyes well up.

"Why is this happening to us?" I go to the window and peer out into the dark. The rain has started up again. Across the street, at Leah's house, I see movement in the top window. I squint hard, but I cannot tell if it is a person or just my eyes playing tricks on me.

"I don't know. Is this why you were calling so many times?" Krystle asks. "In your messages, you said something about Sharon."

"I don't want to upset you, but Sharon's in the hospital." I explain everything to her—what the doctor said, the antifreeze, the gummy candies. "She was convinced some woman was out to get her, but today, I learned that the name she used was actually the relative who left her the house in Westport, so Sharon was clearly confused."

I feel a slight pang of guilt knowing that I won't be able to visit my mother at the hospital tomorrow, but I dismiss it. She's in good hands.

"You still there?" I ask Krystle.

"Who did Sharon say was out to get her?"

"She said it was Margaret Cooper. You know, her aunt?"

"And she said this woman was trying to hurt her?" A note of coolness has crept into her voice.

"Yes." I sit on the bed. "But she has dementia, Krystle. Margaret Cooper died in 2005, right after she gave the house to Sharon."

"No, she didn't."

"What on earth are you talking about?" The radiator clinks, startling me.

"I need to tell you something." Her voice quakes when she speaks. "Remember how you thought that maybe Paul Adamson was behind all the crazy things that were happening to you?"

"He's not, Krystle. He's dead."

"Fine. But what about his wife?"

"What about her?"

"Her name was Margaret Cooper."

52

The room seems to fall away from me. I have to dig my nails into my thigh to stop from screaming.

"Why did Paul Adamson's wife sell us her house for five dollars?"

"She didn't sell it to us. We stole it."

"What do you mean, stole?" I feel sick, betrayed. That my own sister would orchestrate an elaborate scam out of my own suffering.

"Oh, come on, Allie. You never suspected just once?" Her incredulity is a slap in my face. "Like Sharon has some distant relative who lived in Westport? Give me a break!"

"No, I trusted you guys. I didn't question it. You're my family." I feel queasy and confused. The news sits heavy on my chest, making it hard to get my breath.

"I mean, seriously, didn't you ever wonder? How did we, how did Sharon, who couldn't even scrape enough quarters together for the laundromat some weeks, how did she have some distant relative who left her a million-dollar home in Westport?"

"I don't know. I wasn't in Connecticut anymore. I was only seventeen, Krystle." I am furious at the way she has pivoted from her deception to my gullibility. "You lied to me. For years."

"Because you didn't want to know, that's why. You never thought, gee, what a coincidence! A month after rape charges are dropped against Paul Adamson, who lives in Westport, my mother inherits a million-dollar house in . . . wait for it . . . Westport!"

Her nastiness is palpable, and her sobs and pleas have been

replaced by cruel, cutting remarks. I rack my brain trying to recall some hint of this scheme, some clue that this was going on.
But I can't come up with anything. "I don't remember if I knew
that Paul lived in Westport."

"Give me a break. You knew every freaking detail about him.
You knew his zodiac sign. You knew his favorite Dunkin' Donut
flavor. You were obsessed with him, Allie."

"That's not fair. And it doesn't excuse what you did. What
you and Mom did was wrong." But her words ricochet within
me, triggering a cascade of thoughts. Was Krystle right? Had I
tucked away everything about that time in my life out of shame,
because I didn't want to carry that part of my past with me? I
packed it away as if it belonged to another person in another life.
But it belonged to me. It shaped me and who I've become.

But now I need to face it, all of it.

"How did it all happen?" I ask, my tone cool. I can't trigger
a reaction from her now. There will be time for recriminations
later. I need the truth. "Exactly how did we get the house?"

"Sharon and I made it happen, that's how. You can thank us
that you never had to take a single loan out for college or art
school." She takes a deep breath. "I'll never forget when that
lady came to our apartment looking for you. It was a Saturday;
you weren't home. She was borderline hysterical. She wanted to
make the whole thing go away for her precious Paul. She offered
Sharon money to drop the charges."

"What did Sharon say?" I picture a faceless woman at the
doorway to our dark, cluttered apartment, begging a sneering
Sharon for help. How much my mother would have enjoyed that,
holding that kind of power over someone else.

"She told her to get lost," Krystle says. "But then I guess Sharon
changed her mind. The lady left her phone number, and when Sharon called later, she told us to meet her at her house in Westport.
She didn't want to risk anyone seeing her in town again. Paul was
arrested by then. Tampering with a witness is a crime, you know."

"I remember when you guys took that trip," I say. "You told me some story about a job interview, how Sharon had to drive you."

"We drove down there to her house. It was beautiful."

Their duplicity disgusts me. All those secretive talks they must have had—*Don't tell Alexis!* I wonder who cooked up the elderly aunt story. Fury rises in me. All these years that I've been looking after the two of them, they were probably laughing behind my back.

"I only saw it once," I say through clenched teeth. That was five years ago when I moved Sharon out of it and into her first assisted living facility. At the end of the long gravel driveway sat a modest white farmhouse enveloped by a wraparound porch. The house was simple, just six rooms with one full bathroom—it didn't even have central air-conditioning, but what it did boast was a sloping green lawn that stretched down to the Long Island Sound.

"The house was no big deal, but the view was amazing," Krystle says in a faraway voice that makes me want to scream at her, bring her back to reality. The reality in which her and Sharon's actions may be what's led to my life being destroyed. "I knew right away that what Margaret was offering wasn't enough. If she thought Sharon and I would be all cowed, she miscalculated. It was more like, whoa, this lady is seriously lowballing us. So we improvised." Her tone is mischievous, proud.

"What do you mean, improvised?" The word catches in my throat. Dread fills me. This is getting even worse. A glance at the clock on the bedside tells me that I need to get going if I am going to make it to Zucker's office by five. I start down the stairs.

"We told her you were pregnant," Krystle says, pride in her voice. "I even cried, acted freaked out, so concerned for my big sister. And I could see this lady's face doing the calculations. Prison for her precious husband, some bastard kid in their lives forever. Child support. That's a lot of freaking money for the next eighteen years. Then Sharon just went for it."

I inhale sharply and stop short on the stairs. "You did what?"

"Sharon said, 'Give me the house, and it'll all go away. I'll make sure Alexis has an abortion, and you'll never hear from us again.' I couldn't believe when that lady said yes. It was that easy."

"That's when Sharon sent me to San Francisco." At the time, my mother acted as if the only concern she had was for my well-being. I didn't want to press charges, because I still thought I was in love with Paul. And in the middle of all that, Sharon took me aside and said I should go stay with a third cousin in the Bay Area.

That a police investigation would ruin my life.

That, if I stayed, the shame of what I had done would cling to me like a bad smell I could never wash off.

That she was only thinking of me.

She bought me a one-way ticket, drove me to the airport, and gave me one hundred dollars jammed in an envelope to go start a new life. I felt understood and supported by her for the first time, so grateful that she wasn't forcing me to cooperate with police detectives who looked at me like I was trash. One of them told me that I wasn't worth ruining a man's life over but that the notoriety of the case had forced the department to pursue it.

And the whole time, my mother was covering her ass, getting me out of town so I wouldn't ask too many questions. "His poor wife."

"Of course," Krystle says, "I think hormones had, like, everything to do with it."

"What does that mean?" Dread blooms within me.

"She was pregnant."

Krystle's words seize me on a primal level. A realization claws its way up from the depths of my consciousness like a feral animal desperate for air. "If she was around the same age as Paul, she would be in her mid- to late forties now," I say. "And that baby would be a teenager."

53

From below, I hear the familiar jingle of the bell on the back door. I freeze.

"I have to call you back," I whisper. "I think someone is in the house." I hang up and tiptoe down the stairs, on alert for any more sounds. The house is silent, save for the patter of rain against the windows. I cross the dining room into the kitchen. I don't see anyone.

"Hey."

I spin around and face Dustin. He takes a small step toward me, a twisted frown on his face. I search his dark, menacing eyes, his pinched face, for any sign of Paul. Could this be his son?

"You'd better go, Dustin."

"But I want to show you something."

I back up until I am against the wall.

"You lied to me. You gave me the address of my babysitter, knowing I would go there and confront her."

"I gave you the address of the network," Dustin says. "That's all. I didn't tell you to confront someone."

"Well, I did. Based on your lie."

"It wasn't a lie. That network is unsecured. Anyone within range could use it."

"If you don't leave, I'm going to call the police."

He shakes his head. "I can't let you do that. I could get in real trouble. I'm on probation."

I take out my phone. "I'm calling 911." My shaking finger pecks at the small screen. Before I can finish, Dustin is upon me and has my wrist in a tight grip. A searing pain shoots up my forearm as he twists.

"I said, I can't let you do that."

I kick his ankle with my foot, and our legs become entangled. We tumble, landing on the floor. He's on top of me, smelling of sweat and grease, weighing me down, his pointy elbow digging into my ribs. My phone skids away from me.

We writhe together on the dusty floor. I am blind to my surroundings, can see only the black of his sweatshirt inches from my eyes, breathing in his rank odor. If I can only maneuver myself about a foot to my right, I know I can reach my phone.

I hear a thud from above, then feel a sudden jerk. All movement stops. Dustin's body collapses upon mine, deadweight. I grab his head with both hands and push him to one side. I lie there, gasping for air. I feel something warm and sticky on my hands. When I bring my hands to my face, I see the substance that coats my palms is red. Dustin's blood.

I let out a scream.

"It's okay. You're safe now." Above me stands Daisy, our brass-handled fire poker dangling at her side. She drops it, and the clang of metal on wood echoes in the empty kitchen.

"Are you all right, Allie?" She crouches next to me, pulling my legs out from under Dustin's inert body. "I can't believe I did that."

Blood pours from a gash in the back of his head, pooling on the oak floor. I struggle to speak, but my throat has closed. I nod instead.

"Hold on. I'm going to call 911." She stands up, puts her phone to her ear, and begins pacing back and forth. "Yes, an emergency. A boy has been hit on the head, and he's bleeding." I hear her state my address and then repeat it. "Pulse? Hold on."

She stares at me wide-eyed, motioning with her hand. But I am frozen. Daisy drops to her knees and puts her fingers to his neck.

"Yes. He has a pulse." Daisy stands up. "No, we won't. Okay, all right." She pockets her phone. "They're on their way. They want us to open the front door. God, I feel terrible. I just saw him attacking you, and I panicked."

I'm staring at Daisy's hands, which look ghostly. I realize she is wearing clear plastic gloves.

"Are you all right, Allie?"

She follows my eyes to her hands. "Oh, these things?" She laughs her girlish laugh and peels them off, pushing them deep into the front pocket of her jeans. "I was doing a little touch-up painting at the Beckerman place."

My phone pings on the floor where it has landed.

Both Daisy and I look at it.

Neither of us moves.

It pings again, and I reach for it. The message is from Madeline Ashford.

"Found her. Sorry for poor quality."

Margaret Cooper, our tulip bulb expert at work! Below that is a grainy image of a woman on her knees next to a flower bed, wearing gardening gloves. The black-and-white image is of poor quality, but I would recognize that face anywhere. The round apple cheeks. The light, curly hair.

I look up at Daisy. "It's you. You're Margaret Cooper."

54

"Let's see." She grabs the phone from me and squints at it. "Gosh, I look so young." I look up into her wide face, her clear blue eyes that forecast innocence.

"You changed your name."

"Not really. Daisy is short for Margaret; didn't you know that? *Marguerite* means 'Daisy' in French." A small smile appears on the edges of her lips. She exhales deeply as if she's been holding her breath for a long time. "I always hated Margaret. Maggie, Meg, Peg. Such awful stick-in-the-mud nicknames. I always wanted to be Daisy, and when I moved to D.C. after Paul died to start over, I saw my chance. It took a long time, but I finally met Trip. Took his last name when we married. I built a life. Being a stepmom wasn't my first choice, but I had a family, even if things weren't always perfect. I told no one about my past. I put it all behind me. Imagine my surprise when six months ago Sexy Lexi Healy walks into Periscope Realty looking for a house."

"I had no idea."

"Oh, I know. I could tell. To you, I was just another boring, middle-aged woman. You with your perfect husband and child, looking for your forever home. Rubbing it in my face, all the things I didn't have."

"It was a coincidence."

"I don't believe in coincidences," she says with certainty. "It was like God was delivering you into my hands. I had the whole summer to get everything into place. I was ready when you moved in."

A shudder runs through me as reality sinks in. "There's no ambulance coming, is there?" The words come out in a whisper.

"Oh, Allie. Or maybe I should call you Lexi? I told you not to hire Dustin," she says. "I told you to leave him out of this, so this is really your fault."

I brush the hair off Dustin's forehead and stare into his vacant eyes.

"Breathe," I tell him.

"Bludgeoned with your poker." Daisy kicks the mono-grammed fire poker away from us. "I think it's pretty obvious what people will believe."

"You can't think you're going to get away with this." I stand, sizing her up. Daisy has at least thirty pounds on me. I'll have to push past her to get to the back door. Once outside, I'll run to Heather's, to Leah's, to anyone's.

"Would you like some wine, Allie?" She walks to the fridge and takes out a bottle. "I know you love your Matua."

She begins emptying it into the sink. I don't know what she's up to, and I do not wait to find out. I run toward the back door and yank it open. Freedom. I gulp in the cool air.

Then a shooting pain rockets up my arm as she yanks me back. I am struggling to free myself from her grip when a hot stab, like that of a wasp, pricks me in the back of my arm. I shriek and spin around to see her holding a hypodermic needle.

Daisy retreats a few steps, smiling.

"I'm going to the police," I mutter. But even as the words come out of my mouth, my knees begin to buckle. I sway, catching the doorframe for support.

"Are you?" she asks. "I figure with the amount of liquid Ambien you have in your system, you're not going anywhere."

Daisy jerks me back inside and slams the door shut.

328 AGGIE BLUM THOMPSON

"Liquid Ambien," I repeat in a hoarse whisper.

"Just like on International Night," she says. "So easy, you and your wine, your champagne. It will work a lot faster this time, of course, being intravenous. Now, the kitchen isn't a good place to commit suicide. Not what I have in mind at all."

55

"No." The word is heavy in my mouth. With great effort, I stand up straight. I can see Heather's kitchen window through my back door. If I can get outside, if I can get to Heather's, I'll be okay. I reach for the handle on the back door, but Daisy grabs my wrist.

"Oh no, wrong direction." She spins me around so she is behind me, and I am facing the kitchen. I am about to protest when she jabs something hard into my lower back. I don't have to look over my shoulder to know she is holding a small handgun, but I do.

"Let's go upstairs, shall we?"

The Ambien slows me down, making it difficult to walk. We stumble through the kitchen and dining room. In the foyer, a surge of vigor courses through me, and I lunge at the wall where the light switches are, managing to flip them on and then off.

"Sending out a code to the neighbors?" Daisy yanks me onto the stairs. "That's one of the things Paul and I really loved about the Westport house—the privacy. Not like the Eastbrook neighborhood, right?" I pause on the landing, breathing hard. "Everyone up in your business. You can't take a poop in this neighborhood without someone asking you how it turned out." She giggles at her own joke. Her cheer makes my skin crawl.

"Of course, no one in this neighborhood will care what happens to you. And when you are found having OD'd on Ambien, well, will anyone really be surprised?"

My thoughts are muddy and confused, but I need to come up

with a plan, and fast. We continue up the stairs until we are in the master bathroom. My knees buckle, and I drop to the cold, tiled floor. She's a blur in front of me, but I must stay conscious. I must keep her talking.

"You were pregnant," I say, rolling the words out over my fat tongue.

Daisy winces. "Rory. That was his name. Rory."

She bends down and pulls my shoes and socks off my feet.

"Rory," I say.

"Yes. Rory." She is pulling off my pants but pauses. "I lost him when I was more than seven months along. Paul had been fired from Overton, but you know all about that. We had to find him a new job, on top of moving out of our house. Those are two of the biggest stressors in life, did you know that?" She looks at me, unblinking, as if she expects an answer, and when she doesn't get one, she kicks one of my legs. I can barely feel it. I wonder if I can muster the strength to tackle her and knock that gun out of her hand.

"Another woman might have acted differently. Divorced Paul. But I loved him so much." Her voice breaks. "I did what I had to do for my family. Rory needed a father."

She stands up and leans over the tub. Soon I hear the rushing sound of water pouring out of the spigot.

"When you told me Mark and Cole would be gone for the whole weekend, it felt a little too soon for all this. But once Dustin started sniffing around, I had no choice but to act. I got worried, but when I found out he sent you over to Susan's, that was priceless. I knew hopping on her Wi-Fi would be a hoot." She turns back to me and beams. "This is good. Once you're unconscious, I'll post your suicide note. I've already written it— you accept responsibility for everything. Maybe I'll post it on Facebook, or maybe I'll just leave it in your email drafts. I wish you could see it, Allie. It's a doozy."

"Rory," I repeat with great effort. "How did you lose him?"

Daisy frowns. "I never talk about that. No one ever asks. Leah has known me for six years, and she's never asked. Some friend, huh? I listen to her drone on and on about Dustin and Ava, and she doesn't even know Rory's name."

"I want to know." The words come out slurred, barely intelligible, but it elicits a smile from her.

"All right. I'll tell you." She sits on the edge of the large tub, laying the gun beside her. It's only a few feet away. Almost within reach.

"I knew something was wrong the whole day. I had cramping that grew into sharp pains. We had just moved into our new place and were still unpacking. We were starting over, trying to put the whole Overton nightmare behind us. Paul had a new job at a boarding school in Massachusetts. It was all going to work out."

She leans forward and dips her hand in the water. "Bit too hot. Don't want to scald you, do we?" Daisy twists one of the knobs and straightens up. "Where was I? Oh yes. I began bleeding. We went to the hospital. We wanted Rory so much. We needed him. Whenever I thought about what you had done to Paul, to us, I made myself focus on Rory and on how wonderful our life was going to be."

She clucks her tongue and shuts off the tap. The only sound in the room now is the rain beating against the skylight. I'm supposed to be at Artie Zucker's by now. I wonder if he will send someone to look for me.

"Placenta accreta," Daisy says. "Have you ever heard that term? I was in so much pain. Little Rory was stillborn via emergency C-section. When I woke up, they told me I had undergone an emergency hysterectomy."

She sniffs and wipes at her eyes.

"That's right. I didn't just lose this tiny human who had been living inside me. I lost my womb. I had joined this website for expectant mothers that sent an email every month about how your baby was developing. Even after Rory died, the emails kept coming. Oh, now your baby is two months old and might be able to coo. That sort of thing."

"So sorry," I manage to say. I'm losing steam, my energy seeping out of me. I flex my right fingers. If Daisy becomes distracted enough in her reminiscing, then I can make a grab for the gun. It's all I can come up with.

"You can imagine how painful that was. You're probably thinking: *Daisy, why didn't you unsubscribe? Why did you put yourself through this every month?*"

I look up into her large blue eyes. They are glassy and unfocused.

"But I couldn't cancel those emails. That would have been like denying Rory had ever existed. Paul suffered, too. He felt so guilty. He blamed himself for Rory dying, but it wasn't his fault. You know that better than anyone."

I want to keep her talking. I know she wants to. "My sister," I say. "Reverse mortgage."

"Her? She deserved what she got, too. Back then, she wanted more money. The house wasn't enough for that greedy little bitch. She wanted fifty grand, too. Cash. She came to our new place and said she wouldn't leave until we gave it to her."

I try to speak, to tell her I had no idea, but all I can do at this point is part my lips. No sound comes out.

"We didn't have that kind of money, but she didn't believe me. We didn't know what to do. Go to the police in our new town? Tell them what? About Overton? We were trying to start over."

Daisy glares at me.

"Your sister went to the dean of students at Paul's new school. She showed them the pictures. Paul was fired, of course. We had to move in with his mother outside Boston. He couldn't get a teaching job. And we lived with the fear that you or your sister or your mother might come calling. He began drinking. You know the rest, don't you? He died in a car crash. Some people said it was suicide. I was left alone. Widowed at twenty-nine. In debt. No child, no parents, no husband, no womb." She closes her eyes for a moment.

It's my chance.

I can't die.

I can't leave Cole alone to fend for himself. I lunge at the gun, my hand closing in on the cool metal. Before I can raise the gun, she is on top of me, pinning my body to the hard tile floor. Her fingers claw at mine, trying to pry the gun free. I breathe in her familiar, sickly sweet perfume as she falls on top of me, our bodies tangling like sea kelp. The gun falls from my hand and clatters across the bathroom floor. I cannot see it. I hear gasping, unsure if it is coming from me or her. I don't let go. I hold on to her for dear life.

Her hands tighten around my throat and begin to squeeze. The room dims. Gasping for breath, I bring my knee up and connect with something soft. It's enough to loosen her grip on my throat. Choking, I roll to my side. A moment opens, maybe the last one. A low-level rage fuels the fibers of my muscles. I feel around until I've grabbed a fistful of her hair. With one last burst of strength, I wrench Daisy's head back and smash her skull against the side of the porcelain tub as hard as I can.

The world goes black.

56

A nurse is fussing with an IV bag that snakes cool liquid into my arm. The room is dark, save for the bright lights of the monitor beside me.

"You're awake."

I turn to see Mark sitting in a chair by my bedside. He leans over me and plants a kiss on my forehead. "Thank god you're okay."

When I try to speak, my tongue sticks to my parched mouth. He hands me a plastic cup filled with ice chips. The nurse takes my temperature. "Doing okay?" she asks.

I crunch on some ice. "Fine."

"Temperature's normal. That's good."

"Can she go home later today?" Mark asks.

"You'll have to ask the doctor. He'll be by on rounds in a few hours."

After she leaves and the door clicks shut, Mark takes my hand and squeezes it hard. "I'm so sorry, Allie. I had no idea."

"What happened? How did I end up here? The last thing I remember is being in the bathroom. Where's Daisy?"

"Slow down. Daisy's been arrested. Remember the private detective? Jon Block? When you didn't show up at the meeting with Artie Zucker, we called him. Apparently, he had a tracking device on your car. He's the one who found you and called the police." Mark lets out a low whistle and shakes his head. "I can't believe it. All this time, we trusted her. Why would she do this? Do you have any idea?"

I grimace. "I do. I'll tell you everything. Just not now, okay?"
He nods. "I'm sorry I didn't believe you. Or that I doubted you."

"It's okay. I'm just happy you're here. Where's Cole?"

"He's fine." Mark takes a deep breath. "He's still with Caitlin on the Eastern Shore. They're coming back tomorrow. Allie, I would never have . . . The whole Bridgeways thing, I just—"

"It's all right. Really. It's over, right? And Dustin?" I think of him lying in our kitchen, our fire poker next to his head. I brace myself for the worst.

"Poor kid." He winces. "He's in surgery now, but there's a good chance he'll pull through."

A wave of guilt washes over me. Dustin got hurt because of me. "It's my fault."

"No. Don't say that. None of this was your fault."

Tears fill my eyes. I don't deserve his forgiveness. "I want to tell you everything, Mark, all of it."

"Shhh. Tell me later. You need to rest now."

I lie back, exhaustion overtaking me. Unanswered questions pop into my head, but I don't have the energy to chase them down. As if reading my mind, Mark says, "Just go back to sleep. I'm here now."

"Bad luck?" Detective Katz asks and shrugs. It's the next afternoon, and he's sitting in my living room, his long legs stretched out in front of one of those chintz chairs while Detective Lopez stands silently by the window. I am on the sofa, curled up with a blanket over me, hands wrapped around a cup of tea.

"Apparently," Katz continues, "Daisy Gordon—or Margaret Cooper, if you will—had lived here without incident for twelve years. Until you moved in, that is."

"And Rob Avery?" Mark asks from where he is standing at the mantel. "He was just collateral damage?"

"We're not entirely sure," Katz says. "Looks like there may have been some bad blood between those two about a real estate deal. We'll know more as we investigate further."

The mood is entirely different than the last time the two detectives were here, interrogating me. Detective Lopez is the one playing second fiddle, while Detective Katz peppers me gently with questions. They offered no official apology. In fact, they've made no mention of having been entirely on the wrong track. But I guess the fact that they believe me and that Daisy Gordon is in jail should be enough.

"I don't understand how she did everything," I say. "I mean, she's not exactly a computer genius."

"Apparently, she hired some kid from Florida," Detective Lopez says from her spot at the window. We all turn to face her. "We're still piecing it together, but he's the one that created the fake Tinder and Facebook accounts. She fed him the information, including the photos, and he did the dirty work."

"Will he be charged, too?"

Detective Katz shrugs. "It's complicated. He's a minor, and we're hoping he'll cooperate in the investigation. But we can't say for sure. A lot of it depends on how helpful he is, like whether he can help the authorities recover the money from the reverse mortgage."

I take a long sip of my peppermint tea. I'm still astounded at the myriad ways Daisy Gordon, or Margaret Cooper, attempted to destroy my life. Mark heard from a neighbor that Dustin made it through surgery and is expected to fully recover. He'll be in the hospital a few more days; I plan to visit him tomorrow when I go to see Sharon. The doctor said my mother will be all right, but they're keeping her for a few more days until her liver tests come back normal. The police told Mark that surveillance video captured Daisy visiting my mother at Morningside House, not once but several times. Turns out Sharon was not imagining that some woman was out to get her.

I DON'T FORGIVE YOU

I have a feeling it will take a long time to sort it all out.

"Is that all, Detectives?" Mark asks. "I think my wife has been through enough. She needs to rest."

Detective Katz stands up. "That's all for now. Of course, we'll need you to come down to the station for an official statement sometime in the next few days."

Detective Lopez glances at me as she walks by, no sign of remorse on her stoic face. I hear Mark open the front door and exchange a few words with them, although I can't make out what they are saying. I am still groggy; it feels like I am recovering from the flu. The doctor said it would take another twenty-four hours for that much Ambien to leave my system. Cole comes running in and jumps on the couch. He bounces up and down.

"Whoa," I say, putting down my tea on the table in front of me. "Easy there."

"Can we curl up in your bed and watch *Aristocrats*?"

"You mean *The Aristocats*? That sounds good." I can make out low, murmuring voices coming from the foyer. Is Mark still talking to the detectives?

"Can I microwave popcorn?" Cole asks. "I know how to do it. You put the bag in and just press Start."

I almost get up to help, but I'm too tired. "Go ahead."

He runs off into the kitchen just as Mark enters the living room, holding a small woven basket with a checkered cloth over it.

"What's that?" I ask.

"Just a little something from Heather. She wants you to know she's sorry she thought you were a criminal."

I can't help but laugh.

"She figured, what better way to say that than with blueberry chia seed muffins?" He pulls back the napkin and takes a whiff. "They smell good. Want one?"

I narrow my eyes. "You know, I think I'm gonna pass on accepting food from our neighbors. At least for a while."

SIX MONTHS LATER

Margaret "Daisy" Gordon, née Cooper, pled guilty to an assortment of charges from murder to mortgage fraud and was sentenced to life in prison with the possibility of parole after twenty years.

I know this from the Google alerts I received at my new apartment in the heart of the Left Bank, almost four thousand blessed miles from Bethesda. In addition, Krystle sent me links to every story on the internet about the case until I asked her to stop.

Once it was clear that she was in no legal danger and that Sharon would recover completely from the poisoning, Krystle stepped into the spotlight as the representative of our family. She milked every bit out of her role as dear sister and dutiful daughter, and she managed to spin the media interest into a role on a YouTube reality show. A reality show on cable TV can't be far behind.

At least she has agreed to step in as Sharon's caretaker while we are in France. Sharon seems to be holding steady, adjusting to the memory ward. I check in with her caretakers via Skype weekly, which annoys Krystle, but we've agreed to pretend it's because I am a micromanager.

On a late afternoon in April, I am sitting by the window at Le Rousseau, a café around the corner from our apartment on the rue du Cherche-Midi. I'm sipping a café au lait, in violation of the French norm of not taking milk in your coffee after noon.

I search through the images on my digital camera that I've taken today. It's impossible not to be inspired wandering through this city. I started today's stroll in the Marais on the Right Bank, then explored the Latin Quarter and the area around the Quai d'Orléans, and later discovered a quiet street filled with pastel-painted doors hidden in the shadow of the Tour Montparnasse.

For all the pain that my experience with Paul brought me, he was the one who taught me about the concept of *the decisive moment* in photography, when the camera captures elements in life coming together perfectly for a fleeting instant.

And I'm grateful to him for that. Because in the end, our memories are really our mind's collection of such decisive moments. When Mark first kissed me. When Cole was placed in my arms after his birth. When I found the strength to slam Daisy's skull on the edge of that tub.

Sometimes I do this, sit by myself at a café and watch Parisians walk by, trying to make sense of everything that happened last fall.

Reporters swarmed the Eastbrook neighborhood right afterward. REAL HOUSEWIVES TAKES A DEADLY TURN, reads a typical headline. We had to pull Cole from school, move into a hotel. In tears one night, I joked to Mark that I wished we could move to another country, and a few days later, he told me his firm was looking to fill a position in its Paris office. We left before Christmas.

From a safe distance, I've watched Dustin, his now-shaved head lending him the look of a baby vulture, become a media sensation. He made a compelling figure, showing off the angry red scar that ran along the back of his head from ear to ear, a result of surgeons cutting through his skull to ease the swelling on his brain. Last I heard, he had held several ask-me-anything sessions on Reddit.

I learned from the police that Daisy had installed spyware on my computer via an attachment to an email from Periscope Realty back in August. It could have been embedded in any one of the numerous documents Daisy sent me when we bought the house.

I'd clicked on them all, completely trusting.

I finish my coffee and unwrap the small square of chocolate that accompanies it, a French café tradition I love. I no longer ask myself, what if we had moved to a different suburb or even just a different neighborhood in Bethesda? What are the odds that we would move into Margaret Cooper's neighborhood and that she would be our Realtor?

I'm sure she asked herself the same thing when I showed up in her office.

I used to go over all our interactions, wondering if I'd missed some sign. But there's no point in thinking like that. What's done is done.

I've emailed Leah several times. She returned one message, right after we moved here. She said she didn't blame me for what happened to Dustin. Her email was full of exclamation points and forced holiday cheer. She enclosed a picture of the book club—a grinning Heather, Janelle, and Pam, in addition to herself. They were planning to read a novel called *Resilience* for the month of December. Janelle's pick; it's about the Holocaust.

Then Leah stopped returning my emails.

I don't blame her for wanting to move on.

Cole and Mark bang on the window, and I toss a few euros on the small round table. We are off to do our *courses* together. Each Saturday, we attempt as a family to cook a real French meal. We drift in and out of the small shops—first the butcher, then the greengrocer, then the patisserie where Cole can pick from a panoply of glistening desserts. So far, chocolate éclairs are his favorite. Mark and I prefer *opéras*.

Spring has come to Paris, and the sun won't set until after 8:00 p.m. As I leave the café, the mustachioed owner grunts, *"Au revoir, madame."*

"Au revoir, monsieur," I say as I push open the brass-and-glass door. After six months of coming here almost every day, I've merited something resembling a smile in return.

The Parisians cannot be accused of being overly friendly. When we moved into our apartment in a large nineteenth-century building, no one brought muffins. None of Cole's schoolmates' parents have invited me for coffee or to hot yoga.

"Aren't the French unfriendly?" I heard Caitlin ask Mark on one of their Skype calls.

I wanted to poke my face in front of the laptop camera and say, "Yes. Wonderfully unfriendly."

I relish the anonymity.

I have been gingerly dipping my toe back into the photography business—a few portraits and headshots here and there, mostly expats. Recently, the wife of a colleague of Mark's—an Australian writer—asked me to do a headshot for her new book.

Mark and I walk up the rue de Sèvres, Cole running ahead and then back like a dog who doesn't want to lose us. We are discussing whether we should rent a car or take the train up to Normandy when Aunt Caitlin and Uncle Charles come.

They will be here next week, our first visitors, although they will stay in a hotel on the opposite bank of the River Seine. Every six months seems like a nice amount of time between visits with Mark's family.

But I will never forget that I am in her debt. It was her private investigator who found everyone in our house thanks to the tracking device on my car.

That's something. Not love exactly, but something.

Mark and I wrote her a simple thank-you on thick, cream-colored stationery, and she and I have never spoken of it since.

We stop at the greengrocer, where I watch as Mark and the proprietor engage in a detailed conversation about which potatoes to buy. The man wants to know when Mark plans to cook them, and how, before he can select the best ones for us. I watch the exchange, filled with gratitude. Over the past few months, we've had our share of tear-filled conversations and apologies, but they've recently petered out.

Mark turns and asks me what the word for *roasted* is in French.

"*Rôti*," I say. We are both working to improve our French, struggling to be understood.

As the three of us head back to our apartment, we pass a man with auburn hair. He reminds me of Paul Adamson, and for a moment, a wave of emotion washes over me. I make room for that little voice, not the one that has chided me for years—a new one I have been nurturing. This voice does not blame me. This voice comforts me.

It wasn't your fault, it says, soothing me like a mother nursing a wounded child. *You did not set all these terrible events in motion. You were a victim, too.*

Mark hands me the shopping bag as he punches in the security code to our building. I don't hold any grudges against Mark. I wish he had never suggested rehab, but now that I've had time to think about it, I might have done the same.

Wishing things were different has cost me so much—time, energy, peace of mind. I'm trying to break that habit and to form a new one: forgiving. Not only Mark but Krystle and Sharon, too. I'm learning to release a lifetime of grudges and hurts. Forgiveness is not a luxury but a necessity. Forgiveness is the backbone of love. And love makes life bearable.

I hope that one day, my turn will come and I will forgive myself.

ACKNOWLEDGMENTS

While writing can be a solitary endeavor, getting a book into the world is not, and *I Don't Forgive You* would not have been possible without the hard work and support of so many people.

My deepest thanks go to my agent, Katie Shea Boutillier, to my editor, Kristin Sevick, and to everyone at Forge/Macmillan for their generous support and hard work on this book's behalf.

I am indebted to early readers who gave me needed feedback and support—Anne Brewer, Rebecca Title Aretsky, and Julie Coe.

Thank you to my real-life book club—Melissa Grady Pearce, Karen Amatangelo-Block, Chiara Scotti, Janelle Wong, Jackie Mesa, and Valerie Parker—none of whom are secretly trying to murder one another, as far as I know.

Thank you to Fred Brown, who since childhood has fostered within me the insatiable twin passions of reading and writing.

To Assistant U.S. Attorney Steven Snyder and Dana Rice of Compass Realty—thank you both for being generous enough to take the time to provide insight into your professions.

Finally, I am eternally grateful to my loving and patient family, especially my husband, John Thompson: you are not just one of the greatest line editors of all time—your generous spirit lifted me when I was low, and your steadfast confidence in me, and in this book, carried me across turbulent waters. I will love you forever.